UNFAITHFUL

THE DECEPTION OF NIGHT

A novel by

Elisa S. Amore

Translated by

Leah Janeczko

"One last thing I want to emphasize that so impressed me is how Shakespearean this novel is: it's sneaky, cursed, and sublime all at the same time."

"Be prepared for an ending that will make you curse the time you have to wait for Elisa Amore's third novel to come out!"

"It is the kind of book you think about all the time, even when you're not reading it."

"The brilliant love, sweetness, and mystery we saw in Touched begin to turn dark in Unfaithful with the danger that looms over them."

"When I read it everything else faded away and nothing seemed real but the book."

"It's impossible not to fall in love with this story."

"You'll read this book all in one sitting. The author doesn't give you time to breathe!"

"One of the most beautiful parts of this book is when he shows his world to Gemma. It's so fascinating!"

"The story of an incredible love, like few others, Unfaithful will keep you hooked until the final, devastating page."

"I was so caught off guard, it left me breathless, shocked and scared. My question now is: What will happen next?"

"The last chapter of Unfaithful ends in sorrow and mysteries too dark to reveal . . . I used up all my tears reading it. It needs to be made into a film."

To my husband Giuseppe,
who proves to me day after day
that men like Evan really do exist;
I married one.
And to little Gabriel Santo:
no matter how many novels I write,
you'll always be my masterpiece.

PROLOGUE

"Faster! Faster!!!" Adrenaline pumped wildly through my veins as I shouted to Evan, my heart pounding like crazy.

The car swerved dangerously onto the highway, racing at an inhuman speed with a roar so fierce it made the hairs on my arms stand up. Lake Placid was far behind us. My breath coming fast, I stole a glance at Evan's face. It was twisted into an expression I'd learned to decipher: a mix of excitement, determination, and defiance—a combination I liked.

Clinging to the dashboard, I turned back to check out the car we were trying to shake: a smoke-gray Lamborghini Reventón with tinted windows. It was right on our tail, ripping the asphalt off the road. "It's gaining on us!" I cried, trying to control my heartbeat.

"They won't catch us that easily," Evan growled. His eyes narrowed to slits as he gripped the steering wheel, shooting me a captivating smile. "We're faster." He raised his eyebrows, the soft curve of his parted lips mesmerizing me, and jammed his foot down on the accelerator. The engine howled.

The Ferrari 458 Italia we were in shot across the scorching hot asphalt like a missile and I hung on for dear life. The speed took my breath away, pushing me back hard into the leather seat. The upholstery was red and contrasted elegantly with the car's sporty silverstone-gray exterior. I adored the color because it reminded me of Evan's eyes when the somber sky over Lake Placid darkened them.

Although speed wasn't a problem for him, I still hadn't gotten used to it even though being chased on cars and motorcycles had become an integral part of my second life over the last few months, almost a constant. Despite everything, beneath the thin layer of fear there was a stronger, more deeply rooted sensation under my skin: excitement. The emotions Evan had introduced me to were vivid and precious, especially because they were mine alone: no other mortal experienced them. I couldn't live without them any more. Just a few months ago, death had touched me with its icy fingertips, but I'd never felt this alive before.

"Oh my God! Evan! Look out!!!" I shrieked. A huge semi had suddenly pulled onto the road. My heart lurched. It would be impossible to swerve around it and we were going too fast to stop in time. Instead of slowing down though, at the last second Evan boldly downshifted into fifth, making the rear wheels skid. He jammed his foot onto the accelerator, pushing us into the opposite lane as the semi zoomed by like a blurry rocket.

"That wasn't on the agenda!" he exclaimed with a smug smile.

Terror and excitement washed over me. I took a deep breath and let out a whoop, almost shivering. Evan laughed at my enthusiasm and shook his head.

"You're crazy." I smiled, my heart still trembling.

"What can I say?" he shot back, shrugging. His gaze was shrewd, his smile beguiling.

I glanced out the rear window. "We lost them!"

Evan narrowed his eyes, his gaze locked on the road, his proud smile set in an expression as steely as it was dangerous. The car was gone, but he didn't seem at all convinced it was over.

Proving me wrong, we heard the aggressive roar of an engine and a second later the Lamborghini swerved into view behind us. Evan showed no sign of agitation. The car's engine rumbled again challengingly and my heart leapt to my throat when I saw the gray front end of the Lamborghini nosing at our rear wheels. The two cars gripped the asphalt, their engines growling over the tar set aflame by their tires. The roar behind us persisted, more and more aggressive, making my stomach quiver.

"They're too close, Evan! Speed up! They're right behind us!" I shouted, panic gripping me. My excitement was even stronger, though. It raced through my body like electricity, enhancing every sensation.

The sly half smile on Evan's lips spread, his gaze piercing and seductive. "Time to get serious," he murmured with that tough expression that always drove me wild. "Hold on tight."

I instantly understood it wasn't a suggestion. It was a warning.

Before I could take a breath, Evan jammed his foot on the brake and the car abruptly slowed, eluding our pursuer who shot past us like a bullet. Next, he grabbed the emergency brake and yanked it back while turning the steering wheel with his left hand.

I felt a pit in my stomach that spread to my head as the car spun out. I would have liked to catch my breath, but Evan didn't give me the chance. The tires squealed against the asphalt, still damp with early-morning dew, and raced off in the opposite direction, pressing me back into my seat. My chest rose and fell convulsively as I tried to position myself in some way that might keep me from shaking.

Over my shoulder I glimpsed the Lamborghini coming toward us like a missile homing in on its target as our Ferrari zoomed onto Old Military Road at two hundred miles an hour. "Evan!!!" My voice was shrill, almost desperate.

"Brace yourself!" he ordered me through clenched teeth without giving me time to react. The words were still trapped in my throat when he swerved brusquely onto Mill Pond Drive so fast the landscape became a distorted blur of color as the car skidded into the school parking lot, squealing across the asphalt and shoving me against the window. Only seconds later did I anxiously turn and see the Lamborghini behind us copy Evan's maneuver and skid to a halt just yards from us.

I sank into my seat, still shaking, and took a deep breath. At last, everything was still. A car door clicked open, breaking the stunned silence of the students who'd been left wordless by our arrival. My heart was still pounding, my head spinning. My eyes shot to the side-view mirror as the Lamborghini's door swung up like an eagle preparing to take wing. The driver stepped deliberately out of the gray leather and Alcantara suede seat. A shiver ran over my skin, adrenaline still pumping through my veins. As I tried to regain control of my breathing, regular footsteps approached.

"Not bad, little brother!"

Ginevra's long, sensual legs halted next to the driver's door, her voice muffled by the glass. Evan tilted his head toward me and smiled with satisfaction before lowering the window. Ginevra leaned down, gracefully rested her elbows on his door, and winked at me, a smile on her lips. A soft cascade of blond hair hung over her shoulder, hiding part of the neckline of her dress, which was gray with black stripes around the bodice. Its skirt bared her breathtaking legs that, as always, ended in sky-high heels. For some strange reason, her poised, elegant bearing never made her seem inappropriate, no matter what she wore. Quite the opposite: one look and the rest of the world felt out of place and awkward when she passed.

I gave her a little wave, barely raising my fingers, and smiled to myself. My throat was still dry from the race. Although I was dazed and shaken, the thrill won out every time. It was an amazing sensation: pure adrenaline churned out by sheer excitement, totally devoid of fear. It flowed beneath my skin, enhanced by the awareness that at Evan's side I ran no risk. Racing at two hundred miles an hour at the crack of dawn sent an incomparable surge of electricity through me. It was a feeling I'd known for only a short time but one I'd had to get used to quickly. And I would never give it up. Once I'd tasted it, I'd discovered that certain emotions were hard to forget. My body craved it; adrenaline quenched its thirst. I'd lived my life on standby, waiting for Evan to arrive so I could live every moment to the fullest.

Evan hadn't answered Ginevra yet. He just smiled to himself, looking amused. I'd seen this a million times before.

"Don't make that face. I can beat you whenever I want," she insisted with a pout. "You'd better stay warmed up because I want a rematch." Ginevra was totally incapable of admitting defeat.

"Wasn't *this* the rematch?" I put in timidly, imagining that the exact same scene must have played out between them before they stopped by my place this morning.

A sharp look from Ginevra made me bite my lip. Evan let out a laugh, even more amused by his sister's stubbornness. "I'm all yours," he promised, raising his eyebrows.

We got out of the car and Evan walked around the Ferrari to me, but Ginevra was quick to link her arm in mine. "That means I'll keep her hostage until then."

"In your dreams." He grabbed my hand and pulled me toward him, his smile slow and studied. I stifled a laugh, seeing Ginevra frown as we walked off. Turning back toward her, I mouthed *Sorry*. Evan stepped behind me to block me from Ginevra's view. It was incredible how the two siblings competed with each other.

"Once in a while we could show up like normal people, don't you think?" I teased, still trying to recover from the last curve.

He glanced at me, his expression sly. "We could." He squeezed my waist from behind and whispered into my ear: "But that wouldn't be as much fun—don't *you* think?"

The warmth of his breath in my hair sent a quiver through me. He'd found a way to distract me from Ginevra. I shook my head as a murmur spread among the students of Lake Placid High. They cast curious glances at Evan and Ginevra's cars that stood out among all the others in the parking lot. In general I tried not to be bothered by the interest they raised wherever we went in them—unlike Ginevra, I wasn't exactly comfortable being in the spotlight—but cars aside, our spectacular entrance had definitely drawn attention.

"I told you the Ferrari would be overdoing it on the first day of school," I murmured in embarrassment.

Evan tried to object but before he could open his mouth Ginevra swooped in from behind. "This is an important day! We needed to celebrate!" She turned to her brother. "You owe me one."

"Celebrate what, exactly?" I said, though I wasn't sure if I would be better off not asking.

"Today's the first day of your last year of school, Gemma!" she said with surprise, as though the answer were obvious.

I rolled my eyes and decided to humor her. There was no need for Ginevra to keep coming to school, but she'd decided to attend classes anyway. I wasn't totally convinced it was to keep up appearances like she'd said or whether it was so she could continue to keep an eye on me, as my instinct suggested.

In any case, no matter how frustrating it was, Evan was enough to draw attention even without his Ferrari. Their underground garage was packed with flashy, expensive cars they'd gotten who knew where. To Ginevra, money was certainly no issue.

Evan and I usually took his motorcycle. Common sense made him save the Ferrari for nighttime rides when he'd swing by my place and I would sneak out the window at the first light of dawn when Lake Placid was still sleeping. The same thing definitely couldn't be said of Ginevra. Sometimes it was hard to dissuade her once she'd made up her mind. This was probably one of those mornings when Evan hadn't managed to ignore his sister's out-of-control competitive spirit. Ginevra couldn't get enough of standing out.

I spotted some of my friends in the distance: Brandon, walking with his arms around the shoulders of two new girls; Jake, who was getting out of his dad's police car; Faith and Jeneane, hopping off the school bus; and Peter, just arriving on his bike, wearing a Blue Bombers sweatshirt, ready to begin a new lacrosse season. Everything was so familiar and yet so different.

The shrill sound of the bell welcomed us as we walked through the school doors. I forced myself to take deep breaths until the adrenaline had subsided and the annoying hum in my ears was gone. I squeezed

Evan's hand and his fingers returned the gesture. That sound announced the beginning of a new year. A new year together with him.

"O true apothecary!
Thy drugs are quick.
Thus with a kiss I die."

William Shakespeare, *Romeo and Juliet*
Act V, Scene III

GHOSTS FROM THE PAST

A few hours earlier

"The year was 1720. A September night, just like this one." Evan's gaze was distant, his voice deep and melancholy, as if the memory of his past might carry him away at any moment. He struggled to voice the words, as though afraid the events would come back to life in his head. I didn't want to pressure him. I'd never insisted he give me details about his past but he went on, his tone dull. "I was seventeen." He lay down next to me on the grassy lawn on the shore of Mirror Lake, gently resting his head on my lap, and closed his eyes as I looked down at him. "I remember every minute." A twitch under his eyelids told me his mind had taken him back to that distant 1720, but only for a fleeting moment. A second later he opened his eyes again, escaping the memory that was probably too painful for him to experience a second time.

In silence, I waited for him to speak.

"Every single moment of that miserable night is engraved on my memory." He stared at the cloudless sky. His eyes were focused but his blank expression made me doubt he was really there with me. Despite himself, he was lost in the memory.

"Evan, you don't need to tell me if you don't feel ready. What happened to you in the past doesn't matter. All that counts is that you're with me right here, right now," I assured him—though it wasn't true.

A trace of a smile appeared on Evan's face as if he could tell I'd lied. Then he looked me straight in the eye. "I want you to know everything about me. No more secrets, remember?"

"In this case I don't think it counts as a secret," I said. Instinctively, I sank my fingers into his soft, wavy hair, the color of coffee beans.

"I want to tell you anyway."

I waited patiently, continuing to stroke his head during the silence that followed.

"Passing on is a traumatic experience for all of us. Every Subterranean remembers it with sorrow and bitterness, as if we'd hoped for a . . . a better death." He grimaced. "Or a different fate. But we soon learn, one way or another, that if the blood of the Children of Eve flows through our veins it doesn't matter how we pass on. All that counts is our punishment, the sentence we have to serve. That is, if we're even allowed the hope of atonement."

"You aren't damned," I said instantly.

He looked at me. "I know that now. Otherwise I wouldn't have you. I can't imagine any worse damnation than never having met you—or losing you. In any case, those of us who manage to survive never forget."

"Survive?" I gasped, as surprised as I was alarmed. "You mean you risk dying again right after you've just . . . died?" The word sent a shiver down my spine. I tried not to think about the fact that Evan wasn't alive any more. He was so warm, so . . . human.

He smiled, but it was an empty smile. There was no sparkle in his eyes.

More silence.

"My father was a middle-class London merchant. We weren't rich but we weren't poor either. By day he earned a respectable income, but his nights were spent reinvesting the family money in far-from-reputable activities. Alcohol and women were his sole interests and, for my mother and me, our heaviest burden. She meant more to me than anything else in the world. I remember that I saw her through my childish eyes as an angel, and myself as her little warrior. I wanted to protect her from him but that wasn't always possible. You can save someone from any danger, but no matter how important that person is to you, you can't save them from their own feelings. Those are hard to change. In only a few years Father had disgraced our family name."

From time to time Evan stopped, losing himself in long pauses, his breathing deep and labored. Anguished, even. "As a young boy, night after night, my mother's silent weeping was deafening to my little heart. It was as loud as a scream, an unbearable pain that tore me up inside. I would slip into her room to comfort her. She would hold me tight and our embrace seemed to soothe her. It wasn't until later that I realized she was pretending so I wouldn't be upset. I was just a boy, but I felt like the only man in our house.

"I grew older and started to stand up to him. Our arguments became more frequent and uglier, especially when he would come home in the mornings drunk and half dressed. He was my father but I hated him. I couldn't understand why my mother still hoped to see him change, but I gave in to her wishes and instead of making him leave all I did was argue with him. Her happiness was all that mattered to me. Father was handsome, charming, trim, quite tall, with a wisp of a beard as blond as his hair, but his behavior made him unworthy of my mother's good graces."

"What was she like?" I asked, even though I had carefully studied the family portrait that hung in Evan's room. I was curious to know more about the woman Evan had loved so much, but I regretted the question the moment I saw a glimmer in his eyes.

"There wasn't a woman who didn't envy her fair complexion and soft dark curls."

"Like yours," I was quick to point out.

He smiled. "Yes. Like mine," he said, clearly pleased he'd inherited his mother's looks and not his father's. He seemed relieved there was no strong resemblance to the man he despised.

"Her manners were kind and graceful, though her true beauty was in her soul. Her porcelain skin was the envy of all the ladies. Until she met my father, that is. Then their envy quickly turned to compassion. He'd won her heart by hiding love letters in loaves of bread he would send her, but once they were married his attitude changed. It was probably my father's behavior that kept me from returning the attentions of the girls in our neighborhood," he admitted, apparently realizing it only now.

"What *kind* of attentions did they pay you, exactly?" I said, feeling irritated, as if the girls from his past could even matter. None of them had been alive for centuries, but in spite of myself a twinge of jealousy gripped my stomach.

Evan didn't bother to hide a smile. "Nothing that mattered," he reassured me. Looking me straight in the eye, his head still resting on my lap, he reached up and swept a lock of hair from my face, holding my gaze as he did so. "There's never been another girl for me. Back then I had to take care of my mother. I didn't have time for another woman. You've been my one and only, Gemma."

The pause that followed lasted even longer than the others, as if Evan were preparing to reveal the most difficult, painful part. It was so obvious I could almost see the tangle of thorns trapping his words; every time he tried to free them, the thorns pierced his heart before he could open his mouth.

I waited in silence until he was ready to relive the memory. "It was a peaceful September night—but not at our house. In my heart there wasn't a trace of the stillness that filled the streets. Inside I was screaming with rage and frustration. With hatred. I could feel my mother's pain echoing everywhere. In my head, my chest. Every part of me suffered for her. Father had gone out for the millionth time but that night was different from the others. Looking into my mother's eyes, grown dull and weary, I saw something different in the dim light of the candle she kept on the windowsill where she was waiting up for him as she did every night. The look she had on her face is seared into my memory as though with a branding iron. It still burns whenever I remember it. I'll never forgive my father for making my last memory of my mother be that exhausted, empty look in her eyes.

"I decided enough was enough. I went out to find him. I'd never done it before but that night I was determined to bring him home, by force if necessary. I was young, strong, and brawnier than he was. But my good intentions quickly vanished. It took me less than a minute to realize it wasn't worth it; he was in the doorway of a tavern, too drunk to stand, his arms around two bawdily dressed girls. They must have been more or less your age. They staggered down the street, laughing provocatively and behaving scandalously for ladies of that era. When he saw me, my father didn't even take his hands off them. Utterly shameless. I was ashamed for him. I was ashamed *of* him.

"'William!' he chortled as I walked toward him. He was too drunk to notice the disgust and scorn in my eyes. 'Hey! I'm talking to you, lad. Come here. Look what lovely pullets I found in the henhouse. I got one for you too!' He squeezed the girls closer, like a trophy to be shared, and I realized I'd never known true hatred and contempt until then. 'Come! What are you waiting for?'

"Rage boiled inside me as he spoke. 'Come on, laddie! You can do it!' Then he turned to the girls, laughing, not even bothering to lower his voice. 'You must forgive the boy. He's never had a woman before.'

"That's when I got close enough for him to focus on my face. 'And he still clings to his mother's skirts.' He lowered his voice and made a theatrical gesture. 'What's wrong with you? You aren't afraid to know what a real woman is, I hope!' he said in a mocking tone.

"The two girls snickered without taking their eyes off me, as if they were interested in his proposal. But all I could see was that man. I glared at him with disgust as I neared him, trying not to think of the look in my mother's eyes that still set the blood in my veins on fire.

"Suddenly his voice became animated. 'My ladies!' he cried with the enthusiasm of someone about to do someone else a favor. 'Voila! I present to you my son, Evan William James!' He introduced me with a bow that knocked him off balance. The two girls tried to hold him up.

"I didn't lift a finger to help him. With a drunken laugh, he straightened up. 'He came all the way here for one of you two. Who'll volunteer? Or do you want to choose for yourself, William?' he asked before the sneering girls could decide. 'What is it, son? What's wrong? Come now!' he said when I didn't answer. 'These two lassies aren't to your liking?' he said testily, lifting their chins toward the dim light of the only lantern. 'For tonight you'll have to make do.'

"They must have seen the fury in my eyes because the two girls' expressions changed the instant I got close enough. They were so scared they broke away from him and backed up. If looks could kill, my father would have dropped dead on the spot.

"As I stood there, he leaned over and whispered in my ear, 'Choose one so tonight you can finally become a real man.' Then he sneered at me. Wrong move. His words were like gasoline on a fire. I rushed at him, shoved him, and struck him across the face so violently that he landed on the ground yards away from the girls, who were shocked by my brutality.

"'You're no man,' I hissed in disgust. 'You never have been.' Then I walked off, not feeling the least bit guilty about his bloody jaw. I never saw him again."

I shared Evan's silence for a long moment.

"It must have been terrible," I finally said, horrified by his story.

"Not at all," he said. "It was the most liberating, most gratifying thing I'd ever done. The thought of having to leave my mother in his hands was what worried me when I realized I'd never see her again."

Knowing he hadn't finished, I didn't break the silence that followed.

"I went back the way I'd come, running down the cobblestone streets. The places where Father amused himself were in the most squalid neighborhoods, fitting only for the likes of him. It hadn't taken me long to find him. I'd known he would be on the outskirts of town in the most disreputable dens of vice. Now that the burden had been lifted from my chest, the silence inside me was so intense that my footsteps echoed off the buildings in the dark, deserted alleys.

Suddenly the silence was broken by a shriek of terror that sliced through the night like lightning. I was instantly on guard, trying to figure out where the desperate voice was coming from. A woman, at that hour of the night. Imagining she needed help, I rushed in her direction. Although people today think modern society is violent and dangerous, it's actually a lot safer than it used to be, believe me. There were a lot more robbers on the streets of London in the eighteenth century than there are today in New York City. Anyway, I immediately suspected it was a criminal. When I saw them I was surprised. I had just run around the corner and my breath caught in my throat, not from fear—I didn't feel a trace of it—but from outrage.

"There were four of them, all more or less my age or maybe a few years older. They were dressed well, even better than I was, so they must have been from upper-class families. They were all drunk as skunks. Back then noblemen amused themselves by terrorizing people, and the focus of their amusement that night was a young lady. From her clothing, I guessed she was a noblewoman. She wore a full-skirted white lace gown that matched her long gloves and around her neck was a string of pearls. Her face was so innocent, and the terror I read in her eyes when one of the boys slid his hand under her skirt made me run to her rescue. It wasn't unusual for spoiled noblemen like them to rape girls, even dragging them out of their carriages. Their crimes often went unpunished."

"How terrible." Appalled, I could find nothing else to say.

"It was rare for a nobleman to be punished. The art of violence was part of their education. They had the right to carry weapons and they never went without them. I was petrified by the spine-chilling scene I was witnessing in that alley. I was just a boy and it took me a few seconds to react. My presence hadn't disturbed them in the least, or maybe they hadn't even noticed me there, blinded as they were by excitement. I remember one of them covering her mouth with one hand while unbuttoning his trousers with the other.

"It was at that point that the girl looked in my direction. In her eyes I glimpsed the same look I'd seen in my mother's, filled with resignation. Without thinking, I tackled the boy who was forcing the girl against the wall and we fell to the ground. A gun went off and I froze. The boy beneath me wrenched himself free from my grip. I heard the echo of their footsteps, but when I turned around it was too late. The four boys had run off down the alley and the darkness had swallowed them up. I looked down at the hand I'd instinctively raised to my aching chest and realized I wouldn't be going home that night."

I sat there in shock as uncontrollable shivers ran through my entire body. "It's a terrifying story," I finally said, attempting to bring his attention back to me. But Evan was still there in the alley, lost in his memories. In his eyes I could see he'd just relived the tragedy, and I'd done it with him.

"It's just one of many. There were worse crimes in London's deserted alleys in the dead of night. The streets weren't safe. It was what happened afterwards that was unusual."

His words startled me. I hadn't known he had more to tell.

"I didn't have time to realize what was happening. After a moment I fell to the ground and lost consciousness." Evan stopped, lost in thought, reflecting on the distant past. "I felt a profound stillness coming from inside me. It was everywhere, surrounding me, engulfing me. Suddenly a harmonious sound broke the stillness, like music from a harp, but more . . . human. The sound pulled me out of the darkness, back to the surface. All at once I was on my feet again. Confused, I shook my head. The sound came again. I stood still, trying to understand where it was coming from. I wanted it. I longed to reach it with every fiber of my being. I followed it unresistingly. The voice began to whisper my name over and over, like the sweetest of melodies. I couldn't resist it. It was a girl's voice, calling to me with excited giggles like a child playing hide-and-seek. I was irresistibly attracted, like I'd been hypnotized and had no control over my own body or mind. That's when I received the mark."

"Your tattoo," I murmured, stroking the symbols that wound around his left forearm.

Evan nodded. "For a few seconds the burning sensation drove her out of my head. Then I turned the corner and saw her. It was the girl in the white gown. Blinded by my earlier rage, I hadn't noticed how beautiful she was. She wore her red hair up and a few locks hung over her delicate neck. Her voice continued to beckon me until I went to her and instinctively stroked her rosy cheek. I couldn't take my eyes off her full red lips."

I went rigid, not prepared to hear more. A stab of pain had pierced my heart and I wanted him to stop, but Evan went on before I could protest.

"I wanted her and yet I had this strange feeling that I wasn't really in my right mind, like I was falling under some evil spell. Seeing me hesitate, the girl tried to encourage me with her eyes. She lifted her hand and ran it along the curve of her bosom. I thought she might be trying to repay me for chasing off the boys, but I wasn't interested in that kind of reward. Still shaken from having stood up to my father, I wanted to rush home to tell my mother everything. I didn't want the girl and yet I had the strange urge to touch her. She seemed to sense it and, taking my hand, she slid it under her skirt. The contact with her warm skin made me shiver."

A deep ache throbbed in my heart when I heard Evan say these last words. I knew it made no sense to feel such resentment—so much time had passed—but I couldn't help it. The mental images his description was conjuring up were unbearable. No matter how distant they were, Evan's emotions pierced my heart like a dagger.

"A cold shiver," he continued. His eyes locked onto mine as if he'd perceived my thoughts and wanted to reassure me. We were sitting close together, almost facing each other. "An evil chill I'd never felt before, so cold it permeated my bones. It was almost painful, as though someone had trapped me under a thick layer of ice and I couldn't reach the surface. The more I struggled internally, the more it overwhelmed me; I was totally at the mercy of that pain. I couldn't breathe but, against my will, my lips continued to move closer to hers. Shards of ice ran me through every time I tried to resist. My body, in contrast, wasn't offering any resistance. It was attracted to her; it wanted her, but I'd never been that kind of guy. It wasn't that I was indifferent to her beauty, but normally I would have made the decision not to give in to her. I'd always been strong-willed, and my intolerance of those who lacked a sense of decency was probably due to Father's behavior.

"It was only when I looked her in the eye that everything changed, as if I'd unexpectedly found the key to escaping her control. Not caring about appearing rude, I grabbed the hand that was holding mine, doing with it as she pleased, and shoved it against her chest so hard she winced. I had only a second to stare into her sensual, pouting gaze. I saw defiance in her eyes as if, despite my rejection she was still trying to make me change my mind. Then she vanished before my eyes."

As Evan said this it dawned on me. "She was a Witch." I was so stunned by everything he was saying that it came out as a whisper.

He lowered his head in confirmation. "It was a trap. The boys had just been bait. By giving in to evil they'd sealed their fates, but I was her actual target."

"So she wanted them to kill you? But why?" I asked, confused.

"To claim my soul through seduction. That's how they do it. They fog your brain."

"They use sex to steal souls?"

"They use *desire*. Lust is one of the most underestimated sins and the one most often committed. The seductive power of a Witch is so strong it's hard to resist."

"But you did," I pointed out, relieved.

Evan nodded. "It's as though each of us has to atone in our own personal way for original sin by resisting temptation like Adam couldn't."

"Then what happened?" I asked, curious.

"Actually, I still hadn't realized what was going on. I saw the girl vanish and thought I'd taken a nasty blow to the head. I started walking home, thinking about my mother. In my mind, I relived what had happened with my father. I was anxious to tell her about how I'd stood up to him. I wanted to reassure her that from that moment on I'd take care of everything, we'd move away, she'd never be subjected to his humiliations again. Circumstances had forced me to grow up quickly, taking care of the family and the shop when I was still little more than a child. I felt ready.

"Then something caught my eye, something hidden in the dim light at the end of the alley. I moved toward it and began to make out a shape lying on the ground. A body. I ran to help, but when I neared it I saw a pool of blood around the body. There was nothing I could do. Whoever he was, it was too late.

"I was just about to leave when a strange instinct compelled me to move closer. I reached out, turned the body over and saw his face. It hit me like a bolt of lightning right in the chest. It was me. And I was dead.

"I knelt there staring at my corpse, paralyzed, powerless to react and unable to find the courage to leave it and walk away. The bullet had passed through my heart. The shot must have been fired from close range, but it hadn't been the boy beneath me who pulled the trigger."

I cringed at the thought of such cruelty.

"And yet I was too horrified to stay there either. My body was a piece of dead meat lying on the ground. I got up and ran away as fast as I could. I had a strange knot in my throat I couldn't ease. It was as if all my tears had suddenly dried up: tears not for myself, but for my mother. A single thought hounded me: who would take care of her? I had no choice but to leave her to her sad fate, living out her life with that good-for-nothing worm of a husband.

"I was amazed when the following months proved me wrong. My aggressive reaction taught Father a lesson and that was the last time he ever stayed out until dawn. My passing helped bring them together again and their marriage was saved. I couldn't have been happier. They couldn't see me but I watched them whenever possible. They were united in their grief over losing me, but at least they were *united*. If I had to die, I can't imagine a better reason. The happiness in my mother's eyes cancelled out everything else. For years that was all I'd wanted. My wish had come true." Despite Evan's words, his face was stony.

"I think it's best not to think about the past any more," I said, hoping it would improve his mood, and added with a wink, "Let's focus on the future." I was resolved to break down the walls of reserve he'd just talked about. Actually, since I'd known him I'd found his attitude to be anything but reserved.

He laughed, almost as if he'd read my mind.

"What ever happened to that good boy?"

He drew closer, his gaze turning sly. "I'm more of a good boy than you imagine. It's not easy being around you and not . . ."

"And not what?" I asked provocatively.

"And not allowing myself to be consumed by the fire."

"After three centuries, you should have learned to keep that fire under control."

"For three centuries I was surrounded by shadows and ice. *You're* my fire. And whenever I'm near you I risk being consumed."

"Then I might get burned too. I'd better keep my distance."

"Who says I'll let you? We're not in the seventeen hundreds any more. If we'd met back then, you certainly would have had to keep your distance, and only after I'd seen approval in your eyes could I have asked for your hand."

"Right, sure. I just can't see you acting like a fine young gentleman!"

"That's how I would have acted by day," he said, a wolfish look on his face as he sensually drew nearer. "But then I would have tapped on your window every night." He whispered the words directly against my mouth and then kissed me. A long, warm, deep kiss. "No. I don't think I could have managed to stay away from you even by day."

I smiled and rested my forehead on his. "Weren't we supposed to focus on the future?" I asked, still provocative, biting my lip to subdue the fire that burned inside me whenever our bodies touched.

"I'm thinking about the future right now," he murmured, moving his lips closer.

"And what do you see, pray tell?" I whispered, enchanted by his seductive gaze so close to mine.

Evan looked me straight in the eye. "It's right in front of me. You're my future. Nothing else matters." He brushed his lips against my chin, light, tiny kisses that slowly moved to my mouth. "Gemma Naiad Bloom, you're like the sun to me," he whispered.

"You mean you can't look at me for more than a few seconds without your eyes hurting?" I teased.

Evan smiled, his lips so close they tickled mine. "I mean your light is so bright it eclipses everything else." Another kiss, longer and more delicate, at the corner of my mouth. "Not even the stars, no matter how dazzling, how radiant, can shine in the presence of the sun, so they hide, fearing comparison. My sun is you. Your light blinds me and I see nothing—" he whispered under his breath, touching my lips ever so lightly, teasingly, "—but you." Every part of my body trembled from the stolen contact. "You are my sun and my fire. Being near you warms my soul. Without you, I would be relegated to the cold, the dark. I would lose myself forever."

As I was still melting in Evan's warmth, he unexpectedly pulled back and looked me in the eye, smiling like the cat that ate the canary. "Time's up," he whispered, puzzling me.

A loud noise woke me with a jolt.

I opened my eyes groggily. Sadness crept over me as I gradually made out the ceiling overhead. My alarm clock was still blaring, announcing that the day had begun, when I turned and met Evan's dark eyes. He was leaning against my bedroom window, looking vaguely amused. "Good morning," he whispered sweetly, not even trying to hide the smile on his face. Before I could say a word he was lying at my side, his hand brushing a lock of hair from my cheek. My eyes were immediately drawn to the dog tag that glinted on the dark-red, long-sleeved shirt he wore. *Gevan*. My heart still skipped a beat every time I read our names engraved together on the metal.

"You're such a liar!" I punched him on the shoulder, frowning and trying unsuccessfully to sound annoyed. "Why do you keep messing with me? You should warn me when we're inside my head. But then again, why would you, since you've realized that teasing me is more fun than anything else in the world?"

"I didn't just 'realize' it. I've always known it," he said with a grin. All at once his expression grew more serious, verging on sadness. "I'm sorry. It's the only way I can read inside you, Gemma. Plus it saves you the embarrassment of having to hide your feelings. You know it's useless. When you're aware we're in your dreams you're never completely comfortable because you know I can detect all your emotions."

"You should tell me anyway."

"I'll try to remember that. But this time it really was necessary. I needed to sense your feelings while I told you about my past. I didn't want to upset you too much."

Evan's explanation stopped me from replying and I accepted his apology with a simple glance. He grinned at me cheerfully. "You'd better get ready. You wouldn't want to make me late for my first day back at school, would you?"

I couldn't believe time had flown so fast. Five months had already gone by since the beginning of my second life, the night I'd called a truce with death. But a dark feeling inside me made me suspect it wouldn't last forever, that my covenant with fate was destined to be broken. Although the last few months had been the most intense period of my entire life, I'd never stopped jumping at every sound and wondering when Death would come to take me. I'd never lowered my guard and I knew Evan hadn't either, though he tried hard to hide it. Wherever we were, I could sense the concern in his watchful glances. I'd always been good at that, as if Evan were part of my body. And so I drank in every moment, savored every sensation, every breath, afraid it might be my last. I forgot my fears only when I sought refuge in my books, hiding away in other worlds. But then I had to return to reality—a reality where, despite all my fears, there was Evan. I couldn't have wished for better.

"Right." I gave a resigned sigh. "Here we go again!" I pressed my lips together and tried to summon up a little enthusiasm. It was annoying to have to concentrate on anything that distracted me from Evan. We'd become inseparable. We were together all day and at night he would sneak into my dreams. I'd sensed the strength of my connection to him when we'd first met on that March afternoon that was destined to change my fate. It felt so long ago and yet whenever I looked back I found the past following me like a ghost.

"You know, at first no one understood me," I confessed out of the blue, "but I could feel it. I felt deep down that something in my life was about to change, that pretty soon something was going to turn it upside down." I looked him in the eye. "No, not something. *Someone.* I always knew, from the moment I saw that strange light—and then you appeared."

Evan studied my face, puzzled. "What light?"

"The burst of light that lit up the sky just before I met you in the woods," I said, recollecting the memory that I'd thought he shared.

"I have no idea what you're talking about," he said, almost amused.

I blinked in confusion. I hadn't expected Evan to contradict me. He threw his head back and his spirited laughter rang out. "Gemma, there are millions of us and we're constantly moving around. There's no strange flash of light heralding our arrival. If there were, the sky would be an endless fireworks show." His reply threw me so off guard it left me wordless. I'd always been convinced the light was somehow connected to their arrival in Lake Placid.

Evan laughed again, probably amused by my expression. "Don't be silly. It must have been a UFO. Besides, Angels can't fly, didn't you know that?"

Disoriented, I decided to drop it. Footsteps outside my door put me on alert. We exchanged a fleeting glance and he vanished the second my mom came into the room.

"Morning!" she chimed. "Awake already? I came to check. Just wanted to make sure you didn't oversleep on the first day of school."

"Thanks for reminding me," I mumbled, throwing myself back onto the bed and pulling the covers over my face. Actually, I was hoping she wouldn't notice my cheeks were still aflame. Feeling the mattress sag beneath her weight, I uncovered my head. She was sitting beside me, looking at me with a doting expression that made me cringe. My God, Evan was somewhere in the room. I hoped she wouldn't say anything embarrassing.

"Eighteen years old! I still can't believe you've grown up so fast," she said with a sigh.

"Mom, it's not my birthday yet!" I protested, blushing with embarrassment.

"But you're already so *different,*" she insisted, almost with regret. "You'll be graduating this year and you already have a boyfriend . . ."

I stiffened. My face must have been crimson. Evan was probably getting a kick out of my expression. Unexpectedly, he reappeared behind my mom. I cringed and shot him a disapproving look, but he continued to move closer, forcing me to make a face that would stop him in his tracks.

"Gemma, are you all right?" Frowning, Mom glanced over her shoulder and turned back to look at me. Instead of worrying about Evan's presence, I should have been watching my reactions.

Evan continued to shake his head, clearly finding the situation hilarious. Then I noticed his eyes glowing like a diamond of ice. For some strange reason neither of us understood I was the only person capable of seeing him in his ethereal form.

The situation at home had gotten simpler since Evan's endless requests to meet my folks had finally worn me down and I'd introduced him to them, albeit reluctantly. He was used to following a different etiquette. Since then his brother Drake had had to take on my physical appearance and replace me a lot less often but, given his willingness to help, we frequently took advantage of this power of his, especially at night.

Before meeting Evan and his family I'd never seen a bond as strong as the one they all shared. It was a deep, unconditional affection that had instantly extended to me. I could feel it under my skin. For the first time in my life I felt I was part of something. They treated me like I was a member of their family too.

Ginevra in particular had turned out to be the sister I'd never had, probably because she was the most aware of how intense my feelings for Evan were and his for me, which in some way made them her own. Whenever I remembered how convinced I'd been that she was my rival I felt stupid and hoped she wasn't around, otherwise she'd have managed to read it in my mind. It was a relief not to have to compete with Ginevra's exasperating beauty, even though she was always trying to boost my self-esteem. Out of kindness, of course.

"You'd better get ready," Mom said, leaving the room.

"What on earth were you thinking?" I hissed at Evan, shaking, the moment the door clicked shut.

"Did you say something?" She opened the door a crack and peered in.

I instantly froze and stole a glance at Evan's eyes. They were still gray, meaning she couldn't see him. "No, Mom. I'll hurry and get dressed," I stammered with embarrassment.

She shut the door again and I sighed, my heartbeat gradually slowing.

"Are you trying to give me a heart attack?" I whispered, being careful not to speak loud enough to be overheard. I raised my hands in frustration. He gently took me by the wrists, breaking down all my defenses. I tried to free myself but it was no use. Evan was too strong.

"Relax, she can't see me," he murmured, pulling me against him. I melted into his embrace as he stared at me from under his long eyelashes, his gray eyes flecked with gold. "You're so beautiful it almost scares me," he whispered.

"Scares you? Why?" I asked, bewildered.

"Because for the first time I have something to lose."

I pressed my lips against his, parting them gently.

"Give me a few minutes to go home and get my motorcycle. I didn't need it last night. Meanwhile, get ready," he whispered between one light kiss and the next.

"Okay, but come back soon."

Every time Evan had to leave me, even for a little while, I panicked. A strange anxiety filled me, as though I were underwater and someone had taken away my snorkel. I couldn't breathe.

Sometimes Evan had to go away on a mission, the nature of which I didn't want to know. On those occasions—which had been more frequent lately—I avoided thinking about what was going on in who knew what part of the world Evan had been called to to intervene. In general he was never gone for longer than a few hours, but it was long enough to agitate me and reawaken the ghosts that I tried to lock up in the farthest reaches of my subconscious. And yet there they were. They always came back.

When he returned I never asked him for an explanation. I didn't have the strength—or probably the courage—to handle the answers. I preferred not to know.

"I'll ride like a madman to get back to you as fast as I can," he promised. I abandoned myself to the warmth of his lips and he vanished, leaving me with the memory of his kiss.

I sighed, my heart full of butterflies. "You *always* ride like a madman," I murmured. Smiling, I shook my head. My ears were burning and my breathing was rapid, as if I needed more air. Why did Evan always have this effect on me?

I hurried to the closet, took out an old pair of jeans faded at the knees and put them on along with my gray-and-red Nikes and a hooded sweatshirt in the same colors.

Ten minutes later an aggressive roar from outside told me Evan had arrived, but it didn't sound like his motorcycle. I glanced out the window, though my mind had conjured the image even before my eyes could.

Evan beamed at me, leaning against the hood of his Ferrari, and waved for me to join him as another car right behind him—Ginevra's Lamborghini—revved its engine. He shrugged, amused, and I shook my head in resignation.

I took the stairs two at a time and opened the door before Mom could try to make us stay for breakfast, but Evan was right there in front of me, blocking the way.

"Mr. Bloom," Evan said, nodding at my dad, who nodded back. Then he turned to my mom. "Mrs. Bloom."

"Good morning, Evan," she said with her customary enthusiasm. She had no idea we'd just spent the night together. "Care to join us for breakfast? Go on, help yourself to whatever you want."

Evan cordially held up his hands. "Thanks, but I already ate at home," he lied.

I'd never been enthused by the thought of Dad and Evan in the same room. Anxious to get out of the kitchen, I grabbed something from the table and slid it into my army-green backpack. Evan watched me steadily as I zipped it up, a strange look on his face.

"What?! I'll eat it when we get to school!" I said.

"She'll eat it when we get to school," he repeated, resigned, turning to my parents.

I walked out the door and closed it behind us. It was going to be a long day, I was sure of it.

The September morning promised to be hot; the sky was clear and the air still. "You changed your mind?" I asked Evan, nodding at the car. "I thought you were going to get your bike." I tried not to show my embarrassment as I imagined the looks we were bound to attract at school.

Wearing a sly smile that obviously masked something else, he glanced at the tinted windshield of the car behind us. "We have something else planned before going to school."

Behind us, Ginevra rolled down her window. The gleam in her jade-green eyes said it all. There was going to be a race. A shiver ran through my body.

"Don't forget to buckle up," Ginevra said with a hint of sarcasm.

"Good thing I didn't eat," I grumbled.

"Shall we go?" Evan said.

"Do we really have to?" I asked, although I already knew the answer. But my reluctance was probably due more to having to start school again than to the attention we'd draw with their sports cars. I would never forget our summer vacation together, not for the rest of my life. It was hard to face the fact it was over.

Evan opened the passenger door for me and strode back to his side. I sank into the low seat as he and Ginevra exchanged challenging looks in the rearview mirror. Things were looking bad. *Very bad.* I wasn't sure he wasn't communicating telepathically with his sister. His eyes sparked with impatience, as did Ginevra's. I could see her face reflected in the sun visor mirror.

"Hold on tight," Evan told me before zooming off.

THE WALLS OF THE SOUL

Despite my initial reluctance, the first hours flew by in a flash. The thought that I would have Evan sitting next to me during most of my classes was comforting, though his presence did absorb a lot of my attention.

"You busy this afternoon?" he asked as I opened my locker.

What a strange question, I thought, searching for my Spanish book.

Evan peeked inside my locker. "*Forbidden.*" He picked up a novel half-buried under pages of calculus notes and cast me a sly glance, leaning in toward my ear. "I see you've started to enjoy breaking the rules. You don't need to read manuals, though. If you want, I can show you a couple things that aren't exactly allowed." He grinned.

I took the book from his hands and bopped him on the head with it. "Dummy. It's not a manual! It's a beautiful love story between a brother and sister."

"Love story? Where I come from that's called incest. And I thought I'd heard everything!"

"Well, it's wonderful," I said, contradicting him. He laughed.

"Sure it is." He raised an eyebrow and looked at me slyly again. "You didn't answer my question." He banged the locker shut to grab my attention, his biceps taut.

"Hmm . . . Just a sec, let me see . . . Oh, right! There's this boy, you know. I've got to introduce you to him sometime. I think I'm going to hang out with him. If you don't mind, that is," I teased, assessing his face.

"Bad idea," Evan grunted. He leaned in and whispered directly against my skin, "If you did, I would have to kill him." He rested his forearm on my locker, trapping me against it.

I shook my head. "I don't think you'd be able to." His breath on my face was leaving me dazed. "For your own good, you shouldn't try to fight him," I whispered, my voice breaking with emotion as Evan stroked my skin with the tip of his nose.

"And why not?" he asked softly, moving his lips closer to my throat.

The warmth of his breath gave me goosebumps. I swallowed, forgetting where we were. "Well, he's . . . pretty strong. *Incredibly strong*," I whispered, trapped in the thrill caused by the heat of his body so close to mine. Over the last few weeks it was as if a fuse had been lit between us that could trigger an explosion at any moment.

"Oh, really? What else is he like?" he whispered, stroking my neck with his nose.

My eyes fluttered nervously. "This might shock you, but I'm beginning to suspect he's an Angel."

"An Angel?" he replied, shaking his head. "Then I don't stand a chance."

"And he's gorgeous too," I added.

Evan smiled. "Definitely not as gorgeous as you," he quickly said, his gaze both sweet and firm. "Still, I'm afraid you'll have to decline his invitation."

"Why on earth should I?" I asked, bewitched by him, utterly at the mercy of my emotions.

"Because," he whispered, resting his lips below my ear, "I have a surprise for you."

"A surprise? What kind of surprise?"

His face lit up. When he smiled like this, little creases formed under his eyes, driving me wild. "I'm afraid you'll have to wait to find out. That is, if you're willing to run the risk."

"What risk?"

Evan stepped even closer, his breath caressing my skin. "The risk of being alone with me." I swallowed, waiting to feel his lips on mine, but instead he moved them to my ear. "But then," he whispered, "your Angel might get jealous and, again, I would have to kill him."

"No danger of that," I said, shaking myself out of the dreamy state he'd put me in. "I don't think he's the jealous type."

"You don't—you don't think that I—that *he's* the jealous type?"

"*I'm* the one who should be," I said confidently.

He drew a long breath against my neck, wound his hand in my hair and pressed his lips against mine. "You don't know how wrong you are about that." He moved back just far enough to look me in the eye, his hand still in my hair, his tone suddenly serious. "I'd rip the heart out of anyone who dared to even touch you." He caressed my earlobe with his lips tenderly as his voice enraptured me. "You're mine," he whispered. "All mine."

"Definitely," I agreed. I sought his lips but before I could touch them I noticed the silence that ruled in the now-empty hallway. It shook me out of my trance.

"We'd better get to class," I said, tucking my hair behind my ear. Actually, I was afraid I wouldn't be able to control myself any more. "So what can you tell me about the surprise?"

Evan laughed at my curiosity without offering me an answer.

In the hours that followed I didn't manage to get even a scrap of information out of him. But then again, patience wasn't my virtue and he knew it. It wasn't fair of him to lead me on like this. Whenever I asked him about it, he looked at me with a strange smile on his face. My curiosity grew with each passing minute.

"Can't you tell m—"

Evan rested a finger on my lips to cut me off. He looked down at my hand and clasped it in his. Then he slid his thumb through the elastic band around my wrist and slowly slid it back up to my forearm where I always wore it in winter. During the summer, instead, I kept it around my upper arm. I'd had it so long I felt naked without it, but once in a while, when Evan was gone for longer than a few hours, he would take it as a keepsake.

"I think you're ready now," he said, leaving me even more puzzled. "But you'll have to be patient enough to wait a few more hours to find out," he warned, more and more amused by the look on my face.

Classes flew by with the predictable lightness of the first days of school. The classrooms were just as I remembered them, our blue-and-yellow school colors lining the walls, and even in the cafeteria our little group was still the same, with just one enjoyable difference: Evan sat beside me now. It made me happy, but it made someone else unhappy, I was sure of it. Peter feigned indifference, but sometimes when Evan kissed me or held my hand I became aware of his furtive glances and the bitterness hidden in his eyes felt like a punch in the chest. My best friend was suffering because of me and although I was sorry about it, there was nothing I could do.

Giving in to my impatience, the afternoon arrived at last, heralded by Evan's BMW X6, a black shark on the gray asphalt.

"Finally," I exclaimed. After school I'd eaten a late lunch with my parents and eagerly waited for Evan to pick me up.

"Your surprise wasn't ready yet," he apologized, though I was sure he was intentionally being vague just to pique my curiosity. He'd always enjoyed teasing me.

"I imagine you're not going to tell me what that means," I said, resigned.

Evan laughed and tapped me under the chin. "What is it exactly that you don't get about the word 'surprise'?"

I shot him a sidelong glance as I buckled my seatbelt. Evan lowered his head and looked at me. "I wanted everything to be perfect."

With this, another silence fell. Only one thing was clear at this point: his idea of a surprise allowed for no hints or clues of any kind, so I promised myself I wouldn't bother begging for them. His driving was aggressive but I was perfectly at ease sunk back in my seat. All of a sudden Evan laughed and I wondered why.

"Stop chewing on your shirt," he said, grinning.

"I wasn't!" Embarrassed, I hid my fists inside my sleeves.

"Now you need to close your eyes," he ordered after a moment, his tone gentle. "It's part of the surprise." I made a wary face and he shrugged in response. "And no peeking," he warned before I even had the chance to try. In the darkness behind my closed eyelids, I heard his engine being switched off.

"We're there."

"So can I open my eyes?" I asked eagerly.

Evan chuckled. "Your impatience is equaled only by your stubbornness."

"Look who's talking!" I shot back, my eyes still closed.

His door slammed shut, cutting off the last half of my remark. Almost instantly, I heard my door open and felt a wave of fresh air that smelled like the woods.

"Here, I'll help you out." Evan took my hand and I entrusted myself to him. "But don't open your eyes," he insisted.

The seat of the SUV was pretty high up and I held on tight to Evan until I heard the crackle of dry leaves beneath my feet. We had to be in the forest, I was sure of it. I could recognize its scent with my eyes shut. I took a deep breath of the cool, fragrant air, letting Evan guide me for a few yards. Then he stopped and I did the same.

"Now you can open them," he whispered, his tone cautious, as if he wasn't entirely certain what effect the surprise might have on me. I froze, not sure I wanted to open them. I didn't know if my hesitation was a reflection of Evan's or if it was caused by something else. A sense of foreboding. I took a deep breath and, when I felt ready, banished the feeling and raised my eyelids.

What I saw left me petrified, trapped in a body too heavy to drag away even as my mind screamed at me to run.

"You weren't ready yet. I knew it!" Evan cursed under his breath. "Ginevra warned me I should wait."

I shook my head to recover from the shock. "N-no, everything's fine," I said, hoping to wipe the disappointment off his face. My reaction had clearly ruined the surprise for him—and his good mood.

Silently I thanked God Evan couldn't read my mind and realize I was actually fighting back tears. Still, it was something I would have had to face sooner or later. I swallowed and stared at it again: the old lake house. I couldn't take my eyes off the worn walls covered with red ivy. Not a day went by that I didn't think about what had happened that night and not a day went by that I didn't try to suppress the memory and bury it in the deepest reaches of my mind.

Staring at the house that looked so comforting now by the light of day, it was almost impossible to believe it was the place where I'd experienced my worst nightmare. The place I'd been tortured. The place I'd died. A shiver turned my back ice cold. Why had Evan brought me back there? Why inflict such cruelty?

"Gemma, I'm sure you're wondering why I'm making you face the issue, but I'm also sure you already know the answer. At night I can sense your fears and I want to help you overcome them. You said yourself once that you can't go on climbing over all the walls you find in your way—you need to destroy them to be able to say you've overcome the fears—or you'll always end up expecting them whenever you turn around." He paused. "Think you're ready?"

I nodded, worried that if I tried to speak the words might catch in my throat.

"Come on," he whispered, cautiously holding out his hand.

After a moment of uncertainty, I took it. My knees shook with the same intense terror I'd experienced months ago and thought I'd left behind. Reliving it was harder than I would have expected.

I climbed the first step and the contact with the wood triggered a chaotic stream of images that raced through my mind too quickly for me to grasp them. All I could see was blood, shards of glass, terror. And then that face . . . Faust's eyes blinded by hatred, corroded by his thirst for revenge.

I thought I might faint.

Evan urged me forward, climbing the wooden steps to the front door with me. "The surprise isn't over yet," he whispered to reassure me, my hand clasped in his.

It was hard to breathe; I took deep gulps of air as if I were about to go underwater. The door opened by itself.

Inside, however, I didn't find what I'd expected. What my eyes registered had no connection whatsoever to the difficult, painful memory I'd kept hidden in the darkest recesses of my mind. Everything was spick and span, as if that hellish night had never happened. There was no trace of the stage on which the violent battle had been enacted, first featuring me—tortured to a bloody pulp—and then Evan, who'd struggled to defend me and save my life until the curtain had finally fallen and I'd died.

I'd been given a second chance and I owed it all to Evan and his family.

Finding myself in that place again, reliving the memory, was the last thing I'd expected. But the light that shone inside the house gave it a new look, new possibilities. For a moment it didn't even seem like the same abandoned structure I remembered with such bitterness. It was so different.

The dust had been swept away and the walls were no longer gray with age. The coral curtains seemed to glow in the light that filtered through them. Amazed, I let go of Evan's hand and stepped forward, looking around. My action finally seemed to relax him; he smiled with relief and a glimmer of satisfaction.

Anything that might have reminded me of that night had been repaired. The floor was intact and the stair my foot had plunged through, leaving a gash in my flesh, had been fixed. Everything looked shiny and new. The windowpanes had been replaced, the roof mended, even the ceiling beam had been reinstalled. Everything was so perfect and orderly that for a second I almost thought I might have dreamed it all. It was just a comforting lie—I knew it—but it was comforting all the same.

"Thank you," I whispered to Evan.

"I did my best. Actually, we all pitched in so you'd forget, Gemma—in the normal sense of the word, just to be clear. I know you'll probably never be able to erase the memory completely, but I was hoping this might help."

"It does," I reassured him, holding back a pang of emotion, because it was the truth. "It's like nothing ever happened in this house. Thank you, Evan. You've done something I thought was impossible."

"We'll make new memories here. Memories of *us*." He smiled, lost in a thought all his own. "But don't forget to thank Ginevra too!"

"I'll remember. And thanks for helping me get over everything in the more traditional way too. You know what I mean."

"You mean Simon. He would never have done that without your consent."

"I think they're two sides of the same coin. On the one hand, his power to summon any memory and read it through the eyes of the person who's experienced it is fascinating, but I find the other aspect terrible."

"Deleting memories is a painful process, but its effect is even worse. I agree with you that it's terrible. Eliminating a part of your past is like leaving a hole in your mind, a gap that threatens to make you stumble eventually. Memories, even distant or seemingly inaccessible ones, are always there, just waiting for a scent, a gesture, a look, to unearth them from your subconscious. But when you delete them, the process is irreversible and, no matter how crazy it might seem, a part of you, a part of your personality, is wiped away forever. Every instant helps make us who we are. Our minds never stop and every thought is another step toward who we'll become. Simon is very careful with his power. He only uses it in extreme cases, to erase a traumatic experience."

"Like dying," I said.

"Like dying," he confirmed somberly.

"The grand piano!" I exclaimed, walking over to the instrument that my mind remembered as a crumpled heap. It was now intact.

Evan followed me, looking pleased. Feeling like a little girl looking at presents ready to be unwrapped, I ran my hand over its mahogany curves. A shaft of golden light reflected off its surface, making it glow. I rested my hand on the ivory keys, pressing one of them with my finger. The note that played was faint and echoed softly through the room, nothing at all like the out-of-tune senseless series of notes Peter and I would bang out when we were little kids.

"Do you play?" he asked, his voice more melodious than the piano note.

"No, but something tells me you do," I said, looking at him skeptically.

Evan bowed his head, smiling at the veiled compliment, then raised the piano top and searched inside. Just as I was craning my neck to see what he was looking for he pulled out a violin. I stared at him, puzzled, but he didn't give me the chance to speak. "It's part of the surprise," he said, looking amused at my expression of amazement. It was the same violin depicted in the family portrait in Evan's room. I recognized it by the beautiful flower carved into its scroll. He saw me staring at it and stroked it with his fingertips.

"It's an orchid. It was my mother's favorite flower. Our housekeeper Edina would always place a fresh one on our piano. My mother had this violin crafted just for me so I would always remember her. For many years after my death she always kept it with her, and when she died I went back for it."

"It's beautiful," I murmured.

He beamed. "I have an electric one too, but it gets on Ginevra's nerves."

"The one with the hole in the middle!" I exclaimed, remembering an unusually shaped instrument I'd seen beside the piano in their house. The wood was wine-colored and looked solid, but there was actually a hole in the middle of it.

"I like to keep up with the times," he said with a wink, his smile softening. His eyes grew intense as he rested the violin on his shoulder.

I watched him in silence, fascinated. Evan tucked the violin under his chin, his gaze penetrating mine. For a moment I felt naked, as if he'd torn down every barrier between us and was reading me, reaching places not even I knew about. Our eyes, our minds, our souls were irremediably intertwined. He clasped the bow in his right hand and the whole room filled with sound, transporting me beyond the confines of reality.

BEYOND THE LIMITS OF REALITY

The melancholy conveyed by Evan's music was so intense it was almost tangible, a melodious testament to the pain he bore inside — pain he was revealing for the first time. He had closed his eyes with the first notes, drawn in by the stream of emotion, and as my skin quivered to the sweet, sad strains, my heart bled to see the suffering on his face. He was lost in a memory. His fingers moved quickly, striking the bow against the strings almost angrily in pursuit of that dark emotion. Seeing him vulnerable like that disoriented me. For the first time Evan looked defenseless, unprotected by the tough, impenetrable armor I was so accustomed to seeing him wear. He'd taken it off, inviting me closer. I'd relived with him the memory that most tormented him, and now that memory was taking shape, coming alive under his fingertips. Every tiny vibration that rose into the air seemed to return, striking him straight in the heart.

Then the music softened into a slower theme brimming with sadness and nostalgia. Evan knit his brow, lost in the shadows of his past and, slowly, the melody gave way to silence. He opened his eyes, his gaze lost, and I smiled at him because I'd understood the meaning behind his gesture: he'd wanted to give me a part of himself.

"I hadn't played that for centuries," he whispered, the same sadness in his eyes I'd seen when he'd lost himself in the memory of his mother. The sadness of nostalgia, the regret of knowing you'd lost someone forever. "It was my mother's song."

"Danielle." I said her name in a whisper. "It's lovely. Did she compose it?" I asked hesitantly.

Evan nodded, struggling to re-emerge from the devastating memory. "She always used to play it when I was a boy sitting beside her at the piano. When I was too anxious to fall asleep, I would often doze off to the sound of her voice humming that melody."

The melancholy notes mirrored the sadness Evan's mother must have felt night after night as she waited for her husband to come home, playing her song time and time again, pouring her pain into the ivory keys and forcing herself to hide her feelings from her son.

When Evan turned to look at me, a hint of a smile appeared on his lips and I was ashamed of the fleeting emotion I'd just felt. My face had betrayed me, only for a moment, but long enough for him to detect my mild disappointment. It wasn't like me to be so self-centered but I hadn't been able to keep a thought from forcing its way into my head. Evan had glimpsed a glimmer of hope fading inside me—the hope that he'd improvised those notes right then and there for me. I forced a smile, embarrassed by how easily he'd managed to probe my feelings. He rested the violin on his shoulder again, his gaze locked onto mine.

Seconds later, notes returned to fill the silence as his fingers moved quickly on the ebony fingerboard and the bow being drawn over the strings conveyed the intensity of a different emotion: frustration. Almost as if the notes could talk, nostalgia had been replaced by dismay.

I recognized the piece instantly. I'd heard it only once before but my brain had jealously guarded the memory, bringing it to the forefront of my mind a thousand times, conjuring the magic of our first dance together when Evan had confessed his feelings and our bodies had touched for the first time.

I looked at him, surprised, but Evan smiled at me calmly. "Remind you of anything?" he whispered, a sly look on his face.

"You said it was our song," I murmured, blinking. "You mean you composed it yourself?" I stared at him, amazed by the revelation.

"Just for you," he whispered, his eyes focused on me. The melody rose into the air, intense and full of harmonic nuances. A motif that I now knew was all mine—all ours.

"I often played this back when I thought I had no choice," he explained as a light tingle swept over my body. "I felt oppressed, but I still hadn't figured out why. I couldn't understand why it hurt so much to think about you," he went on as the intense, heart-rending music yielded to a sweeter, calmer melody, releasing a river of emotions inside me, hot and cold at the same time. I could never forget how that night had changed my life—the night that should have been my last. "I added this part only after I'd saved you. It sprang from my fingers without my realizing it, like it had always belonged here. It showed me that my decision was the only one I could possibly have made." His hands came to rest, finishing the song.

"Why didn't you ever tell me you could play so well?" I asked after a few seconds.

"Bragging isn't one of my virtues. But that night at the dance I dedicated it to you, remember?"

"Yes, but I could never have imagined you'd written it for me."

"It all seemed so complicated back then," he murmured, stifling a bitter laugh. "When actually"—he brushed a lock of hair from my face and tucked it behind my ear—"it's so easy to love you, Gemma. It's like breathing, something so automatic, so natural, that you can't survive without it unless you're searching for death."

I half closed my eyes at the warmth of his lips on mine. He barely touched them, withdrew slightly, then kissed me again in a sensual game that threatened to drive me crazy. His dark eyes probed mine, hiding another, deeper desire. Physical contact with Evan had always triggered strong emotions in me, but over the last few weeks the invisible cord that connected me to him had caught fire and I was in danger of losing my way. My longing for him was becoming harder and harder to contain, especially when his gaze met mine and I could see his desire for me in his eyes. I felt a primitive yearning whenever he touched me, whenever he kissed me. I longed to feel his hands on me, his body against mine. I was afraid I'd catch fire every time his kisses intensified, expressing what we weren't able to reveal aloud.

Evan leaned his head over my shoulder and caressed it with his nose, barely touching my skin, then kissed it tenderly as I melted in his warmth.

"Y-you should teach me sometime," I stammered, desperately trying to control myself.

"To do what?" he whispered as his lips continued their slow exploration of my neck.

"To play. I'd like to learn how to play."

My eyelashes trembled as his mouth slowly curved into a smile. He slid behind me and, still holding the violin firmly, raised my arms. "Why not right now?"

His voice caressed my ear, making me quiver. "Not a bad idea," I replied, dizzy.

"Hold it like this." He gave me the violin and positioned it on my shoulder. As I leaned toward the instrument the back of my head brushed against his chest, making my heart flutter. I closed my eyes and Evan swallowed, standing behind me in silence for a moment. "You need to rest your chin here. It'll feel awkward at first, but later on you won't even think about it." He clasped my right hand in his, holding the bow, and drew it across the strings. "Now close your eyes and let the music guide you."

I did as he said and another slow melody filled the silence. Evan's hand guided mine, moving it slowly as his hot breath tickled my ear. I couldn't think of anything but his body behind mine. I could feel his every breath, every muscle, every movement.

"You're pretty good," he whispered, a sly smile painted on his face.

"I am—unless we consider that you're the one who's playing; you're only using me. Your hands are moving the strings," I said sardonically. As usual, he was teasing me.

"Then maybe I should move them somewhere else . . . Onto you, for example," he said provocatively, tracing a line across my neck with his nose.

My eyelids fluttered as his meaning sank in. Evan laughed out loud and moved away from me. Without him to lean on, I felt dizzy for a second. Or maybe it was my untamable longing for him. "I'd better sit down," I said as I lowered myself, straddling the piano bench.

Evan laughed again, no doubt aware of how he was making me feel. He sat down on the bench facing me, one leg on each side. "All this music must be having a strange effect on you," he said, his smile turning into a grin. Before I could breathe he grabbed my rear with both hands and pulled me toward him. "Or maybe it's me," he whispered against my lips, his wild gaze locked onto mine as I melted, burning with desire. Resting his forehead against mine, he attempted to control himself, but his unsteady breathing betrayed him, faithful testimony of his emotions.

I was dazed, trapped in a dreamlike state. His lips were so close, his body so hot. The heat between us had grown so intense it left me feverish. I stared at his mouth and he at mine as our tormented breaths merged. His lips brushed a corner of mine, and again, igniting my longing for him as our tongues touched ever so slightly. The touch of him on my lips was paradise.

"I could faint from pleasure at the touch of your mouth," I whispered, utterly under his spell.

Evan's hands clasped my waist and his thumb slowly slid beneath my top. My skin burned beneath his fingers. Our mouths wavered a millimeter from each other, exploring a new desire, almost as if they'd never touched before. We stared at each other's lips, intoxicated by the same thought. "Maybe we need some fresh air," I suggested, trying to calm my heartbeat. The electrical connection stretching from him to me threatened to electrocute us with each breath.

Evan smiled, leaning back slightly. Although he never pressured me in these situations, he always made me be the one to stop us. "As you wish," he replied, sounding resigned, his gaze on mine. He took my hand, led me to the door, and paused on the threshold. "And so he took her hand and clasped it in his own because she knew he would never leave her," he said, his breath uneven, running his thumb over my lip. Sometimes we had fun speaking in the third person like we were characters in a book.

"And she felt as though her heart would burst," I said, my head spinning.

Evan sought my mouth again, unable to subdue his desire. "We risk setting the house on fire," he whispered with a smile.

"That would be a shame." I shook my head, trying to recover from the surge of emotion he'd triggered in me.

Evan noticed and smiled again, seeming proud of the effect he'd had on me. "Ginevra would never forgive us," he exclaimed, amused. "She worked so hard to make everything perfect."

"Well, I know how we can avoid it."

"Interesting," he said with a sly smile. "What do you suggest?"

I bit my lip, shot him a look that dared him to follow and pulled him through the trees toward the lake.

"Where are you taking me?" he asked, curious.

"I want to show you something," I said, intentionally vague. It was my turn to surprise him. Something had crossed my mind: a place Peter and I used to go to a lot when we were children breaking the rules. It wasn't far from the old lake house. Evan followed me without protesting until the calm waters of Lake Placid were spread out before us. I stopped, satisfied.

"Are we there?" he asked, letting slip a hint of impatience. Unsure of my intentions, he looked at his car, parked nearby.

"Not yet," I said, keeping him in suspense to get back at him. With a smile, I jerked my chin over our heads at the cable that stretched across the mirror of water.

"You can't mean—" Evan shot me a glance and I confirmed his suspicion with a nod, looking him in the eye. He laughed, understanding the crazy idea I had in mind. To reach the uppermost point of the cable, we had to climb to the top of a rugged slope where it was tied to a big tree. Although I hadn't been there for years the old wooden steps were just like I remembered them. Hanging from the zip line were thick handles that would slide down the cable all the way to the small clearing on the opposite shore. It was an experience I'd always found electrifying.

I grabbed one of the two handles and turned to face Evan.

"Looks like fun!" he exclaimed without a trace of hesitation.

"Follow me," I dared him, my gaze sensual, and leapt into the void.

I plunged downward. When I was close enough to the water, I stretched out my legs so my feet grazed its surface. Evan leapt after me, catching up in no time. We twirled through the air, one beside the other, as Evan pulled my cord closer to him, hanging on with only one hand.

Moments later we'd reached the opposite shore. I barely felt my feet touch the ground. Evan was holding me gently in his arms, almost like we were levitating. He relaxed his grip and for a moment I lost my balance.

"Well?" I asked him, studying his expression. "Fun?"

Evan shot me a strange look and grabbed my hand. "I know a way that's even more fun." He reached over his head, grabbed his red T-shirt, and pulled it off. His dog tag jingled against his white undershirt that was so tight every muscle showed. He smiled at me, his eyes locked onto mine for a moment with that penetrating look that made my head spin. My heart skipped a beat as I thought of us back on the piano bench just minutes ago, but before I could ask him for an explanation he grabbed me, cradled me in his arms, and carried me up to the top.

I was about to take hold of one of the handles but Evan stopped me. "Wait." He moved closer. "I want to try something first." He grabbed both handles in one hand and opened his other arm to guide me over. "After you," he whispered, holding my gaze.

"What do you have in mind?" I asked warily, casting a sidelong glance at his teasing smile. I grabbed the first handle and after a moment felt Evan's body against mine.

"Ready?" Evan whispered, his lips behind my ear.

I tilted my head and my cheek brushed his, right behind me. The light contact between us rendering words impossible, I half closed my eyes as his breath on my neck made my heart tremble. He took firm hold of the handles supporting us both and leapt into the void.

Considering the combined weight of our bodies, I prepared to hold my breath, certain that the wind would make the crossing more difficult and we would end up in the lake. I expected the descent to happen quickly like last time, but instead we seemed to be moving slower. I heard Evan's low laugh vibrate through our bodies and guessed why, basking in the pleasant sensation the thought triggered in me: Evan was controlling the air to make us move slower, to prolong the interval when our bodies were pressed together. Almost in slow motion, the surface of the water came nearer until our feet were inches above it. Evan's warm voice caressed my neck. "Now let go."

"W-What?!" I exclaimed, shocked. What was he thinking?

"I'll hold you." Evan let go with one hand, encircling my body from behind with his arm as he held on tighter with the other to support us both. "Trust me, Jamie," he insisted in a tender voice.

An uncontrollable impulse made me obey him. I cautiously relaxed my grip and let go. Evan held me up with one arm without any apparent difficulty. I squeezed his hand as the surface of the water slowly ran beneath our feet. He let go of the handle with his other hand and I froze in panic, my breath caught in my throat, but his arms held me tenderly. The breeze softened as we gradually slowed down in a way that defied the laws of physics and then stopped halfway across. My foot was touching the liquid surface but I wasn't sinking.

"Evan!" I exclaimed, frightened and amazed.

We were floating, suspended on the mirror of water. "What's— How is this possible?" I clung harder to his arm, which was rock solid, his muscles flexed, as my eyes shot nervously to the lake beneath our feet. Evan raised me slightly, turning me to face him. Though I knew I wasn't running any risk, my body refused to relax and continued to move cautiously.

"Well? Fun?" he said, echoing my question.

I slowly raised my eyes and found his smiling ones waiting for me.

"Evan! We're suspended on top of the water!!!" I cried, my fingers clutching his arm.

"Yes." He smiled as if it were the most natural thing in the world. "Isn't it electrifying?"

I looked for the right words but it was no use. It all seemed so bizarre yet it was real. "It's incredible," I said in a barely audible whisper.

It was as though Evan's coming into my life had brought down all the barriers between the real and the imaginary. There was no border between them any more; the two worlds had merged, bound together by a gossamer thread of magic—the same thread that had bound me to him since the very first day.

Evan pulled me closer to him and held me tighter.

"We're hovering on top of the water," I stammered, still unable to wrap my head around it. "It's illogical, *impossible*. How did you—?"

His laughter interrupted my babbling. "I'm an Angel, Gemma. Once in a while I like to remind you of that. I want you to be part of my world."

I leaned in to kiss him and his fingers tenderly stroked my back. Sometimes it was so natural—so *human*—to be with him that I forgot about the power intrinsic to all Subterraneans like Evan: the ability to control the elements. Fire, water, earth, air—they all obeyed his commands so he could carry out his orders.

Suddenly doubt gripped me. No, it wasn't doubt. It was a sense of foreboding. My eyes shot to Evan's. "How do we get back to shore?" I said, worried, looking for the two handles. They were long gone.

The mocking smile that spread across his face gave me the answer. All at once I realized why Evan had taken off his shirt. He'd planned this. Before I had the chance to object, the support under my feet vanished and I plunged into the cool water, still in Evan's arms that didn't let go of me for a second.

DANGEROUS EMOTIONS

"Woohoo!" Evan shouted, whipping back the dripping-wet hair that fell over his forehead. God, was he a sight to behold.

"It's freezing!" I shrieked as we treaded water in the lake.

Evan grabbed my hips and pulled me to him. "I can always warm you up," he whispered, his tone sensual. A laugh escaped him.

"You think this is funny?" I said indignantly, pretending to pout. The water wasn't actually so cold. "I can do it on my own." I pushed him away.

Evan raised his eyebrows and stared at me with a sly expression. "I never doubted you could swim." He pulled me against him harder and my heart leapt to my throat at the rough contact with his body, his face a fraction of an inch from mine. His moist lips rested softly on my mouth and the warmth they filled me with penetrated all the way to my bones. He kissed me again and again, twining his fingers in my wet hair. My hands slid up his shoulder blades, squeezed his hard shoulders, stroked the skin left bare by his undershirt.

The minutes ticked away, heedless of our longing for time to stand still, until the sunlight began to fade behind the dark mantle of forest. The sunset was our backdrop as we came out of the water. My fingers were wrinkly and my sopping-wet clothes clung to my skin as I shivered in the cool September air.

"You're cold," Evan said, thoughtfully warming my arms with his hands.

"Just a little," I stammered, forcing my teeth not to chatter.

"Take this." He leaned down, grabbed the red shirt he'd left on the grass, and offered it to me. "What are you waiting for?" he said, his eyes on me as I hesitated. "Take off your clothes and put this on. It's dry."

I took it, embarrassed. "What about you?" I asked shyly, pointing at his clothes that were as soaked as mine.

He grabbed his white undershirt by the neck and pulled it over his head. My heart skipped a beat as I stared at his bare chest as though seeing it for the first time. The reason for the quiver deep in my heart became clear to me: desire. The fierce desire to touch him, to stroke his smooth, tanned skin without the hindrance of clothing.

"I won't catch a cold if that's what's worrying you," he assured me.

From his smile, I guessed my dazed expression must have given me away. I instinctively looked away and made myself turn around, but Evan took my wrist firmly in his hand.

"Come on." He pulled me against him roughly, his gaze sensual. His voice took on the warm tone that made me melt every time I heard it. "Don't tell me you're still embarrassed to see me undressed."

I babbled something incomprehensible and lost all control as Evan held me close. His body was so warm. I tried hard to find my voice, trapped in the flow of my emotion, and opened my mouth only to close it again, powerless.

Evan's grin broadened at my awkwardness. "I was only kidding! Come on, Gemma!" he said, relaxing his grip. "I'll wait for you here. Go change or *you'll* be the one who catches a cold."

I must have been a statue of embarrassment because Evan touched his fingertip to my nose to snap me out of my daze. I blinked and stared at the red shirt. "Yeah, I guess I should," I murmured, heading toward the car.

"Everything okay back there?" Evan's voice reached me behind the door of the BMW as I took off my wet clothes, dropping them to the ground. I wasn't sure whether the trembling in my chest was because I was afraid he might take a peek in the mirror—or because I was afraid he might not.

"I'm naked and wet and going home wearing only your shirt. Is that 'okay' enough for you?"

"Hmm . . . an interesting prospect. I'd say it's okay enough." He smothered a snicker.

I got into the car and shot him a look brimming with sarcasm. "I'm really happy you're having so much fun teasing me today."

Evan leaned toward me, his face inches from mine, taking my breath away. He reached across my body and shut the door, then sat back and started the car. "Who says I was teasing?" he said with a grin, looking at me out of the corner of his eye. He stared at my mouth for a second and then, clearly unable to resist the impulse, slid his eyes down my body in a slow exploration of my legs, barely covered by his shirt. He began to move closer, his face growing serious, uncontrollable desire in his gaze, and I understood that the game threatened to become dangerous.

For the first time, his movements seemed hesitant, cautious, almost embarrassed. He slowly swept back my wet hair on one side, baring my neck, and gently caressed my skin, his face inches from mine. Tenderly, he drew his lips to the curve of my neck and rubbed his temple against my cheek. After a moment he sought my gaze, a tortured look on his face, and his forehead came to rest on mine. With a deep breath he closed his eyes, his chest trembling, revealing his desire. Was it possible he was experiencing the same emotions I felt in my heart?

"God, you're so beautiful," he whispered against my lips as his hand hesitantly slid down my skin to where the shirt didn't cover it. I half closed my eyes, pervaded by a quiver of uncontrollable heat.

"It's your shirt," I murmured, lacing my fingers with his. "You should lend it to me once in a while."

Evan smiled, his forehead resting on mine. "But then I'd have to kill anybody who saw you," he whispered, stifling a smile before growing serious again. "Do you realize you risk driving me crazy?" he murmured, narrowing his eyes.

I sought his lips with mine and ran my fingers down his bare chest, letting myself be swept away by my uncontrollable desire for him, to feel his hands on my body. I felt feverish as my mouth melded with his, my heart ready to burst. My skin wanted him. Driven by the need to eliminate the distance between us, I moved closer, lifting myself a little without taking my lips off his. My body brushed his and my need for him overwhelmed me.

In the middle of the blaze of passion that enveloped us, a glimmer of lucidity made me pull my lips away from Evan's and rest my forehead against his, forcing myself to regain control of my breathing.

We'd never spoken about it openly but I could sense how intensely Evan wanted me. At times I had the feeling his human body couldn't contain the passion that set his blood on fire. And yet he always managed to control himself, leaving the decision about when to stop to me.

Forehead to forehead, our eyes expressed our desire, locking for a long moment as our breathing grew steady again.

"We'd better go back so you can dry off," he said, my hesitation checking his impulses. I nodded without saying a word as my heart rebelled, continuing to race.

"Where are we going?" I asked as we drove, breaking the silence. Probably neither of us had ever experienced such feelings before.

"My place. That way you can put on something"—he cleared his throat and I thought he was about to say *dry*—"less dangerous." He shot me a glance.

"Less dangerous . . . " Interesting choice of words.

Contact with him had lit a fire inside me that burned silently day after day, blazing up whenever his body was close to mine. Sometimes all it took was one look from him to set it aflame, like gasoline.

A few minutes later the car stopped in Evan's driveway. I dried my hair in the bathroom and went to join him in his room but unexpectedly found it empty. I fell onto his bed. On the ivory-colored walls, the old family portrait caught my eye. It had always been there and I'd studied it down to the last detail, but his parents' faces, gazing at me from the canvas yellowed by time, had taken on a new meaning now that I knew their story. In the portrait Danielle was seated beside a piano in blond wood. Soft dark curls cascaded to her shoulders, partially obscuring Evan's hand as he stood behind her. On her lap she held a pair of long gloves in white lace. Her face looked strained, her smile dictated by circumstances. I studied her more carefully, looking into her eyes, and was startled by the depths I saw in them. It was almost as if they were actually looking at me.

The elder James stood on the other side of the grand piano, his haughty posture effectively conveying the clear-cut division between him and his family.

Evan had one arm hanging at his side, his shirtsleeve rolled up, holding his violin, of which I could see only the flower carved into the scroll. I stopped to examine it and thought how bizarre it was that this was actually him in the centuries-old painting. He hadn't changed at all except that his hair was bit shorter and less rebellious. The defiant look in his eye was the same. His dark, austere, fearless gaze stared at me from the canvas, taking my breath away. I would have loved him back then too, I was sure of it.

"Does it frighten you?" Evan's cautious tone startled me. Who knew how long he'd been watching me from the doorway.

"Not at all," I reassured him. "I wish I'd known you then," I admitted.

Unexpectedly, my answer made him laugh. "I brought you some dry clothes." He came into the room and laid them on the bed.

"I imagine I have Ginevra to thank for these."

"I'll wait for you outside so you can change."

The gallantry of his words, no matter how forced, reminded me that this was the same Evan who'd posed for that portrait three centuries ago.

"Evan," I said, causing him to pause in the doorway. "After your—" I searched for an alternative to the word *death*. "After your transformation, your appearance didn't change. I was wondering if the rest stayed the same too," I mumbled, awkwardly trying to make myself understood—though at the same time I wasn't entirely sure I wanted him to realize what I was getting at.

"That depends. What do you mean, exactly? What is it you want to know?"

Why the hell did he always have to be so direct?

"Um, well, I was wondering if—compared to when you were human—I mean, if an Angel can—" Could I manage to make him understand? I wasn't so sure.

"If he can . . . ?" he prompted, though the smile he was trying to hide spoke volumes.

"If he can still feel the same emotions, act like a human. I was wondering if your sensations have stayed the same like your body."

He came over and sat down beside me, never moving his eyes from mine. "I can't feel human emotions any more, Gemma."

The disappointment on my face made him smile. I'd felt his desire growing along with mine day after day, but maybe I'd been completely wrong. Maybe it had just been a reflection of my desire for him, a delusion. Was that what he was trying to tell me? "I thought—so you'll never feel what I feel when I'm with you," I murmured sadly. There was no point in asking him. A bitterness that I tried unsuccessfully to hide rose in my throat. I'd been fooling myself.

"I can't feel the same emotions I did when I was human," he continued, looking at me intently, "but only because the ones I feel now are much stronger."

My heart skipped a beat, allowing me to breathe again.

"They're feelings a human body isn't capable of containing. My perception no longer depends on imperfect human senses. But you should know that, Gemma. You've experienced it yourself."

I flinched at the memory Evan was evoking. Although I kept it deeply buried, it only took a moment for it to re-emerge: the sensation I'd felt when I'd left my body. I had felt freed of an enormous burden; all my perceptions—even the simple touch of Evan's hand—were amplified hundreds of times. Every impact was stronger, more vivid, more intense. So that was what Evan must feel.

I nodded in silence, shaken by the revelation.

"When there's no body to contain them, feelings expand infinitely, like they're exploding, and they're a thousand times more intense. It's like the body's an obstacle that muffles every sensation, every emotion, every desire."

I looked into his dark eyes and a new worry made its way to my lips. "How does it work when you're in human form, like now?" I asked, puzzled.

"For me it's almost the same. It doesn't matter what form I'm in. By now I've lost my original human body. In *this* body the spirit prevails over the flesh. I can materialize when I want to, but it's like I no longer belong to this world. I'm made of different matter, as if the spirit can take on corporeal form. It's hard to explain."

"No, I get it. That's why you can be injured but not killed."

"Exactly. My wounds heal in no time. I think our bodies are made of some supernatural substance that's more similar to the soul. It looks and feels like flesh but its structure is different—it's a stronger, indestructible alloy." He smiled to himself before going on. "So you don't have to worry about my not feeling the same sensations you do, Gemma." He moved his face so close to mine it touched my forehead. "Because what I feel is even stronger," he murmured against my lips before brushing his over them. "Sometimes I'm not even sure I can control it," he whispered and then swallowed, his Adam's apple rising and falling.

"What if you decided not to control it? Could you . . . *behave* like a human too? You're still an Angel," I insisted, trapped between hesitation and the need to know. I hoped he could see what I was getting at because I really didn't know how else to ask.

Evan's lips smiled on mine and the exasperating sensuality of his gaze suddenly became more decisive. He grabbed my hips and pulled me to him, taking my breath away. In a split second my back was flat against the bed, my legs—still bare—trapped beneath him. "Didn't I make myself clear?" he whispered in a smothered sigh of repressed desire. With one hand he held my wrists and pinned them to the pillow while with the other he pulled me against him so I wouldn't try to escape the contact to which the only thing stubbornly offering resistance were his jeans.

All control abandoned me as the whirl of arousal I sank further into with each breath swept me away. It was too strong to resist or ignore. I closed my eyes and surrendered as Evan's soft lips explored my neck. My hands slid under his shirt and he muffled a groan. "You want to send me to hell."

"You've discovered my plan," I replied, dizzy with desire.

"He wanted to resist, but by that time he'd lost all control."

"You want to play that game again?" I smiled against his lips. For a moment he fell silent and stroked my belly. My heart exploded in my chest.

"He looked at her with the eyes of one who had never loved before. His hand trembled as it slowly slid under her shirt. Not because he was afraid, but because he feared he wouldn't be able to stop himself this time."

"Then don't stop."

"*Ahem . . .*"

From the door came the noise of a throat being cleared and we froze. Ginevra.

"Get lost," Evan growled in exasperation. "We're kind of busy here in case you hadn't noticed."

Ginevra smiled. "Didn't it cross your mind to close the door? I tried knocking, but evidently you were too busy to hear me." I could have died from embarrassment. "I'll leave when I've gotten what I want, Evan," she said, determined, crossing her arms over her chest like a little girl.

"She wants to race," Evan explained under his breath.

"Well? You promised!" she retorted. Ginevra simply couldn't handle losing.

Evan shot her a furious look, trying to make her give up the idea. "We're not going to have a rematch right now, G. Maybe you haven't realized it, but you're not the center of the world. I've got other things on my mind right now," he snapped, glaring at her.

"I can see that," she said, looking at me as Evan shot her a look, begging her to leave. Or, more likely, telepathically ordering her to leave.

The door slammed shut behind Ginevra.

"You shouldn't have," I told him, feeling guilty about how he'd treated her. "We can go, if you want." I hoped he wouldn't take me seriously.

"You're more important than a stupid race," he whispered, moving closer again. "Besides, unless I'm mistaken, we started a conversation, and I don't like to leave things half-finished."

I smiled, ready to pick up where we'd left off. "You're right," I whispered as his mouth touched my neck, "one should never leave things half-finished."

"So did you get the answer you wanted?" he murmured against my skin, a sly smile forming on his lips.

"I *think* so," I began, pretending uncertainty, "but I'm not entirely sure."

Evan raised my thigh and pinned me against the bed with his body. A shudder surged through me as he kissed me passionately. Suddenly he stopped, still on top of me, and looked me in the eye. "Not a second goes by that I don't want you, Gemma."

I nodded, dizzy, my heart thumping against his chest.

"I don't want to rush you," he whispered, his hand gently caressing my bare thigh. "Although it feels like I might go insane whenever I touch you." A frustrated sigh escaped him as he rested his forehead against mine, trying to regain control of his breathing.

I closed my eyes, stunned by what he'd said because I felt the same exact thing. "Then I'd better get dressed now before I risk making you give in to temptation," I said, teasing.

He shot me an irresistible smile. "People of my bloodline aren't exactly known for being able to resist temptation. You know, with Eve and all that."

"God, no! I don't want to condemn the world to catastrophic reprisals," I said, laughing with him.

Evan raised himself on his palms, his body suspended over mine, his hands framing my head. His hair hung down and his gaze softened on mine. "Condemn me, then, with a kiss," he whispered against my lips, "and I'll be forever damned, if you wish it so, in exchange for that one kiss."

He touched his lips to mine but I pulled back. "Never would I wish you damned—not for my sake nor any other reason in the world," I said, playing along, my eyes locked onto his.

"Alas, you condemn me to a far worse torment by denying me your lips," he went on as I tried to elude him. "Seal our pact with a kiss, my lady, and I'll willingly accept damnation," he whispered in the sweetest tones I'd ever heard.

"How could I not indulge such a heartfelt request? Then I condemn you, Evan William James, with this my kiss." Gently, I rested my lips on his.

Evan looked at me for a long moment, his expression uncertain. "If I'm damned now, can you explain why I feel like I'm in heaven?"

His irresistibly tender gaze made me smile. "I don't know. I think that kiss condemned both of us because I feel like I'm there too." I bit my lip, the longing for him to kiss me again making my head spin.

"Did I condemn you?" He withdrew, tormented. "Forgive me, my love, and give me back my damnation." He kissed me again to take back his pledge, a groan escaping him. "Damn me again, I beg you. The desire for your kisses is too great a pain to bear."

"And so, just as I damned you, with this kiss I absolve you of your sins. Here." I kissed him delicately. "Now you are free."

"Cruel deception! I don't want to be free!" He grabbed me by the hips and swiftly rolled beneath me, inverting our positions. "I entrust to you my freedom, my queen. Bind me with the chains of love. Kiss me again, I implore you, and I will be your slave," he whispered, raising his head to kiss me.

I smiled against his lips, considering his offer. "Hmm . . . my slave, huh?" I bit my lower lip, still smiling. "That's an interesting prospect. But watch out—if you keep saying it I might take you up on it."

"Romeo, I'm still waiting!" Ginevra reprimanded him from behind the door, making fun of the game he and I often played, improvising reinterpretations of scenes from books.

Evan fell back onto the bed, exasperated. "Unbelievable!" he grumbled. "She never gives up! Can't a guy have any privacy in this house?" he shouted through the wooden door as I held back a laugh.

"I think you should go," I said, encouraging him in spite of myself.

"Giving in to her will only make her more stubborn. She needs to learn she's not the only person here."

"Come on, Ginevra isn't that demanding." Evan shot me a skeptical look. "Okay, maybe a little," I admitted.

"The problem is she can't think of anything but herself and her own interests."

"Guys, I'm right here!" Ginevra exclaimed from behind the door.

"Come on in, Gin," I called to her, amused.

"Can I? Are you sure? You aren't naked or anything, are you?" she asked, making me blush, then walked in without giving us the chance to reply because her mind had already read the answer. "Please oh please oh please," she wheedled, trying to persuade him, her voice theatrical and her big green eyes disarming.

Evan smiled and shook his head, his answer the same. "You know I love you but I can't, really, G. It's already nine o'clock."

I glanced nervously at the clock, surprised it was already so late. "You'd better take me home. My mom and dad will be back soon and you know how my dad gets when I come home too late."

Ignoring Ginevra, Evan inched closer to my lips, resuming the tormented mask he'd worn a moment ago. "What affliction you cause me by depriving me of your presence," he whispered, stroking my cheek.

"Oh God!" Ginevra groaned, rolling her eyes. "Who are you and what have you done with my brother? I'd better leave you two alone." She turned her back on us.

"You'll have to go through three centuries of PDAs before we're even. I've had to put up with a whole lot worse. In case you've never realized it, you and Simon are as inseparable as doughnuts and icing."

"Ha ha, very funny!" she responded sarcastically. "I hope I'm the icing! Or do I seem more like the doughnut to you?"

Trying not to laugh, I decided to intervene before the room caught fire. "Believe me, you look nothing like a doughnut."

"Thank you, sister." She winked at me and left the room.

"She's hopeless," Evan said, a smile on his face, resting his hands on my waist.

"Yeah, but it's impossible not to love her."

"That's true too," he said, still lying underneath me.

"Can't you stop time?" I whined, refusing to let him go. "You're an Angel, you should be able to do that."

Evan smiled and squeezed his eyes shut. "Here, let me try." He screwed up his face, tightening every muscle as I watched with bated breath. Then he opened one eye and peeked at me. "Did it stop?"

He raised an eyebrow and I hit him with the pillow. "You're a clown, you know that? When are you ever going to stop teasing me?"

Evan let out a laugh and pinned me beneath him again, his gaze becoming tender as he kissed me. "I really *did* try," he said, hiding a grin.

"Yeah, right. Well, we'd better go before my dad comes to take me home by force."

"I'll take you, though it'll be hard to be away from you tonight." He locked eyes with me, serious again.

I instantly knew what he meant. "So you were being serious. You have to—"

Evan tightened his lips, confirming my fears. "I can't get out of it."

"Okay, don't say any more." I didn't want him to go into detail. That dark aspect of his life gave me the shivers. Evan wouldn't be spending the night with me. He wouldn't be joining me in my dreams because while I was sleeping, somewhere out there—who knew where or how far away—someone else would lose their life. By Evan's hand.

Another shiver, cold and unexpected, froze my heart. All it took was a wave of Evan's hand to extinguish a life—and yet it wasn't his fault at all. Fate moved the strings in our lives while he carried out orders like a soldier. So why did that aspect of him still scare me so much? Why couldn't I accept that it was life taking its natural course? I knew the answer, no matter how hard I tried not to think about it. Deep in my heart, I was still afraid of the moment when someone would come for me. Another Reaper Angel like Faust. Or like Evan. Sometimes it seemed impossible that the shadow of death lurked in the depths of his gaze and the warmth of his touch. And yet neither he nor any other Subterranean decided whose time had come. The fact that I'd survived certainly didn't give me the right to judge them. I owed my life to Evan; he was the one who'd forged a path that diverged from the fate I'd had in store for me. I had no right to judge his dark side just because it scared me.

"Hey." Evan snapped me out of my thoughts. "Everything okay?"

"It's just— Will you be gone all night?"

Evan slowly slid his hand up my sleeve and pulled off the elastic band I wore around my forearm, claiming it as his own. He held it tightly in his hand and looked at me. "Yes, unfortunately, but you'll find me when you wake up. I'll stop by and take you to school. Now get dressed." A light kiss on the lips. "I'll go down and get the bike ready."

I nodded regretfully as I watched him walk out the door.

I'd had no idea how quickly time had flown until I felt how cool the air had become that September night. I looked at the dark sky hidden behind a leaden veil of clouds that promised a storm and tried not to think of it as an ill omen since Evan wouldn't be with me that night. I was safe now—I just had to find a way to convince myself.

I walked over to the black MV Agusta, squeezing my eyes shut at the wild roar that filled the courtyard as Evan gunned the accelerator with a smug expression on his face. Stroking the leather seat before climbing on, I experienced the thrill I always felt before we went out on his bike. I readied myself for the charge of pure adrenaline waiting for me, sitting behind a wild, totally out-of-control Evan. The adrenaline went to his head too.

"Shall we?" He flashed his foxiest smile. I slid forward on the seat and wrapped my arms around his chest. "Hold on tight," he said, tilting his head, but I already knew what to expect.

I rested my chin on his shoulder, giving in to my insane, never-ending desire for his body. "Sooner or later we should buy helmets."

Evan grinned as if this were a joke. "We don't need helmets," he said. His laughter shook his chest.

"That might be true for you, but in case it's slipped your mind, I'm still delicate and fragile!" I teased, and his expression softened.

He lowered his hand and stroked my calf while perceptibly slowing down. His touch was so gentle it made me tremble. "If you were alone, I would *insist* you wear one. No one knows better than me how dangerous the roads can be for a mortal. But when you're with me you don't need one, Gemma." He flashed a smile, tilting his head back until it touched mine. "Nothing could ever happen to you. I wouldn't allow it. I'm an Angel. You're safe with me," he said comfortingly. His tone made me melt. "We could take a spill at two hundred miles an hour and nothing would happen to you," he added with a smirk.

"Don't you dare!" I warned, instinctively holding him tighter.

"That I can't promise you," he murmured with a grin, giving me a sly glance. His hand left my calf and I had only a split second to register his warning before he gripped the handlebars. "Hold on tight, babe," he said. The instant Evan felt my arms tighten around him, he twisted the throttle, hauling the bike up onto its back wheel.

There was no denying the excitement that ran through me whenever he did a power wheelie like that. His wild riding style thrilled me and I surrendered to the exhilaration that filled my head, the adrenaline that flowed through my veins. The sensations left me dizzy. At times like this I could sense every detail with incredible precision. It was as if my vision became sharper, triggering a sort of super high-res optical zoom in my brain.

The air was chillier outside Lake Placid, far from the glow of the streetlights that made the roads seem warmer, but I didn't care. As long as I was holding Evan tight I was in heaven.

Unfortunately, reality always returned to tear me away from him and there was never enough time. To my regret, Evan pulled into my driveway and turned off the engine. The knowledge that he would be gone that night returned to frustrate me. I climbed off the seat, pushing my hair to one side. It had gotten tangled in the wind and I tried to comb it out with my fingers, but it was futile. "Well, good night, then." I raised my lips to his in a shy kiss.

"That's what I wish you. As for myself, I already know it won't be good, not without you." He kissed me back.

"So don't go." The words escaped me even though I knew it was impossible.

"I'll stay if you ask me to," he said tenderly.

"Don't get my hopes up. You know you can't," I reminded him in a whisper.

Evan sought my lips, smiling. "True. Still, I'll be back soon. I promise," he murmured, his face inches from mine.

"I'll be waiting on pins and needles."

"Dream of me." He kissed me again and started the engine.

"That's like wishing me good night."

He winked at me and rode off, trailed by the sound of his engine. When the echoing roar faded, the darkness sank into my bones.

I was outside, all alone and in the dark.

EVAN

THE HUNT

"No way! Young Casanova, back already? Aren't you spending the night with your babe?"

I smiled, switched off my motorcycle in the driveway, and turned toward Drake. He was bare chested, hanging upside down from the branch of an oak tree.

"Trying to turn into a bat?" I asked—jokingly, because my brother had the power to change his human appearance but couldn't transform himself into an animal.

Drake laughed and flipped off the branch onto his knees. He looked up at me, his icy Subterranean eyes glimmering in the darkness. "Did you mistake me for a vampire?"

"Same difference, isn't it?"

"You need to keep up with the times, bro. Vampires aren't the same as they used to be. Speaking of which, I hope you didn't come to ask me to fill in for Gemma. I've been spending more time with that mutt of hers than with you guys lately."

"He isn't a mutt, he's a pug."

"He's a rat with a pig's tail. If that's not a mutt I don't know what is."

I laughed. "Gemma loves him. You'd better not go calling him that in front of her or she might sic him on you."

"Can't promise you that. I don't get it. How can she love the thing? It's a monster. The other night it tried to bite my finger off! I can barely keep myself from throwing it out the window when it growls at me. Stupid dog, don't you see I've got your owner's face?"

"If he recognizes you he's not so stupid after all. When you take on Gemma's appearance, not even I can tell the difference."

"Where is she, anyway?"

"It's midnight. Where do you think she is? I dropped her off at home. I'd still be with her if it were up to me. But no, I get to spend the night with a bunch of drunk teenagers instead."

Drake threw his hands up, annoyed. "I knew it! They always give you the fun missions."

"What on earth could be fun about a group of sixteen-year-olds?"

"Don't ask him that." Simon had appeared, leaning against the doorway, his hair wet. "You'd be shocked by all the answers he'd manage to come up with."

"Look who's back. Finally risen from the ashes, I see," Drake said.

"Did I miss something?" I asked, looking at Simon who had a smug smile on his face.

"I went for a little swim with Ginevra, that's all," he said.

"Yeah, right. A little swim in a fiery pool of passion. Why do you think I was training outside?"

"If you didn't want to hear us you could've used the workout room. The walls are soundproof," Simon pointed out.

"Not when the two of you are around."

Simon laughed out loud just as Ginevra sprang up behind him. "I finally found you! Were you hiding from me?" She bit his earlobe and whispered something I tried hard not to hear.

Simon grinned and took her hand. Turning to Drake he said, "Maybe you should stay out here a little longer." He winked as Ginevra led him away, shutting the door behind them.

"I'd better take his advice," Drake grumbled. "C'mon, bro, *please* let me come with you."

"Forget it. I already know what you're thinking. I'll do a nice clean job and be back before dawn."

"Come on, you want to leave me here with those two? Don't forget I always cover for you while you're out having fun with your girlfriend."

"You bastard—you thinking of bailing on me?"

Drake flashed a crafty smile. "Not if we have a little fun tonight like back in the old days."

"Sounds like extortion."

"Seems more like negotiation to me."

I sighed. Drake could be stubborn. "Okay, as long as you don't overdo it."

"Shit! I think I stepped in something," Drake cursed, making me laugh. The mission had taken us to the fields of Kansas. Nearby we could hear the excited voices of a group of teens. Drake and I drew closer and watched them for a while.

"No fair! Layla pushed me out into the open!" said a blond with dark eyes.

"It's not my fault you got caught, Audrey! Now you're it," said another girl. Her hair was raven-black hair with a silver streak on one side. She wore black eye makeup and her neck was tattooed.

"Forget it, Layla. I'm afraid to go around looking for everybody," Audrey said. She grabbed the hand of a guy who must have been her boyfriend, instinctively seeking his protection, but he just smiled.

"What are you scared of, possums? You can always use your claws on them," he said, grinning. "Sometimes you leave me with some pretty nasty scratches."

"Whoa!" chorused the other kids.

"Asshole." Audrey dropped his hand, annoyed. "It's dark out and this place gives me the creeps. I'd rather hide. Is there a problem with that?"

"What did I say? I just wanted to reassure you. No ghosts around here."

"I'll be it," another boy told her. He was tall and lean and had just been staring at her hand as she'd reached for her boyfriend's.

I looked him in the eye and instantly understood what he felt for her: he was jealous. It made me think of Peter, the way he stared at Gemma and how his face changed when she looked at me instead of him. I decided I might have a little fun tonight after all.

"You can't, Adam. We have to follow the rules," said a black boy with cornrows.

"What do you care, Jarret? Mind your own business. You heard Audrey—she's afraid of the dark. You want to force a girl to wander around the fields in the middle of the night? I said I'd take her place, so you all go hide."

"I'll do it, then," Audrey's boyfriend said. "It's not your job to protect my girlfriend, McGrent."

"You could have thought of that before, Ron. Or maybe you're afraid of the dark too," Adam sneered.

Ron grabbed him by the shirt. "This is my place and I make the rules. You want to look all brave in front of the girls? I'm not afraid of anything," he snarled. His eyes were glazed over. Judging from the smell in the air some of them had been drinking.

"Okay, chill. Whatever," Adam said, holding up his hands. Ron let go of him.

Drake laughed as he watched the scene. "I've always loved hide-and-seek!"

Five guys and three girls had gathered in the clearing in front of the house. Two of them had snuck off to one side, their intentions evident on their faces, while a third was fiddling with his iPhone.

"Aren't they a little old for this game?" I said.

"They're teenagers, Evan. Most of these guys have more testosterone in their systems than gray matter in their skulls. I bet none of them can wait to find a spot to hide with one of the girls—two, if they're lucky."

Drake reached down and took a brownie from a plate resting on a low stone wall. He inhaled its aroma deeply and closed his eyes before slipping it into his pocket.

"Did you really just put a pot brownie in your pocket?" I scoffed.

"You're right. I'll grab one for you and Simon too. Think little Gemma would want one?"

"Forget it. I'm not giving her one of those things."

"Why not? You two could really get down with one of these."

"Gemma and I don't need to get high for that."

"Your loss." He tucked another one into his pocket.

"You're unbelievable," I said, shaking my head. Meanwhile, the yard had grown silent. The kids had gone into hiding. "Anyway, let's focus on the mission now. Let the hunt begin."

"I'm ready to play."

I smiled. Our eyes were gray as molten silver.

When we walked by the kids, some of them shuddered and peered around uneasily, but none of them could see us. Drake followed Ron, who was wandering through the tall grass in search of his hidden friends, unaware that he was being hunted as well. The boy moved slowly, trying not to make a sound, but now and then something—a sinister shiver—make him look over his shoulder.

A wooden swing hanging from a maple branch moved. He flinched and whirled around. "Who's there?" Taking a few steps toward the swing, he stared as it swung steadily back and forth as if someone were gently pushing it, though there was no wind. The boy gulped and grabbed the chains to stop the ominous creaking that filled the night. He walked away, but after a few steps the noise began again, freezing him in his tracks. When he turned around he saw the swing moving back and forth even faster than before. Smothering a scream, he raced to the house, threw open the door, and slammed it shut after him. Drake was already inside, hidden in the shadows, with no intention of cutting the poor boy any slack.

I could hear Ron's heart beating wildly in the silence. It seemed he'd perceived something sinister. What he didn't know was that it was Death, passing right by him.

Drake knocked over a pot and the boy stifled a scream, his eyes shut tight. He curled up on the floor, panting, his knees clasped to his chest. A chair passed in front of him, scraping against the floorboards with a menacing sound. Next, a wooden spoon flew across the room, followed by another and yet another, almost hitting Ron, whose eyes bulged as they whizzed past him, colliding with the walls. He covered his ears with his hands, doubtless more terrified than he'd ever been in his life.

A sudden silence fell. Drake materialized but remained hidden in the shadows. Though the room was shrouded in darkness, the boy could sense something. "Who's there?" He drew closer, one slow step after the other. From out of nowhere a cat leapt at him, making him jump. He whirled around to run away but found himself face to face with Drake. With a shriek, he ran in the opposite direction, but in the darkness hit a wooden beam head-on and fell to the floor, unconscious.

Drake's laughter filled the room. "God! I haven't had this much fun in days!"

"You were pretty rough on him. He's going to have nightmares for the rest of his life."

"You're saying I scared him? And I thought he wasn't afraid of anything! Shame he doesn't have claws like Audrey," Drake laughed, his gray eyes glittering. "There are four of them left. Want to find out who's bravest?"

"Drake, we agreed we wouldn't overdo it."

"What do you care? Let's let them have a little fun!"

"Let *them*? I don't think *he* was having any."

"Relax! I'm just trying to make their night more interesting. Look on the bright side: after all those brownies they ate, they'll figure they were hallucinating and will never eat them again. So in a way I'm doing this for their own good."

"Yeah, right. Go ahead and kid yourself."

Drake grinned sheepishly. "In a few years they'll look back on this and laugh," he assured me.

I grew serious. "I doubt they'll remember any of this after I do what I came here to do."

"Yeah, so there you go. I'm not the bad guy. You're the one who's going to spoil their party."

He was right. Years would pass but only one memory of that night would haunt them. Drake had had some fun, but in the meantime I'd made sure all the kids were where they were supposed to be.

The time had come for me to play. Only mine wouldn't be just a game.

"Hey, keep those hands where they belong!"

A guy and a girl had hidden in the hayloft, but I had the impression they were more interested in another kind of game. They were the two who'd been ogling each other the whole time. I recognized them from his black ponytail and her red hair.

"Shh, quiet or they'll find us!" he whispered, pulling her against him.

She laughed and pretended to fight him off while actually guiding his hands onto her, her breath coming fast as he kissed her neck.

"Oho! I knew you were a killjoy! Him or her?" Drake asked, watching them with a gleam in his eye.

"Neither. They can have a little more fun. At least for now."

"Then if you don't mind I think I'll join them."

"What do you mea—No, wait. I don't want to know."

Drake had already transformed. He looked like a younger version of himself. "The more the merrier in this kind of game." He winked at me and went to lie down behind the girl.

She gave a start and turned toward him. "Who are you?" Her eyes were still misty with desire and the brownies were no doubt taking effect.

"Shh," Drake whispered, sweeping her hair back behind her ear. "I'm only a figment of your imagination." Believing him, she relaxed and let herself be kissed on the mouth while the other boy touched her all over.

"What a bastard!" I shook my head and chuckled. I went out of the hayloft, leaving Drake with the couple. Outside the night was silent. I listened, sensing every hidden sound, every heartbeat, every breath. None of the kids could hide from me; I could track down even the most cunning. Only one was keeping my senses alert, however. I concentrated on him and his soul led me to the place he'd hidden—to the place *I'd* made sure he'd hidden.

Standing on the roof of the little wooden house, I stared at Adam, sitting on its edge, his back to me. He was smoking weed and watching a few of the others hidden below. He seemed older than the rest of them. Maybe he was in a higher grade at school or, more likely, he'd been held back a few times. In some way the guy reminded me of Peter and this made something boil inside me, something I had to struggle to push down. Maybe it was his curly hair or his lacrosse jersey. Or more probably it was the way he'd been staring at that girl. Yeah, that must have been it. But I had to focus on my mission and carry out orders.

A creaking noise broke the silence and Adam spun in my direction. "What was that?"

I turned the rooster-shaped weathervane slowly as he watched, frightened not just because there wasn't any wind but because I was turning it first in one direction and then the other. When I abruptly stopped, he peered around and listened to the renewed silence. He sighed and stared at the half-smoked joint in his hand, shaking his head, then stubbed it out next to his foot. I flicked it away with my invisible touch, making it bounce. His eyes darted around again and another creak interrupted the sound of his rapid breathing.

"What's going on? You're playing a joke on me, aren't you, guys? C'mon, it's not funny!"

He couldn't see me, but I let him hear the wood creak as I moved toward him. Adam heard the sound coming closer and looked around like a cornered animal. I could hear his heart beating like a drum.

His wasn't the only heartbeat on the roof, though.

I clenched my fist and the beam beneath Adam's hands snapped in two, leaving him without support. He instantly lost his balance, but someone hidden in the darkness leapt out and grabbed him by the leg just in time. With incredible strength he pulled Adam back up but slipped and fell in the process. Adam lunged over the edge in a useless attempt to grab him.

The thought ran through my mind that I would have preferred it if Adam had been my target.

"Connor!" Adam screamed, clutching his hair.

I walked to the edge of the roof and looked down at the boy lying motionless below us. Drake appeared beside him, looked up at me, and smiled. "We done already?"

I smiled back. "We've only just begun."

DANGEROUS GAMES

"Connor!!! Oh my God! Is he dead?"

The girls rushed to him, shrieking. Adam knelt beside his friend as the others watched, frozen with terror.

"Adam, what happened?"

"Do something!" Audrey screamed. "We can't leave him there like that!"

"I, I w-was falling off the roof. He caught me but then he fell instead."

"What were you guys doing on the roof?" asked the pony-tailed guy I'd seen in the hayloft.

"What do you think we were doing, Preston? We were hiding!"

"Nice fucking hiding place! Can't you see the house is ready to collapse?"

"You saying it's my fault? I didn't tell him to hide up there. I didn't even know he was there."

"Guys, cut it out! Stop fighting!" Layla said.

The redheaded girl fell to her knees beside Connor and began to sob.

"Paige, get up! Let's go," Layla said to her anxiously.

"Connor! I've always been such a bitch to you and now you're dead." Paige took him by the shoulders and started to shake him. "Forgive me, Connor! Forgive me!" she sobbed.

Connor opened his eyes wide and let out a whoop, making everyone jump. He propped himself on his elbows and started laughing as his friends stared at him in shock.

"You freaking moron!" The girl punched him on the shoulder and he fell back, still laughing.

"Fuck, man! You scared us half to death!" Adam said. "What were you doing hiding there?"

"Saving your ass." Connor shot out a hand and the others helped him up.

"So you didn't die. It was all a joke," Audrey blurted as Connor put his glasses on.

"No shit, Sherlock."

"We thought you were dead! How could you play a prank like that on us?"

"I just wanted to see how much you guys love me!"

"Five more minutes and we would have buried you," one of the guys said, chuckling. "In fact, what do you all say we bury him anyway? C'mon, grab him!"

"Whoa, whoa! Hold on! What are you doing?" Connor said, but the guys grabbed him by the wrists and ankles. "C'mon! It was just a stupid joke! Put me down!"

"On three, we dump him in the water," said Jarret, the boy with the cornrows. "One, two—"

"Wait!" Layla stopped the boys before they could throw Connor into the water tank. "I've got a better idea. Why don't we play Truth or Dare? It's more fun! Each of us gets asked a question, and whoever refuses to answer it honestly has to do a dare."

"I'm down!"

Connor protested as the guys dumped him on the ground. He touched his head, stifling a groan of pain. "Somebody bring the brownies. Looks like we're going to need them. Hey! What happened to Ron? Anybody seen him?"

"Hey, you're right. I haven't seen him for a while now. He was supposed to come find us."

"He's in here!" There was a splash followed by a shout.

"Hey! Are you crazy?" Ron shook his wet hair as he came out of the house. One of the guys had dumped a bucket of water on him to bring him to his senses—or maybe just for fun.

"What happened, Ron? You decide to take a nap right in the middle of the party?" Adam said, grinning.

"I passed out, moron. I don't even remember what happened."

"Have a brownie. It'll help you remember," Jarret suggested. Everyone laughed.

"If I eat another one of those things I think I'll puke."

"Then we need to find a different punishment for you," Layla said. "You go first. Truth or dare?"

"Hey, why me? I don't even want to play!"

"You said it yourself: this is your place, so you go first," Adam said.

"Okay then. Truth."

"Brave! Let's see . . . Confess: when was your first time and who was it with?" Layla asked.

"What, you don't remember?" Ron said, winking at her with a sly smile.

"You lying asshole! It's not true! Don't listen to him. I'm still a virgin!" In the silence someone whistled while someone else faked a coughing fit to hide their laughter. "Time to pay, smartass. It'll teach you a lesson." Meanwhile, Audrey was glaring at Layla as if she didn't believe her.

"What, do I have to eat another brownie?" he asked with a sneer.

"You'd like that, wouldn't you? I've got a better idea," Layla said. "You'll do sit-ups, dunking into the water tank. You're already wet anyway."

"What? Are you crazy? You must have eaten too many edibles."

"You can't say no. Those are the rules. Or aren't you sure you can do it?" She shot Ron a challenging look, but he was already grabbing the back of his shirt. The whole group cheered as he pulled it off without taking his eyes off Layla's. He sat on the edge of the tank and Jarret and Preston held his legs down.

Drake appeared at my side, watching them. "That Ron guy reminds me a lot of myself when I was his age."

"Yeah, you seem barely older than him."

"I wasn't talking about my appearance," he said.

"I wasn't either."

Drake laughed and slapped me on the stomach.

"GO! GO! GO! GO! GO!" The whole group cheered Ron on as he dunked his torso into the water and resurfaced. One, two, three . . . ten times. When he was done he popped up, shook his wet hair, and let out a battle cry as the other boys pulled him out and the girls cheered.

From time to time Connor raised a hand to his head. Though he hadn't admitted it to his friends, the impact had been brutal.

The girls all opted for the dare, refusing to bare their sins. One was told to do a belly dance on the edge of the tank. Another had to kiss everyone present. When she tried to refuse, the others threatened to throw her into the water, so she had no choice but to agree to the long round of kisses.

Then it was Connor's turn. He chose truth but then refused to answer the question. When Ron complained that his dare had been the hardest, they decided to force Connor to do it too. He stumbled to the edge of the tank and took off his glasses, determined to look brave, but when he saw his reflection in the black mirror of water he tried to get out of it.

The others barred his way. "Don't be a wuss! Just do five!"

All at once a sinister shudder ran over me. I looked at Drake and we exchanged a long look. He'd felt it too. We turned around. Behind us stood a Witch.

"Kreeshna," Drake murmured, a flame in his eyes.

The Witch had dark skin and long hair in a braid that hung over her right shoulder. A smaller braid wound around her forehead like a diadem. Her black eyes glittered like a cobra's and for a second her pupils narrowed to slits, strengthening the impression. She vanished and reappeared behind the kids.

I heard Drake snort and gripped his arm. He seemed on the verge of attacking. An eerie whisper drifted to us on the wind; the Witch was murmuring her dark litany into the kids' ears, planting the seed of evil in those willing to listen to her.

She stopped behind Layla. "Come on, what are you waiting for? Push him down!" the girl was saying.

"What? No! What the hell do you think you're doing?" Connor protested, but it was no use. "Wait! I'm not feeling so good."

"Don't listen to him, it's just another trick," Layla shot back.

"Down! Down! Down! *Down! Down! Down!*" The kids cheered as they dunked him.

"One!"

Connor struggled, panicking. He re-emerged and attempted to take a deep breath but before he could they pushed him back in, counting the dunks.

"Two!"

"Down! Down! Down!"

"Three!"

"Down! Down! Down!"

"Wait, guys! Stop!" Adam shouted in alarm.

Everyone froze. Connor had stopped struggling. I glanced at Drake and was worried to see he couldn't take his eyes off the Witch.

"Fuck! Get him out of there, quick!" Jarret ordered.

"Connor! Connor, can you hear me?" Adam ran to him.

"He's just kidding again," Layla said.

"Shut up!" Adam snapped. "He's not breathing! Maybe he hit his head when he fell from the roof. Why didn't I think of that?"

"Oh my God! You mean he's really dead?" Audrey whimpered. No one replied. They all stood there, petrified, staring as Adam tried to resuscitate Connor.

He gave up and looked at his friends. "He's dead."

A wail of dismay rose from the group.

"What have we done?" Paige grabbed her hair.

Audrey covered her mouth and stared at her friend's corpse in shock. "It can't be. He can't be dead."

"But he is. And now we've got to decide what to do."

Behind Layla, the Witch smiled and continued to whisper into the girl's ear, her eyes on Drake's face the whole time.

A sudden warmth rose in me. I took a deep breath and closed my eyes. When I opened them again I was at the center of the group. Connor was standing at my side and his motionless body lay on the ground.

THE ALLURE OF DARKNESS

Connor looked around in fright. His friends were panicking. When he saw his body he froze, backed up, and looked at me. "Go away," he whispered.

"Connor, listen—" I said in an effort to reassure him, but he took off across the fields. Drake materialized in front of him. The boy jumped and changed direction but Drake foresaw his every move. He took on Connor's appearance and when Connor saw him he let out a scream and tumbled backwards. I approached him as he scrambled away across the ground.

"I don't want to hurt you," I said, trying to put him at ease.

"You sure the same goes for him?" Connor asked, lifting his chin at Drake. My brother's shaved head gave him a threatening air.

Drake snorted, finding it funny. "You should be more worried about your friends."

"What do you mean?" Connor shot to his feet and ran to the middle of the group where they were having a heated debate.

"We've got to hide him," Layla was saying. "Let's bury him somewhere."

"No!" Connor was shocked. "What are they doing? Are they out of their minds?" He walked around them, shouting to get their attention, but it was no use—they couldn't see or hear him.

Everyone froze. "Did you guys hear that?" They'd heard him. How was that possible? The Witch smiled. She must have let Connor's voice reach his friends. To scare them, maybe, or—more likely—to defy me, after reading my mind, as all Witches were capable of doing.

"It was Connor! I'm sure of it!" Layla exclaimed. "He's going to curse us. He's going to curse all of us! We've got to burn the body!"

"Are you insane?" Adam said. "We've got to call the police. Maybe there's still time to help him."

"No!" Ron said. "No police. They'd find my brother's weed. I can't bring the cops here. I'd be fucked. He's dead. There's nothing more they can do for him now. Layla's right—we've got to hide him."

Evil breathed more of its poison into the girl's soul. *You'll go to jail because of what you've done. No one will ever talk to you again . . .*

"I don't want to go to jail," Layla murmured in a tiny voice.

You're better off hiding him. You can just say he disappeared. No one will ever find him . . .

"We'll say he disappeared," the girl repeated, under the Witch's sway. "It'll work as long as we all tell the exact same story."

"That bitch!" Unaware that she was under the influence of evil, Connor could barely keep himself from rushing at her.

"Connor." I rested a hand on his shoulder and used my powers to calm him. "It doesn't matter. It's not your problem any more. Don't worry about it."

"How can I not worry? They're talking about my *body*!"

"It's not your body any more. All that matters now is your soul, your essence. That's all you'll need in the place I'm taking you. I'm here to guide you to the other side."

Connor swallowed, curious. "It's just that—I thought she was my friend. How can she be saying this stuff?"

"She's scared and weak. There are times in life when you need to make decisions. Those who are strong can make them on their own and resist the temptation placed before them. Those who are weaker, on the other hand, decide to give in to it. You made the right choice. You should be happy because you're coming with me."

"But Layla won't?"

I clenched my jaw. The girl's soul had already been poisoned. "No. She won't belong to our world."

"Hold on." Connor shuddered. "Who's that woman?"

In his current form, I could sense how strong his emotions were. He felt fear, but also fascination. The Witch gazed at him and smiled.

"She's here for the girl, not for you."

"Is she going to kill her?" he asked, worried.

"No, but she'll slowly take her soul. When Layla's time comes, no one like me will be there for her."

"So could she take mine too?" he asked, frightened.

"No, I wouldn't allow it. The fate of your soul has already been determined. Layla could still resist—there's always time to redeem oneself until the soul leaves the body. At that point, nothing more can be done. If her soul is corrupt, evil will claim it."

"We've got to warn her! Layla, don't listen to her!"

"It's too late. Only she can decide whether to listen to evil or renounce it. Each of us is fully in command of our choices, just like you were. It's called free will."

"But that woman's influencing her! She's *making* her say all those things!" he protested.

"Not exactly. She's putting options in front of her, sowing the seeds of doubt, pushing her to follow the path of least resistance. It's called temptation. Layla could resist but she's choosing not to. Temptation is an evil that humans don't often recognize."

Connor looked at his friend and sighed in resignation.

"Now we need to go."

"What if I don't want to?"

"You have no choice. I'm here for you, to show you the way. I need to carry out my mission. Not even I have a choice. Besides, if I left, sooner or later darkness would come to claim your soul—and you wouldn't want that to happen. I don't want it to either. I need to help you pass on. That way you'll be safe."

"What about my parents? I don't want to leave them. I'm not ready yet." Connor was distraught. I could sense it.

"You don't belong to this world any more. You feel confused right now because you're trapped between two worlds. Where you're going, your soul will be at peace."

"But . . . will I see them again?"

I flinched. That question was the one that worried me more than any other: not seeing Gemma again once she died. But Connor wasn't condemned to solitude like I was. He wasn't a Subterranean but a mortal soul that would soon have life eternal. I swallowed and looked him in the eye to reassure him. "Yes. One day, when the time comes, you'll see them again."

He smiled at me, turned to look at his friends one last time, and then took the hand I was holding out to him. "Goodbye," he whispered, and disappeared.

His soul was at peace.

I sighed and looked around for Drake, but my smile soon vanished because he wasn't there—and neither was *she*. In the distance, a bolt of lightning lit up the sky.

"Damn it!" Drake was under the Witch's influence.

I materialized behind them, clenching my fists. I had to move with extreme caution or it would be the end of Drake. She had pushed him against a tree and demolished his defenses, and was now using his own power against him by taking on the guise of another woman. Drake seemed so entranced by her that I instantly realized what had happened: the Witch had taken on the appearance of the fiancée Drake had lost and he'd surrendered control of his mind to her.

I stared in alarm at the sight of the Witch's serpent. It had slithered up to its mistress's neck and was hissing into Drake's face, poised to attack.

"Drake!" I shouted. The Witch turned toward me, her eyes two black pools, her face a mask of rage. She raised a hand to the sky and brought it down. A bolt of lightning shot toward me, but I deflected it onto a nearby tree that exploded in a million sparks.

The explosion snapped Drake out of his trance. Freed from the Witch's spell, he struck her just as she was hurling another bolt of lightning. The movement distracted me and I didn't see it in time. It zoomed straight toward me, blinding me, but Drake instantly appeared at my side, held out his hand, and raised a shield. The thunderbolt crashed against it, dispersing its energy. We were safe behind the barrier, but blue and white beams of electrical energy darted back and forth over it like anxiously pacing animals ready to pounce.

I joined my powers with Drake's and together we hurled the thunderbolt back at the Witch, who disappeared and reappeared right in front of us a split second later. We exchanged defiant looks. Everything—nature itself—went still in the presence of two Subterraneans and a Witch. She couldn't defeat us on her own, just her against the two of us. Her serpent hissed a threat and the Witch smiled, training her black eyes on Drake. Blowing him a kiss, she vanished.

I grabbed Drake by the shoulders and shoved him against the tree. "What were you thinking?!"

"I've got a score to settle with her," he said, looking grim.

"Yeah, I realize who that Witch was. I was there too, remember?" Of course I remembered her: Kreeshna, a woman of Amazonian proportions with dark skin and a lethal gaze. She'd killed a lot of Subterraneans the day I first met Drake, but I'd managed at least to save him. "Christ, Drake! She could have killed us both!"

Drake sighed and rested his hand on my shoulder. "I know. I'm sorry, man."

We gave each other a rough hug, easing the tension in the air.

"No problem. You're my best friend. You okay?"

"I was so stupid!" he said. "I'm sorry. I don't know what got into me. I put your life in jeopardy. If it hadn't been for you, that Witch would have taken mine. She came on to me. I was sure I had it all under control. I pretended to play along but then she clouded my mind and . . . that's all I remember."

"She used your power. She turned into someone else," I said.

Drake's eyes wavered and it was like the Witch's thunderbolt had returned from out of nowhere and struck him. My hunch had been right: it was the girl Drake had lost, the one he never stopped grieving for, no matter how hard he tried to hide it. I knew he didn't like to talk about her. He pushed that part of him deep down so no one would see it, withdrawing into himself. He looked at the world from behind a tough outer shell and let everything else roll off his back. Sometimes I envied him; other times I thought it must be terrible.

"Thanks, bro. You saved me," he said.

"Once again," I reminded him with a laugh. Slapping him on the shoulder, I said, "That's what we do, though, isn't it? We've got each other's backs."

"I'm not risking my life when I cover for you with Gemma's parents."

"I wouldn't be too sure about that. Iron Dog is bound to attack you one of these days."

"Let's hope not or we'll find out what the little rodent tastes like roasted."

"That's disgusting!"

"What did I say? Everybody knows I can't stand the thing. If it were up to me, I'd already have gotten rid of it. You don't know how hard it is for me not to smother it in its sleep!"

"Poor Irony," I murmured. For a long moment neither of us said anything, then I took my phone out of my pocket and punched in Gemma's number.

"She awake already?"

"No. I just let it ring once. She'll find the missed call when she wakes up. That way she'll know I was thinking about her."

Drake didn't reply. For a moment he seemed lost in thought . . . or in his memories, maybe. "Ever wonder what things would be like if you'd decided differently?" he finally asked.

"I don't know how I would feel if I'd decided not to save Gemma," I admitted. It was impossible to imagine my world without her in it. I looked at the sky. The clouds were gathering, churning and brimming with energy, ready to unleash a downpour. "To me, Gemma is the storm, the thunder, the lightning . . . but she's also the sun and the stillness of the moon. She's all those things and without her I would be an empty sky. No sounds, no colors. I'd be lost in a black universe. She's my energy."

"I know the feeling."

I turned to look at Drake, then lowered my head and stared at my shoes. He probably beat himself up every day about the choices he'd made. The wrong ones, the ones he would never stop regretting. No, I had no doubts. If I had chosen not to save Gemma that day in spring, I would have regretted it forever.

"I—I'm in love with her. I love her with all my being," I confessed.

"She's so beautiful it would be hard not to love her," he said, teasing me.

"Hey, stay away from her!" I punched his shoulder, laughing.

Drake raised his hands. "I meant for *you* not to!"

"Drake, you think one day you might find another girl to make you forget your bad memories?"

"Nope," he replied without hesitation, " . . . but I never get tired of trying." He wiggled his eyebrows and we both burst out laughing.

For a Subterranean, love went beyond mere mortal emotion. Once our spirit had united with someone else's, it was impossible to sever the bond. But Drake had bonded with his fiancée when he was still alive, so maybe there was still hope for him, though I wasn't totally convinced.

We talked for a long time, sitting at the foot of the pine tree. I liked hanging out with Drake. Everything seemed simpler when he was around.

A glimmer appeared in the sky, heralding the dawn. I looked at my brother, absorbed in his thoughts, and rested my head quietly against the tree to watch the rising sun.

GEMMA

ANCESTRAL CALL

Blue. I was surrounded by nothing but an intense, unvarying, infinite cobalt blue. It seemed to dominate everything, extend everywhere, as far as I could see. I had no idea where I was nor did I care. I felt the soft, grassy, slightly damp ground beneath my back. The sound of lapping water in the distance filled me with a feeling of tranquility. The blades of grass rustled softly as they danced in the light breeze. They caressed my hands as I moved them over the soft mantle, feeling its consistency.

I heard every sound around me, even the remotest. Every whisper drifted through me as if I were part of it. My mind lost itself in the infinite cobalt that hung over me, protected from the outside world by the melody that lulled me into a pleasantly peaceful state. Lying there, the feeling that I needed nothing else became more and more of a certainty, as though the sky were a void that absorbed all my thoughts, carrying them farther and farther away to a place where nothing else existed.

All at once a whisper, so delicate and hypnotic I was sure it must belong to some enchanting creature, entered my consciousness. I closed my eyes and focused on the sweetness of the sound, forgetting everything else. The breeze lightly brushed my skin as if a ghost were passing over me, and the sound resolved into a voice.

"Naiad . . ."

No one ever called me by my middle name. Confused, I propped myself up on my elbows. The voice vanished, carried away on a breath of air. I lay down again, filled with a sense of peace too profound to worry about it, and it returned, whispering my name, lulling me with its tender melody. I half closed my eyes, almost as if the voice had trapped me in an enchantment in which oblivion summoned me, forcing me to forget the world. I was sure I'd never heard a sound so imbued with power, and deep in my mind I heard the promise that if I managed to reach it, that power would become mine. Driven by the desire for it, I opened my eyes and listened closely without moving a muscle for fear of losing it again.

Who could such a soft, enchanting voice belong to? And how did they know my middle name? The desire to know spread through my mind until it became unbearable. My body rose impulsively, guided by the sound of my name whispered in the wind.

"Naiad . . ."

Like a siren's hypnotic song, the enchanting call was impossible to resist. I barely noticed my body drifting toward the lake. Cool water wet the tips of my toes and awakened me from the trance that had led me to its edge. I looked down and frowned to see my bare feet lapped by the waves that danced on the lakeshore. Raising a hand to my head, I experienced the strange feeling that someone had crept into my mind, leaving behind the mark of their trespass. My eyes wandered over the clearing, confused about how I'd reached the shore without realizing it.

"Naiad . . ."

I shivered as the call insinuated itself into my brain. As if I were under a spell, all hesitation suddenly seemed illogical. I forgot everything except the visceral desire to reach that voice. It was as if some instinct buried deep inside had taken hold of me. Nothing in the world was more important.

I lifted my bare foot, expecting it to sink into the water, but it stopped short of the lake's surface. I raised the other foot and then the first one again, moving forward without wondering why my body was suspended on an unmoving pane of glass.

A flurry of cool air shook me out of my dazed state. It was as though part of me were struggling against the desire that had gripped me. Confused, I stared at the mirror of water offering me its support. The shore was far behind me and my body was completely dry.

"Naiad . . ."

Like a deadly poison, the voice unexpectedly took on a sinister edge that eroded my will to resist its call. It was more somber now and seemed to be coming from the depths of the lake. I didn't care what I had to go through to reach it. I took a step and this time my foot entered the water, which wet it up to the ankle. Another step. And then another. The farther I went, the stronger the voice became, seeming to come now from within, like a part of me. It was a breeze that blew gently on my worries, clouding them. I had the vague sensation the place had changed, almost as though the shores of the lake had been replaced by a grotto in which I was being held prisoner, but I couldn't perceive it clearly. The surface of the lake glowed with strange, pearly reflections.

The cold water wet my wrists . . . my arms . . .

"Naiad . . . let yourself go . . . Don't resist us . . ."

The whisper filled my head, trapping me in its melody until the water reached my chin, jarring me out of the enchantment. The veil that had led me to that place dissolved. Then why did I *long* to go further? Why did I covet the promises hidden in the voice? The yearning to reach it had grown so powerful I wasn't even frightened of the darkness drawing me into the depths of the lake—I even forgot to grant my body one last breath. What could a breath be worth compared to what awaited me under the water?

My nose, cheeks, eyes disappeared beneath the surface of the lake as the water underneath solidified into a crystal staircase that guided me ever deeper. The water engulfed me to the ends of my hair and the cold penetrated my flesh as darkness enveloped me.

Sporadic air bubbles floated up from my body toward the surface and I watched them helplessly, feeling emptied of breath. Even so, I continued to descend, driven by the dark force possessing me. The voice was ever present in my head, urging me on. I couldn't give up, not now that it had become so intense, so *close*. It was so kind and comforting, full of a promise I couldn't relinquish.

Suddenly I felt I was sinking, my body too heavy to hold up. The water was crushing me, the pressure squeezing my chest, preventing me from going further. I felt suddenly weak, wanting nothing more than to surrender to the arms of darkness and let myself be cradled by the water caressing my skin.

All at once, a gleam of light illuminated the shadows that clouded my mind and the abyss into which I was sinking, deprived of all strength. I found myself staring at it, forgetting all else except the desire to reach it. It was so radiant. If only I could find the strength to attain it I would be saved, I knew it.

"Naiad . . . You'll be safe here . . . Don't resist and no one will be able to harm you any more."

The voice bound me to it. I blinked and another puff of air escaped my mouth when I saw its source, close enough for me to reach out and touch. It was a breathtakingly beautiful woman with long dark hair that flowed and drifted in the currents. She wore a long white gown that swayed around her, enveloping her pearly skin.

"Come to me." She held out her hand.

I tried to bring her into focus but the image split into two and then merged back into one. Her lips curved in a sweet smile, her features so harmonious that the only thing that prevented me from taking her hand was my weakness. I suddenly felt on the verge of fainting.

I tried to extend my arm but a sharp, baffling pain gripped my chest before I could touch her fingers. Seeing my hesitation, her face instantly metamorphosed into the most evil expression of power and mastery my eyes had ever beheld. I flailed in the water, trying to get away, but a jolt of terror forced the last bit of air from my lungs and I lost myself to utter darkness.

"Gemma! Gemma!"

"Evan!" I woke with a start, crying out his name.

"Everything's fine," he said, drawing me to him. "I'm here now."

I hid my face in his chest, shaken and breathing convulsively. I could still feel the need for oxygen and my forehead was beaded with sweat as the memory faded little by little. No—it wasn't a memory. It had only been a nightmare.

"You really scared me," Evan said, brushing the hair from my forehead. He looked concerned. "You were tossing and turning like crazy when I got here. I was just about to join you in your dream when you woke up." The torment hidden in his eyes told me he hadn't forgiven himself for the time Faust entered my dream and convinced me to run away from him.

"I dreamed I was drowning." Although I wanted to reassure him, I could still feel the sensation of the water closing in around my throat.

"I'm sorry I wasn't there to prevent it," he said regretfully, stroking my hair.

"What a strange dream," I murmured, still dazed.

"It's not so strange. We went to the lake yesterday. Your mind must have combined that information with your fears, your emotions. That's how it happens. The brain never stops working. While you sleep, logical thinking gets broken up and memories get confused with things that have never happened."

"I saw a woman," I said, clinging to the memory that was rapidly vanishing as if it had just occurred to me that the information might be important. "She was waiting for me at the bottom of a lake, or maybe it was a spring inside a cave, I'm not sure. She wore a white gown. She wanted me to follow her."

For some reason the worried look on my face made him smile. "Calm down, Gemma. It was just another nightmare. It has nothing to do with the real world. I bet it's already fading."

I made a face that confirmed his assumption.

"Good," he said with a satisfied nod.

The fact that Evan was right relieved me a little. It was different when he visited me in my dreams. His being there blurred the line between the dream world and the real world and in the morning I woke up with a new memory—not a faded image created through mere imagination, but an actual memory, crisp and indelible. A real circumstance experienced in my mind together with him.

"You know dreams don't fade when a Subterranean establishes contact with you."

The words "Are you sure of that?" escaped me. I was more worried than I'd thought, and still not entirely convinced. For some ridiculous reason, my instinct continued to contradict him. "You're right," I said, capitulating to the look on his face before he could answer. "I'm just afraid they—"

"Don't even say it. They're not going to find you, Gemma. It's not going to happen." I hid my face in his chest and he hugged me tightly, as if by doing so he could hide me inside him. "It's over now. If they wanted to find you they would have done it already. No one is coming to look for you."

I heaved a deep sigh at his words, remembering the fear I'd felt day after day, so gut-wrenching I hadn't been able to breathe. "I hope you're right," I said uneasily. A whimper escaped me, revealing the anxiety that gripped my stomach.

Sensing my dismay, Evan cupped my face in his hands and rested his forehead on mine. "I'm not going to let them hurt you," he whispered against my lips. "I'll always be at your side to prevent it. Trust me." He looked at me as though he could enter my very essence. I nodded and buried my face in his chest again.

DANGEROUS REVELATIONS

"I was still thinking about yesterday," I told Evan as we walked through the school doors.

"About what, exactly?" he asked, curious.

"I can't figure out why you never told me you were such a good musician."

He smiled. "I already said I don't like to brag. You'd seen the piano before in the music room by the garage. The violin's always been there too. It's not my fault the only time we went in there you didn't ask any questions. If I remember correctly, you didn't feel much like looking around."

I blushed, remembering his hands on me and how he'd distracted me from everything else. So actually, it *had* been all his fault. Besides, that day was the first time I'd seen Drake, Simon, and Ginevra training in the workout room next door and it had left me shocked. Evan had told me several times that it was the only place they could truly let it all out without all of Lake Placid thinking there was an earthquake, but deep down I knew the real reason: they were keeping themselves prepared.

"Only because you never mentioned you liked playing it. How could I have known?" I shot back, trying not to show how much the memory had shaken me.

"Um, by asking?" He raised an ironic eyebrow.

"After all the insane things I saw you do over the summer, you didn't seem like that kind of boy," I said, grinning.

Evan opened his mouth in astonishment. "Well, they weren't insane enough to make you talk me out of them. In fact, you seem to like all the excitement," he said teasingly. He stopped and wrapped his arms around my waist, a sly smile on his lips.

"Only in those extreme cases when I don't know if I'm going to come out of it dead or alive," I said, entertained.

"Hmm, I have one in mind right now." He leaned in and kissed me lightly.

"Have I ever told you you're crazy?" I kissed him back just as tenderly.

"Only a couple times."

"Clearly not often enough. At first I thought you were trying to kill me, you know. That you regretted saving me and wanted to get rid of me. Confess!" I said with a grin.

"Okay, you got me." He laughed, but a trace of seriousness flickered in his eyes. "I don't know what sense it would make to keep you in a glass case when I know nothing can happen to you when you're with me. Emotions should be lived to the fullest, Gemma, or you run the risk of them fading away. And there are some sensations you can never experience unless go you out and look for them. The important thing is to be in control of them instead of letting them overwhelm you."

"Fading away?" I asked, amused, casting a sidelong glance at him.

"I mean the spark. That charge that makes little kids throw themselves headlong into things before fear puts the brakes on their impulses. Few people still have that spark by the time they're adults."

"Oh, you mean irresponsibility," I teased, even more entertained by the conversation.

"I mean courage."

"You're forgetting that my time is up."

Evan squeezed me against him more tightly. "And you're forgetting that you have an Angel to protect you."

I freed myself from his embrace and looked at him. "No. I never forget that." Rising onto my tiptoes, I rested my head against his for a moment.

"Feel like going to my place?" he asked me point-blank.

"Now? But what—"

"Don't worry, I'll ask Drake to fill in for you at lunch with your folks." He smiled. "He owes me a favor."

I glanced at him, curious. "What did he do to deserve such a punishment?"

"Him? Nothing! I saved him from Simon and Ginevra. And then, let's just say something that wasn't on the program came up."

"What sort of something?"

"Something that'll keep him in our debt for a long, long time."

"Hmm, that doesn't sound bad. But poor Drake! I feel a little sorry for him. I wonder if Irony will ever get used to him."

"He'd better!" Evan laughed at what seemed like a private joke.

I chuckled and nudged him with my shoulder.

"I think I'm about to explode," I told them. The food was always sublime when Ginevra was the one taking care of it.

"At least warn us first, sunshine, and give us a chance to duck for cover," Drake joked from the living room where he was lounging on the couch watching a documentary about arachnids.

"I thought I just had," I shot back.

"You'd better get to Gemma's," Evan told him. "You're already late. Make yourself useful instead of loafing around."

"Sir, yes sir!" Drake winked at me. "I definitely like this Evan better than the gloomy version of him back when he had to—Well, you know."

"Shut up, Drake!" Ginevra threw some food at him, smiling. "Pass me another slice of pizza, hon," she said to me. We all turned to stare at her in disbelief. "What?" she retorted, a puzzled look on her face.

"How many have you had already?" Evan asked, aghast.

His sister shrugged and glared at him. "It's authentic! It came all the way from Italy!"

"You're disgusting."

"I've always said so but nobody ever believes me," Drake said.

Among all of Ginevra's abilities, being able to pig out on anything without gaining an ounce was the most incredible of her magic powers—not that I'd ever worried about my weight, but who wouldn't love to be in her shoes?

"You're just saying that because you have such a jaded palate," Ginevra told Evan, making me curious.

"Wish you did?" he shot back.

Something in their exchange must have gone over my head because Ginevra cast Evan a far-from-reassuring look. "I guess my palate will just have to settle for this delicious, flavorful, piping hot slice of pizza," she teased him, biting into it with a theatrical gesture. I couldn't really tell whether their usual kidding had actually been replaced by veiled insults.

"What does she mean, 'jaded palate'?" I asked Evan under my breath. "So you *do* eat, after all?" He'd never mentioned it to me.

His expression softened as he looked into my eyes. "It's based more on need than pleasure, although the two aren't mutually exclusive."

"You never told me you *needed* to eat," I said, still surprised.

"I don't need food as you know it. What I eat is—Well, it's a pretty thorny topic, to be honest. We've never really discussed it."

I started to wonder how many other unexpected details would crop up. "You can't always use that as an excuse!" I said acidly. I was suddenly shocked by the tone I'd taken with him.

Evan turned to me and lowered his voice reassuringly. "We've never talked about where I come from."

His answer caught me off guard. "I thought you were forbidden to talk about it," I said, almost accusingly.

"No, it's because you're discreet. You never asked me about it and I didn't want to force you. I thought you didn't feel ready to know more yet. You've already had so much to handle."

Evan's explanation made me decide to drop it because I honestly couldn't blame him. He'd always been one step ahead of me. By reading my emotions he could perceive with perfect timing what I needed even before I realized it myself. Sometimes I had the impression my subconscious revealed as much to him as it hid from me.

For seventeen years I'd known a world that now seemed so distant. It felt like it had totally disappeared, eclipsed by Evan's world. Angels, Witches, heaven, hell . . . If I stopped to think about it, it all seemed so insane that part of me was still terrified—the part that Evan had access to whether I liked it or not.

Lost in these thoughts, my eyes shifted to Ginevra's hand and glimpsed it reaching for the last slice of pizza. Suddenly I felt dragged into another dimension, struck by a devastating, uncontrollable emotion. A violent one.

Rage.

Rage that rushed up from deep inside me. Furious. Unexpected. Unstoppable. "What the fuck do you think you're doing?!" I had no control over the words that spewed from my mouth. As if it had a life of its own, my hand snatched the food from hers and flung it across the room. It was like someone had taken over my body. Something dark and evil was stirring inside me. I could feel its strength. "You think you're entitled to everything just because you think you're *better* than the rest of us?" I screamed, horrified by the ungovernable impulse that was driving me to say these things. A little voice hidden in a corner of my brain begged me to stop.

Icy silence descended on the room. My insides mirrored the frozen faces of the others. I rubbed my arms, ashamed of my reaction. Simon and Drake stared at me in shock. I wished the earth would open under my feet and swallow me up.

"Everything's fine," Ginevra whispered cautiously, probably reading in my mind how ashamed I was. But nothing was fine, not at all. What the hell had just happened to me? I stared at the floor. Emptiness filled me. None of it seemed real.

"I . . ." I stammered, my voice lifeless. "I don't know what got into me." I was disgusted with myself. "I'm not even hungry. I have no idea why I reacted like that." I looked up at Ginevra. "Forgive me, Gin," I begged, mortified. I hid my face in my hands and found they were trembling, as if some violent energy were surging through them.

"It's no big deal, Gemma," Evan said to dispel my obvious embarrassment. "Everybody loses their temper once in a while. Besides, we all know Ginevra's a total glutton. It does her good to be reminded of it once in a while." He said it lightheartedly enough to clear the tension in the air, but in my heart the fog hadn't budged an inch. Still, I forced a smile, masking the agitation that still threatened to consume me.

With a jerk of his head, Evan invited me to follow him upstairs. Unable to look Ginevra in the eye, I barely glanced at her and followed him to his room.

"What do you think got into me?" I asked Evan, leaning against the desk in his room.

"What do you think?" he echoed, slowly moving closer.

"Honestly, I don't know how to explain it. All this anger flared up inside me and I couldn't keep it from exploding. It was overwhelming, Evan. I've never felt anything like it."

He reached for my hands and pulled me to him. "It's nothing you should worry about. You're making too much of it."

As soon as Evan's lips rested on mine I felt relieved and the last remaining traces of the terrible memory instantly vanished. I pulled back to look at him, filled with the suspicion that he'd caused the soothing sensation. "Was that you?" I raised an eyebrow, even more convinced he'd used his powers to guide my thoughts elsewhere and ease the tension.

Evan moved his lips closer to mine. "Don't know what you're talking about." But the smile he tried to hide gave him away.

He watched me as I slipped out of his embrace and went to the built-in bookcase that took up an entire wall. Rows of well-worn books were lined up side by side like little soldiers. Their pages were yellowed by the centuries, their smell comforting. The first time Evan had showed it to me, he'd had to drag me away by force. I scanned it, studying the titles on their spines. "So many books," I said aloud.

Evan shrugged. "They were the only things that gave my life meaning before I met you."

"Not counting your car," I teased. "And your motorcycle."

He laughed and hung his head, probably because I always replied with something sarcastic when receiving a compliment. I realized it but couldn't do anything about it. "Not counting those," he agreed.

I grinned and turned back to look at the books more carefully. With an affectionate smile, I remembered when Evan had given me his 1847 edition of *Jane Eyre*. I hadn't been able to sleep for a whole week after that. Lost in this memory, I didn't notice that in the meantime I'd begun to trail my finger over the meticulously organized books. I'd almost reached Shakespeare when I stopped, curious, on a dusty book that looked older than the others.

"*Tristan and Iseult*," I murmured as I carefully took it out, my eyes filled with fascination. I blew across its top edge, raising a cloud of dust. The leather cover was worn. "I've always loved this story," I told him eagerly, resting one knee on the mattress and sliding down onto my belly facing the foot of the bed.

"That makes the list of things we have in common even longer," Evan said, clicking on a playlist on his laptop that was sitting open on the desk. "Actually, it's a legend of Celtic origin that dates back to the Middle Ages." He lay down beside me on the bed, staring at the ceiling as the soft notes of Hans Zimmer's *And Then I Kissed Him* filled the room.

I leafed through the book, my fingers brushing the fragile, yellowed paper. Evan gently took it out of my hands and turned the pages, a confident look in his eye. He was clearly searching for something. I could tell he'd found it when he stopped, rolled onto his side, and gazed at me. Then he looked down at the old yellowed page.

93

They were like the honeysuckle vine,

Which around a hazel tree will twine,

Holding the trunk as in a fist

And climbing until its tendrils twist

Around the top and hold it fast.

Together tree and vine will last.

But then, if anyone should pry

The vine away, they both will die.

My love, we're like that vine and tree;

I'll die without you, you without me.

He recited the verses with a sad awareness in his voice, as if they were his own. When he was finished I lay there in silence listening as the echo of his words faded inside me.

"The verse reminds me of a couple I know," he said softly, a bitter smile on his lips. "Constantly hounded by a fate that tries to divide them, forcing them to repress their love. But not even death manages to separate them." His gaze lingered on mine. "It's the two of us, Jamie. Together," he whispered in a low voice, touching my lips. "Like the hazel and the honeysuckle. Like Tristan and Iseult."

"No!" I protested, realizing his meaning.

"I couldn't go on living without you," he said, closing the book with a little puff of dust.

"But you *have to*," I said, a pleading look on my face. "You can't— you can't even *think* of something like that, Evan!" My fate was uncertain and Evan had already planned his if worse came to worst. My life could end at any minute, but his couldn't come to an end because of me; I would never allow it.

"I've already made up my mind."

"Change it," I ordered him with a determination I didn't know I had.

94

"I can lie to you if you want, but I'm not going to change my mind. I can't even stand the thought of losing you. *I'll die without you,*" he said slowly, looking me in the eye.

A shiver ran down my spine and I looked around, sensing something.

Evan looked at me, frowning. "Something the matter?"

"I have a bad feeling. A sense of foreboding." He stared at me and the serious look on my face caused concern to appear on his own. "Something's wrong, Evan. Their strange lack of interest in me and especially in *you*. Why weren't you ever held accountable for what you did?"

"I don't know. I imagined I would be denied entrance to Eden, but there must be some reason behind their apparent disinterest. I'll pay for my decisions, you can be sure of that. The Elders never go about things directly. They're far more subtle."

"I don't know. It's like I can feel something brewing. The uncanny silence that comes before a storm. Doesn't it seem odd to you too?"

He put his arm around my shoulders and rested his forehead against mine, driving off the anxiety threatening us both. "We'll face it together," he whispered tenderly.

"All right," I made myself reply even though I wasn't convinced. I got up from the bed, his eyes still on me, and went to the bookcase to put the book back. Another book fell off the shelf but I caught it before it hit the floor. "*Paradise Lost.* The irony of fate." I chuckled and looked at the book for a long moment, lost in a silly thought. "You think Milton's vision of heaven did it justice?" I asked casually, hoping his answer might reveal to me what mankind had always been forbidden to know.

Evan looked at me with a strange smile. I frowned. "What did I say?" I asked, at a loss.

"You can ask me . . . or you can see for yourself."

"See for myse— What are you talking about, Evan?" I asked, stunned.

From the way he laughed out loud, I guessed this particular book hadn't ended up in my hands by coincidence. "Actually I've been considering it for a while now and I think you're ready."

I began to worry that I'd actually understood what he was saying, but the thought that flashed through my mind was too ridiculous to take seriously.

"I want to show you my world," he said matter-of-factly.

Another shiver spread all over my body, giving me goosebumps.

"I want you to be part of it."

My thoughts blurred and I tripped over my words. "You—No, wait, y-you want—oh, no! You can't be serious. This is another one of your jokes. You're talking about—" I stared at him in shock as Evan nodded with a little grin on his face.

"We're living in *your* world. It only seems fair for you to know the place I come from too."

I sank onto the bed. Evan took my hands as his enthusiasm grew. "You don't know how long I've waited for you to be ready, Gemma. You've got to see it!"

"Do you think it's really possible?"

"Why shouldn't it be? It's like home to me. It's hard enough not being able to see the other souls there. I want at least to show it to the one person who matters to me."

"It could be dangerous," I said. The idea was as tempting as it was frightening.

"It won't be. Trust me, no one will see us." He knelt down in front of me and made me look at him. "It'll be just you and me, in heaven." I rested my forehead against his. "The two of us against the world," he added. "What do you say?"

Sometimes it was impossible to talk him out of his recklessness and just as impossible to resist that look in his eye, as wild as it was tender. "I feel like I'm already in heaven," I whispered, my eyes closed and my forehead against his. Even so, the idea made me tremble and I couldn't refuse. I bit my lip, my unspoken acceptance sending a tremor of excitement through my heart. A glance at the clock told me it was already five in the afternoon.

Evan squeezed my hands and pulled me to my feet. His lips brushed my ear. "Close your eyes," he whispered. "Empty your mind of all thought and let me guide you. Trust me completely."

A strange tingle filled my head. Instinctively, my lips sought his to dispel the fear that, in spite of myself, was mixed with excitement. Evan held me in his arms and the tingle spread all over my skin. It was a pleasant sensation that made me dizzy. When he relaxed his grip on my arms, I wasn't completely sure I was ready to open my eyes, so I hesitated. A sweetly scented, intoxicating breeze caressed my skin and I understood at once that we weren't in his room any more. A fresh delicate fragrance filled my nostrils, arousing my curiosity.

I opened my eyes and everything I had known up to a moment ago ceased to exist. The sight was so astonishing I realized nothing would ever be the same—because *I* wouldn't be the same any more. Everything I'd feared, everything I'd always believed no longer made sense; but then again nothing had ever made sense until this moment. It was a new reality that my spirit drank in thirstily. No, not new. A part of me trembled under my skin, as if this world were all I knew. It belonged to me, I could feel it deep in my soul. I belonged to this place. *I wanted it.* At all costs.

I inhaled deeply. The air had a different aroma, new to my still-human earthly senses. Still, part of me recognized it as familiar. It must have been my soul. This was where it had come from and where it wanted to return. I could feel it.

The reward . . . Eden.

"My God," I murmured, looking around, astonished by the landscape that exploded in a myriad of colors, shapes, scents beyond my wildest imagination.

"Well?" Evan's pleased voice snapped me out of my daze. "What do you say about Milton's description?"

My mouth opened and closed convulsively before I finally found my voice. "This is even better than Pandora!" I exclaimed, unable to believe it was real. My eyes widened, trying to take it all in.

"The first woman created by Zeus to punish mankind?" Evan asked, looking confused.

I made a face at him. "The film created by James Cameron at a price tag of two billion dollars!" From his expression I guessed he had no idea what I was talking about. "Come on, haven't you ever seen *Avatar*?" His eyebrows rose higher. "You must at least have heard of it!" I insisted. He shook his head, a bewildered look on his face.

I continued to get waves of goosebumps. Clearly my body wasn't used to being in that place and handling the intense emotions it triggered in me. Or more likely, my soul was struggling, begging to be allowed to return there where it felt it belonged. The sensation was both electrifying and frightening.

The air had a strange, almost tangible consistency. I found myself moving my hand through it, studying it. It was hard to perceive colors as I knew them; brilliant silver particles filled the air, flowing over every surface. Everything shone like a diamond struck by moonlight or the harmonious shimmer of a mirror of water at sunset.

"This is why people on earth are so attracted to everything that sparkles." I looked at Evan. He'd just answered my thoughts. "A part of them still remembers," he whispered. I drank in his explanation, too entranced by my surroundings to wonder how he seemed to be reading my mind.

The light was warm, like the moment just before sunset or just after dawn. It must still have been daytime there in paradise and yet there was no sun in the sky. In its place, a warm moon watched us from above with its silvery rays reflecting a delicate shimmering light. It was so close and so immense it felt like I could reach out and touch it.

It was as if day and night, sun and moon, darkness and light had agreed to coexist in perfect harmony. A happy medium between the golden rays of day and the pale diamond reflections of night. It occurred to me that on earth our sun and moon were also being punished, forced to chase each other without ever meeting, while here they could unite, melting together in their love.

The particles in the air reflected the moonglow, filling the sky with incredible colors like the northern lights. I couldn't take my eyes off the sky: a warm, delicate mantle of red and golden shades that glowed above us like stardust, flowing like a silk scarf stirred by the wind. This place seemed to have been carved out of the inside of a diamond with light shining through it.

"Come with me." Evan took my hand. "I want to show you something."

"Where are we going?" I asked, following him without protest.

"You'll see." Evan was bursting with enthusiasm and I was drowning in my emotions.

The vegetation around us was lush, an infinity of harmonious colors. Evan led me through a thick patch of woods full of massive flowers. I stopped to study one from close up, too fascinated to resist. There were hundreds of them, all as tall as me, lined up one behind the other like sentinels, forming rows of contrasting colors from deep purple with pink streaks to cherry red sprayed with golden reflections to night blue with silvery speckles.

Evan watched me silently, pleased by my enthusiasm. I couldn't imagine how he must be feeling. This was the first time he'd ever shared the emotions this place instilled with anyone.

I stroked a silky flower bud for a few seconds and something seemed to stir inside it in response, making me pull back instinctively in alarm. To my amazement the flower slowly opened before my eyes with a graceful movement. The next moment, the other buds opened as well, forming a fan of colors that extended as far as my eye could see. I stared with fascination at the rainbow that had come to life at my touch. In a matter of seconds the entire host of flowers had awakened, releasing shimmering specks of stardust that sparkled on my skin.

Something glowed inside one of the blossoms, catching my attention. I frowned, repressing my urge to touch the silvery light.

"Those are Sephires," Evan whispered at my side. I could feel him looking at me, enjoying my wonder.

"They're amazing." My voice was only slightly louder than his.

Evan seemed to hold his breath as I said this. Had I done something wrong? Before I could ask him what, the light glimmered and moved. Then, as if each flower could communicate with its neighbor, they all lit up in unison, trembling. Countless luminous points rose into the air like a silent swarm of bees, whirling around us without making a sound.

My mind was lost in the dazzling display. Tiny, beautiful creatures danced around us like fireflies in the night. I couldn't remember seeing anything more spectacular in my whole life. My skin tingled as the tiny stars drifted past and it felt like the sky was at my fingertips. Evan and I exchanged a look that said more than a thousand words. His eyes glowed like moonstones.

"Tell me I'm not dreaming," I whispered in a tiny voice.

"You're not dreaming," he replied, smiling.

"It's all so incredible. And magical. How can a place like this exist?"

"It always has," he whispered, reluctantly leading me away. "Deep in their hearts, everyone keeps a memory of it. They've simply forgotten to believe in it."

"I feel like I could stay here forever," I confessed.

"I can sense that," he said, looking at me out of the corner of his eye, seeming slightly worried that I felt that way. After a few steps he chuckled and I looked at him suspiciously.

"What's so funny?" I asked.

"You are," he said, earning himself a sharp look from me. "Don't get me wrong, it's just that here I can read you more clearly than anywhere else, even more than in your dreams." His lips brushed my ear. "Here, your soul is completely naked to my eyes," he whispered with a hint of mischievousness. "The energy your spirit draws from this place is so strong it keeps your body from hiding what you're feeling. Every single emotion is revealed to me like a reflection in a mirror."

"And reading my emotions is that amusing?" I asked, embarrassed.

"I can't deny it." He laughed. "Don't get mad. To me this world is as real as yours is to you, and I love sharing in your excitement, Gemma. I'm happy I can read your emotions just now. Couldn't be happier, in fact."

I opened my mouth but closed it again. "Is this what you wanted to show me?" I asked after a while.

"No, but we're almost there," he said.

The path we were on grew steeper. Although I felt an explosion of emotion, something suddenly worried me—an unusual sense of uneasiness. "Evan!" I noticed my voice trembling. "Are you sure there won't be consequences for this?" After all, who was I? Why should I be granted such a privilege? "Don't you think we're overdoing it? Maybe we shouldn't be transgressing in this way," I murmured as my uneasiness rose. I held my breath in the silence preceding his reply.

"I can't lie to you." I paled. "I'm not entirely sure there won't be consequences for me for bringing you here. But I'm willing to run the risk. Let them punish me. It's worth it," he said solemnly.

"You're crazy," I said, shaking my head.

"Love has made me crazy but it's the sweetest form of madness and I accept it willingly." He winked at me, his smile tender.

I tried to take in as much information as possible, hoping to remember this place forever. Even the colors glowed with hues that didn't look natural to me—or more likely the ones I was used to were the unnatural ones.

Everything suddenly made sense in my life. Who I was, why I existed . . . what was in store for me. No matter what happened, this was my fate.

I would have remained in this state of unconscious exaltation if meeting Evan's gaze hadn't pulled me into his melancholy. As long as I was human and mortal, I could never be part of his world, but once my fate had made this place my home, Evan would be the one who couldn't be part of it. Death would separate us forever because Evan had been banished and would never be able to see me again. The sadness of this reality overwhelmed me. Within moments his pain had become mine and together we slid into the dark pit of that awareness.

"It's not fair," I whispered bitterly. Something that had eluded me, obscured by my excitement, now crashed down onto me like a deadly wave: we were all alone.

"It's so quiet. No one's here." I listened carefully. All I could hear was the sound of flowing water somewhere not far away. The breeze drew my attention, caressing my skin with its rich scent. I saw a moose raise its head, interrupting its grazing. "Can't you Subterraneans even see each other?"

"It's no problem for me. I'm used to it," he said, but his tone of voice belied his words.

"It can't be forever," I protested, as if my opinion mattered. "It can't, really." My frustration was replaced by guilt. My presence in Evan's life had led him to give up everything that was dear to him, to give up hope. "What you did was done out of love. That should make some kind of difference."

"No one can know for sure," he murmured, sounding defeated, his tone as distant as his gaze.

"But they give you missions, orders to carry out. All this must have some kind of purpose!"

"I've been telling myself that for centuries," he said.

"That can't be *it*. It can't. Every flame eventually dies out. It's inevitable. And my life won't last forever," I reluctantly reminded him. For the first time, the words took on new meaning in my mind. If dying meant belonging to this world, death per se didn't frighten me any more. What terrified me was the thought of what it would inevitably take from me: *Evan*. Although my soul longed to return to this place, I would give it all up without a second's hesitation if only it meant having the chance to stay with Evan. And wasn't that exactly what he'd done for me? Until now I probably hadn't fully understood what his sacrifice meant.

"You'll manage to redeem your soul. I'm sure of it," I promised him, resolute. No one deserved it more than he did.

"It's not so important—not as long as you're still alive." For a moment I thought I heard a quiver in his voice. "And maybe I'll find a solution for this too." He forced a laugh, then stopped abruptly as if he wasn't really convinced.

"It's not so important?" I replied, annoyed. "How can you say something like that? I don't need to read your subconscious! You think I don't know you well enough to understand what you're feeling?" His eyes narrowed to slits. "I know perfectly well how much you want to atone and see your mother again." His gaze wavered as if he hadn't been expecting that. I tried hard to hold his eyes. "You've never told me that but I know it's true."

"No." He looked away. "It seems you don't know me well enough. Otherwise you'd know that you're the only thing that matters to me now. Maybe there was a time when my soul being damned was a burden, a time when I felt lonely, useless, empty, and my only goal was to cling to the thought of the one person I had ever really loved. But then you arrived." His hand slid into my hair and his eyes on mine grew tender. We were forehead to forehead. "What sense is there in living without a heart, Gemma? Because my heart beats with yours," he whispered. "My very breath is bound to yours." Holding my gaze, he laid his hand on my chest over my heart. I felt it beat under his fingers. "If your heart stopped it would silence mine forever too. I couldn't live even one minute knowing you were gone. I wouldn't be able to stand it—not in this world or any other."

"Don't say that! Don't even think it!" I cried, devastated. Now I was sure he was telling the truth. "You would be the one to break my heart. I wouldn't be able to bear it. I need to know you exist and that you're alive somewhere in the world or it would be like losing you all over again." I realized how self-centered it sounded only when I'd shared the thought with him. It was strange how the prospect of spending my whole life with him—if I was allowed to live it—wasn't enough any more in view of his immortality.

Evan wrapped his arms around me and his voice caressed my ear tenderly. "All these centuries spent without you have been so meaningless," he whispered. "If I'd known I would find you one day, I'd have lived just to see you breathe, Gemma. I can't lose you now that I've found you. I won't let it happen. No one will ever separate us without killing us both. Not even death. That's a promise." He held me close and I breathed in his scent.

We were alone, he and I, lost in this paradise all our own.

DIAMOND NIGHT

Evan led me through an area dotted with trees of all different sizes. Their branches spread out, weaving harmonious motifs along the path as if playing together. The leaves reflected the silvery light of the moon, and the strange heat it emitted warmed me to my bones. My senses were intoxicated by the trail of aromas and the smell of fruit that filled the air. The flowing water wasn't far away any more; the sound was louder now.

"You still haven't told me where we're going," I reminded him.

"It's a surprise," he said with a smile. He ducked his head under a large oak branch and turned back to make sure I didn't run into it.

The forest was full of fragrances. I could already smell the scent of water, fresh and heady. A cool, invigorating breeze caressed my skin and I closed my eyes. When I opened them again Evan was standing in front of me, his hand resting on a long branch that hung down from what I guessed was a willow tree. "Ready?" he asked. I looked at him, full of anticipation. There was no need for me to answer. Evan pulled the willow back as if it had been a natural curtain and the sound of water became deafening. I moved forward, pushing the branches aside, and stopped short, stunned.

Spread out in front of me like a treasure guarded by the forest was a majestic crescent-shaped waterfall that plunged into a river stretching as far as the eye could see. The rock ledge over which the water flowed—a jagged semicircle edged with white foam—was far, far overhead. I cast an incredulous glance at Evan, who took my hand.

"Come with me." He squeezed my fingers, almost as if afraid to lose me as he moved toward the cascade.

The cool breeze left my skin damp. "What are you doing?" I shouted, puzzled.

Facing the rock wall, Evan pointed at its top and smiled. "Time to climb." It sounded like a warning.

"What?!"

"Don't worry. I'll hold you."

I could barely hear his voice over the deafening roar of the waterfall. No matter how dangerous his suggestion seemed, my trust in Evan moved my feet forward. When we reached the slippery wall he stood behind me, pointing out handholds in the rock. I doubted anyone else ever climbed it to reach the top—there must have been a different, less dangerous way—but knowing Evan, I was sure he wouldn't even consider it.

My fingers slipped on the wet rock, but Evan acted as a safety net behind me, pressing me against the wall as if we were one being.

"This way," he shouted when we were halfway up.

I did a double take when he pointed not up but over at the center, right in the middle of the white inferno. Resisting the urge to look down, I tried to focus on the mossy wall instead.

You can't fall," his voice whispered in my head. *"I'm right behind you. If you slip, I'll catch you."* He held me from behind, accentuating the contact with his body to let me feel he was there. I nodded and began to move cautiously toward the center. The horizontal climb turned out to be harder than the vertical one. I began to worry after few yards when the rocky surface became even slicker and the water splashed onto me from every which way.

"You sure this is the right direction?" I shouted, unable to restrain my anxiety. The sound of the water was too loud for Evan to hear me, but his body shook as if he was laughing.

A few steps farther ahead, my heart in my throat, I found a broader ledge to rest my feet on. I was almost afraid to look but Evan stepped in front of me and held out his hand. When I grabbed it he pulled me to him and held me tight. I let myself take a deep breath and stared at the darkness behind him, puzzled. "Where are we?" I asked.

The sound of the water had grown fainter and my voice echoed with unexpected volume against the walls. I glanced behind me and saw a thick layer of water, as transparent as a glass wall, separating us from the outside, enclosing us in a rocky cavern.

"Why didn't you carry me here on your shoulders? I wouldn't have slowed you down—or risked having a heart attack," I grumbled with a hint of sarcasm.

"The only thing you would have risked would be missing out on all the excitement. Don't deny it—I could sense it," he shot back confidently. "You can't separate powerful excitement from the fear generated by the risk involved. That's what pumps the adrenaline into

104

your system. You have to take the whole package," he said, a mocking look on his face.

"What is this place?" I whispered, still shaken. Giving in to the urge to touch the crystal curtain, I reached out my hand, wanting to feel the water flow through my fingers.

"No!" Evan grabbed my wrist before I could. "The current's too strong. It could drag you down." His firm voice echoed against the rocks.

I looked over his shoulder. It was totally dark. Dense shadows seemed to be crowding forward to swallow us up. A shiver drew my thoughts to the ominous darkness and he smiled as the water thundered behind me, forming a barrier as invisible as it was impassable. Looking me in the eye, Evan cupped his hands together. I frowned, not understanding, but in the blink of an eye, a silvery light came to life in his palms, glowing like a firefly in the night. Amazed, I stood there staring at the little speck in Evan's hand as it grew into a sphere of soft white light about the size of an apple.

"This is angel fire," he explained, watching my reaction.

"It's white," I whispered, fascinated. Although I'd heard about it, I'd never seen it with my own eyes.

"That's because it's pure," he said.

Inexplicably drawn to its light, I stared at it for a moment and reached out to touch it, but something distracted me. Another light, a sparkle coming from another direction. I instantly sensed its power. The hazy, silvery light from the fire that burned on Evan's palm—as delicate as a will-o'-the-wisp—had lit up the darkness of the grotto and reflected against its walls, taking my breath away.

"Oh my God," I exclaimed, turning around and around to study the rocky ceiling. The universe seemed to have sprung into life above us. A multitude of stars twinkled in the darkness of the cave. Night sparkled with its silver mantle in this tiny corner of heaven.

"Are they . . . stars?" I murmured, my gaze lost in this night with no firmament. I pivoted slowly, fascinated by the twinkling specks that completely covered the rock walls. A mantle of stars that sparkled within reach, shining with their own light. "It's impossible . . ."

"They're not stars." The second Evan finished speaking, the fire he held in his hand glowed brighter. Its rays bathed the walls, revealing their secret.

"Diamonds," I whispered, fascinated, as the white light was refracted off the crystals in the rock, casting silvery prisms that chased each other across the walls.

Evan nodded, happy to have surprised me. "I used to come to this place a lot when—" He stopped, trapped in a memory that still seemed painful for him. "When I thought I had no choice. I've never been so happy to be wrong," he sighed, his gaze melancholy.

"You would come here," I murmured, studying the sparkling walls. I imagined him all alone in that twinkling grotto, reflecting on our secret encounters in my dreams—reflecting on my death.

"I didn't understand what I was feeling. The emotions were too strong for me to ignore and I couldn't explain why I was suffering at the thought of having to—" He looked away, his fist clenched at his side. "I just wanted the pain to go away. Not understanding it made me desperate."

"Evan—"

"So I would come here, listen to the water, watch the gems sparkle, and try not to think about it, try to forget. But every time my light struck one of the diamonds, I would see your eyes reflected in it. It was torment. I was obsessed with you." There was anger in his face. For a moment I thought I saw his eyes glitter with unshed tears, as though the memory was still too painful for him. "I already loved you, I just needed to realize it," Evan said, smiling now to himself.

I slid my hand into his. He lifted his other hand, the one holding the flame, and the light rose into the air, floating above our heads and illuminating the cave. I resisted the urge to press my lips to his; I felt uncomfortable expressing my feelings in that place, as though it were forbidden, but Evan sensed my desire and came closer. I raised my chin, moving just in time to avoid his mouth as it sought mine.

"Don't go there. We'd better not attract too much attention," I said, sealing his lips with my finger. Although I was the one who'd done it, the refusal drove me wild and I couldn't tear my thoughts away from Evan's lips. All I wanted was to enjoy their soft fullness, their delicious fruity flavor as he moved them against mine and the whole world revolved around us.

He took another step toward me and our bodies touched. His tone became velvety, challenging my self-control. "You can't reject me like this," he whispered, stroking my lip with his thumb. "Come on, just one kiss," he whispered directly onto my mouth.

I stood there, paralyzed by his hot breath as the need to kiss him trembled under my skin. He moved toward me slowly but I pulled away at the last minute. "This is no place to sin. It's like being in church!" I stammered, dazed. "I would never kiss you in a church!"

I composed myself as Evan straightened up, unsatisfied but smiling. "At least let me give you a present." He raised his arm.

"What kind of present?" I asked, worried.

He drew a semicircle in the air over his head and lowered his closed hand. When he opened it, a speck of light sparkled on his palm. A diamond. An instant later I saw another sparkle appear on the rocky crust as a new diamond silently formed in its place as though created by the rock itself.

"Don't worry," Evan whispered, sensing my fear that someone would discover us. The diamond rose from his palm, dancing in the air, and floated toward me before my eyes. With a wave of his hand he guided it to my neck, from which hung the butterfly pendant on which he had engraved our names. I looked down to follow the diamond's movement and watched as it incrusted itself in the white gold.

"Evan—"

"Shh." He rested his finger on my lips and winked at me. "It'll be our secret."

I touched the cold, sharp-edged jewel that sparkled under my fingers. "I'm speechless, Evan. It's really too much."

"You could always find a way to show me your gratitude," he said provocatively, raising an eyebrow.

"You're so stubborn!" I tilted my head, holding his gaze. His face was right in front of mine.

"I've heard that before," he whispered, drawing his lips closer for a few electrifying seconds.

"It's a shame I'm even more stubborn than you," I said, stepping back and leaving him hanging. "Does Ginevra know about this place?"

His face turned unexpectedly serious. "She's a Witch. There's absolutely no way she could ever set foot in here. They would detect her presence immediately. All hell would break loose."

"That's too bad." I shrugged and moved toward the way out. "I'm sure she'd love it. She's crazy about sparkly things."

Evan snickered. "Yeah, she'd love it, all right. But instead of admiring the diamonds, I think Ginevra would spend hours staring at her reflection in them."

I laughed at his joke, but doubt gripped me as I glanced at the transparent curtain a few steps from us. "I know that at this point you're probably going to consider this a rhetorical question, but how do we get down from here?"

Evan looked at me with a raised eyebrow, hiding a grin that instantly struck panic into my heart.

"Oh . . . no," I whispered. My eyes widened. "You can't mean—" I stammered. I looked down, refusing to believe what I suspected he meant.

"Scared?" His challenging tone triggered a rebellious reaction inside me. "You're excited about the idea of jumping. I can feel it," he added, his tone even more mocking, his cunning gaze fixed on mine.

His remark triggered a vortex of confusion in my brain. Conflicting, indecipherable feelings rebelled in me, evolving and changing an instant before I could control them.

"You need to decide what to listen to, Gemma." Suddenly his voice sounded far away. "What's stronger?" A strange impulse tickled my skin. "Fear? Or—"

The impulse was stronger now and it drove me to react. Before Evan had finished his question, I succumbed to it and rushed past him.

"—excitement?"

My body hit the cold, crystal-clear wall of water as Evan's last word reached me. It hung in the air, conveying an equal mix of amazement and admiration. And then the void. The cool breeze caressed my skin as I fell through the air, surrendering to its comforting embrace.

Right behind me, Evan whooped with excitement.

"It's like flying!" I shouted, trying to make myself heard over the roar of the waterfall as we plunged down, almost gliding through the air. A surge of adrenaline shook me from within, its intensity matched only by the force of the water as it thundered down into the pool. We were so high up!

I felt light, free, as if the whole universe belonged to us.

Then, impact. The water enveloped me and carried my body up to the surface. It was pleasantly cool, slightly below room temperature, and my skin instantly adjusted to it.

I was still trembling from excitement as another sensation rose up inside me: wellbeing. A deep sense of peace spread over me as I floated just below the surface, drifting in the current. I bobbed up just a second before Evan resurfaced, shaking his wet hair. "Woohoo, was that awesome!" he shouted, swimming toward me.

The water was calm except for the spot, marked by churning white foam, where the waterfall plunged into it. Frightened by something moving below us, I flinched and jerked my feet up. I squinted through the water but couldn't make out what it was. "Are those fish?" I asked Evan, amazed. They didn't look at all like fish—I couldn't tell where one began and the other ended.

Evan laughed. "No, those are more diamonds." I admired them, fascinated by the kaleidoscope of color that wavered beneath us as Evan trod water next to me. "Here they're worth about as much as a flower. The lakebed is full of them and when light hits them they emit shafts of colored luminescence that blend together in the current." He stopped at my back, barely touching me. "Just like when you came into my colorless life." He breathed the words against my neck and I turned around, floating in front of him.

"They're beautiful," I whispered, looking down at them again.

The lights darted around in the water and I tried to follow them, fascinated. Streaks of cobalt blue merged with iridescent currents ranging from pink to purple to light green to orange. Shafts of pearly light that moved toward me, pushed by the current as though alive. I instinctively dodged to the side but Evan grabbed me from behind and held me tightly against him.

"Don't worry," he whispered into my ear. For a moment the water felt warmer. Then I noticed where the heat was coming from: me. I began to burn up whenever Evan held me against his body. He clasped my waist. "You're out of your mind, you know that?" he said, amused. "You jumped out of that cave. I didn't think you'd actually do it." My reaction had been so instinctive even Evan hadn't expected it.

"I made up my mind, like you told me to," I replied, extricating myself from his embrace to grin at him. I floated in the water, moving myself with one hand around his body, as if he were the fulcrum of some imaginary circle I was tracing.

"Looks like you made the right choice, then," he murmured, turning slowly to follow me. His eyes rested on mine. "Never let fear or insecurity make decisions for you." Something in his tone suggested he was talking about an entirely different subject. Darting toward me, he abruptly pulled me toward him, his hand against my back so I couldn't escape, and spoke softly, a fraction of an inch from my mouth, enunciating every word. *"Always follow your instinct."*

"That can be risky sometimes, don't you think?" I murmured, letting him hold me up in the water. I realized my voice had dropped to a low whisper, driven by the sensations the contact with his body was causing. It was a dangerous game. I stared at his mouth as it drew closer almost imperceptibly.

I swallowed, so spellbound I couldn't move, and he pressed his lips to mine.

"Risk is part of the game," he whispered. "You need to be willing to run risks or you'll never be able to say you're in command of your choices. Fear will take control of them instead. Never let it stop you." For a long moment his eyes lingered on my mouth and then he looked me in the eye again. "Never let your fear stand between you"—he brushed his lips against mine and I felt a world of emotion—"and what you want." His gaze was a mix of sweetness and naughtiness.

"I see you know exactly what I want." The words trembled in my throat. "You're pretty convincing."

Evan brushed his cheek against mine, claiming permission for what I'd denied him so long: a slow, sensual, incredibly tender kiss. I parted my lips and let his soft tongue gently touch mine as his full lips, wet from the water, enveloped my mouth.

My head spun. I loved him. I loved him with every fiber of my being. I could feel it even there, in that corner of heaven where my soul was more exposed than anywhere on earth. It didn't matter where I was—to me, Evan was the only world that existed.

MOON MAIDENS

"Why you—" I opened my mouth to protest, but then decided to bop Evan on the head instead. He laughed. We'd explored the lakebed, touched the diamonds lodged in the rocks and chased the shafts of light they emanated. We'd had splash fights. At first I'd only defended myself from Evan's attacks, but then a real battle had broken out. Now Evan had swum down in search of something. While I was waiting for him to return, listening to the stillness all around me, he suddenly popped up in front of me, giving me a start.

"Find what you were looking for?"

"I made sure everything was all right. Let's go."

"Where?"

Evan smiled. "To the most beautiful place you'll ever see."

"*This* is the most beautiful place I've ever seen!"

He held out his hand, his eyes alight with enthusiasm. "I'm going to change your mind."

"Why do I have the funny feeling I should say no?" I asked, recognizing the impish tone he used when teasing me.

Evan threw his head back and laughed. "I wasn't sure about showing it to you, but after that leap you took a little while ago I decided you might be brave enough," he said to provoke me, raising his eyebrow.

"Brave enough for *what?*"

"To cross the rocks beneath the waterfall. There's an underwater tunnel connecting the river to a little—"

My eyes opened wide. "What?! Forget it. I'm claustrophobic!"

Evan took my hand, a smile on his face, ignoring my concerns. I knew why: he could tell how much I longed to see the place.

"It's the only way to get there. It's not so narrow. It'll be worth it. Besides, I'll be there with you."

It was a good thing Peter and I had grown up playing in and around the lake. "Okay. But only if you stay close."

Evan ducked under the water, my hand still clasped in his, and pulled me down with him. *"Of course I'll stay close to you. You'll need air,"* he told me with his mind.

I came to an abrupt halt, releasing air from my lungs as I made sounds of protest. Evan grinned. He'd waited until we were underwater, when it was too late for me to turn back, to mention that detail.

"Don't waste your breath," he warned me telepathically. *"You need to ration it. Let out little puffs through your nose once in a while. That will make it last longer. I'll give you more when you need it. I'll be your personal air supply."*

Even though I could only hear his voice in my mind, I could still perceive his mocking tone. *How long do you plan to keep me underwater?* I wanted to ask, but couldn't. Evan laughed again at the funny expression I must have had on my face.

He motioned for me to follow him, diving so deep that the light above us disappeared and darkness swallowed us up. Before I had the chance to feel afraid, though, Evan's hand began to emit a soft glow. The sphere of light illuminated the way for us like a beacon. Suddenly I stopped, afraid I would run out of air.

Evan sensed what I was feeling and was instantly by my side. *"I'll give you some air,"* he told me with his mind. Stroking my neck, he sank his fingers into my hair and pulled me to him. *"When I exhale, take a deep breath and hold it in tight."*

I nodded. He put his lips to mine and blew. When he thought he'd given me enough air, he turned to move away, but I pulled him back against me, pointing to my mouth and putting my hands around my neck as if I were suffocating.

"You want more." He guessed what I was doing and smiled. *"All right, if it'll make you happy."* He came closer and this time kissed me passionately before giving me more air. *"How's that?"* Evan looked at me through the darkness illuminated only by the sphere of light and I smiled. Sensing my anxiety, he grabbed my hand and led me through the tunnel in the rocks. The walls seemed to be moving, as if they wanted to close in around me and crush me. I stifled the thought and closed my eyes. Having a panic attack without being able to breathe was something I wouldn't wish on anyone. But then Evan stroked my palm, making me feel safe.

"Hang in a little longer, babe. We're almost there."

I screwed up my courage as a glow in the distance lit up the darkness and the rocky passageway gradually widened. Fascinated, I admired the walls in the new light. They were studded with crystals, fused with multicolored rock and strange, glittering stalagmites.

A moment later we left the tunnel and emerged into a small lagoon. Even though we were still underwater it felt like I could breathe again. When we finally resurfaced, I couldn't believe my senses. I took a deep breath and quivered with pleasure. The water was hot. I dunked my head, smiling at the pleasurable warmth.

"You never told me there were hot springs in heaven," I said. Something occurred to me and my eyes shot open wide. "There isn't a volcano around here, is there?"

Evan laughed. "Nope, no volcano."

"Then why is the water so hot?"

"That's exactly what I want to show you. Come with me."

We swam to shore. The delightful little lagoon was ringed by waterfalls and slabs of pink limestone. The water was so clear I could see the rocky floor, composed almost entirely of diamonds except for some strange, spherical, red stones that glowed softly.

"Come on," Evan said, coaxing me out of the water. I followed him, laughing in excitement like a little girl. Onshore, I turned in a circle, fascinated by everything there was to see. The lagoon was a pearly shell set amid an expanse of gorgeous ruby-red flowers that extended in all directions like a mantle. No. They weren't flowers. They were strange stemless mushrooms that swayed gently, the same ones I'd seen underwater.

"Save a little enthusiasm for later," Evan said, grinning. I closed my mouth, only realizing just now that I'd been gaping. He guided me through giant rock archways hung with red vines into what appeared to be a forest. For a moment it felt like we were back in the woods in Lake Placid, but then something up in a tree sparkled, bringing me back to reality—or better said, back to the dream.

Evan had stopped and was looking at me, waiting to see my reaction. We were in the center of a circle of trees. I was left speechless. This had to be the surprise he had mentioned before we crossed from one world into the other.

"Like it?" he asked, his eyes as excited as a child's.

Ruby-colored mushrooms grew upward in a spiral around each tree trunk, forming an artificial stairway. From time to time they glowed, pulsing with their own light. Then a melody broke the silence, a gentle *oooh . . . oooh* followed by a breath of warm air.

The sudden change in temperature made me shiver. "What was that?" I asked.

"It was them, the moon maidens."

"I thought they were mushrooms."

Evan laughed. "No. They're spirits of fire and air. They're heavenly creatures."

"Oh! Sorry," I murmured to them, embarrassed, and in reply they glowed one after the other.

"Moon maidens." I stepped over and touched one. It moved, let out a melodious sound and sent a puff of warm air onto my face. Meanwhile, Evan had leaned down to pick some flowers. "What are you doing?" I asked, watching as flowers grew back in the spot where he'd picked them.

"Watch." He opened his palm, showing me the little red blossoms, and stood there, listening.

"What—"

He rested his finger on my lips and the air filled with the melodious sound again: *Oooh . . . oooh . . .*

A current of warm air wafted the flowers from Evan's open palm and the petals scattered, whirling higher and higher overhead until they disappeared. For a moment I had the impression the sky above us rippled, drawing the petals into it.

"How beautiful," I whispered. "So *they're* what's doing it. It was them in the lagoon, too. That's why the water was so warm. It's the mushrooms emitting the heat!"

"Moon maidens," he said, correcting me.

"Oh, right. It's such a funny name. Why are they called that?"

"Because they emit minute pink and silver particles that sparkle, just like the ones given off by the moon."

I turned to look at the huge moon. It dominated the sky, lighting up the air with its colors.

"They say God was so entranced by the moon that she offered Him the gift of her handmaidens, celestial creatures that populated her, on the condition that He allow her to watch over them. That's why the moon is so much bigger here than she is from earth. But that's just a legend." Evan took my hand and led me to the center of the circle of trees. "I've got an idea." He walked away and came back with a moon maiden that pulsed in his hands with soft light.

"Evan—"

He stood behind me and let me be the one to hold it as he swept my hair behind my ear and I shivered at the touch of his breath.

"Make a wish," he whispered.

I closed my eyes as the echo of his words reached my heart. Together we held up the moon maiden, waiting for the fascinating creatures to make the sound that announced the puff of warm air. When we heard it, we let it go. The maiden lit up, floated into the air and disappeared, carrying my wish with it.

"That was incredible," I exclaimed softly.

Behind me, Evan moved his lips to my ear. "Now it's our turn," he murmured.

I frowned and he slowly raised my arms. "Ready?" He grabbed me around the waist and before I knew it our feet were a handspan above the ground. Another breath and the maidens sent forth their melody, blowing one after the other, as we rose higher, twirling in a circle. The long chains of maidens in the trees and their puffs of warm air created a vortex that pushed us ever higher until we were twenty feet above the ground.

I looked up, hoping to discover how the flowers had disappeared. Overhead, above the perfect ring of trees, there was a layer of water instead of sky. When I reached up to touch it, its surface rippled.

"It's a wishing well," Evan murmured behind me.

"Seriously?" I asked, excited.

Evan laughed. "No, but it might be for us."

All of a sudden the current of warm air keeping us aloft ceased and we plummeted to the ground. I landed in Evan's arms. He stared at me for a long moment before setting me down.

"And he continued to gaze at her, enchanted," he whispered. "Of all the creatures in heaven, she was the most extraordinary."

"Only because he was looking at her through his heart," I said.

"It was his eyes that looked at her and not his heart. He no longer had a heart, because she'd taken it from him as a keepsake, making him her prisoner."

"And you will continue to be my prisoner," I murmured, biting his lip, "because I have no intention of letting you go." I rubbed my nose against his and gazed at him intently. He could read inside me, but I didn't need to probe his soul to know how excited he was to be showing me all these wonders.

"Let's go," he said. "I can't wait for you to see some of the other places."

PROMISES

We reached a cave from the mouth of which a waterfall tumbled hundreds of feet through rings of rock located at different heights. We walked along a rocky path, climbing toward the top of what looked like a natural skyscraper. Fascinated, I stared at red-leafed trees that grew upside down, their branches reaching toward us. As we made our way along the path I heard the sound of falling water that gradually became closer and more deafening. When we finally reached the small summit I teetered and clung to Evan for support. The rocky ledge we were on broke off abruptly, plunging into the void as if we'd reached the limit of the world. Curiosity drove me on to the edge and I discovered where the sound of falling water was coming from. I held my breath as I saw below us a vast city all of alabaster. An infinite series of waterfalls flowed from the mountain into the river surrounding the city.

Evan looked at me, curious to see my reaction. The giant alabaster palaces towered over everything, streams of water flowing through them and small waterfalls pouring from their windows.

"What is this place?" I murmured, amazed.

"Come with me. I'll show you."

I stared at the waterfalls thundering down. "How do we get there?" I asked, afraid to hear the answer.

Evan nodded at a large tree trunk that lay among the rocks. "We'll ride down on that, but you'll have to hold on tight." My eyes went wide with terror and he laughed out loud. "Just kidding! There's a path." He winked at me and led me by the hand down a stairway carved into the rock that passed behind the waterfalls. For the first time I was grateful he'd only been teasing me; Evan was capable of anything.

We reached the bottom and I realized I'd been wrong. It wasn't alabaster. The city that rose from the water was made of unrefined diamond, so opaque it looked white. From below, the buildings looked even more majestic. Surreal waterfalls flowed here and there, reflecting the glow from the enormous moon above. A light mist cast a mysterious halo on everything, making the atmosphere gothic. I recognized features from different eras. Bridges with spires and pinnacles stood on rocks protruding from the water. Overhead was a statue of a dragon with its wings spread. I remembered seeing something vaguely like it when we'd studied French gothic cathedrals at school. In the distance atop tall, tall pillars were two more giant statues of lions that seemed to be guarding something. The buildings were of different sizes. The larger ones looked like sixteenth-century baptisteries complete with surrounding colonnades and Michelangelo-style cupolas, while the smaller ones had more Asian-looking domes. One in particular caught my eye. It was smaller than all the others and looked like a wedding gazebo, ivy-covered with carved floral motifs.

"We call this place Diamantea, the Celestial City," Evan explained. "Some simply call it the City. We don't really know what it's for. It's not small, but it can't be home to many souls, and it's the only building complex in all heaven. We think it's a place where souls meet, go for walks, or spend time together. This is where we appear when we cross over for the first time."

"Does the same thing go for mortal souls?"

"I think so but I'm not sure. No Subterranean knows. We can only guess. We help souls cross over, but once we get here our senses can't perceive them any more. There. That's the spot where I appeared." He pointed to his right at a roofless colonnade that reminded me of an arena.

I tried to imagine Evan in this place, lost and alone, but I couldn't visualize him any way other than the way I knew him: fearless and confident. Suddenly I started and spun around, alarmed. "Did you see that too?" A shiver lingered in my spine; for a second I thought I'd seen a shadow.

"There's nothing here, Gemma. Relax," Evan reassured me, sensing how nervous I was.

The city was both enchanting and eerie to me, knowing as I did that at this very moment hundreds, maybe thousands, of other souls filled the palaces that to our eyes appeared empty. Knowing that this was probably the spot souls from all over the world went after death.

"It's not a good idea to stay here," I murmured grimly. "Let's go."

"Okay," Evan said. "Let's go."

I took his hand and followed him. Not far away I glimpsed what looked like a cave covered with purple ivy suspended over the river at the edge of Diamantea. It turned out to be a natural passageway made of plants and artistically interwoven vines, a tunnel of lavender flowers.

I let go of Evan's hand and hurried to it, laughing. The scent was intoxicating. I turned toward him and opened my arms wide. "God, this place is enchanting!" My voice echoed with a strange melodic effect and I clapped my hand over my mouth. Evan held a finger to his lips. I crouched down, peering through the branches at the water that flowed beneath the tunnel. The world all around us was lilac-colored.

Delightful interlaced flowers covered everything, their shape like nothing I'd ever seen on earth. They were round and so full they looked like they were about to burst, but one end had a sort of doubled-over neck. I breathed in their scent and stood up. "I would love to lie down here and read for hours on end," I told him dreamily.

"Read me instead," Evan dared me, a roguish glint in his eyes.

I clasped the pendant I always wore and touched the stone Evan had given me, my diamond. It was still unfamiliar to my touch, but knowing it was there warmed my heart. Evan sensed this thought and held me close, pressing me back against the wall of flowers. He nuzzled my neck as if the scent were coming from me, then brushed his nose against my ear, sending a shiver down my back. "Did you know," he asked, "that when a male penguin chooses a mate, he scours the whole beach in search of the perfect stone to offer her? If she accepts it, they stay together for life."

"Are you saying you're a penguin?" I joked, even though he was so close it left me dazed, but he remained serious and kissed me right below the ear.

"I'm saying I've chosen you," he whispered.

I stroked the gem as a shiver spread his warmth through me. "Then I accept your stone." Suspecting that Evan was on the verge of forgetting where we were, I rested my hand on his upper arm to remind him.

"Don't stop me," he protested. "This is the tunnel of love."

"How would you know?" A smile escaped me.

"But it's true! Enamored souls come here and swear their eternal love for each other."

"You can't know that," I reminded him. He was teasing me, but it was a game I didn't dislike in the least.

Evan rested his hands on either side of my head, blocking my way. "Look, I'm the expert here," he insisted. He leaned in to kiss me, but I slipped under his arm and ran down the tunnel, unable to hold back the laughter that produced a strange echo.

"Where are you going?" he scolded, laughing as he chased me. I kept running. "Come back here! I still have to show you the surprise."

I stopped in my tracks and turned to look at him as a sly smile spread across his face.

SECRETS REVEALED

"What, do you mean that wasn't the surprise? But you said—" I was confused.

Evan led the way, quickly climbing a steep promontory. "I never said it was." He cast me a sidelong glance, grinning.

My wet clothes clung to my skin, but the warm air lessened the discomfort. My legs seemed to be holding out well though we'd been walking for hours now. How many, I couldn't say. I'd completely lost track of time, among other things, and the fact that the moonlight hadn't changed since we'd arrived didn't help me gain my bearings.

We'd walked across bridges of intertwined branches and crossed the river below them inside a giant water lily, blue streaked with silver, that had immediately closed over our heads. Evan had seized the opportunity to try to kiss me, but I'd dodged his every attempt, jostling the flower, which had begun to emit a soft glow, as if ticklish. We'd climbed rocks so high I had the urge to fly. Finally I glimpsed a pinkish sky beyond us, revealing that the peak was near. A rich floral scent filled my nostrils at all times. A breath of air caressed my hair and when I looked up, a shiver ran down my arms. I wasn't sure whether it had been caused by the gentle breeze or the breathtaking view that had opened up in front of me. I held my breath as the entire valley revealed itself to my eyes in all its glory.

An incredible, primeval glory.

Nature bloomed in splendid profusion, painting a surreal landscape whose colors and shapes formed a harmonious whole. Yet the valley contained something even more magnificent that held sway over everything else and riveted my attention. Despite the distance I grasped its vital essence as it stood tall, challenging the sky, towering over all the rest, ruling all that surrounded it. Majestic. Eternal. Ancient.

"The tree of life," I whispered, almost without realizing it.

"And of the knowledge of good and evil," Evan said.

Still mesmerized, I sensed a movement to my right and jumped when I saw two beautiful, tawny-furred creatures grazing on the red grass. They had thick lion's manes and two thin horns that curved back toward their long tails. They looked like big, prehistoric dogs. Then I remembered: these were the same creatures depicted in some of the statues in the celestial city. Evan went over to the two animals and one of them bowed before him, allowing him to stroke its fur.

"Tyadons are shy but loyal creatures that are always found in pairs. It's said that God placed the breath of life of one of them in the other so nothing could separate them and then sent them to earth to protect mankind. But then it was discovered that if one of them died, the other lost its *prana*, the spirit that dwelled within it. The battle for survival led to their extinction so God—seeing man's cruelty—decided to keep them for Himself," Evan explained. He laughed and leapt onto the tyadon's back.

I opened my eyes wide. "Oh no . . ."

Evan looked at me as if he'd just climbed onto a scooter instead of a giant prehistoric dog-lion. "We need a ride," he said, shrugging and smiling to himself. Before I could reply, he nudged the animal with his heel. It took off at a gallop, but he stopped it a few yards away. "You going to take much longer?" he joked, turning back to look at me.

I pressed my lips together, not about to give in, and quickly climbed onto the other animal. Once I'd mounted it I wasn't sure how to ride it. I grabbed its horns, which were spread out like handlebars on a motorcycle, but the tyadon shook its head, seeming annoyed, so I wound my hands in its thick mane, hoping I wasn't hurting it.

"I'd hang on tight if I were you," Evan warned me a second before the air was sucked from my lungs. The landscape became a blur and my brain finally caught up: my animal had shot off behind the one Evan was riding and we were racing like the wind. Their steps alternated rapidly, barely touching the ground, and at times they leapt so far forward I wasn't sure they couldn't fly. It was an electrifying, otherworldly experience. Racing at two hundred miles an hour on Evan's motorcycle had never left me as breathless as I was now, even though Evan controlled the air around us so I wouldn't suffocate. It was an indescribable thrill I knew I could never get used to.

I opened my eyes again when the air stopped lashing my skin. My animal had come to a halt right behind Evan's. I dismounted carefully, not because I was afraid I'd fall but because all my attention was riveted on what my eyes beheld. The colors were so intense they dazzled me. I looked up but couldn't see the sky. The tree towered over everything.

A mighty network of interlaced trunks rose majestically into the sky. The branches swooped down in dense and impenetrable arrangements, snaking across the ground. It was almost impossible to believe that the tree was a single living organism.

I looked at the opalescent, unusually colored leaves that clothed its branches. My neck craned, I swiveled and peered toward the sky. Silvery light winked through the sparse gaps among the leaves.

"It's so . . ." No matter how hard I tried, it was impossible to find words.

"Ancient?" Evan suggested.

"Magnificent. I feel its energy," I told him. A steady tingling coursed through me from head to toe.

"Is this how you imagined it?" Evan already knew my answer. There in that place, I was an open book to him.

"Not with all these colors," I admitted, fascinated by the incredible hues that covered it. Evan chuckled and for some reason I had the impression he was laughing at me again. A moment later, he pursed his lips. A soft melodious sound like a gentle whistle issued from his mouth and I started when a dense shadow moved over our heads. I looked up in alarm and my breath caught in my throat.

Butterflies.

His whistle had stirred them. Countless butterflies, as big as my hand, had risen into the air, leaving the trunks on which they'd been resting. The sky was filled with their incredible colors: red, purple, deepest blue, amber, even bright pink; opalescent shades that blended together to create new ones. The sight left me breathless.

Watching their colorful wings flutter around us, I tried not to make a sound that might scare them away. As they passed, a delicate floral fragrance lingered in the air, the same one I'd perceived in the distance. It was an irresistible scent.

Now that the leaves were uncovered and the tree stood before my eyes in its true form, I glimpsed the round shapes that grew from its branches like golden flowers.

"Is that . . ." My voice trailed off. I was awestruck.

"The fruit." Evan looked at me. "The one Eve ate despite being forbidden to do so." A shadow of sadness clouded his face, taking me by surprise. "The same one I'm forced to eat in order to survive," he added, trying to hide his bitterness.

Fascinated, I moved closer to the amber fruit. It was streaked with red, the color of pomegranates. I reached out but Evan's shoulders instantly stiffened and his face tensed. The message was clear: I wasn't allowed to touch them. I suppressed the urge though the yearning to give in to the temptation writhed under my skin.

An intricate network of veins ran along the branches, extending into the fruit as if they were one and the same. Though I knew it was impossible, it almost seemed to be pulsing, beckoning to me like a beating heart. The longing to touch the fruit washed over me and suddenly, holding it in my hands became the only thing that mattered. It smelled so good . . . It dawned on me that it wasn't the butterflies. The scent was emanating from the tree itself. The power it held over me was fascinating and frightening in equal parts.

"Gemma." Evan snapped me out of my trance, concern in his voice.

"It seems alive." As if hypnotized, I moved closer, feeling I could lose myself in this desire.

"Don't touch it." His tone was cautious and he was clearly trying to hide his nervousness.

I shook my head to dispel the urge clouding my mind and tried to focus on something else. "How is it you're 'forced' to eat it? What do you mean?" I asked.

"It might seem paradoxical to you, but it's one of the punishments my race has to endure."

"I wouldn't call it a punishment." I smiled. "I mean, it can't be so terrible. It looks scrumptious." I couldn't take my eyes off the fruit, as if it were absorbing my essence. It was almost like it could control me.

"It is. We only feed off its juice: ambrosia. Its taste is soft to the palate, creamy, rich, and intense on the tongue, an explosion of flavors that makes everything else taste bland. Its juice strengthens us and nourishes our souls and our powers. But without it—" His gaze grew hard, his tone grave. "No Subterranean would live for long. And death is a long, painful process. First it drains you of your powers." His eyes were unfocused, trained on some distant spot as if reliving a memory. "Then your strength, until you disappear entirely."

"That doesn't sound fun." I bit my lip.

"It isn't. Other souls, pure ones without the curse in their blood, are immortal and don't need anything to preserve their immortality. But for us it's a constant struggle for survival. Eve's transgression left us with a high price to pay, a burden for anyone who has the blood of the Subterraneans running through their veins. That's why we receive her mark, so none of us forget it."

"It's not so terrible," I repeated in an attempt to cheer him up. My throat was dry and I was consumed with the desire to taste the flavor of ambrosia.

"You don't know what you're talking about," he said severely. "In the beginning it is. It's beyond terrible, in fact." His gaze turned inward, lost in the distant memory. "We're put to the test from the start." A veil of painful memories descended over his eyes.

"Try to describe it," I said.

"You already know what happens when a mortal's life ends: a Subterranean comes to save them and bring their soul here so it won't get lost and no one else can claim it. But there's no one waiting for my kind. We're left alone, adrift, helpless. Forgotten. Hidden." His gaze darkened as he struggled against the bitter memory.

"'That which has been hidden from me will be hidden from the world,'" I murmured, thinking of the story Evan had told me—the punishment God had given Eve for hiding the children she hadn't yet bathed in the river. Water represented purification and, fearful of God and His power, she hadn't wanted to show him the children who hadn't been purified yet.

The same water I swam in. A shiver ran through me.

"No one comes to help a Subterranean when his mortal life ends, but a Witch is there to try to tempt and kill him. If he manages to survive that first trial, his soul wanders aimlessly, ignorant of the fact that he needs to eat of the tree to survive, for months, until his strength begins to diminish. And while his soul is growing weaker, the Witch is waiting for a second chance. She watches the Angel from afar, ready to steal his soul in exchange for promises which at that point the Angel can't refuse."

"But why do Witches long so intensely for your souls? What sense does it make?"

"We're not their real objective. *You* are." I shivered as he fixed me with a piercing gaze. "Imagine if they managed to get rid of us. Imagine if they killed all of us. There wouldn't be anyone left to help mortals travel here and their souls would be lost to evil. They would belong to it. It would be the end," he murmured, staring into space. "The end of everything."

Another shiver, colder and sharper. "You were right. It is terrible," I whispered, my voice trembling.

Evan smiled. "But that will never happen. They kill a lot of us, but they'll never manage to exterminate us all."

"Why bother killing you if you disappear anyway for lack of nourishment?"

"Killing a new Subterranean right away lowers the risk that he'll be found and helped to grow stronger. But that's just one of the reasons. Witches are capricious creatures and the Children of Eve are tempting prey."

"How do you find out what it is you need to survive?" I asked, more and more curious.

"Chance. Pure chance. If you're lucky, you run across another Subterranean to guide you before it's too late. No one else cares about us. It's only when an Angel eats the supreme fruit for the first time that he's officially recognized by the members of the Brotherhood and begins to receive orders in his mind. It's a sort of natural selection process. Learning to break down the barriers between the two worlds is too complex an operation for someone to do on their own. That's why your souls need us. Moving from one dimension to the other is a delicate undertaking. You need to know how to breach certain barriers without disturbing the balance."

"From the way you describe it, becoming a Subterranean must have been a painful experience for you."

"You can't imagine how painful." His voice was a murmur of sadness.

"But if it's all a question of descent, shouldn't your parents have been like you?" I asked.

"That's what I thought too, but evidently not. There's no handbook that explains the secrets that connect us to each other, and no Subterranean realizes what he is until his mortal existence comes to an end. My parents were mortal; I saw them grow old and die. I expected them to join me, but it didn't happen. It's like the gene is active only in some of us. Actually, I only saw their lifeless bodies. I was even deprived of my chance to say a final farewell because when it happened I was on a mission and didn't get back until they'd passed away."

"How terrible! But why didn't you ignore the orders? It meant so much to you."

"I've never broken the rules," he replied, his expression solemn.

"For me you did." Evan locked his gaze on mine, a tender smile hiding behind his eyes. "You said you had to come across another Subterranean to survive. Who was it that found you? Who saved you?"

Evan smiled as he sat down on a large branch that reached almost all the way down to the grassy ground and invited me to join him.

Casting me a sidelong glance through his long eyelashes, he said, "It doesn't always happen like that. At least it didn't for me. In fact, it *should* have, but let's say my case was the exception that proves the rule."

I stared at him uneasily, waiting for him to go on.

"I didn't know who I was any more, what I'd become. It was like I'd been returned to the primordial human condition. I was famished but my instinct wasn't strong enough to help me find food. I went weeks without eating and had no strength left. Ginevra's the one I owe everything to. She's the one who found me. She saved my soul and that's why I'll always be in her debt."

"Ginevra? You were saved by a Witch?! I thought Witches were out to kill you! Wasn't she supposed to?"

He smiled at all the questions I'd bombarded him with. "Fortunately she'd already met Simon, though at that point she hadn't betrayed her Sisters yet. Simon and Ginevra would meet secretly and she was making a huge effort to keep the others from finding out about their relationship. She had to learn to control her thoughts so she wouldn't be discovered because all Witches have telepathic powers, including her Sisters. They communicate with each other through their minds. You have no idea how powerful the bond among them is—it's almost impossible to break."

"But she broke hers for Simon," I contradicted, searching for answers.

"That's true, but it wasn't easy for her, and there's no saying it's permanent. She managed because there's only one thing stronger than the power of evil and the bond that unites Witches: love. True, pure love . . . like ours," he whispered, squeezing my hand. "When Ginevra found me, I was close to death, on the point of vanishing entirely. Ginevra's relationship with Simon had made her more compassionate." For a moment I had the impression he was lost in that memory which almost didn't belong to him. "When she discovered that her Sisters were keeping their eye on me, preparing to attack me, it was a difficult decision for her but in the end she took me to Simon, who immediately had me eat of the tree. It took weeks for me to recover. Since then, we've all been together. We've become inseparable, a family. Although," he said, smiling to himself, "living with Ginevra can be pretty weird sometimes. All that pomp and luxury!"

"Yeah, right, sheer torture!" I said, nudging him with my shoulder.

"We don't need all that, actually, but for her it's fundamental. Just because she broke the bond with her Sisters doesn't mean she's less of a Witch. She uses her powers now to satisfy her whims. She can manipulate any material object simply by controlling it with her mind. Her power," he said, pointing at his temple, "is all right here, in her head. Ginevra can have anything she wants."

"Is this where I say I feel sorry for you? Forgive me, but I can't."

Evan laughed. "No, you don't have to. I never said I dislike it—I just said we don't need all that. Not that it's not nice."

"Nice?" I teased him again. *Nice* seemed like an understatement.

"All right, I can't complain. I must admit I got used to it pretty quick," he added, chuckling. "Living with a Witch has its advantages in the end. I know she seems tough, but she's actually really thoughtful toward us."

"And what can you tell me about Drake?" I asked.

"He showed up a lot later on."

"And your trio became a quartet."

He looked me straight in the eye and his expression softened. "But only now, since you've arrived, can we consider our family complete." Hearing those words filled me with warmth. It was nice to feel like an integral part of their family. "You are," Evan said, replying to my thoughts. "We all think so, you know. You're one of us. You always were for them, from the moment they realized how much you meant to me. Especially Ginevra. I didn't expect her to bond with you so strongly. You'd be amazed to know how much. She probably sees in you the reflection of the Sisters she had to abandon."

The bittersweet thought made me frown. I felt deeply connected to Ginevra too, as if we were sisters, and for the first time I realized everyone could see our bond.

Evan jumped off the branch, startling me.

"Is it time to go?" I asked, almost regretfully. A primitive instinct made me breathe in the fragrant air, to engrave its scent in my mind. Not far from the tree the river I'd first seen at the base of the waterfall flowed slowly, filling me with nostalgia.

Evan stopped and faced me while I was still sitting on the branch. He rested his hands on my knees and I took them in mine. His voice filled my head, soft and velvety. *"I want to make you my promise here,"* he told me, his lips perfectly still and his eyes locked on mine.

"What promise?" I asked, my voice coming out in a squeak.

"This tree is sacred. I can't imagine a better witness," he went on without answering my question.

"Evan, what—"

"Don't worry. I just want you to know what I feel for you."

"I already know what you feel for me, and I feel the same."

"No, let me finish," he insisted, his eyes probing mine as he took my hand and turned it over gently, as if afraid to break it. He stroked my palm and raised it to his chest. "You can't feel my heart."

I looked at him, confused.

"But I can. I feel it pulsing inside me whenever you look my way, whenever you breathe." His tone was so intense and tender I couldn't say anything. His expression tuned serious, his eyes filling with awareness. "I know that what I do scares you. I'm not perfect, Gemma, even if you think I am. But when I'm with you I feel like I am because I don't need anything else." His eyes burned into mine, filling me with emotions I'd never felt before. "I would be nothing if I lost you. I've known that since I realized the love I feel for you. You can't know you're incomplete until you find your other half. Alone I'm worthless. I'm just a broken soul, an unfinished painting, a starless sky. And what's the sky without its stars?"

"Evan—"

"It's a giant black hole. Like I would be without you," he said, cutting me off. "I don't want to tell you I love you—the word is so overused it's lost its meaning in your century and I'm afraid you wouldn't understand the magnitude of the feeling I'm trying to describe to you. No, it wouldn't express enough. What you need to believe is that I'm a part of you as much as you are of me. You're here inside me. Always remember that," he whispered, squeezing my hand on his chest.

I smiled at his tenderness and leaned against him. "And you're inside me," I agreed.

"Kiss me," he ordered me in his mind, his gaze sensual and commanding.

I widened my legs, allowing Evan to move in closer. He slid his hands around my waist, rested his hips against mine and kissed me. I forgot everything but his lips on mine, even where we were. His kiss made heaven and earth move for me and I was swept up into an infinite sky studded with stars.

"Hold me close," he whispered in my mind. I felt an urgent need to look him in the eye. I didn't want it to end, I didn't want to go back. "We can't stay here forever. It's risky," he said, trying to convince me.

"If we must." I resigned myself to the idea of leaving.

The tingle filled me again, and again it felt as if the world were revolving around us, as if Evan and I were at the center of a vortex that would have pulled me in if I'd opened my eyes. In a matter of seconds everything became stable again.

I opened my eyes, squinting cautiously at the walls of Evan's room as a frightening feeling of anxiety rose in my stomach. Now that heaven was far away again, only the memory of a waking dream, the seriousness of what we'd just done burst on me in all its gravity. After all, who was I to have a secret like that revealed to me?

"Maybe we overdid it this time," I whispered to Evan, but the sound of the door opening drowned out my words, startling me.

Standing in the doorway, Ginevra and Simon stared at us, puzzled.

"Why are you guys all wet?" Simon asked, frowning.

Evan tried to hide a smile. Ginevra raised an eyebrow. "Don't get too used to breaking the rules, you guys," she warned us, making Evan and me exchange a complicit look. He still couldn't wipe the grin off his face.

"It's really frustrating to always be the last one to know what's going on," Simon grumbled.

My eye distractedly fell on the alarm clock. It read 5:01. How was that possible? "Evan, there's something wrong with your clock," I pointed out.

He laughed, looking amused. "It works fine," he whispered into my ear. "It's just that where we were, time doesn't exist. I'll explain later." I blinked nervously as I took in what he'd just said.

The impatience in Ginevra's voice brought me back to the room. "You owe me something and I've come to demand it," she told Evan. "If you win, I'll give you an R8," she said persuasively.

"Thanks, but cars are like girls: once you find the right one, having lots of them doesn't matter." Evan winked at me with a little laugh.

"Speak for yourself!" Simon said. "I want an R8!"

I smiled, but Evan wasn't giving in. He spoke in a mock-threatening tone. "If you want victory, you'll have to earn it." He sought approval in my eyes.

"You can't put it off any longer," I encouraged him, despite myself.

"Okay, okay." He waved his hand in resignation.

Ginevra's face lit up with a satisfied look. "Careful you don't catch fire. I've heard that under extreme conditions your little toy tends to overheat," she warned him in a seductive tone, referring to his Ferrari but poorly concealing a clear double entendre. "Seems to be a pretty sticky problem."

"I've already modified the fastening of the bulkhead that protects the wheel well from the heat of the exhaust manifolds, but thanks for the heads-up." Evan exchanged looks with Ginevra and then focused his attention on me, his gaze softening. "Coming with me?"

"Or you could come with me," Ginevra said, raising a superior eyebrow. "Waiting for the others at the finish line is always more fun."

I shook my head with a smile. "I'd rather wait here if you don't mind," I replied, still in a daze.

Evan nodded and turned to Simon. "Drake?"

"I just left him in the workout room. We were going to fight but Ginevra insisted."

"Only because I want a witness there when I make him eat my dust." She narrowed her eyes at Evan and then cast a sly glance at me. "Don't worry. I'll bring him back to you in no time," she assured me, her smile captivating.

"Make sure he's still in one piece when you do!" I admonished her as they all walked out the door.

"Can't promise you that!" she shouted from the hall.

Once silence reigned in the room again I lay down on Evan's bed and realized I was hungry. All that adrenaline had whetted my appetite, leaving me with the urgent need to munch on something. I went down to the kitchen, explored every compartment of the fridge, and pulled out some strawberry ice cream. I spread it on a slice of bread I'd already covered with Nutella. Thick and thin. Hot and cold. The combination had an explosive flavor that Evan thought was as interesting as it was bizarre. I called it *Strawtella*. Ginevra loved it.

Grabbing an apple from the fruit basket on the table, I sank my teeth into its shiny, crunchy surface. For some strange reason I felt like I hadn't eaten in days. When I was done I opened one of the upper cabinets, still looking for food.

All at once I felt a tingle beneath my skin. A cold shiver. Someone was there with me, I could sense it. I whirled around and my heart skipped a beat when I saw him right in front of me.

"Drake!" I gasped, breathless from fright. Evan's brother had appeared behind me so unexpectedly. "You almost gave me a heart attack. What are you doing here?" I asked, still uneasy but happy it was only Drake.

He had a serious look on his face, his expression unusually wary. "You alone?" he asked, no expression in his voice, tilting his head to the side.

"Yeah," I said, confused. "Evan went out with Simon and Ginevra. I don't think they'll be long. In fact, they're probably already on their way back." I blinked nervously, unable to figure out why he was staring at me so steadily. He seemed to be studying me. I'd never seen this look in Drake's eyes before. I felt my cheeks flush and looked away, uncomfortable. "Um . . . Sh-shouldn't you be at my place? Evan said you owed him a favor."

My question seemed to confuse him and he hesitated before answering. "My presence wasn't needed any more," he said coldly, reminding me that my parents must have gone back to work. He stared straight into my eyes, making me feel even more embarrassed, then looked up at something behind me.

Puzzled, I turned around, but nothing was there. "Drake, what—" I stopped dead and the words hung in the air in the empty room.

Drake had vanished.

I shook my head, bewildered, as the sound of voices came from the front door. "You're back," I murmured, trying to overcome my embarrassment. Finding myself alone with Drake had never made me uncomfortable before. It must have been something in the way he'd looked at me. With Simon it was different—he had Ginevra. Drake, on the other hand, was the only one of the three brothers who didn't have a girlfriend. I was aware of this, of course, but it had never bothered me until I'd seen it in his eyes.

"Were you talking to someone?" Evan asked, curious.

"Wasn't Drake supposed to take your place?" Ginevra had already read the thoughts crowding my mind.

"I asked him that myself. Seems he had something else to do, I guess." I glanced shyly at Evan who was leaning his arm against the doorframe, a victorious look on his face. "He came looking for you," I explained. "He probably needed to tell you something."

"So why didn't he wait?" he asked, looking perplexed.

"Maybe it wasn't so important," I stammered.

"Mmm, delicious!" Ginevra groaned with pleasure. She'd sunk her teeth into my slice of bread spread with Strawtella. She opened her eyes again as we stared at her. "What?!"

I laughed and took the bread out of her hands, earning an aggrieved look from her. "Well? How'd it go? The race, I mean."

"How do you think it went?" Ginevra sounded satisfied, but her tone of voice clashed with the triumphant gleam in Evan's eyes. I shot him a sidelong glance and he winked at me with a sly little smile he didn't even try to hide.

Ginevra went over to him and whispered in his ear: "What did I tell you?" He stared at her steadily, the grin still painted on his face. "What does dust taste like, little brother?" She shot me a glance, looking pleased. "He's all yours now," she said, walking out of the kitchen.

I followed Evan up to his room. "You let her win," I said in a low voice when he closed the door and I was sure we couldn't be heard.

"I had to, otherwise she never would have left me alone. She was starting to get on my nerves. She's good, I'll admit it, but the road is my domain." He raised an eyebrow, a proud look on his face.

"Let's hear it for modesty!" I cheered sardonically.

"There's a subtle difference between arrogance and self-confidence," he said with conviction.

"If you say so. Anyway, how'd you manage to hide your intentions from her?" I asked, curious.

"You underestimate me. I can influence her thoughts with my powers. All I had to do was convince her of my sincerity."

"Shrewd."

"Pushing it, you mean! But she gave me no choice. At least for a while she'll stop trying to compete with me constantly."

"I wouldn't be so sure about that." I glanced at him and his expression turned mysterious.

"I think the winner deserves a prize," he whispered, approaching me. "Don't you?"

"Are you sure? Because in that case I'll have to call Ginevra. Technically *she* won the race," I teased, stepping back as Evan inched toward me, seeking contact. I took another step back and came into contact with the desk. Helpless, I stood there, trapped, as Evan kept moving toward me until our bodies touched.

"Technically," he whispered, his gaze locked onto mine. He brushed his nose against my cheek, grabbed me firmly by the hips and thrust me against the desk. "That means I'll just have to take what I deserve," he whispered in my ear.

The heat of his words ignited the fire inside me. The flames rose under his dark, seductive gaze until they consumed every inch of me.

Evan lingered, his hot breath tickling my skin as he pushed me up against the desk in an attempt to intensify our contact, forcing my legs open wider. His hands pulled me against him, closing the distance between us. The contact was so passionate and intense it shook me, igniting my desire. A shiver swept down my back and fire filled my head. Every part of me was begging for him not to stop.

Evan grabbed the back of my head with primal urgency and raised his mouth from my neck to my lips. His ragged breathing mingled with mine, impatient and tormented.

"So," I gasped, caught up in his spell, "does this mean my lips are a prize worth fighting for?" I was at the mercy of my emotions.

"Your very breath is reward enough," he whispered without hesitation, his mouth moving down the curve of my neck.

"You settle for so little," I said provocatively. He pulled my hips against him again, lifting me impetuously, his hot breath on my mouth. Impulsively, I followed his movements, wrapping my legs around him as he pushed me down onto the bed, his hot body on top of mine as his mouth touched me below my ear, causing electric tingles with every breath.

"Do you think it'll always be like this?" I whispered as his hands moved over me.

"Like what?" he said without missing a beat.

"Will I always feel like I lose myself when your hands are on me?"

"As long as I live, we'll lose ourselves together." He stopped for a moment, seeking my gaze. "Far from everything and everyone. I'll challenge anyone for you. I'll take on the whole world." He rested his forehead against mine and his cold chain brushed my chin. "You're safe with me," he murmured, slowly kissing the curve of my neck again. "Here, just you and me against the world," he whispered against my skin.

A quiver ran through me all the way to the tips of my toes.

SOUL SISTERS

Light streamed rudely through the window, waking me from a long, dreamless night. "Ow," I groaned, lifting my head from the pillow and instinctively touching my temple. My head felt like it was being squeezed in a steel vise while a giant jackhammer tried to pierce my skull. There was no sign of Evan in the room. If this was how my day was starting out, the best course of action would be to climb under the covers and go back to sleep.

The beep of a horn nipped that idea in the bud and made me get up. My head throbbing, I staggered to the window. The roar of an engine reached me before I could look outside, and when I did, I quickly recognized the gray fairing and sleek shape of a motorcycle. It wasn't Evan's.

"Need a ride?" With a jerk of her head, Ginevra invited me to join her.

I fought down my disappointment and got ready as fast as I could, wondering where Evan was. Clattering down the stairs, I found Ginevra in the kitchen chatting with my parents, who were crazy about her and her charismatic personality. Like everyone was, for that matter. If she'd asked them to, they would have let me blast off in a rocket to help colonize Mars.

Over tight-fitting jeans tucked into tall, black high-heeled boots she wore a white shirt that hugged her generous curves. A black silk foulard scarf was draped around her neck and tied in a knot on her chest, making it look like a tie. *Or a snake*, I thought instinctively.

Outside, Ginevra put on a figure-flattering leather jacket in the same shade as her boots. She shook her voluminous hair that was always perfectly coiffed, emanating a cloud of floral perfume.

I climbed onto the rear seat. "Don't you have a helmet for me?" I asked, my nervousness showing in my failed attempt to take the edge off my voice.

"What's with the fixation on helmets?" she chided me before gunning the throttle. I grabbed hold of the gas tank, my fingers gripping the steel just in time.

"Where's Evan?" I tried to ask, but the fierce roar of her Aprilia RSV4 drowned out my voice.

"His intervention was needed," she said promptly, showing how superfluous words were with her since she could read anyone's mind. "His and many others', actually. Simon's with him."

I trembled at Ginevra's unexpected confession and at how easily she could talk about the subject.

"What's going on?" I asked, as surprised as she seemed to be that I'd been brave enough to ask.

"I don't know, but I think it's something big. An emergency in the Middle East."

"The Middle East?! But there's a war going on there!" I said, alarmed.

Ginevra looked at me in the mirror. "Exactly."

I opened my mouth, shaking off a shudder, and sorrowfully closed it again, staring blankly at the streaked asphalt that raced by beneath us. I couldn't come up with anything else to say, but Ginevra still gave me the answer I was looking for.

"He said he wouldn't be back before tonight."

"He'll be gone all day?!" I groaned.

Ginevra nodded and parked the bike in the school lot. Time wasn't as important to her as it was to me and I doubted she could understand my resentment. I didn't know how much time I had left before death returned to claim me. Because it would, I was sure of it.

"You'll have to settle for me." She yanked me by the shoulder and we made our way down the school corridors.

I was so used to Evan's company that the thought of him being gone all day long made me queasy. In a flash, the suspicion I'd had months ago became a certainty: Ginevra had enrolled at my school specifically for situations like this. My instinct had been right.

"C'mon, it won't be so bad," she teased, probing my thoughts.

I threw her a disapproving look but actually she was right. Her being there made Evan's absence less bitter. It was surprising how the bond between her and me had grown so strong in such a short time. Sometimes I actually missed her when I hadn't seen her for more than a few hours. Not even for Peter had I ever felt anything like it, and it was an extraordinary sensation. It wiped away the loneliness I'd grown up with. Evan's love, my connection with his brothers and Ginevra . . . I'd never hoped to find everything that had unexpectedly filled my life. Sometimes it seemed like too much.

In the past, I'd often felt like I was searching for something, as if, even with everything I accomplished, it was never enough. And now the tiresome dissatisfaction I'd always felt inside had finally been completely eclipsed. For the first time I didn't need anything else.

"Well? What do you want to do this afternoon?" Ginevra asked, her voice hopeful.

She'd already decided everything, I was sure of it, but still I tried to talk my way out of her plans. "No offense, but I think I'm going to stay home and read."

"No offense? Of course I'm offended!" she said in an annoyed voice, loud enough that people in the hallway turned to stare at us. "You want to leave me alone all day long? Forget it!"

"Really, I wouldn't be good company. I'm in a terrible mood this morning and have a splitting headache," I insisted though I knew it was useless.

"I don't think your bad mood is because of your head," she grumbled, shooting me a glance.

"You know everything," I said with a sigh, shrugging. "I couldn't lie to you even if I wanted to. Evan's never been away for so long before," I said sadly.

"Oh, come on, you won't die from going one day without Evan. You'll be too busy having fun with me!" she exclaimed, carried away with enthusiasm about her plans.

As we walked down the corridor, a freshman was so dazzled by Ginevra's very presence that he walked straight into the lockers, making us wince. I held back a laugh as he picked up his books and looked at her sheepishly.

"Hello to you too," she said, giving him a come-on look as she strode by, moving her long legs with feline grace. The boy continued to stare at her, babbling something incomprehensible, but Ginevra didn't slacken her pace. I shot her a disapproving look.

"What? I was just being nice!" she said.

I couldn't keep from laughing. "And you're going to end up in his fantasies for the rest of his life."

"Who says I'm not there already?" She stifled a laugh at what only she knew for certain.

In the cafeteria the only empty chair at our usual table did nothing but remind me how much I missed Evan. I took a seat next to Peter. Seeing that Evan wasn't there, he moved his chair closer to mine. "Hey Gemma! You alone?" he asked, a little surprised.

"Hey Peter! Do I look transparent to you?" Ginevra said sourly.

"N-no," he stammered. Ginevra's allure had an effect on everyone, especially when she decided to flaunt it. "Come on, you know what I meant," Peter said, turning back to me. "I'm talking about your boyfriend. Is Prince Charming off repairing the carriage?" he asked, unable to contain his sarcasm, which was actually directed at Ginevra.

I wished I could warn him to keep quiet because I was a little afraid of how this might turn out. Ginevra was sweet with me, but with other people you never knew what she might do.

"Watch what you say. He's not crazy about you as it is," she told him.

"Whoa, I'm not gonna be able to sleep, I'm so scared. So is the white knight off feeding his stallion?" Peter was really pushing it.

"I wouldn't call him that." Ginevra stared at him, an evil smile on her lips. "Black is definitely more his color."

A black knight. That's what Evan was. Deep down, Ginevra was right. Everybody around the table had fallen silent, tension spreading from one face to the next.

"There was something he needed to do," I said, hoping to make them stop.

"Will he be gone long?" Peter asked as though for a specific reason.

"Kind of," I said, crestfallen. "He'll be gone all day."

Peter's eyes lit up. I knew him well enough to understand that look, though I was sure I was the only one to notice it—except for Ginevra, of course. "We were just talking about going for a walk in the woods this afternoon. If you don't have plans you could come with us, Gemma."

I couldn't read minds like Ginevra could, but I didn't need to. Peter's hopefulness couldn't have been more obvious if it had been written on his forehead. Ginevra glared at him. "The two of you could come with us," he quickly corrected himself. "Of course I meant both of you," he stammered as Ginevra's expression became even haughtier.

"What walk in the woods?" Faith asked, surprised.

Someone cleared their throat to cover a laugh and Faith jumped in her chair. "Ow!" she exclaimed, shooting an angry look at Peter. Then she blinked nervously. "I meant 'Oh! The walk in the woods!' We were just talking about it a second before you guys showed up," she said awkwardly.

Ginevra and I exchanged a look of understanding as someone else stifled a laugh. "Sounds like fun," Ginevra said, looking at me to see if I liked the idea.

"I don't know," I grumbled reluctantly. "I don't feel so good today."

"Come on, just say yes!" Jeneane said. "When's the last time we all spent an afternoon together?"

"I can't even remember," Faith agreed, hoping to put her gaffe behind her.

"You guys went camping together all summer long!" I said accusingly, weighing their expressions.

"Yeah, but you weren't there. This is our chance to finally have you all to ourselves! Come on, Gemma, I know you don't have anything better to do," Jeneane said.

Their silent faces were hopeful. I'd had no idea they'd missed me. I hadn't really missed them. Was it all my fault? Evan absorbed all my attention, along with my new family. All of a sudden I felt horribly guilty for having neglected them.

"All right." The answer slipped out. After all, what could happen to me while spending an afternoon with my old friends?

"Great!" exclaimed Peter, who'd been holding his breath.

"Then it's decided," Brandon said.

"Okay if we meet at my place?" Faith suggested. "We can reach the woods easily from there. Shall we say three o'clock?"

"Sounds perfect," I said, resigned.

Ginevra was there to pick me up with the punctuality of a Swiss watch. Sitting behind the wheel of Evan's BMW X6, she was bubbling with enthusiasm about our spending a few hours together, since I usually spent most of my time with Evan. And yet it was so weird how she and I felt a need for each other. An invisible bond drew us together like the two poles of a magnet, me tending to underdo things and her to overdo them.

As always, she was impeccably dressed: casual boots laced up to the calf, tight jeans, and a brown vest that matched her boots and revealed the sleeves of her beige top. I climbed into the car, put my dark-red sweatshirt in my backpack, and pulled the white-gold butterfly pendant out from under the green, short-sleeved top that I wore with jeans and dark hiking boots.

"Still have a headache?" she asked me considerately.

"It *had* gone away, but thanks for reminding me," I replied sarcastically. My mood hadn't improved much since that morning, though my headache had relented, disappearing almost completely.

The sun was warm, though temperatures had dropped quite a bit compared to summer. The car's tinted windows muted the light.

"Hi, Mrs. Nichols!" I said, rolling down my window when we reached Faith's house. Her mom was bent over some bushes with red blossoms, holding a big, dangerous-looking pair of hedge clippers. Short, with dark hair, she didn't resemble her daughter at all. Today she wore a big straw hat to protect herself from the sun and green rubber knee-high boots.

"Hi, kids," she said warmly, raising her head slightly. She looked tired.

"We came to pick up Faith," I said.

"Oh, right! I think she's with Jeneane. I saw them heading toward the stable." The woman pointed at the large wooden construction a few hundred yards away.

"Horses give me the creeps," came a whisper from the back seat. I didn't have to turn around to know who it was or the reason horses scared him so much. "What?!" Peter protested, noticing the guys' raised eyebrows as they looked at him, surprised. "They're huge! They could kill you with a single kick, you know."

"Wuss," Ginevra teased.

I rolled my eyes, a faint smile on my lips. This was going to be an interesting outing. "I'll go get them," I said, pushing open the heavy door.

"I'll come with you," Ginevra said instantly.

"I don't need a bodyguard!" I said scathingly, immediately feeling guilty when I saw the looks everyone gave me. All Ginevra's concern about my safety was doing nothing but making me even more anxious.

"All right, sorry. I just wanted to keep you company," Ginevra said.

Some strange instinct made me slam the car door and stride off in irritation without even turning around. I headed toward the stable, as shocked by my own reaction as the others no doubt were.

The stable was clean, although stray wisps of hay covered the wooden floor. I inhaled the smell of the hay with pleasure.

Freedom. There were few situations my mind associated with this feeling, but among them was the image of a herd of pure-white wild horses, their manes flowing as they galloped across an infinite landscape chasing the wind.

Then I saw the horse in the stall Mr. Nichols was standing next to and the image instantly vanished, replaced by a stronger feeling: uneasiness. It was black, as black as pitch. And from the way its hostile eyes fixed themselves on me when I walked into the stable, it didn't seem to like me.

"Gemma!" Faith welcomed me with a giant smile. "You guys are here already?" She and Jeneane wore impeccable hiking outfits, Jeneane's in pink and Faith's in dark green.

"We didn't hear you drive up," Jeneane said, standing next to Mr. Nichols who was busy stroking the horse's huge black head over the top of its stall.

"Mr. Nichols," I said, nodding at Faith's dad who returned my nod. "The others are waiting in the car," I told her, hoping she would get the hint without my seeming rude to her dad. I had a bad feeling and suddenly all I wanted was to get out of there.

"I haven't seen Mr. Bloom in quite a while. How is your dad?" Mr. Nichols asked me politely.

The horse snorted nervously through its big nostrils, making me jump. "He's just fine, thanks for asking. It's because of work. He's always really busy. More than usual lately. I barely see him myself," I replied, trying to suppress my anxiety.

"Tell him I said hi."

"Will do. Nice horse you've got there. It's, um, *huge*," I said, as fascinated as I was frightened by the massive beast's black eyes. They riveted me like a black hole dragging me into its depths.

Jeneane coughed awkwardly. Had I said something wrong?

"His name's Mustang. He's my champion." A proud twinkle in his eye, Mr. Nichols stroked the animal's nose.

"Oh no, here we go again!" Faith groaned under her breath.

"Now you've done it," Jeneane whispered in my ear, biting her lip. She'd probably put up with Mr. Nichols's obsession with his horse long enough already.

"He's a stallion," he continued, oblivious to the looks on our faces. "He's won more races than Casey Stoner!"

"Who?" Jeneane whispered, making me smother a laugh.

"He's a champion MotoGP motorcycle racer," I explained, still smiling at Faith's dad who proceeded to rattle off the technical and aesthetic qualities that made his precious horse a champion. Mustang didn't seem interested in all the praise; he didn't take his eyes off me.

"I'm telling you, young ladies, in all my years I've never seen any horse run like Mustang. He's a force of nature!" he exclaimed proudly as Faith rolled her eyes.

"I bet he is," I mumbled, pursing my lips.

"Dad's fanatical about that horse," Faith whispered in my ear. "Sorry."

"No problem," I reassured her. "I think it's nice."

The horse snorted again and tossed his head, jerking Mr. Nichols's hand as it held the reins. Mustang seemed spooked. Like me.

"Wow! He's a real brute," I said, my voice edged with anxiety.

Mr. Nichols tugged on the reins, trying to hold him still, but Mustang didn't seem willing to obey his owner's commands. He kept snorting with his big, black, damp nostrils and skittishly pawing the hay-covered floor, his black eyes fixed on me with what looked like a malevolent expression. My heart skipped a beat as I gazed into their depths. I instinctively stepped back, trying to make it seem casual. For some strange reason the horse seemed to have it in for me.

"Easy," Mr. Nichols said softly. "Mustang! Easy! What's wrong?" He stroked the horse's nose as if expecting him to answer. "He's usually so gentle. I don't know what's gotten into him today," he said, clearly uneasy.

My eyes didn't leave Mustang's. The horse neighed and I backed up even farther, a terrible feeling flooding through me.

"Easy," Mr. Nichols continued to whisper as the animal moved in his stall, agitated, snorting through his giant nostrils.

It was like he hated me. His dilated eyes made me shudder, but no one was paying attention to me. Jeneane, Faith, and Mr. Nichols were all focused on the animal's strange behavior.

"Girls, maybe you should go and have fun," Mr. Nichols said. "He's probably just nervous because there are so many of us here. How odd. He's never acted this way before."

His words pulled me out of the pit of agitation into which I'd sunk. I nodded and waved goodbye, more anxious than ever to get outside and away from Mustang. The moment I walked out of the stable I took a breath of fresh air and noticed my hands were trembling.

Faith stopped in her tracks. "I left the flashlight in the kitchen!" she said.

"Flashlight?" I said, surprised. "You're planning to stay out that late?" More than a question, it was a protest.

"What, didn't they tell you?" Jeneane said, always eager to supply information to people who didn't know everything she did. "The guys are going to make a campfire when it gets dark."

"I'm bringing marshmallows!" Faith cried eagerly, gesturing at her pink backpack as I tried hard not to let my jaw drop.

"I wonder why they forgot to tell me," I said sardonically. Actually I knew perfectly well why. Peter had been the one to plan everything and I was sure deep down he was still hoping something might happen between us. It would have been harder for me to turn down spending a couple hours with my friends, which was what he'd told me, than going on an outing that lasted until late at night.

I mechanically reached for my elastic band to put my hair up in a ponytail but it wasn't around my arm. Then I remembered Evan had taken it as a keepsake and a hot shiver ran through my heart. At least he'd taken a piece of me with him.

"I'll go with you!" Jeneane caught up with Faith who was walking to the house. "I have to go to the bathroom before we leave. The bushes irritate my skin."

"I'll wait in the car," I called after them, unsure if they'd heard me. I began to walk quickly away from the stable but Mustang's furious screams startled me. My heart contracted in my chest and I began to shiver, totally in the grip of an unexpected anxiety. Although I was already a hundred yards away, the noise of his hooves resounded in my ears: the horse was out of control and, judging from the nervous reaction of his owner who was trying uselessly to hold him, not even he knew why.

The earth beneath me began to tremble and my heart raced: Mr. Nichols had let Mustang out of his stall. I was glued to my spot, my eyes locked onto the horse's as he neighed and snorted furiously. All at once I had a glimmer of lucidity: Mr. Nichols was leading Mustang into the paddock, so I had no reason to be afraid. The fence was newly constructed, its posts and bars thick and sturdy. The possibility that the horse might escape was all in my head.

Then something made me tremble: the tension in Ginevra's voice. "Gemma!" she called, leaning out of the car door. My alarmed gaze shot to hers just as a neigh far louder than the others put my instincts on high alert. I spun around and froze, registering only confused scraps of information.

Mr. Nichols was on the ground and Mustang was up on his hind legs, out of control. He kicked at the fence so violently that the sound of his hooves striking the hard wood echoed through the yard, making me shudder.

A primitive fear shook me to my core. Panic clouded my mind and suddenly everything happened so fast I didn't even have time to breathe. A ferocious black mass raced toward me like a raging bull in an arena. It would trample me in a matter of seconds. Everything around me became muffled and confused. My friends' terrified voices faded into the background as my mind focused on one sound: the thundering of hooves against the ground as Mustang's wild eyes bored into mine. No one else was around. It was just me and him.

"GEMMA!!!"

Ginevra's scream was like a sledgehammer breaking me free from the block of ice in which my body had been encased. Mustang was only a few feet away by the time my brain gave the order for me to duck. He was too close for me to elude him and it was too late for me to run.

I curled up on the ground, closed my eyes, and held my breath, bracing for the impact. A blast of sandy earth struck me and I heard the deafening silence of the others holding their breath. The echo of wild galloping grew fainter as, numb with terror, panting and trembling, I slowly raised my head and saw Mustang racing into the trees. Mr. Nichols, on Faith's small brown horse, galloped after the stallion in a desperate attempt to catch him.

I shuddered, the hairs on my arms standing on end as the sandy earth settled to the ground around me. In the moment of silence that followed, I looked at my friends. Motionless, they stared at me, pale and speechless.

Ginevra was the first to run to me. The look in her eye told me how difficult it was for her to limit herself to a human pace in this bizarre circumstance. The others followed her as if waking from a nightmare, and an instant later the silence was replaced by a frantic jumble of worried voices.

"Are you okay?" Ginevra rested her hand on my arm, her tone apprehensive and her expression more worried than anyone else's.

I wasn't sure I could speak. "I—I think s-so," I stammered, my eyelids fluttering. I raised a hand to my temple, which throbbed beneath my fingers. Everybody surrounded me, staring as if I'd just survived a shark attack. If Mustang had trampled me, it probably would have been even worse than a shark attack.

"What did I tell you guys?!" Peter exclaimed. "Horses are dangerous." He shot me a glance, looking almost reproachful, and in his eyes I could see how worried he was. No one else paid any attention to him.

"I'm taking you home," Ginevra said matter-of-factly.

"No!" I said quickly in a determined voice.

For a moment my tone made everyone fall silent. They were all studying my face, their own still full of concern. Unjustified concern, because the worst had passed.

"I don't want to ruin the outing for everybody," I insisted.

"But Gemma!" Ginevra shot me a pleading look.

"Everything's fine, all right?" I hissed. "Let's go."

Faith was still as pale as a wax statue. She seemed to want me to go home more than anyone else. "It could have been a tragedy," she murmured dully as she stared at nothing. As she lifted her face to mine I saw tears shining in her eyes. She probably felt guilty because the horse belonged to her dad.

"But it wasn't," I reassured her, looking at Ginevra.

Was it you who stopped him? The thought sprang spontaneously from my mind. Ginevra looked at me, nodding almost imperceptibly, replying in a conversation no one else could take part in. *Thank you*, I thought, so only she could hear.

"You sure you're okay?" she asked me out loud.

"It was an accident. It could have happened to anyone," I reassured them all, forcing myself to speak convincingly. The truth was I wasn't sure. Something inside me continued to say it wasn't true: the memory of how ferociously Mustang had looked at me. He'd wanted *me* and nobody else, I could feel it in my gut. "I just happened to be standing in his way, that's all," I added, trying to persuade myself as well as the others. "If it had been Peter instead of me, I'm sure it wouldn't have gone any differently," I lied. Peter shuddered at the thought.

The others were already convinced: the one I needed to reassure was Ginevra.

"Except he would have had to go home and change!" Ginevra taunted him in an effort to relieve the tension. Peter shot her a withering look and she took it back. "You're right. It's more likely you would have fainted," she added. She'd probably read this in his mind, because when Peter heard her say it his eyes went wide. "Come on! No need for you to get mad."

She rested her hand on Peter's shoulder but he continued to glare at her. He didn't realize Ginevra could hear all the insults he was keeping to himself out of politeness.

"I was only kidding!" she said, amused.

"Wow. You're hilarious," he shot back sourly.

Faith still couldn't get over it. "It's so weird! Nothing like this has ever happened with Mustang. He was calm before you showed up and he's usually gentle with everyone. My little sister rides him without any problems," she said, mortified. I stopped listening to her and focused on the strange uneasiness stirring in my gut.

"The important thing is that it's over," Jake said, "and nobody got hurt." He walked toward the car with the others. I started to follow him, but Faith held me back, still visibly shaken. She slowed her pace and we fell behind the rest of the group.

"You shouldn't feel guilty!" I insisted, already assuming that was what she wanted to say. "I'm fine, really. Don't worry about it."

"I wanted to ask you something," she said point-blank. I slowed down even more, surprised. "It's not your time of the month by any chance, is it?" she whispered, almost embarrassed.

"Am I having my period? No. Why?"

"I don't know if it's actually possible. I'm no expert. My horse is female." She hesitated a moment before going on, encouraged by how curious I looked. "It's the only explanation that comes to my mind. Mustang's reaction was so unusual because, well, I mean, I think the smell of blood might have set him off." She rolled her eyes and imitated her dad's voice. "He's a stallion."

"I'm sorry to prove your theory wrong but I'm not on my period. Besides, honestly, I don't think it's possible. I mean, come on!" I exclaimed. Her idea was crazy. "Mustang must have just been in a bad mood," I said, trying to reassure her. "It happens to everybody, doesn't it? Or maybe it *was* something about the way I smell." I pulled the edge of my collar to my nose and sniffed it. "Stop torturing yourself and let's go. Nothing happened. That's all that matters."

"Right," she said, still shaken.

"Ready to have some fun?" I cheered to the group as I strode over to them.

"Well, at least you're in a good mood again," one of the guys said from the back seat.

Ginevra and I exchanged glances. Only she knew the truth.

REAWAKENED INSTINCT

"You sure we're not going too far?" Peter asked Ginevra, who was leading the group along a rambling path none of us knew well.

"Afraid of the big bad wolf?" she teased, a feral look on her face. Her lips twisted into a sardonic smile. "Or witches, maybe?"

I shot her a disapproving look. I didn't know exactly what Peter had done to end up being the butt of all her sadistic jokes, but it wasn't hard to guess.

"Witches!" Peter snorted. "Aren't you a little big to believe in stuff like that?"

Ginevra leaned in close to his face. "Aren't you?" she said in a sinister whisper. Something about the look in her eye made Peter fall silent, almost as if he'd grasped the veiled truth behind her words.

"It was your idea to go for a walk," Brandon said. "At least we'll see something new."

"Yeah, sure we will!" Jeneane shot back, annoyed. "New trees, new rocks. And look down there! A new stream, all our own!" she said sarcastically. "So is it going to take much longer? My feet are starting to ache," she whined, panting like someone who's just scaled Mt. Everest.

"Exactly five minutes less than the last time you asked," Ginevra said.

"Hey, chill! Did you just get stung by a wasp or what?" Jeneane stared at her almost defiantly.

Behind them, Peter laughed. "I don't think so. I don't see any dead wasps lying around," he said. "I doubt there's anything that could survive after stinging her." Ginevra glared at him, a challenging look in her eye, surprising the rest of us who had expected a more elaborate answer.

"We're almost there," she said, responding more to my thoughts than Jeneane's grumbling. Her lips curved into a sly smile. "There's just one last push," she told us, looking amused, her eyes on a steep slope to our right that led away from the path.

"You can't mean—" Jeneane's incredulous voice trailed off.

Ginevra looked her up and down. "You can always stay here and wait for us," she suggested spitefully, not leaving Jeneane much choice.

"Or," Peter whispered in her ear as he passed her, "you can come with us and follow the queen of the witches."

Ginevra turned to look at him. "Thanks. You finally said something nice about me." Peter didn't realize he'd just paid her a compliment. I bit my lip to keep from laughing.

"Can't we follow the path?" Faith asked cautiously as if Ginevra made her nervous.

Surprisingly, Ginevra answered nicely. "That would take a good two hours. I'm offering you guys the chance to get there in fifteen minutes, tops. If that's okay with you."

"Hang in there just a little longer," Jake said to Faith considerately, resting a hand on her shoulder. Looking resigned, she nodded at the tenderness on his face.

As we made our way up, the slope grew even steeper. The ground was covered with leaves, dry pine needles, and gravel. An occasional rock lodged in the ground or a tree trunk jutting out the sandy soil offered us a foothold.

Peter led the group, followed by Jeneane and Faith who were being helped by Brandon and Jake, while Ginevra and I brought up the rear.

"It's been over twenty minutes, Ginevra!" Jeneane groaned, looking tired and fed up.

Ginevra smiled and looked at me, shrugging. "It's not my fault she's a slowpoke!" I shot her a reproving look. "Fifteen minutes would have been enough time for me," she said in a low, amused voice.

I stared at her, open-mouthed. "I thought you meant fifteen *human* minutes!" I said reproachfully.

"Nobody asked."

"You're unbelievable," I teased her affectionately. I didn't mind climbing uphill through the trees at all. I could have kept going for hours. The strong smell of moss in the air relaxed me. My girlfriends, on the other hand, seemed exhausted.

"We're almost there!" Peter called. He was standing on a large trunk half-buried beneath layers of earth. Faith joined him on top of it and so did Jeneane.

As I trudged uphill, absently staring at the ground beneath my feet, my heart unexpectedly leapt to my throat for no reason at all. Instinctively, I raised my eyes to the trunk that Jake was now climbing onto, then looked back at my feet, moving forward, then again at the trunk, as if something were beckoning me. My instincts were strangely on alert, and yet the tree trunk was a perfectly sturdy foothold. It had been lying there on the ground for who knew how long.

A strange cracking sound rent the air. I looked up, alarmed, but no one else seemed to have heard it.

It was Brandon's turn to climb onto the trunk, a dozen yards up the slope from me. My eyes darted to his foot as he rested it on the trunk and the blood suddenly drained from my face. Before I could open my mouth, the trunk tore itself violently from the earth and began to roll downhill, dragging Brandon with it. He clutched at the ground, his fingers sinking into the earth. Shouts came from above but they were lost among the trees.

The blood froze in my veins as I watched the trunk barreling toward me, out of control. Panicking, I stepped back and lost my balance. The trunk bounced off the ground and came flying at me. As I fell someone yanked me out of its trajectory. It crashed against a tree and rolled down the hill. I suspected Ginevra had diverted it from its path and I hoped the others were still too much in shock to have noticed. Shaking from head to toe, I forced myself to take a breath. Ginevra had saved me again. Our eyes met, mine still filled with terror, and I saw she was petrified too. The others raced down the hill toward us as the trunk hit the bottom and smashed into a thousand pieces.

"Are you okay?" Peter shouted, breathless with worry as he rushed past the others. The question was starting to become a constant part of my life. Before I could answer him, he smothered me in a desperate hug as Ginevra looked on uneasily. "I thought you were done for," he whispered into my hair. Peter couldn't imagine I'd already survived far worse situations.

"Gemma!" the girls cried in concern when they finally reached us.

"It's okay, I'm fine," I reassured them, still looking at Peter. Of all of them, he looked the most shaken. I locked eyes with Ginevra in an attempt to let her know how thankful I was. "Well?" I exclaimed, trying to appear nonchalant though my heart was about to burst out of my chest. "Are we planning to put down roots here?"

Jake surprised me by resting a hand on my shoulder. "Girl, either you're jinxed or this is totally not your lucky day!" he kidded as my brain processed what he'd just said. My instinct had tried to warn me. I forced a smile and said something in reply.

Meanwhile Jeneane had stopped to stare at Ginevra, who looked back at her out of the corner of her eye. "Nice move. I didn't know you were so strong," she said, almost accusingly.

"Just lucky, that's all." From her tone, Ginevra seemed to have lost her sense of humor.

The minute the others turned around we exchanged a knowing look. Ginevra had to be careful not to attract attention like that.

After a few more minutes a small clearing surrounded by trees opened up before us. It didn't look much different from the one I was used to, but Ginevra insisted that the trees around it formed a perfect circle. No one seemed convinced it was a good enough reason to have dragged us all the way here.

I rummaged in my backpack for *Forbidden*, a novel by Tabitha Suzuma that I hadn't been able to put down for days now. "Book!" Brandon's warning cry made me flinch and I looked up. "Hey, hey, hey! No books allowed! Confiscate that book from Gemma!" I felt like a cornered animal. Before I knew it, Peter had pounced on me.

"All right, all right, I'll put it away!" I protested cautiously, a little alarmed by his impulsive behavior.

Peter fixed his eyes on me and said in a mock-threatening voice, holding back a grin, "We don't need some you-might-see-me-but-I'm-on-another-planet zombie version of Gemma!"

"It's bad enough having to put up with that at school," Jake chimed in sardonically.

I'd planned to finish the novel but had no choice but to hide it before my friends actually took it away from me. Instead, I pulled out my camera and took snapshots of them. Then we tossed our backpacks on the ground, split up, and went into the woods to gather firewood.

"Hey, Gemma!" Peter walked toward me.

At my side, Ginevra rolled her eyes. "Such a pain in the neck," she murmured in exasperation. "He needs to *talk* to you."

Do you mind? I asked her with my eyes so Peter, who hadn't reached us yet, couldn't hear.

It was clear from the look on Ginevra's face how irritated she was. "But he wants to be *alone* with you!" she exclaimed, surprised by my openness toward him.

"He's my friend," I reminded her.

Ginevra clenched her jaw and quickened her pace. Catching up to the rest of the group, she strode past the boys with a toss of her head, her wavy hair cascading over her shoulders like molten gold.

"Close your mouth, Brandon," Jeneane warned, seeing his expression. "You've got all day long to drool." Ginevra smiled to herself and I shook my head.

"So she finally gave you some room to breathe." Peter walked up to me. "I was starting to think your boyfriend had appointed her as your bodyguard. She never leaves you alone for a second!"

"We're really close," I said, bothered by his sarcasm.

"Like you and I used to be?" he asked bluntly.

His question hit me straight in the heart. I searched his gaze, feeling a pang in my stomach I couldn't express, then looked away, focusing on the path we were following. "It's different," I said in a small voice.

"Right." His tone was resentful. "But what we had was special too." I said nothing, but Peter wouldn't take my silence for an answer. "You think so yourself, don't you? Tell me you do."

"Pet . . ." I couldn't find the words. "You're a big part of my life. An important part, and that's never going to change."

He pressed his lips together in a bitter smile and said, "But I'm part of the past. That's what you're trying to tell me."

Since when had he become so straightforward? I hesitated. "I'm with Evan now. Don't be upset about it. That's just how things turned out. I don't want to lose your friendship, but I'll understand if you don't want me around any more. Don't misunderstand me: you'll always be a part of my life. I want you to be, even in the future," I reassured him. I felt guilty for being so direct, but I needed to be clear with him. "But only as a brother—like it's always been for me."

The look on his face finally expressed what he'd never managed to say in words: Peter didn't feel the same way about me. My confession seemed to have crushed his heart. I took comfort in the knowledge that the flame of false hope was more devastating—because it burned stronger and longer—than the flame of cold, hard truth, which flared up initially, but was soon extinguished by resignation.

"You're wrong." The sudden change in his expression confirmed it. "I'll *always* want you around." Peter tried hard to keep his disillusionment off his face, understanding how pointless it was to insist. Then he smiled at me as if the conversation had never happened. But a person's smile can be called sincere only when it's their eyes doing the smiling—and his were dull. "So what did you do over the summer, you and . . . your boyfriend?"

I looked at him sadly, unsure whether I should follow his lead. He'd changed the subject so abruptly it worried me. Rubbing salt in the wound I'd just inflicted didn't seem like a good idea, so I dodged his question. "No, tell me about you. I mean, you guys spent three whole months camping while I was stuck back here. Tell me everything! Was it fun?"

"It would have been more fun if you'd been there."

"Aw, I bet it wasn't all that bad."

His smile broadened as he tousled my hair. He knew I hated it when he did that. "Don't let it go to your head! We had a blast even without you." He grinned.

I gasped, feigning shock. For a moment I was glad of how easy it was to talk to Peter, just as if nothing had changed between us. But then he turned serious again. "It was just what I needed, to get away from . . . Lake Placid," he murmured, casting me a sidelong glance. *To get away from the sight of you and Evan together all the time* was what I read on his face, which was more honest than he was.

"Oh, man!" I shook his arm. "I leave you alone for one summer and you turn so serious! Where's the Peter I used to know? He would be dying to tell me every detail. What have you done with him?" It was my desperate attempt to get through to my friend, hidden somewhere behind this new Peter I barely recognized.

Unexpectedly, it seemed to work. He laughed at some memory that crossed his mind. "Would you believe it if I told you Jake managed to shoot spaghetti out of his nose?"

"Oh my God, how disgusting!" I exclaimed, grossed out.

"The guy would do anything to get Faith's attention."

"I doubt it worked. They should offer courses for guys like him who don't know how to pick up girls."

"Well, he *did* manage to make her laugh. In fact, she was laughing so hard she could barely breathe," he said.

"Good thing Brandon didn't have a brilliant idea like that. I don't think Jeneane would have reacted quite so well."

"You're probably right." For a moment I recognized my old friend, the one I missed so much, in his carefree expression. "But then again, Brandon got a laugh out of Jeneane too," he said.

"Oh, I've got to hear this."

"You'd better sit down first," he warned. "I'm not sure you'll be able to stay standing." He doubled over in laughter. "One night there was a party at the campground and Brandon picked up a girl." Peter was laughing so hard there were tears in his eyes. It was contagious; my lips curled into a smile. "She was gorgeous, no doubt about it, and he was strutting around because she even seemed older than us. They . . . they started dancing . . . and he found out . . ." Peter gasped out the words between laughs, "he found out it was a dude!"

"Brandon picked up a transvestite?!" I asked, astonished.

Peter nodded, unable to speak for hilarity. "He wanted to make Jeneane jealous but instead he made her pee herself laughing!"

"I won't ask how he found out it wasn't a girl."

"That's the funniest part!" he said, throwing his head back. "They danced all night long and then went off behind a tree and he tou—"

"Okay, okay, no need to go into detail!" I said quickly. "I wish I'd seen his face."

"He couldn't look us in the eye for two whole days."

"Poor Brandon. I'll try to go easier on him," I said, happy I'd erased the sadness from Peter's eyes. Unfortunately, it wouldn't begin to erase the sorrow he carried in his heart, I was sure of that. His hand accidentally brushed mine and our eyes met awkwardly. We both stopped laughing. Embarrassed, I nudged him. "Sounds like you had a good time."

"Yeah, it was fun."

I felt a sudden flicker of selfishness in my heart. Who was I to keep Pet from getting on with his life? I'd spent the most wonderful time in my life while he was off camping, so why did the idea that Peter was pulling away bother me? It wasn't like me. What was happening to me?

A jingle in my pocket startled me. My phone. I didn't need to check it to know I'd gotten a text. My stomach in turmoil, I slid my fingers into the back pocket of my jeans and pulled it out.

Evan. My heart skipped a beat and the expression on my face didn't escape Peter. "That him?" he asked, his tone flat.

I stared at the ground as guilt gripped my throat. "We'd better get back to the others," I said, hoping we could drop the subject. Deep in my heart, I was bursting with impatience to find some isolated spot where I could read the message from Evan, on the other side of the world.

"We haven't gotten enough firewood yet," he said.

I could see in his face how much he wished to keep me there with him and by extension, keep me away from Evan as well, just this once, but it was a wish I refused to grant. "The others have probably found enough for all of us," I said, prodding him to go back.

We walked back into the clearing just as the rest of the group emerged from the trees on the opposite side. Jake and Brandon carried logs for us to sit on and arranged them in a big circle. Jeneane held a handful of twigs, careful not to ruin the decorations on her nails. Faith and Ginevra's faces, on the other hand, were barely visible behind the huge armfuls of firewood they carried. They dumped them into the center of the circle and brushed off their clothes.

"Nice work," Ginevra told Faith, high-fiving her. Faith had also collected dry pine needles to use as tinder. She'd once explained that her grandfather, a beekeeper, used them as a natural fuel in the smoker. They emitted a thick, white, sweetly scented smoke that helped placate the bees when he was working with the hive. Their fear of fire made them fill up on honey until they were sated, which calmed them down.

"Who's got a lighter?" Faith turned to Brandon, who searched his pockets. "I thought you smoked."

"I was sure I brought one. It must have fallen out along the way," he apologized, looking around.

"Do I have to do everything myself?" Ginevra complained, making the whole group look at her.

"What are you going to do about it?" Peter said. More than a question, it was a provocation. He smiled at her sardonically and Ginevra gave him a crafty smile.

"I never reveal my secrets," she said, shutting him up. Peter turned his back to her.

I watched silently as Ginevra patiently waited for Jake to stack the wood, leaving a space in the center for air and scattering clumps of dry pine needles that would instantly catch fire.

"Gin, what are you—"

She winked at me and I left the question unfinished. Leaning over the pile of wood with a haughty little smile on her lips, she grabbed a small stick and pretended to rub it between her palms while the others waited, full of curiosity.

"You've got to be kidding!" Peter scoffed immediately. "There's no way you'll ever light a fire with that!"

Ginevra ignored him and shot me a fleeting glance, her lips moving quickly. "Distract them," she murmured, her tone firm, so fast I was amazed I'd been able to understand what she'd said.

I obeyed without hesitation. "Brandon, isn't that your lighter down there?" I signaled vaguely with my finger. Like marionettes, they all turned their heads to look where I was pointing. Everybody except Ginevra, who was concentrating on the fire. I watched her, fascinated, as the green of her eyes lit up, producing a spark.

"That's just a rock," someone said. By the time they turned back, the fire was burning.

"Wow! How the hell—" Brandon stammered, the first one to feel the warmth spread over his face.

"Oh. My. God!" Peter said, his tone caught between amazement and disbelief.

"No. Just me," Ginevra replied, grinning.

"Great job!" Faith said, as astonished as the others.

"*Magic*," Ginevra exclaimed in response to the incredulous looks on their faces. Behind her wild, provocative expression hid a smile only I could decipher. She was telling the truth, but no one would ever have guessed it.

The flames rose higher, coming close to Ginevra's face. Something Evan had once said crossed my mind as if he were whispering it in my ear right now: *Fire is the only weapon capable of annihilating a Witch.* Panic washed over me. "Gin, look out!" I shouted, shoving her away and crashing to the rocky ground as the fire crackled behind us.

"Hey! What's wrong?" she whispered, not a trace of resentment in her voice.

"Evan told me that—"

Words weren't necessary. Ginevra burst out laughing before I could finish my sentence. "Thanks for the thought, but there's no need to worry about me. Don't you think I can take care of myself?" she said with an affectionate grin.

Softly, so the others couldn't hear, I whispered in a tone that was almost reproachful, "Aren't you afraid of burning to death?"

"I certainly can't be killed by *your* fire!" she reassured me in a low voice.

"But I thought—"

"The fire that can kill a Witch is no different from yours, actually," she explained, "but it's only effective if an Angel is using it to purify evil. That's the only way it can keep its purity."

Embarrassed by my reaction, I lay back and spread my arms out on the ground. "Evan didn't mention that!" I said with a smile.

Ginevra lay down beside me and we both stared at the sky, neither of us worrying about dirt on our clothes or hair. Although the sun hadn't set, a few brighter stars were already shining in the twilight. The air smelled good. The scent of the forest was gradually replaced by the aroma of the campfire.

"I'll go sit with the others," Ginevra said unexpectedly, getting up. "That way you can read your message," she added, shooting me a little smile.

Sometimes her ability to read minds was an incredible advantage. I could never have come straight out and told her to leave me alone even though my eagerness to read Evan's text tingled beneath my skin, but she'd sensed my wish all the same. I smiled to myself, still impatient. I wanted to wait until I was alone.

"Gin?" I called after her.

She turned gracefully and waited patiently for me to ask the question she'd already read in my mind.

"Was it hard for you to leave your Sisters?" Given the closeness I felt between us tonight I thought it was safe to ask.

"The bond among Witches is ancestral," she said solemnly, "but love is stronger than everything else." She gave me a sweet smile, turned, and left.

I took the phone out of my pocket and my heart skipped a beat as I read Evan's name on the display. I unlocked the screen and it came to life, lighting up the night that was encroaching on the forest. My chest rose and fell with the agitation of my heart.

I miss you to death. I'm on the other side of the world, but my thoughts are captive back there where I left my heart. All I have to do is close my eyes to feel you're with me. Wherever I am, you're inside me, my love. See you tonight. Evan.

I closed my eyes and took a deep breath, filling my heart with his words. Then, opening it to him again, I typed a reply, my fingers flying over the keys.

Holding my breath for a whole day would hurt less than being away from you for this long. But all I have to do is lift my eyes to the heavens and look at my star to know that you're in my heart. Come back soon. Jamie

"Where's Gemma?" A distant murmur of concern reached me as I realized night had fallen, surrounding me with darkness without my noticing. In my heart, the sun was shining. When I sat up, dazed by the brightness of the fire I'd been staring at, Ginevra was sitting on a log just far enough away to keep an eye on me. I got up and joined them as the light from the flames flickered on their faces.

"Good news?" Ginevra asked as I sat down beside her.

"You mean there's something you don't already know?" I said in a low voice.

"No, you're right. I tried to mind my own business, I really did. It's not that I want to listen to your thoughts, but I can't help it. It's what I am. Sometimes it's hard to block them out."

"Yeah, right. In any case, no one asked you to." I smiled at her affectionately.

"Well, what now?" Brandon's voice rose over the crackling flames. "Come on, guys! We're in the woods, sitting around a campfire. Don't you think something's missing?" he said, studying our expressions. "Like ghost stories?"

"Any better ideas?" Faith was quick to say.

"Faith, don't tell me they scare you," Peter teased.

"What if they do?" Jake spoke up in her defense. "You're afraid of snakes, after all."

Ginevra stiffened, though no one noticed but me. My relationship with her probably wasn't the only reason Peter instinctively felt so negative toward her.

"What the hell? It's not true! Who told you that?" he shot back uncomfortably.

"Come on, everybody knows it," Jeneane said.

"Well, now you know it's not true! I'm not afraid of anything," he said in a low voice, almost to himself. Everyone could see the embarrassment on his face.

Ginevra looked at me out of the corner of her eye, a strange little smile on her lips. There was no need to read her mind to understand what she was thinking. I started to shake my head in protest, but she didn't stop to consider my objection; she seemed to have already made up her mind. Unable to stop her, I buried my face in my hands. A second later, Jeneane, sitting across from us, let out an ear-piercing shriek. "A snake!" she screamed. Peter burst out laughing.

Poor Pet, I thought.

"You think I'm stupid? We were just talking about it a second ago, Jeneane. You could at least let a few minutes go by before pulling a prank like that. Awesome performance, though, I'll give you that!" he said, annoyed.

"There really *is* a snake!" Faith burst out, looking horrified. "And it's moving straight towards you, Peter! Get away from there! It's a poisonous one!"

"Don't be stu—" Peter heard the hiss and paled violently before he even looked at the ground. The snake was inches from him.

"This isn't funny," I whispered to Ginevra. The smirk she was trying to hide made me nervous.

"It is to me!" she said under her breath.

Peter sat like a statue, careful not to move a muscle. Frozen with terror, the others watched the snake slithering across the ground in Peter's direction. None of them knew he actually had nothing to fear, but how could I explain that it was just a sadistic practical joke Ginevra was playing on him?

"What do we do?" Brandon whispered between clenched teeth, as if afraid to draw the snake's attention onto himself.

"Somebody do something!" Jeneane cried, tears in her eyes.

I saw the fear on their faces and didn't know what to do. Why did Ginevra have to be so vicious?

Peter was petrified. The fire flared, lighting up his face, and I could see he'd broken out in a cold sweat. Seeing him so powerless and panic-stricken triggered something violent inside me. I couldn't bear to see the terror in his eyes. Ginevra was going too far. I had to do something. I switched off my brain, followed my instinct, and rose to my feet, but Ginevra immediately grabbed my wrist so tightly it hurt.

"That's enough, Gin!" I ordered her with all the authority I could force into my voice.

A corner of her mouth rose, her expression sly. "I'll take care of it," she said aloud so everyone could hear her. She could have made the snake slither away with her powers, but she chose not to. Instead, she moved gracefully toward it as the anxious group stared at her, looking as amazed as they were worried.

"Ginevra, are you crazy?" Jake shouted from the other side of the fire. "It's poisonous! Stay away!"

She continued to move toward the snake, completely unaffected by his remark, amused by her little game. The flames writhed in the air and her long eyelashes cast shadows on her face.

"Stop, damn it!" Peter shouted, furious because he'd been unable to do anything himself. All of them were powerless, but Ginevra continued to smile as she crouched down until she was face to face with the snake.

Paralyzed in an unearthly silence, we watched Ginevra lock eyes with it as if she were communicating with it telepathically. Actually, she was just showing off. The others watched her with bated breath. The snake responded by interrupting its hostile hiss. The silence was eerie; all we could hear was the ominous crackling of the fire. All at once she snatched the snake up, holding it behind its head and lifting it into the air as a murmur of surprise and admiration rose around the flames.

"He's just a little creature," she said proudly. "He's more afraid of us than we are of him."

"Funny, none of us are poisonous," Brandon said, his pride wounded.

"He doesn't know that," Ginevra said, raising an eyebrow. "He would never attack except in self-defense," she added, moving the snake from side to side to show us.

I stole a glance at Peter. He was still frozen with fright, his eyes locked on the snake in Ginevra's hand. As if she wanted to twist the knife in his open wound, she held it toward his face to show him, then walked to the edge of the woods and let it slither into the darkness. "He's gone," she told us smugly.

"You are fucking awesome!" Jake exclaimed as Ginevra returned.

"You sure it won't come back?" Jeneane asked, her face still pale.

"Don't worry, he won't," she said. "Sorry," she whispered to Pete as she passed him, "but we all need to overcome our fears. They're limitations we impose on ourselves."

"What a coincidence," Brandon said. "We were talking about your fear of snakes and then one showed up right next to you."

"Good thing you're not afraid of bears!" Jake said, breaking the tension. Everyone laughed and began to relax.

Ginevra sat down next to me as the rest of the group murmured admiringly about her. "Congratulations," I said acidly, watching Peter's face, still slack with shock. "You got what you wanted."

"It's not like you think. I did it for him," she said.

"For him?!" I retorted bitterly, feeling a wildness hidden deep inside me come to life and burst out at Ginevra. "What were you thinking? Look at him! He's terrified!" I said, shocked by the anger in my voice. Ginevra stared at me as if she didn't know me, as stunned as I by how I'd blurted out the thoughts I'd been holding back. *But I couldn't stop them.*

"All right," she admitted. "Maybe I overdid it a little, but now you're the one overdoing it. What's gotten into you? It was just a stupid joke! Would you chill?" she hissed.

Like a slap in the face, her words snapped me out of it, awakening my conscience. For a moment I found myself watching the scene from a distance. I'd felt it again: the uncontrollable impulse that drove me to react this way. *It was inside me.* I opened my mouth to speak but closed it before my thoughts took shape. Ginevra studied my bewildered expression and rested her warm hand on my leg.

"Sorry," I whispered. "I don't know why I reacted like that. You're right. Deep down I knew Peter wasn't in any danger, right?"

"Of course not," she said. "I was in complete control of the situation. I knew exactly what Peter was feeling. I could hear his thoughts. I wanted to help him overcome the trauma that's haunted him since he was little, when his horse got spooked by a snake and threw him from the saddle."

My mind filled with memories. "You're right," I said in a low voice, shaken. I well remembered the episode with the horse and the snake. "I thought he'd gotten over it."

"No, but tonight he was on the verge of doing it. He was about to face that snake, you know."

"I had no idea. I'm sorry," I whispered, mortified.

"That's okay. There was no way you could have known."

"Why don't you just use your powers of persuasion instead? I've seen what you can make people do."

"My power, like Evan's, can only make people act against their will. I can't eliminate a deeply rooted fear inside them. It would just keep resurfacing. Only Simon can work on such a deep level."

"I'm such an idiot! I ruined everything!" I groaned, burying my head in my hands.

"Don't worry," she reassured me, stroking my knee.

"You wanted to do him a favor and I thought you were just being a bitch! I'm such a mess. Forgive me! I've been losing control so easily lately and—" I covered my mouth with my hand and silence fell, a silence all our own. Meanwhile the voices of the others in the background faded into the distance.

"Speaking of which . . ." I looked up at her. "You know how much you mean to me," Ginevra said, "and I know you're the nicest person in the world, but lately there's something about you I can't figure out. It's like you've got a split personality. Your thoughts stop dead, you have mood swings, even the smallest things totally set you off. Maybe there's something worrying you that's making you react like this. We can talk about it if you want." She looked at me thoughtfully. It was so strange for her to ask me to talk to her about something she didn't already know.

"Believe me, I have no idea what's going on. You're probably right. Maybe I haven't totally overcome the whole death thing. Maybe I just hid it somewhere inside and when I get too emotional I can't handle it any more—I feel overwhelmed and lose control," I confessed regretfully. "It's like I'm constantly afraid an Executioner is out there waiting for his chance to attack me, and the feeling is wrecking my nervous system."

"I don't think you have anything to worry about. Months have gone by and nobody's come looking for you," she said, trying to reassure me.

"It would be great to believe that, but I can't control it. There's this tingling sensation under my skin like my instinct has reawakened, and I keep getting a terrible feeling in my stomach. It's cold, creepy."

Ginevra wrapped her arm around my shoulders affectionately. The others weren't paying any attention to us. "Sooner or later you'll put the whole thing behind you, you'll see. No Subterranean who isn't one of us will ever manage to get near you."

When I rested my head on Ginevra's shoulder she lowered her voice. "You're safe with us, Gemma. Take my word for it, no one's going to hurt you."

I felt sleepy and her words became fainter. My eyelids grew heavy and I could barely keep them open. I finally surrendered, closing them.

"You're not going to die . . ."

The words echoed in my head, sweet and soft, as my eyes opened, dazzled by the blinding sunlight reflected off the lake—a perfectly still mirror of water that stretched to the horizon like a pane of glass.

I rubbed my eyes, filled with an unusual feeling of lightness. It soon vanished, overpowered by a stronger emotion—a strange and now familiar sense of uneasiness. It gripped my mind as soon as my gaze landed on a distant figure veiled in white. It was a woman. She had her back to me and was clad in a pearly gown. Her hair flowed down her back like molten gold with a strange hint of copper that made it gleam with an unusual light. As if she'd sensed my presence, she turned her head and met my gaze, startling me. Her honey-colored eyes summoned me like an ancestral call. I felt something deep within me awaken, something new and intriguing. It battled the instinct that was warning me not to give in to the primitive need I felt to draw closer to the enchanting woman. But the need was stronger than the instinct and it prevailed.

The closer I came, the clearer the woman's outline appeared. When I was quite near her I discovered she wasn't alone. Another figure, hidden by her gown, was facing her, perfectly still. A shiver ran over my skin like a premonition.

"Evan," I whispered, bewildered, barely moving my lips. He didn't look at me or even acknowledge my presence, but focused all his attention on the woman. "Evan, what are you—"

The words died on my lips when the woman closed her eyelids, fringed with long lashes, and opened them again gracefully, fixing her gaze on mine. She rested her hand on Evan's neck and walked around him slowly, almost as if they were dancing. Her long legs made the white silk flow with each step until she stood behind him. She peered at him with a strange light in her eyes. *Desire.* With a satisfied expression she raised her amber eyes to mine. I couldn't move a muscle. Her hand moved slowly over Evan's skin and he tilted his head, following the movement as though it gave him pleasure, still paying no heed to me. I frowned, disconcerted. The woman smiled at me again and moved her lips to him, slowly sliding her finger down his neck and touching her mouth to his ear as if whispering something to him. Evan half closed his eyes with pleasure.

"No!" I screamed at the top of my lungs. I tried to reach them but couldn't move. Something was keeping me glued to my spot. My heart skipped a beat, then shrank back as Evan took the woman's hand, lifted it to his lips, and kissed her palm like he always did mine. "Evan . . ." I could barely breathe.

They gazed at each other for a long moment while I—powerless, trapped in my body—watched the woman rest her lips on his neck again. Evan encouraged her with his eyes. Desperation flooded me. Overhead, the clouds slid by quickly and the sun sank beyond the lake, dragging my heart with it into the darkest depths.

"Evan!" I shouted, but he couldn't hear me. My muffled voice echoed against the walls of my brain as if I were sealed in a crystal sphere. "Don't do it!" I shouted with all the desperation I felt.

She heard my cry and her eyes sought mine. A shudder ran through me and I squinted at her. Something about her looked familiar, almost as if I were staring at my own distorted reflection in a pool of water. I had the feeling that part of me had always known her. Suddenly my surroundings blurred and a stabbing pain in my head doubled me over. Confused images began to revolve around me as I writhed in pain.

They suddenly stopped, showing me a serpent with yellow eyes, two narrow slits that stared at me. I flinched.

The image vanished, replaced by another that was even more dangerous: the woman's sharp, seductive gaze locked on mine. Eyes closed, I pressed my fingers to my temples to banish her cunning smile from my mind and the image of the serpent took its place only to disappear again, alternating with that of the woman. Now Evan's dark eyes filled my head and gripped my heart and again, the serpent. I covered my ears with my hands, unable to stop the rapid sequence of frozen images tormenting me; it was as if my brain had gone haywire and no longer responded to my commands. I felt like I was going insane as the flashes alternated faster and faster. The woman. The serpent. Evan. The serpent again. *Enoooough!* My screams pounded against the walls of my mind, blowing them up, but not a sound came from my lips. Again the woman. Evan. Again the serpent. *Stop it!*

The flashes suddenly focused on Evan's face. His eyes went wide as if someone had just struck him in the chest. He looked at me and I knew he could finally see me. "Evan," I murmured, but his eyes of ice were frozen in dull pain. "Evan," I whispered again.

The picture in my head blurred and disappeared, replaced by an image of Evan's arm as it fell heavily to the ground. Unbearable pain gripped my chest and the blackest darkness swallowed me up.

"Evan!" I screamed, panting, as a knot in my throat choked me and tears burned my eyes.

"Easy, Gemma," Ginevra whispered, brushing back the hair that clung to my damp face.

"Ginevra," I whispered in a daze. Neither the burning sensation in my eyes nor the pain in my chest had faded.

"Everything's fine. Evan will be here soon, you'll see," she said, trying to calm me down, but the feeling in my heart was stronger.

"He's dead! Evan's dead! Don't you see?" I hissed, confused, as tears continued to stream down my face. I clung to her comforting gaze in an attempt to climb out of the pit into which I'd fallen.

"Evan isn't dead. You had a bad dream, that's all."

My lips were trembling. I had a terrible presentiment. "Do you—do you think it's possible I can see things before they happen?" I asked, still shaken.

Ginevra looked at me with compassion. "Evan can't die," she said softly. "Gemma, you're just a little stressed. Try to relax." For a moment she fell silent and stared back at me, matching the intensity of my gaze. "I'll admit that at first I didn't think you'd be able to handle all this, but then I found out how strong you were, Gemma. You're stronger than you think. It's perfectly understandable for you to be so stressed. In fact, it's the least we expected. And I know you're shaken because Evan brought you into his world and shared things you thought were forbidden, and you're right. Sometimes my brother just doesn't think things through. Still, you have no reason to be so worried. It's just fear awakening your instinct and it seems my prank shook you up more than I thought it would."

Her words crept into my mind like a cloud of fog as my gaze, lost in the darkness of the woods, spotted something moving. My heart leapt to my throat and I cringed. A shadow. Ginevra read my thoughts and followed my gaze to the trees, then looked back at me, her expression calm, and squeezed my hand. Maybe she was right. I was starting to get paranoid.

I forced myself to take a deep breath and glanced at the clear sky. My star smiled at me, twinkling. Evan was fine and in a few hours I'd see him again.

"That was my mom." Faith's voice shook me out of my thoughts as I put my phone into my backpack. "Seems something horrible has happened in Iraq. She said there were massive casualties, including a lot of our soldiers. My brother called to say he's okay."

I shuddered so violently Ginevra sensed it through my skin. We exchanged a glance and a chill descended on us. "We'd better go," Ginevra told the group, squeezing my hand. "It's late."

SUBTLE JEALOUSY

When I woke up, I had a hard time remembering how I'd made it to bed. The light streaming through the window told me it was daytime, but that meant Evan should be there with me. I looked around, frustrated. No one was in the room with me except Irony, snoring on his cushion.

I dragged myself out of bed to get ready for school. My head was a heavy mass that weighed on my neck and my thoughts wandered, fleeting and muddled, leaving me in a daze. When I was ready I opened the door to leave, my stomach in a knot, ignoring the table laid for breakfast. The ice-cold air lashed at my face. It was strange no one had come to pick me up. There was no sign of Evan or Ginevra on the deserted street. What could have kept them?

I started to chew on the inside of my cheek as a multitude of questions filled my head. It had been so long since I'd walked to school that I had a terrible sense of foreboding.

Something caught my attention: a butterfly. I'd never seen such a pretty one before. It was big and black. *Completely black.* Its wings looked like velvet. I had the impression it was frightened, but it didn't fly off. Instead it came closer as if it knew me. I obeyed my urge to touch it and it moved its wings. Cautiously, I pulled my camera out of my backpack and took a few snapshots for the photography assignment Mr. Madison had given us a few days ago.

The sound of a car horn made me jump. I spun around, but saw no one on the street, so I turned back. The butterfly was gone—I looked around, but there was no trace of it. I set out again for school and another blare of a horn, closer this time, made me start again.

I shook my head, not recognizing the green pickup truck that had honked at me, and kept walking. The horn blared again insistently. I stared at the truck, but the light reflecting off the window kept me from seeing the driver. As if in response, the window slid down with a hiss.

"Need a ride?"

"Peter?" I squinted, frowning. "Pet!" I crossed the street with long strides. Peter rested his hand on the steering wheel, a satisfied smile on his face. "You've got a pickup?!" I exclaimed, amazed. "Since when do you have a pickup?"

"Get in," he invited with a jerk of his head. "I'm going your way." He shot me a glance as I sank into the low seat of the Ford Ranger. I still remember how excited I'd been the day we got our driver's licenses, but neither of us had ever had a car all our own before.

"Wow, this is awesome!" I said, stroking the black dashboard.

"It's not much—it's already a few decades old," he said, "but it's something—and it's mine." His lips curved into a proud smile.

"Are you kidding?" I asked, happy for him. "Remember how we used to play inside cardboard boxes, pretending they were cars?"

"You always wanted to drive but I never let you," Peter said, making me laugh.

"You said you were the *man* and that one day you'd take me for a drive in a real car."

"Yeah." Peter looked down and gripped the steering wheel. Looking at his fingers made me think of yesterday when our hands had accidentally touched. I didn't want Peter to suffer. He was a part of me—an important part. "That was a long time ago. We were just little kids. What we said back then doesn't matter." His tone was dull. Silence filled the truck as Peter pulled into the school parking lot.

"Hey! We're here now, right? You kept your promise."

"True," he said. We both laughed out loud just as my eye fell on Evan's BMW, parked almost directly in front of us. My heart raced. Evan was glaring threateningly through the windshield at Peter. I tensed. I'd never seen his eyes so dark before. He seemed to be trying hard to keep himself from killing Peter.

Evan got out of the car, slammed the door, and canceled the distance between us with long strides. His face wore a caustic expression that was far from reassuring. "What are you doing with him?" he asked me, cutting to the chase. His tone was cold, his gaze dark.

"He offered me a ride, that's all," I stammered.

"You could have waited for me. Do you have any idea what went through my mind when I found you weren't home?" he admonished me, a note of desperation only I could understand in his voice.

"Thanks for the ride, Peter," I mumbled quickly before walking off with Evan in an attempt to keep the two of them apart.

"See you in class!" Peter called after me.

"And do *you*," I shot back once I was sure no one could hear us, "have any idea what went through *my* mind when you didn't come to my house after telling me you would?"

Evan's face relaxed and his expression turned sly. "You missed me." He raised an eyebrow and lifted one corner of his mouth in a smile. "I thought you wouldn't even notice I was gone," he said, satisfied. But it was a challenge, I was sure of it.

"You can't—how can you even think something like that?" My eyelids fluttered nervously. I couldn't believe he'd just said that. "Maybe that's true for *you*," I said, throwing the insinuation back in his face.

"Sorry, but I had no choice. I should have gotten back last night, but I was delayed."

"Delayed?"

"It was more difficult than we'd expected," he said.

"Okay, okay. That's all I need to hear," I murmured. A strange tic had begun to pulse in my eyelid.

Evan looked away, a brooding expression on his face. "I know it's hard for you, but I can't change what I am," he said regretfully.

"All those people—" The words caught in my throat as I stared straight ahead.

"Each of them will have what they've earned, so you shouldn't feel sorry for them. You've seen with your own eyes what's on the other side. Those who went with us were lucky. We weren't the only ones recruiting souls in the trenches."

"W-what? You mean there were Witches too?"

Evan's face darkened. "When there are so many deaths all at once, they're almost bound to show up. Not all mortals have a Subterranean waiting to help them cross over. It's a privilege that has to be earned by resisting evil during their lifetimes. Otherwise they sign an unspoken agreement with the Witches who can't wait to claim the souls of mortal sinners. A lot of people lost their lives last night, but it was something that had to happen," he said, trying to convince me. "It was their fate. No one can do anything about it. You know what happens when you try to elude death."

"It always comes back looking for you," I said.

Evan squeezed my hand. "I didn't mean that. That's not always how it goes. And it's not our problem any more," he stressed reassuringly. "Anyway, you haven't answered my question."

"What ques—"

"I asked if you missed me," he said.

I shot him a glance. "What do you think?" I raised a flirtatious eyebrow. "And what about you? Am I mistaken or did I just witness a jealousy scene?"

He mimicked my expression. "What do you think?"

"Oho!" My jaw dropped and my eyes opened wide. I couldn't believe he was actually worried about Peter. "*You?* Jealous? Of *Pet?*"

"Why not? You were in his truck."

"Come on, it's only *Peter*. He's like a brother to me! You can read my emotions so you should know that already. Besides, he was just giving me a ride," I said, my cheeks pleasantly aflame because of his unexpected admission.

"That doesn't mean I can't be jealous of him."

"Why should you be?"

"Ginevra told me what he feels for you."

I opened my mouth and then quickly closed it, embarrassed. "I don't feel the same way about him," I said reassuringly.

"But he's still important to you. He's a part of your life—the life I had no part in—and that makes me crazy."

"Evan, I only want to be with you," I said as I stopped at my locker. "You have no reason to be jealous. Of Peter or anyone else."

Evan raised an eyebrow and took a slow step in my direction, forcing me back until I felt the metal pressed against my shoulders. "I can't help it if I'm jealous when it comes to you," he whispered. "I want you all to myself." He rested a hand beside my head.

"But I'm already yours," I said slowly, gazing into his dark eyes.

He pressed his lips together as if he didn't completely agree. "If that's true," he whispered tenderly, breathing the words a fraction of an inch from my skin, "explain why you haven't given me a kiss yet." He stared at my lips as if he wanted nothing more in the world.

"Do you mean to say you're asking me to kiss you?" I asked provocatively.

Evan smiled, just as provocative. *"I don't need to ask,"* he whispered in my mind, his mouth on mine. He coaxed my lips apart and suddenly my head was spinning. I wasn't sure if it was because of the deep, sensual tone of his voice inside my mind or my repressed desire for him. Being away from Evan for so long had been harder than I'd expected, especially because his absence had caught me unprepared.

"Next time remember to warn me when you'll be gone for so long," I whispered. I took my lips off his, but immediately pulled him back toward me by the shirt and kissed him again.

"Sounds like you weren't bored without me. Ginevra said you had a pretty lively evening." He smiled and I pretended I didn't understand what he was talking about.

"Nothing out of the ordinary, actually," I said, holding back a smile.

"I can't leave you alone for a single day! Tell me, are you trying to get my attention? Is that what you're trying to do?" he asked under his breath, his elbow resting on the locker and his body close to mine.

"Now that you mention it," I said, biting my lip sensually, "I can't rule out that possibility. You know, I have to say you made a big mistake, getting me used to all those strong emotions. Hasn't anyone ever told you bad habits die hard? You weren't here and I had to find some way to kill time," I teased, my voice low.

Evan brushed his lips against my neck, making me tremble. "The important thing is for you not to end up killing yourself."

"I'm not so sure I wouldn't be doing you a favor." I slipped away from him and grabbed his hand. We headed down the hall to class. "Or are you saying you'd miss me?" I cast him a glance, but his eyes were already on me and he smiled.

"Which brings us back to where we started," he said. In a flash he was in front of me. Grabbing me, he lifted me up, pressing my body against his. Our faces were at the same height, almost touching. "I would miss your every breath," he whispered, looking into my eyes.

My mouth sought his as I slid down against his body until my feet touched the floor.

"Let's skip school," Evan proposed under his breath.

"What?"

"Let's leave!" he said excitedly.

"And go where? Are you out of your mind?" I said in astonishment.

"We have a whole day to make up for," he said, assuming a seductive look to convince me. It was hard to ignore.

"Evan William James!" I said, pretending to be scandalized. "What kind of Angel are you?"

He moved his mouth close to mine, one corner curved in a sensual smile, and shot me a look that made my head spin again. "A dark one." He raised an eyebrow. "Be careful; I might even be dangerous."

"And crazy too," I purred.

"You're right. Guilty as charged."

"Oh, really?" Our voices were whispers murmured on each other's mouths. "Then you admit it."

"You should know. You're the one who made me lose my mind." He kissed me tenderly.

"You're saying *I* made you crazy?" I asked.

"Completely. I'm a slave who is mad with love, and you're my queen," he whispered, ensnaring me in his dark spell.

"No one should know how to kiss like this," I murmured, amazed by the softness of his lips.

"What do you say to my proposal now? Want to run away with me?"

"Slaves shouldn't be allowed to make proposals."

"Not unless they're dying with longing for their queen." He grew serious again and looked me in the eye. "Let's go to our hideaway, Gemma," he whispered. "I want to spend some time alone with you."

A warm sensation trembled deep in my chest and filled my head. The lake house had become our refuge. I began to consider the proposal but continued to toy with him. "You know, I'm not sure that's a good idea. If you're as dangerous as you say, maybe I should run away from you instead," I replied, challenging him with my eyes.

A corner of his mouth curled into a smile. "I don't think you could." He tightened his grip around my waist. "I'm too strong."

"And I'm not so sure I want to run away." The words escaped me, my mind clouded by his scent. "The truth is, you're my demon. You should let me get to class," I said, my breathing irregular. I wasn't very convincing.

"I could do as you say, or"—his lips were right next to mine—"I could ignore what you want and follow my instinct."

"What does your instinct say? I've gotten the impression your intentions aren't exactly honorable," I said accusingly, my voice seductive.

"Honorable intentions are for good boys."

"And you're not a good boy?"

"Not at all." He shook his head and looked at me through his narrowed, long-lashed eyes.

"You should have told me that before, don't you think?" I said as his hands tightened on my back.

"I thought you knew," he whispered. "You're still in time to escape," he warned, his smile sly.

"I think I'll run the risk."

"Careful . . . I might take advantage." He raised an eyebrow as his hand sensually made its way toward my rear. There was something irresistible in his manner and tone, a spell that made my head spin.

"I might even enjoy it," I whispered, biting my lip to provoke him. I raised my mouth to Evan's to seal the deal just as the last bell sounded, throwing a bucket of cold water on our bodies that were burning with desire.

"Too late," I whispered. "Someone else has decided for us."

"What makes you think I'm willing to give up so easily?" he warned, looking at me stealthily. Smiling, he took me by the hand and headed toward the Spanish classroom.

What are you doing? I mouthed. Evan had taken my hand and rested the tip of a black felt-tip pen on my skin. The teacher was explaining something, his back turned to us. Evan moved the pen across my palm, drawing a little heart.

"You're the only subject I can focus on." He smiled.

I raised my pencil to my lips and nibbled on it. "That's because languages are easier for you. You know more than the teacher does," I said, trying to follow the class.

Evan smiled at me with his eyes.

"So tell me, how many do you know, exactly?"

He laughed under his breath, counting on his fingers. "Hmm . . . Let's see . . . There's English, Italian, German, Nahuatl and—"

"Nah*what*?"

Evan shot me a sidelong grin.

"You're just making fun of me," I said resignedly, nudging his shoulder.

"You said it, not me." He laughed again and then tried hard to be serious. "I know *all* languages, even the extinct ones. We need to in order to communicate with the souls entrusted to us," he explained softly. "We acquire all knowledge with our first bite of—"

"A-*hem*." The teacher cleared his throat and shot us a threatening glance.

Evan craned his neck toward me and I looked at him warningly. "I can always help you study . . . on the condition that you accept my proposal." He batted his eyes at me, his face inches from mine.

"What proposal?" I whispered, puzzled.

"That we skip school. We still can."

"You know, you were right about that business of being crazy," I said, grinning, "but I'm afraid you'll have to wait until after school to be alone with me." I shot him an alluring look.

He leaned toward my ear and breathed words through my hair, giving me goosebumps: "I'll hold my breath until then." His tone was sensual and provocative.

My eyelids fluttered and it took me a few moments to regain the power of speech. Evan seemed to enjoy causing difficulties for me; he was well aware of the effect he had on me. "Ooh, what a sacrifice," I stammered, trying to come across as sarcastic. "You don't need to breathe." We both smiled as the teacher began to write letters with strange symbols on the board. During the silence that followed, Evan sought my hand under the desk and squeezed it. I returned the gesture, feeling a shiver run down my spine.

ADDING FUEL TO THE FIRE

Empty.

How was this possible? I was stunned. "Gin! Remember to restock the fridge after you empty it!" I yelled from the kitchen, smiling to myself. Ginevra had finished all the food again.

"Order whatever you want, hon," she replied affectionately from her place on the red leather couch as I continued to smile. "Home delivery!" she exclaimed, amused, as she abstractedly stroked Iron's wrinkly head. Ginevra had been bringing him home with her ever since I started spending most of my time with them and now she couldn't live without him.

"A cheese pizza wouldn't be bad, actually." I peeked around the three overlapping walls that separated the kitchen from the living room to look at Ginevra. Simon was lying on one end of the couch, his leg thrown over the back of it, and Evan was sunk into the cushions.

"One cheese pizza coming up!" she chimed.

I opened the fridge again and jumped back as a package of chocolate muffins tumbled from the top shelf, pushed forward by the mountain of food that had appeared. I blinked in surprise. "Don't you think you overdid it a little? I'm not *that* hungry!" I said teasingly.

"Oh! Don't worry, some of it's for me."

I shook my head and chose a carton of pineapple juice from the second shelf along with two candy bars and a slice of pizza. I shut the refrigerator door but heard Ginevra grumbling from the next room. "Hey!" she complained. I got the hint and opened the fridge again, taking out a second helping of everything, then awkwardly nudged the door shut, trying not to drop the food I was holding.

"While you're at it, get some popcorn too! It's in the top cabinet," Simon called. "Oh, and don't forget the soda! Hurry up! The movie's about to start!"

"I've only got two hands!" I protested, joining them in the living room, my arms full of food. "You could help, you know." Juggling the various containers, I shot a look at Ginevra.

"All you have to do is ask," she murmured with a laugh. They all got a kick out of my human awkwardness. Sometimes I wondered if they asked me to do things just to have fun watching me do them. Relaxed, she continued to stare at the screen in front of her as the food floated out of my hands. Alarmed, I tried to grab it, but then saw it drifting through the air toward her and realized it hadn't fallen—she'd taken it from me. I still wasn't completely used to her magic and often felt like I was in a Disney movie.

Ginevra's food moved straight toward her and she plucked it out of the air as the rest of the things continued to hover, waiting for someone to claim them. With a tinge of uneasiness, I reached out, took the slice of cheese pizza, and sank my teeth into it. "French fries would be good on this." I sat down next to Evan and watched the food arrange itself on the crystal coffee table in front of us. Although it was all so unusual, I'd come to feel I was part of the family. Our closeness reassured me.

"Oh, I forgot to turn off the light," I said. "Gin, would you mind?"

Ginevra gracefully flicked her pointer and middle fingers as if shooing away a pesky insect. It was an automatic gesture she didn't need to make—she could exercise her powers using nothing but her mind—but sometimes she liked to be a little theatrical. The room instantly went dark though we were all still in our seats.

The movie was almost over but I'd only managed to pay attention to a few scenes. Having Evan's body so close to mine distracted me from everything else. The way he stroked my hair and never took his eyes off me spoke volumes. A sort of static electricity surrounded us and in his eyes I saw the desire to leave the others in the living room and shut ourselves up in his room to break the rules a little.

That afternoon I'd turned down a trip to our hideaway so I could dedicate myself to a nobler pursuit: studying. I'd soon abandoned that, however, in favor of Ginevra's far more enticing proposal that we all watch *Vampires Suck*.

"Anybody know what happened to Drake?" Simon asked as the credits filled the screen.

"I haven't seen him since yesterday," Ginevra said. "To tell you the truth I have the funny feeling he's avoiding me. Is it the same with you guys?"

"I saw him a few hours ago. Why would he avoid you, G?" Simon asked.

"Feel like going out for some air?" I whispered to Evan, taking advantage of their conversation.

He had one foot on the floor and the rest of his body on the couch, his other leg draped over mine. "Where do you want to go?" he asked, the gleam of desire in his eyes mirroring his thoughts.

"I don't care. You choose. Anywhere's fine," I said in a low voice.

An unspoken proposal glinted in his gaze. "Don't tempt me," he whispered, tilting his head. "If you do, I'll have to take you up to my room." He raised an eyebrow, his expression provocative.

"I was thinking more of getting some ice cream at Ben & Jerry's."

"Do you ever think about anything but food?" Simon looked at me, amazed.

"Yeah, Gemma, what's been going on with your appetite lately?" asked Ginevra, who was sitting next to us.

"She's been spending too much time with you," Simon told her, grinning.

"This was actually supposed to be a private conversation," I said in a mock-threatening tone.

"What a witch you are!" Ginevra accused me, pinching my side.

I opened my mouth, taken aback but smiling. "Look who's talking."

"Want to come with us?" Evan asked them, but only to be polite.

"Spare me the pleasantries—I'm not buying it." Ginevra rolled her eyes. "I know what you're thinking. In fact, please spare me that too!" she said sardonically. "Just, when you get back, can you take a look at my car? There's something wrong with it."

"What's wrong with it?" Evan asked.

"If I knew that, I wouldn't be asking you, would I?"

"Very funny! You might as well admit you like the idea of me being the one to take care of it," her brother scoffed. Ginevra threw a piece of popcorn at his back. "I'm sure I'll have to change the brake pads too," he said. "Last time you literally burned up the brakes. Again."

"Make sure not to add too much pressure to the back tires to try to destabilize me or I'll burn the tires again too."

"I don't need to sabotage you when I can beat you fair and square."

"Don't be so sure about that. The drifting brakes I had you install will help me beat you around the curves, little brother."

"I've told you a thousand times you've got to downshift before entering a turn. When are you finally going to start heeding the advice of an expert?" he asked with a grin of satisfaction.

"Just as soon as an expert gives me advice," she shot back.

Evan laughed out loud. Ginevra would never give in.

"Were you really serious about going to Ben and Jerry's?" Evan whispered as if hoping to hear a completely different proposal.

I nodded as we left the house. "Why not? Let's go for a drive, soldier," I replied, making my way down the walk.

"As you wish," he murmured, holding back a smile as he opened the door of the BMW for me.

I looked out the window as we drove back from Mirror Lake a couple of hours later. It was strange how the place I was born and raised appeared in a new light now that I was sharing it with someone important. What was even odder was how everything appeared normal and unchanged. The shop windows, the people walking down Main Street . . . nothing seemed to have altered in the Lake Placid I'd always known. And yet nothing about the way I perceived the world was the same, as if Evan had lifted the veil from my eyes that had prevented me from seeing the reality hidden behind the appearances. Evan was an Angel, Ginevra a Witch, and I knew the true purpose of human life. I knew the answers mankind had sought for millennia. I'd seen Eden; I knew what awaited us. I'd been given a gift. If only I could share it with others, spread the incredible awareness. How would it change the lives of every other person on earth? The world would never be the same again.

"What are you thinking about?" Evan's voice pulled me out of my thoughts. His expression was serious, his hands gripping the black leather-covered steering wheel. Not knowing what was going on in my mind frustrated him.

"Just people-watching." I paused, staring through the closed window, my eyes unfocused. "They have no idea what's actually happening."

"Just like you not so long ago." He smiled, but I remained serious.

"What's so special about me? I don't deserve to know more than anyone else does," I acknowledged, my tone pensive.

Evan smiled again in satisfaction. "You deserve it because of what you just said." There was a long silence. "Hungry?" he asked, tilting his head and deliberately changing the subject as he turned onto Main Street.

"A little," I said, shrugging.

"What do you want to eat?"

"I wouldn't say no to a cheese pizza," I said. This was confirmed by a low grumble in my stomach even though I'd just inhaled a double scoop of Ben and Jerry's two hours ago. What could I do? I wanted more.

"Of course you wouldn't," he said, amused. "You would never turn down a cheese pizza."

"How could anyone turn down a cheese pizza?" I said.

A laugh escaped Evan as he parked outside Bazzi's Pizza on Main Street and turned off the engine. In the silence that followed, he propped his left elbow against the steering wheel, leaned toward me, and stroked my cheek with his right hand. His eyes turned serious again as he returned to our discussion of a moment ago. "Never underestimate yourself, Gemma." I shook my head, ready to contradict him, but he rested a finger on my lips, preventing me from speaking. "There's something special about you. I think I understood that the first time I saw you," he whispered, staring at my lips. "Something extraordinary that makes me lose control. I'd never met anyone with such power over me," he whispered.

"The only thing I have that's extraordinary is you. There's nothing special about me," I mumbled, looking at the dashboard.

"If you could see yourself through my eyes, you'd realize you're like a diamond in a pile of broken glass. The fact that you don't realize it makes you sparkle even brighter in comparison."

I continued to shake my head in disagreement. Evan sought my gaze and drew closer. "You have so many things inside you; you just need to let them out." He stroked my chin.

"Don't expect so much from me, Evan. I'm afraid you may end up disappointed," I warned. His eyes narrowed on me as if I'd just said something unacceptable. "No one can know better than me what's inside you. Not even you," he replied confidently.

I blushed. "Okay," I said, embarrassed. "Too many compliments make me dizzy."

"I think it's just hunger," he said, getting out of the car. A moment later he was looking in through my window, his hands resting on the roof. "Was it me or did I hear your stomach grumble a minute ago?" he said, grinning. Instinctively I rested my hand on my belly. I'd hoped he hadn't heard it. "What's it been, two hours since you last ate? How on earth do you stay in such good shape?"

"I don't eat *that* much," I said sheepishly.

"Wha—You don't eat that much?" he repeated, looking astonished.

"It's just—I eat often and my metabolism is fast," I stammered, to Evan's amusement. Still smiling, he walked away from the car. Through the rearview mirror I watched him head toward the pizzeria, a white stone building on the corner, until he disappeared behind the big red awnings. I switched on the radio and sank back into my seat while from the street came the chatter of people dining on the balcony of Generations, the restaurant across from Bazzi's. The melodious voice of Evanescence's Amy Lee filled the car. The CD was still in the player from the last time we'd gone camping.

I was just beginning to lose myself in the notes of *Hello* when an uneasy shiver crept across my skin. A frightful sensation. Cold.

Again.

Alarmed, I scanned the street. The sensation came again and I recognized it as it ran over my neck. It was an old feeling, as familiar as it was bone chilling: someone was watching me.

I peered around nervously, leaning over to get a better look around the Northwoods Inn sign and the tree-lined parking lot. Everything looked normal. As I checked out the cars my heart began to pump at an accelerated rate. The blood throbbed in my veins, agitating my breathing as my panic mounted.

"You okay?"

Evan's voice made me jump in my seat. Consumed by the fear that had returned to torture me over the last few days, I hadn't even noticed he'd walked back to the car. As he closed the door, I sank back in my seat and forced myself to breathe, my skin still cold and clammy. "That was fast," I said, not answering his question.

Evan flashed me a smile and pulled a French fry from the pizza box. "I can be convincing," he said with his sensual grin. "I had them put fries on it, just the way you like it." He raised an eyebrow.

"You trying to bribe me?" I said accusingly, returning his gaze. My panic had subsided.

Evan laughed. "If I wanted to do that I'd definitely be on the right track."

I lowered my eyes, embarrassed. What was he insinuating? "Yeah," I admitted, "pizza with fries works wonders with me—can't deny that." I lifted the lid and inhaled the aroma that instantly filled the car. The pizza box warmed my lap as I took out a big, piping-hot slice dripping with cheese. "Where are we going?" I asked, checking the clock on the dashboard. "It's almost seven."

"I promised Ginevra I'd take a look at her car." Evan raised a finger to his temple and twirled it. "If I don't she'll go out of her mind, and who can stand her when that happens?"

"Why doesn't she fix it herself? She's a Witch, she should be able to do it."

"Who said she couldn't?" he asked, glancing at me. "She likes having me as her mechanic, and deep down I don't mind being the only one who puts his hands on her engine."

"Your hands are amazing on anything."

"Is that so?" he whispered, a big grin on his face.

Oh my God. I thought I'd only said it in my mind! I felt the blood rush to my cheeks.

He tilted his head to look at me with his hands resting on the steering wheel, his smile seductive. "On anything in particular?" His voice had softened.

I decided to play along. "On me, for example."

"This is getting interesting."

"On my neck in particular, if you really want to know." It was the truth and I hadn't been able to hold it back. Feeling his hand on my neck always made me tremble.

Evan stopped the car in his driveway and immediately leaned toward me. He extended his hand, slowly drawing lines of fire on my skin. "Like this?" he whispered, slipping his fingers through my hair to my nape. A shiver of pure energy spread down my back, giving me goosebumps. God, the feeling made my head spin. I half closed my eyes, my body quivering, his face close to mine. "Exactly," I whispered, swallowing. His hot breath tickled my ear.

"And what do you say"—he gently slid his fingers across my skin—"if I move my hand like this?" He brought his fingers to the base of my neck.

"Perfect," I murmured.

He slowly brushed his thumb across my lips, igniting in me the yearning for his mouth, barely an inch away. Evan's cheek moved over mine, brushing my skin, and I let myself be swept away by the sensations. He raised his chin slightly and our lips touched. I parted mine, seeking contact, but Evan lingered, keeping his a fraction of an inch from me, limiting himself to light, fleeting touches.

I took a deep breath and lifted my own chin higher. His kiss was sweet, his lips full and soft as his fingers moved again to my neck, seeking shelter in my hair, filling my body with shivers.

"Now it's your turn," I whispered, not completely sure I'd regained control of myself. "You have to tell me something you like," I said to arouse him.

"That's easy." He took my hand and rested it on his chest over his heart. "I like it when you put your hand here." His voice was a low murmur as if someone might hear us.

"I do that all the time," I said, realizing it only then.

"True. And whenever you do it takes me back—back to when I kissed you for the first time, thinking it would be the last," he confessed. "I was desperate at the thought of giving you up. Feeling your hand on me devastated me. It made something explode inside me, an untamable fire." Evan squeezed my hand against his chest.

"Has that changed?" I asked under my breath.

"Never," he said firmly. "I feel the same emotion every time." I rested my forehead against his and touched his lips with my own. "We'd better go before your pizza gets cold," he said. He vanished and reappeared a second later, opening my door and holding out a hand to help me down, since the seats of the SUV were quite a bit higher than those of the other cars.

"Wait for me in the garage. I'll be right back." Evan headed toward the front door, leaving me outside. I nodded and walked around the corner, my eyes on the dark path.

The garage was in the left wing next to the kitchen's huge picture window and had two massive doors in dark wood. On the opposite side, another picture window revealed the vast room downstairs that housed the swimming pool.

Something made me look up, a fleeting movement behind the thick patch of trees beyond the path. It was too fast for me to see what it was. My heart constricted as a dark figure darted toward me and halted a few steps away. I gasped and dropped the pizza box from my trembling fingers.

"Mmm . . . pizza!" someone exclaimed, catching the box an instant before it hit the ground, opening it, and taking out a slice.

"Drake! You think it's funny, scaring me like that? Do you want to give me a heart attack?" I scolded him, my voice shaking. "Can't you show up like everyone else?" I said scornfully as my voice grew steadier and my knees stopped knocking.

"Hey, it's not my fault you're out here in the dark all alone," he shot back, arching an eyebrow. His dark gaze sharpened on mine, almost as if he wanted to probe my thoughts. It was the first time his eyes had studied me like this and part of me felt seriously uncomfortable.

My instinct told me there was something different about him though I couldn't put my finger on it—it was something beyond my understanding. "Are you letting your hair grow out?" I asked bluntly.

The question seemed to confuse him. "Nope, it's the same as always," he said. On closer inspection I realized he was right. It must have been something else.

"Evan's not around?" he asked, avoiding my searching look. I suddenly got a feeling of déjà vu.

"I'm right here," Evan said behind me. "Where've you been, Drake?"

"Here and there. Slaughtering souls as always." Drake winked at me and I shuddered. "Where else would I be?" He shrugged as if we were chatting about the weather.

"Watch how you talk in front of her," Evan warned.

"Hey, chill. I've had a lot on my plate recently. That better?" He threw me a surly look and then looked back at Evan. "Were you looking for me or something?"

"No. I didn't want to interrupt you in your—um, interrupt what you were doing." Evan also cast me a grim glance. It was clear what he meant and he was trying to talk his way around the subject to avoid upsetting me.

Drake shrugged again. "Just carrying out orders. We have no choice," he said, his eyes fixed on his brother's.

"Yeah, as if I didn't you know better than that."

Drake spread his arms. "Have you been drinking?" I asked him, smelling Scotch on his breath.

He narrowed his eyes and held up his hand, the thumb and forefinger an inch apart. Looking at me through the space between them, he said, "Just a little."

"You'd better go freshen up," Evan told him, grinning. "You're always a mess when you drink." Drake burst out laughing as he turned to go, his hands clasped behind his head, while Evan and I headed to the garage, following the path that skirted the house. Something made me turn around. I saw that Drake was still looking at me, his face more serious than I'd ever seen it. I stared back for a second and squeezed Evan's hand, suddenly uncomfortable. Seemingly without effort, Evan raised one of the two garage doors and lowered it again behind us.

"Has Drake always been alone?" I asked point-blank, a thread of bitterness running through my voice.

Evan frowned at me, surprised by my question. "Why do you ask?"

I struggled to find a more acceptable word than the one that had come to mind: *excluded*. "I think he might feel a little . . . lonely."

"What makes you say that?" Evan didn't sound convinced.

"Come on, don't tell me you haven't noticed. I get the impression he's changed a little lately too. Haven't you realized it?"

"What do you mean, exactly?" he asked with a puzzled look as he laid out his tools on the workbench.

"It's like all the life's gone out of him. He barely ever hangs out with us and when he does it's almost like he's not really there. I don't recognize him any more, he's like a different person." Evan listened carefully, a surprised look on his face. "So yeah, I think he might feel lonely. I mean, you and Simon both have someone, but he's all alone."

"He has us," Evan said innocently.

"It's not the same. You had them too before you found me."

Finally he seemed to understand. "I'd never thought of that. So you think he's jealous?"

"Hmm. Jealous might be overdoing it, but yeah, I think being constantly surrounded by couples might make him feel left out. It's just a theory," I was quick to add.

"Ginevra would have realized it," he said, thinking aloud.

"If I'm right, that might be why Drake's been avoiding her, like she said. Maybe he doesn't want her to know how he feels."

"What's made you think all this?" Evan asked thoughtfully.

"His face," I said. "The way he was looking at me tonight was odd."

"What do you mean?" I didn't know if it was a good idea to tell Evan everything Drake's look had made me feel. "What kind of look did he give you?" he insisted, as if sensing my hesitation to explain further.

"Well, if I didn't know Drake was your brother, I would have said there was a bit of slyness in his eyes. Like he was, kind of . . . coming on to me." It had sounded better in my head. Saying it out loud made me feel like such an idiot.

Evan burst out laughing. "That's crazy! Drake would never think of you that way." Then his expression changed as if he were considering the idea seriously for the first time. "He's my brother. It's ridiculous." He shook his head to drive off the suspicion.

"You're right. I don't know how I could have thought something like that," I admitted sheepishly. "It really is ridiculous." *Please God, let the earth open and swallow me up.* If only I could go back in time and erase that last embarrassing moment.

"I'll talk to him about it," Evan said, his tone serious.

"No!" I said quickly. "You can't. He would realize I'd said something to you. I already feel like such an idiot. Please, Evan. What I said was crazy—I misread everything. That's at least as clear as the fact that you're my boyfriend!"

"Hmm . . ." He drew closer. "That sounds so good. Say it again."

"Don't tell me I've never said it before," I teased, relieved I'd managed to change the subject.

"Not recently, you haven't." He held me close.

"Then I'd better fix that," I whispered, my face a handspan from his. "You, Evan William James, are my boyfriend."

"Say it again." His eyes were locked onto mine, his tone firm, almost commanding.

"You're. My. *Boyfriend.*"

He squeezed me tighter and rested his lips on mine. "I like hearing you say it." His voice softened to a sigh.

"I like saying it," I said, abandoning myself to him.

"Sounds like we're agreed, then."

"Sounds like we are." Another gentle kiss. "You know, I'm starting to think you're jealous," I teased him. The provocation worked.

"Jealous? Who of, this time?" He frowned, surprised, and I bit my lower lip.

"Of my pizza, of course! You keep putting yourself between us!" I exclaimed, pulling away from him and grabbing the pizza box.

Evan smiled and shook his head. "You got me. Want me to leave you two alone?" he said, grinning.

"It's the least you could do."

"If that's really what you want," he shot back, tucking his foot under the workbench and pulling out the dark-gray creeper, his gaze never leaving mine. Lying down on it, he rolled himself under Ginevra's car.

Still smiling, I stood on tiptoe and hoisted myself onto the metal workbench where Evan had laid out his tools. I gave myself a few minutes of silence to chew on the now-cold pizza and study the garage, which looked like a cross between a well designed, well organized auto repair shop and a racecar showroom.

Suspended from the ceiling was a fluorescent tube that ran around the entire perimeter of the garage and also branched off toward the center. The result was a bright white light that illuminated everything, dazzling my eyes whenever I looked at it.

The light-colored walls were accented by a row of black pillars that also ran down the center of the garage. Lining the walls were dark-gray panels hung with all kinds of tools. Evan was the one who took care of all the cars and motorcycles in the house. Although he'd never told me so, I'd realized right from the start that engines were his passion. It was easy to see from the twinkle of satisfaction in his eyes.

The BMW was parked outside, but its absence was barely noticeable in the huge garage filled with vehicles. Parked right in the center, the gray Ferrari shone like a starlet in the spotlight. The other cars followed it, lined up in an orderly, well-spaced row.

At first I'd been able to tell them apart only by their color but over time I'd learned their names. By the end of summer I'd spent so much time in the garage with Evan that I'd become a bit of an expert myself. The Bugatti Veyron Super Sport with its elegant carbon-blue trim was Simon's, and I'd learned that its 1200 horsepower allowed it to reach a top speed of 267 miles per hour, going from zero to sixty in 2.4 seconds. Drake, on the other hand, preferred Italian cars to French and had opted for a black Maserati GranTurismo S.

Despite Simon's ability to erase people's memories and Evan's power to control the mind of anyone who might be too interested in them, they rarely went out with all three cars at once in order to avoid drawing too much attention. They were safe to a certain extent—that is, except for Ginevra's obsessive tendency to put herself in the spotlight. She didn't at all mind being the center of attention.

Lined up on the far left of the garage were four motorcycles that confronted me menacingly, perfectly representing the sporty, aggressive riding styles of the four family members, as if even they knew no other way to express themselves.

Evan's MV Agusta CC seemed to be trained on me like a black panther ready to pounce. At first I'd been surprised to learn that the ferocious-looking gray Aprilia RSV4 belonged to Ginevra; no one had warned me the first time I'd seen her on it at dawn in a clandestine race where I'd been on the back of Evan's bike, clinging to him. Drake, instead, had a Yamaha R1 Laguna Seca, parked next to Simon's Ducati Desmosedici with its unusual black and white design.

To the right, just in front of the workbench I was sitting on now, on top of the retractable platform car lift was Ginevra's gray Lamborghini. Its elegant lines were reflected in the glass wall opposite it that held tires in all sizes. The futuristic design of its carbon fiber and steel body had been inspired by a fighter plane's fuselage and perfectly expressed Ginevra's sensual, provocative nature. Flowing lines and angular surfaces created a fascinating play of color further enhanced by sunlight. There were only twenty of these custom-built sports cars in the whole world, and it was worth over a million dollars.

Lying on the flat, four-wheeled creeper, Evan was working under the rear of the car where the engine was. From where I was sitting, I could see only his legs, as if the car had swallowed up the rest of him.

"Everything okay down there?" I asked, gulping down the last bite of pizza. Until now, the clink of his tools had been the only sound in the garage.

"Sounds like you're done." Evan's muffled voice stifled by laughter echoed between the car's wheels.

I loved the smell in the air—a mix of gasoline, new tires, and motor oil. I hopped down and went over to him. His knees were raised. I pulled off my burgundy sweatshirt, my necklace jingling against my army-green tank top, and sank down cross-legged beside the back wheel of the Lamborghini. It was elevated a foot or so off the black quartz floor that glittered as if studded with rhinestones.

"Okay if I sit here?" I asked.

"Sit wherever you like."

"Find the problem?" I added, peeking under the wheels.

"It was the alternator drive belt," he said as if I had any idea of what he was talking about. "The spring was almost broken and that was making the car vibrate. I replaced it. There, almost done."

A few minutes later Evan planted his foot on the floor and rolled himself out from under the car until he was lying next to me. Just above his right cheekbone was an oily black streak that gave him an even tougher look. The position I was in relative to him made the temptation to kiss him irresistible. Surrendering to my instinct, I rested my palms on the black floor and lowered myself to his mouth, but Evan pulled me roughly against him and held me tight. He smiled, lying beneath me, and pressed his lips to mine.

I opened my eyes only at the sound of his suave voice. "Careful," he whispered, "there's gasoline nearby." He raised an eyebrow and fixed his gaze on mine, leaving me defenseless.

"We'd better not play with fire," I said breathlessly.

"I could always try to control"—his eyes went to my mouth as if it had summoned them—"the fire." He swallowed. Then a sparkle appeared in his eye and a proposition in his sly smile. He slowly drew closer.

"Think you could manage it?" I asked as he tenderly kissed my chin.

"I'm not sure. Things might get out of hand . . ." Another kiss, just below my jaw.

"You know, someone once told me that sometimes you need to run risks," I murmured with pleasure, my skin pulsating beneath his hot lips.

"Whoever told you something like that must be crazy."

"I think so too, but maybe I should give him the benefit of the doubt."

Evan's eyes lingered on mine as he searched my words for implied permission. He began to kiss me again even more passionately, lifting his torso off the creeper without taking his mouth off mine. Before I knew it we were on our feet, our lips glued together, his hands on my hips as he thrust me against the car door, kissing me again and again.

My head was spinning. Our bodies sought each other, the awareness that I wouldn't be able to control myself much longer growing more intense by the second. I stopped to catch my breath without moving my face away from his. The air in the garage seemed scorching hot. Evan closed his eyes and rested his forehead against mine, drawing a deep breath.

After a minute, his hands found mine again and he swallowed. I watched his Adam's apple rise and fall, his eyes half closed as he struggled to control his overwhelming desire. He reached behind me, the silence between us alive with unspoken passion, and I heard the car door click and swing up. My heart beat wildly as his eyes probed mine, seeking my consent.

I followed him with my gaze as he slid down into the Lamborghini's upright leather and suede seat, still holding my hand. I leaned in under the scissor door and raised my knee to rest it on the seat next to Evan's leg, but he grasped it in a firm yet delicate movement, his eyes fixed on mine. Sliding his hand up my thigh, he guided it until I was straddling him.

Our fingers entwined and I felt feverish at the touch. Every movement, even the tiniest breath, seemed slowed down by a delicious tension. His body heat was intense against my thighs and I tried to keep myself raised slightly above him to avoid direct contact, but Evan had other ideas. My heartbeat accelerated as his hands slid down my back, making my skin tingle. He gripped my waist and fervently pulled me down onto him, his body trembling with yearning. The contact made me dizzy, melting me like warm honey as my legs spread open on top of him. His mouth touched my shoulder, opening and closing again, his tongue lightly brushing my skin.

I was aflame. The small space we were in emphasized the intimacy our bodies were claiming. The car was filled with Evan's hypnotic scent that made me even dizzier. He and I were a ticking time bomb that threatened to explode whenever we were alone. The detonator had been set and there was no way back. I felt it inside me whenever Evan touched me or his lips caressed my skin.

His hands held the backs of my thighs firmly so I couldn't move away from him, and every so often they pulled me closer in an attempt to erase even the distance created by our clothes. Responding to a primitive instinct, he ground his pelvis against mine. My body was on fire, the flames licking up from my belly, igniting every part of me.

"Evan . . ." I panted as our breathing merged. His desire shut out my voice as his firm, full lips moved down my throat, his hot breath warming my skin.

"I think . . ." Pleasure, hesitation, and yearning combined in my murmur. "I think you should stop." I took a deep breath.

His breath tickled my skin. "Do you?" he whispered, his tone sly. He didn't sound very willing to believe me.

"I thi—I think you should."

"Uh-uh." He shook his head. "I don't agree in the least," he murmured.

"Then I'm afraid I'll have to insist," I whispered back, my tone far from convincing.

"Since you put it that way," he replied, his voice barely audible, "where would you like me to stop?" His full lips parted against my shoulder, sending an electric charge surging through me. "Here?" He lightly sucked my skin. "Or"—his mouth moved to the curve of my neck, making me tremble—"here?" It slowly slid down to my collarbone. "Personally," he whispered, caressing my shoulder with his hand, "I think it would be better"—his fingers pushed aside my bra strap, which fell over my arm, baring the skin right above my breast as he followed it with his eyes—"if I stopped right . . ."—his hot lips moved down my chest, following the curves of my top—"here," he finished, hovering his mouth over my breast without touching it.

A jolt shot up from my back, rose to my neck, and filled my head. "Evan," I stammered, closing my eyes, my body longing to surrender to the sensations.

"Gemma . . ." His voice was an exasperated murmur that enveloped my name like black velvet as his hands returned to my hair and his mouth, tired of waiting, sought mine. Putting out this fire was going to be both impossible and painful—I might as well burn with him. I abandoned myself to the heat of his lips, losing myself in another dimension, when a cheerful melody suddenly vibrated in my pocket, reverberating inside the car and breaking the spell, a bucket of ice water on our fiery bodies.

I buried my head in Evan's shoulder, groaned, and pulled out the phone. "It's my dad," I told him, panicking when I read the time on the display. "Shit! How did it get so late?" Evan hid a satisfied smile. I pressed the call button. "Dad?"

My father's furious voice shot through my head from one eardrum to the other, booming inside the car. *"Gemma! Where the hell are you? It's midnight!"*

Feeling my face turn bright red, I lowered the volume on the phone as if that would help. "Dad," I said, but he didn't give me the chance to speak. I shot Evan a look. *Where's Drake?* I mouthed. For some reason I always took it for granted that he was filling in for me, but it wasn't like he was my babysitter. Besides, it was my own fault I lost all track of time when I was with Evan.

"I—I didn't realize it had gotten so late," I blathered. "I'm with *Evan*, Dad," I added, hoping he would hear the discomfort in my voice and lower his own. Dying with embarrassment, I looked at Evan. "He wants to talk to you," I whispered, cringing as I handed him the phone.

Judging from his expression Evan didn't seem the least bit concerned. I stared anxiously at his face, but saw no trace of nervousness as he spoke in monosyllables, nodding. "Yes. Right. Fine."

Silence. Evan handed the phone back to me.

"Well? What did he say?" I asked, worried. There were times when my wish for super hearing was as pressing as my need for air.

"I'm taking you home," he said calmly.

"What did he say to you?" I insisted nervously as Evan moved into the driver's seat and the car lift silently lowered the wheels to the floor.

"I don't think you want to know." He fell silent, his expression still relaxed as he turned the steering wheel. I sank into my seat, turning bright red with shame. Evan smiled at me as the Lamborghini's headlights flashed on, casting their light on the wall. The door began to rise and the car came to life with a roar that filled the garage. Aggressive, elegant, fierce. Like Ginevra.

"Won't she get mad if we use her car?" I asked, turning toward him as he continued to stare straight ahead. The last time we had, she hadn't taken it well.

He revved the engine, impatiently waiting until the garage door had slid all the way into the ceiling. With a tilt of his head he shot me a complicit, sensual look. "We need to take it for a road test." He winked at me and the Lamborghini let out a low, ferocious purr, then leapt into action with an even more aggressive roar, its wheels squealing against the shiny floor that was as black as the darkest night.

UNSCHEDULED ADVENTURE

"Good morning." Evan's velvety voice greeted me the moment I opened my eyes.

"What time is it?" I mumbled, groggy. The light coming in through the curtains was already too bright compared to what I was used to since school had started.

"I turned off your alarm. Don't worry, it's Saturday," he reassured me when I sat bolt upright in bed.

Taking a deep breath to release my tension, I slid down again and rolled onto my side, resting my head on my palm. Evan was in front of me, lying in exactly the same position. His hand stroked the edge of my army-green cotton top, moving sensually from side to side. His gaze told me what he was thinking.

"Meaning no school," I sighed blissfully.

"Meaning you and I can—"

The door abruptly opened.

"Gemma, what are—"

"Mom!" I bolted upright in bed, panicking. She looked at me, puzzled. My heart thumped as my thoughts chased each other desperately through my brain in search of some plausible explanation for Evan being in my bed so early in the morning.

She stood there in the doorway. "Who were you talking to?"

Her question surprised me and I spun around. Evan wasn't there. I heaved a sigh of relief, babbling something incomprehensible as my eyelids fluttered. Whatever came out of my mouth now, the only thing she could possibly accuse me of was talking to myself. Explaining how my boyfriend had managed to sneak into my room would have been far more complicated and embarrassing. Seeing that she wasn't really paying attention anyway, I caught my breath and relaxed. "You're still here?" I asked, trying to distract her.

"We were just about to leave. I came to say goodbye." Her expression changed. "And to make sure you won't come home so late again. Your father was furious last night. I'm surprised at you—you're behaving like you don't know him." She lowered her voice, not wanting him to hear us from downstairs. "I ran out of excuses trying to calm him down."

"Thanks," I stammered sheepishly. "Really, it was the first time I—"

"Just make sure it's the last time too," she said in a low voice, winking at me.

As the door closed behind her I anxiously turned to look for Evan. He was exactly where I'd left him. I saw his eyes were gray. If my mom had come back in, he would have been invisible to her. I sighed with relief.

"You knew," I accused him, narrowing my eyes. He was trying hard to keep a grin off his face. "You knew my mom was coming, you knew it!" I was annoyed.

At this point he couldn't help but laugh. "I have to admit, it was hilarious."

"You want me to be sent off to the loony bin? My mom thought I was talking to myself." Evan's lips quivered as he tried to hide how funny he thought it was. "Would you mind warning me next time? I'd like to avoid my parents having me locked up." His mocking grin was putting me on edge.

"In that case, I couldn't blame them, could I? It's not normal for someone to talk to themselves." Evan's voice faded as he disappeared before my eyes. Teasing me was one of his favorite pastimes. He reappeared a second later, smiling. "Or you could always tell her your boyfriend's an Angel, that he's here watching over you even when no one can see him." He spoke in a whisper in spite of the fact that we were alone in the house now and moved his face very close to mine.

"I'm not sure how she would take it." I stifled a smile, playing along. "Plus, I'm starting to think the word 'Angel' is used inappropriately where you come from."

"You think?" He lowered his head and tickled my ear with the tip of his nose.

"I'm more convinced by the day."

"You've never exactly seemed to mind my trespasses," he shot back boldly.

"I never said I did," I retorted.

"Because if you're complaining I can always force myself to keep my distance," he said, brushing his cheek against mine.

"I think I'm capable of resisting your sinful behavior."

He nibbled my earlobe as his voice caressed me. "Get dressed. I'll take you out to breakfast."

"I can just eat here. The house is empty now," I said, though he knew it even better than I did.

"That's not what I had in mind," he admitted, one corner of his mouth raised slightly.

"And what did you have in mind, exactly?" I eyed him suspiciously.

"There's something you've absolutely got to see," he said, a glint in his eyes as they turned dark.

Knowing Evan, I was sure I wouldn't be able to pry any information out of him. It was clear from the grin on his face. Resigned, I held his gaze for a second and then let it drop. There was one thing I was certain of: whatever Evan had in mind, it had to be dangerous. It always was, when he had that glint in his eyes.

"You still haven't told me where we're going." I tried to get an answer out of him again but my attempts went nowhere.

"And I have no intention of telling you." Evan smiled, his eyes fixed on the road ahead.

"I figured," I murmured.

He cast me a sidelong glance, the smile never leaving his lips. He seemed pretty pleased with whatever was on his mind. I wasn't entirely sure it would have the same effect on me. At least not immediately. We were riding in his Ferrari—that was enough to alarm me. Usually Evan only used this car for the clandestine nighttime races in which he almost always beat his siblings. Only in rare instances did the car's gray body gleam in the daylight. There had to be something special about this morning. I could tell from his occasional glances my way, brimming with excitement. I guessed he had high hopes about my reaction to his mysterious surprise.

When the car gradually slowed down I looked around curiously but didn't see anything particularly interesting. We seemed to be at an ordinary travel-service plaza.

"Are we there?" I asked eagerly.

"If you're talking about breakfast, then yes, your stomach will be grateful." He looked at me. "But if you're talking about our final destination, then no, not yet." He stifled a smile.

It was ridiculous how much he teased me.

The Ferrari pulled into a small parking lot, its metallic gray body reflected in the picture window of a café as we passed it. I wasn't completely sure where we were. We'd left my house about twenty minutes ago, but with Evan driving I could never judge distances based on the time it took us to get anywhere.

Through the window I glimpsed rustic wooden tables. Evan parked in a spot where he could keep an eye on the Ferrari from inside. He hadn't actually given me his reasons for parking where he did, but by now I was used to deciphering the look on his face, almost as if I could read his mind. It was pretty comforting that more and more often I was able to guess what he was thinking.

The bell by the café door jingled as we walked in. The interior was welcoming, done in warm, cozy hues. The cream-colored floor contrasted with the dark wood of the ceiling and furniture. Hanging from the windows were thick, soft curtains gathered to the sides, offering a view of the outside. The fabric was rust-colored, as were some of the walls.

The window at the far right looked out onto the parking lot with the road behind it. Not far beyond, next to the on-ramp, stood a gas pump.

"What do you want?" Evan studied the pastry case in front of us. It was small but had a good selection.

My stomach growled at the sight of it. "I can't decide." I bit my lip, the inviting aromas confusing me. I'd always loved food, but lately something in my metabolism seemed to be changing.

"Want me to get you one of everything?" he asked considerately.

"No, no!" I quickly replied as he gestured to the waiter behind the counter. "A chocolate doughnut will be just fine, thanks." Before I could stop him he ordered three of them and then pointed to a free table by the window.

"Worried about the car?" I teased, drawing a look of surprise from him.

"Just habit," he said. Despite the look of perplexity on his face, his eyes went to the Ferrari. "It's because I need it to take you to where we're going, that's all," he added with an air of mystery.

I looked at him out of the corner of my eye as the waiter came to our table. "Yeah, right! That's all," I echoed with a grin, leaning back in my chair so the waiter could place our order on the table. He was young, with skin as dark as his hair, an athletic build, and dimples in his cheeks that reminded me of Peter. Smiling at me politely, he handed me a tall glass of piping-hot steamed milk with a shot of espresso and a sprinkle of cocoa on the thick layer of froth. Just how I liked it, though I hadn't even noticed Evan ordering it. I shook my head and took a sip. With Evan there was no point trying to follow any form of logic.

He was sitting to my right, straddling his chair, his elbows resting on the back of it. "Is it good?" he asked, studying me as I dunked one of the doughnuts into the warm milk and chewed with relish. "There's no rush," he reassured me. "We've got all day."

"No way—I don't believe it! It's filled with strawberry ice cream!"

My enthusiasm made Evan laugh. "And covered with chocolate," he said. "I heard some kids talking about this place and these special doughnuts of theirs. It made me think of that stuff you make with Nutella."

"Strawtella!"

"Right, Strawtella. So I thought you should try them."

"These are the best doughnuts I've ever had in my life," I said, my mouth full, and swallowed another bite. "Oh! Don't tell my dad I said that." I bit into another, shooting Evan a glance. He laughed at the look on my face. "Seriously," I insisted, picking the crumbs from the plate and eating them. "Mmm, I definitely have to convince him to make these at the diner. Strawtella doughnuts. They're amazing! People will be lining up around the block!" The doughnut was warm and the ice cream melted on my tongue with every bite. It was an intense, delicious taste.

"I'll go order you some more," he said.

I stopped him before he could. "No, no! That's enough for today, but we have to remember to come here more often."

Evan smiled and stood up. "I'll go pay so we can get back on the road. We've still got a ways to go." He walked off before I could reply. For Evan the idea of me even taking out my wallet was inconceivable. In five months he hadn't let me pay for so much as a piece of gum.

Turning my head to the left, I looked at the Ferrari outside in the parking lot. The yellow logo with the black horse on its wheel caps sparkled in the sunlight against the anthracite-gray body. The café had only a handful of clients and their murmurs of admiration hadn't ceased for a second since we'd walked through the door. On top of that, a group of girls sitting in the corner kept looking in our general direction, though it wasn't entirely clear whether they were staring at the Ferrari or at Evan. From where I was sitting I could occasionally make out their low whispers and was pretty sure their admiration wasn't limited to the car.

A twinge of jealousy tied my stomach in a knot and my gaze instinctively went to Evan, casually leaning against the counter, wallet in hand. As if I'd called his name, his eyes met mine. It had been hard to resist the urge to glare at the girls at the table to intimidate them, but when my eyes locked with Evan's all my insecurity slipped away. I could tell he hadn't even noticed them. As this realization warmed my heart, he smiled at me, triggering the same reaction in me, and our gazes remained entwined.

Only a couple of seconds later his face altered radically, becoming a mask of horror. Though his eyes were still on mine, a veil of darkness dropped over them and I could tell he was no longer seeing me. All at once, a loud screech grated on my ears. My eyes shot to the parking lot and a shudder of terror seized me, trapping the breath in my lungs. I felt my heart bursting from my chest as my brain registered a blurry blue-and-white shape spinning through the air like a Frisbee or an enormous, out-of-control top hurtling directly toward the window.

It was a huge sport motorcycle, and I was its target.

"Gemmaaaa!!!" A roar of desperation drowned out the customers' cries of alarm. Evan tackled me with all his strength, knocking me to the floor and holding me tight. Despite my disorientation, I looked over his shoulder as, shielding me with his body, he raised his arm toward the window. A massive burst of energy shot from the palm of his hand and hit the glass like a tornado. There was a deafening explosion inside the café and the window shattered before the motorcycle could make impact. The deafening noise of the thousands of shards falling to the ground pierced my eardrums.

Trembling like a leaf, I felt Evan's hand rest gently on my hair. The explosion had thrown the bike abruptly off course, sending it hurtling in the opposite direction toward the gas pump. Inside, a murmur rose among the customers but Evan didn't seem to notice anything but me. "You okay?" he asked, stroking my forehead with his thumb, clearly shaken.

My heart was in my throat and I could barely breathe, but my first thought was of him. "Evan, you shouldn't have. Everybody saw you!" Concerned, I peered around at the looks on everyone's faces.

"I don't give a damn!" he growled. "Are you okay?" There was desperation in his voice and his eyes burned into mine as he caressed my cheek. I nodded. Taking a deep breath, he held me against him and kissed my forehead. "I wasn't expecting that. If I hadn't seen it in time—" He was so upset the words caught in his throat.

"Evan—" I stopped, suffocated by a bone-chilling foreboding.

He gritted his teeth and clenched his fists. I was sure my fear had communicated itself to him. One look was enough for Evan to grasp it. Neither of us paid any attention to the other customers who had gathered around the window, murmuring in shocked concern. Only Evan and I existed.

I saw a flash of hesitation in his eyes before he looked at me decisively. "No," he said firmly, answering my unspoken question. "It was just a coincidence." Fire rose in his gaze. "An accident."

Although there wasn't a trace of doubt in Evan's voice, a nagging thought throbbed at my temples until my head ached: *There was no such thing as coincidence.* He'd told me that himself.

"Incredible!" someone in the crowd said.

"Did you see that?!"

"It was that guy, I'm sure it was," someone else whispered, gesturing in our direction.

"How on earth did he do it?" another person wondered aloud.

I looked at Evan with concern but he instantly reassured me, whispering in my mind: *"Don't worry. I'll take care of them. I'll convince them they never saw us. They'll think there was a gas leak."*

I nodded and his hand squeezed mine as he helped me to my feet. All at once, there was a deafening roar. The gas pump the motorcycle had crashed into burst into flames, sending a violent wave of heat our way.

Everyone ducked and backed away, covering their faces with their arms. Evan wrapped his around me, shielding me with his body. "Come on. We've got to get out of here," he ordered me, pulling some hundred-dollar bills out of his wallet. He left them on the table and led me toward the door without sparking the least interest in the crowd who suddenly seemed to be looking through our bodies. He hadn't even needed to glance at them to convince them we weren't there. We'd become ghosts, invisible to their eyes.

"Evan." I stopped him and pointed at the security camera.

He stared at it and in less than two seconds the metal melted. Only when we reached the car did he let go of my hand. My heart was still pounding. I looked toward the road and caught my breath. The lifeless body of the motorcycle rider lay on the asphalt. Everything had happened so unexpectedly no one had noticed him.

All at once an unnaturally fast movement froze me in my tracks.

"Evan." I stifled a whimper, my gaze riveted on the other side of the street. "Someone's there." A shudder of terror slowly spread through me.

Evan's eyes shot to where I was looking. He frowned and turned back to look at me. My human sight couldn't make out the details of the figure across the street—not like Evan's could. Or had all the confusion just clouded my senses?

When he spoke, his voice betrayed anger rather than concern. "It's Drake." He pressed his lips together, his face full of fury. "He came for the rider."

Another shudder shook me, more violent than the last. I'd never seen any of them in these circumstances. Unable to look away, I swallowed, trying to moisten my parched throat.

"Christ, Drake! You should have been more careful!" Evan growled in his brother's mind, allowing me to listen in.

The blood froze in my veins and I couldn't take my eyes off Drake. Although he'd become like a brother to me over the last few months, right now it felt like I was seeing him for the first time. He wasn't alone any more in the middle of the empty road. A less attentive glance would have told me there were three people there, but I knew there weren't. Until a moment ago, the lifeless body lying on the asphalt and the young man beside Drake kneeling over it had been the same person. But then again, a less conscious glance would never have been able to fathom the ghastly sight.

I felt Evan's eyes on me. He was frowning and studying me carefully. "You can *see* them?" he asked. From the look on his face I couldn't tell if he was more stunned or upset. "Both of them? You *can see them?*" he whispered, not taking his eyes off mine.

"Is that bad?" I asked timidly. My hands were trembling.

"No. But it's not normal." Evan looked at me as if he were looking through me. I would have given anything at that moment to know what he was thinking. He licked his lips and came back to reality just in time to realize how much his answer had shaken me.

The Ferrari drove onto the on-ramp as unspoken words filled the space around us. Neither of us could find the courage to break the profound silence. Though I was confused, one thing stood out in my mind: Evan's remark and the look on his face had upset me more than everything else that had happened.

Before I could torture myself again with the memory of his expression, his voice pulled me out of my torment. "It's not bad," he assured me, as though I'd just repeated my question. His fingers caressed the red leather of the steering wheel. "At least I don't think it is. It's just strange—and incredible." He sought my gaze. "But there's nothing wrong with you," he repeated to make sure the message had gotten through.

I looked at him, pressing my lips together, and then gazed out the window. Silence returned.

Miles later, as the car roared along at such a speed it would have been virtually invisible to anyone we passed, I began to realize how ridiculous it was for me to be so uneasy. I couldn't blame Evan for being shaken up by something he'd never seen before in his whole life. Especially since it had something to do with me.

"Do you think we should be worried," I asked timidly, "if I can see all of you sometimes?"

His comforting smile broke the tension tingling under my skin. "No, not at all. I've always told you you're special, Gemma. Besides, if it hadn't been this way, if you hadn't noticed me that time in the woods, who knows? Right now we probably wouldn't be here talking about it. This *strangeness* of yours changed my life." He turned to look at me. "Because it let me fall in love with you."

I tried to convince myself. "You're right, it's stupid to get all worried about nothing."

Evan nodded confidently. "I agree." His words ushered in another moment of silence, this one calmer. His hand slid off the gearshift and touched mine, resting on my seat.

A corner of his lips curved seductively upward, forming a crease on the right side of his mouth. "Well." He drew my hand to his mouth and kissed my palm, then rested it on the gearshift. "Ready for your surprise?" He winked at me and his half smile broadened, wiping away every last trace of concern from my mind. Sometimes I wondered if Evan occasionally used his powers on me.

I waited a moment before replying. "You mean we're there?"

"I mean we're *almost* there," he said.

In the silence that followed I tried to interpret his answer. I decided it was best to pick up the conversation where I'd left off. "When you say 'almost,' what do you mean, exactly?" I said, starting to blather. "Because, you know, the meaning of the word can be totally subjective. You can interpret it in different ways depending on your point of view, so do you mean in ten minutes or half an hour or an hour or what?" I raised an eyebrow.

Evan held back a smile as we turned onto a small, steep road. I had absolutely no idea where we were. He tilted his head and looked at me as the car came to a halt. "I mean *now*."

Impatient, I freed myself from his gaze and looked out the windshield, surprised and confused when I saw where we were. Confused, mostly. There was nothing around us except an arid, sandy stretch of uninspiring land. I honestly didn't know what to think, but I tried hard not to let Evan's attentive eyes see my bewilderment. I studied the desolate landscape, still not understanding why he would bring me there. Out of the corner of my eye I noticed that in the meantime he was studying *me*. There was a mocking grin on his lips that was starting to exasperate me. Clearly something had escaped my notice.

We got out of the car. All at once Evan disappeared, reappearing at my side so fast the dirt beneath our feet didn't even stir. It was like when someone yanks a tablecloth off a table without disturbing the objects on top of it. He nodded at something behind me. "That way," he said, pleased, his eyes fixed on mine. At least the nerve-racking wait for the mystery to be revealed had finally come to an end—whatever the surprise was.

I looked over my shoulder and started, not sure whether I was amazed by the size of the building behind me or the fact that I hadn't noticed it before. Still, it was nothing that really enthused me. Was this the surprise? The structure seemed to be constructed of metal and looked a lot like an old abandoned warehouse. I honestly couldn't imagine why Evan had been so enigmatic about bringing me to a place like this. In any case, it seemed best to wait before telling him how puzzled I was.

He held out his hand to me. I took it and followed him toward the building. Something in the façade started to move and a low rumble grew stronger the closer we came. In seconds the entire façade broke into two equal halves from top to bottom as the two giant doors opened toward us without anyone touching them, revealing the entrance. The sunlight at my back prevented me from distinguishing the dark shapes I glimpsed in the vast interior. From the distance they looked like embalmed giants.

"Evan, what's in there?" I asked, curiosity getting the better of me.

"Your surprise." His tone was finally serious.

I stared at the huge building, wondering what might be hiding behind all those layers of dust. The air was damp, despite the desert-like surroundings, and billowy clouds had built up overhead, almost obscuring the amber-colored sky. The scant rays of sunlight that peeked through them didn't follow me as I crossed the threshold and the darkness swallowed me up. It took my eyes a minute to adjust and I realized that what Evan meant to show me was something enormous hidden beneath a thick canvas tarp that was covered with so much dust I could barely tell what color it was. I opened my mouth to speak, but my voice was drowned out by a different noise. Evan had grabbed the green tarp with both hands and yanked it off with a single jerk, a cloud of white dust rising from the fabric and filling the air. When it cleared I saw what it had been concealing.

The words died in my throat and I swallowed.

THE TERROR OF THE SKIES

"What on earth—What is it?" I asked, bewildered.

Evan smiled, finally satisfied. "I didn't think I would need to explain," he said, a sly, amused look on his face as I squinted at it.

"No, I, I mean, what—" All I could do was stammer. "Evan, that's a *plane*! Where on earth did you get a plane?" I asked, still confused.

"It's a fighter plane, to be exact," he said, smiling.

I stared at it, totally at a loss, then walked over and touched the fuselage, studying the details, running my hand across the gray paint faded by time. There was no denying it was magnificent. I flinched when I felt deep holes as big as nickels in its front end. My blood ran cold. They must be bullet holes. I tried not to imagine why they were there and instead focused on the picture on its side, by its left wing: the words KILROY WAS HERE and the doodle of a man peeking over a wall, his big nose sticking out. I smiled faintly as Evan studied my face with a pleased expression. Beneath the wing, "*U.S. ARMY*," stenciled in white letters, still stood out against the dark background. I had no idea how the plane had gotten all the way there or how long it had been hidden under the thick military tarp. It almost looked like it had always been there.

"What do you think?" Evan's voice rose in a whisper like the cloud of dust that had settled on the floor.

"It looks really old," I said after a moment of hesitation as I looked for the right words.

"Older than you think," Evan said. He joined me by the plane and silently stroked its painted surface, deep in reflection. "It's a P-51 Mustang. The terror of the skies during World War Two," he went on, serious, as he patted the side of the plane with his hand almost affectionately. His gaze seemed lost in memory. "It was Drake's," he said before I could ask. "Once in a while I like to come here and polish it the old-fashioned way, even though he doesn't like it. The others don't even know it exists, of course—otherwise Ginevra would have fixed it up her own way. But I like to use more normal methods just to relax from time to time. Or maybe, without realizing it, it was a way for me to try to feel more human before I met you."

"You *are* human," I replied instinctively. "Your emotions are human."

"No, they're not." He lifted my chin and kissed it softly, then looked me in the eye again. "And I've never been happier about it."

The electric charge his mouth sent through me when he whispered those words against my skin left me so dazed I couldn't reply. My eyelids fluttered as I tried to regain control. "How did you manage to block your thoughts about it from Ginevra?" I asked, fascinated by his ability to control his own mind as well as others'.

"I learned over time." Evan hid a sardonic smile, clearly understanding from the twinkle in my eye what I was about to ask him.

"Think you could teach me?"

He laughed. "Ginevra would go nuts! But"—he glanced at me, a sly smile on his face—"I guess I could. Anyway, we're not here to talk about that right now." The eagerness in his voice was evident.

"What are we here for, then?" The look on his face made me uneasy and a wave of emotion rose up in my throat, making it difficult to breathe. Still, I wasn't entirely sure it wasn't because of something else. Worry, maybe. "Evan, you can't be thinking of—" I blinked and steadied my voice. "You can't be thinking of going up in that thing?" I couldn't see his face, but I was more than sure he was smiling. I watched with alarm as he grabbed hold of the wing and nimbly swung himself up onto it. He climbed into the cockpit and looked down at me. "Why do you think I brought you all the way here?"

A mix of emotions churned inside me, rising to my throat. I stared at him for a moment and his sexy, enthusiastic smile made something tremble inside me, something in my chest that quivered with each breath. The sight of him behind the controls of a fighter plane was something I never would have expected to see, and yet for some reason he perfectly fit the role of a soldier. The clothes he wore—a black military-style jacket with patches and an army-green sweater—strengthened the impression even more. It was as if we'd gone back in time and Evan was there in that warrior eagle, ready to take off and soar through the skies to do battle like a soldier. An Angel of the skies.

"You think it's capable of flying?" I asked as the sputter of the engine drowned out my voice. The propeller on its nose came to life, more dust rising in a cloud from its whirring blades. A delicate wind blew on my skin and stirred my hair as Evan jumped out of the tiny cockpit and looked at me with satisfaction. He walked across the wing to where I was standing, knelt, and held out his hand.

My heart skipped a beat and pounded in my ears, challenging the roar of the airplane. It was *really* about to happen. Part of me was already aware of it, even if my brain was having a hard time ordering my hand to take hold of Evan's. I wasn't sure which was making me hesitate: fear or excitement. Evan always said that in certain situations one couldn't exist without the other. This must have been one of those times. And yet I wanted with all my might to take his hand, so why was I hesitating? I had nothing to be afraid of when I was with him—I knew that perfectly well—so it must have been because of my emotional reaction that was so powerful it paralyzed me when I saw this Angel hold out his hand to take me into the sky with him.

His voice resonated inside my head as he answered. *"Want to find out with me?"* It enveloped me like the rays of sunset. *"Fly with me, Gemma,"* he whispered in my mind.

I grabbed his hand and squeezed it with all my strength. A second later I was standing on the wing, wrapped in Evan's arms. Releasing me from his embrace, he took off his jacket and draped it over my shoulders. The dog tag he wore around his neck glinted against his green short-sleeved shirt. "So you won't get chilled," he whispered to me, forehead to forehead. He wouldn't need it.

Evan's arm muscles flexed as he grabbed hold of the metal rim overhead and slid down into the single-seat cockpit.

"It doesn't look big enough for more than one person," I pointed out warily.

Evan didn't respond, but sat me down in front of him so we could share the cramped space. In the end, being so close to him wasn't uncomfortable. He tucked his chin over my shoulder. "That just means we'll have to stay closer together," he whispered sensually in reply to my thoughts. He carefully shut the glass canopy above us.

Fascinated, I stared at the control panel without recognizing any of the levers that Evan was moving confidently. "This is the throttle," he explained, his voice calm, resting his hand on a lever to our left. He gripped it in his fist and smoothly pushed it forward. "This gives the plane power. Think of it like the accelerator in a car."

I watched him in silence as he used his other hand to grab a larger lever that looked kind of like a car's stick shift. I couldn't find words to express the emotions that filled me when the plane began to move and the hangar disappeared behind us. In spite of my excitement, though, all I could focus on was the heat emanating from Evan's body, snug against mine. I leaned to the side slightly to give him a better view of the controls as the landscape beyond the canopy raced by ever faster. Only my heart, maybe, was keeping up with its pace. I held my breath and his smile tickled my neck, his arm muscles flexing as he pulled one of the controls toward him.

"And this is the control stick," he said, speaking close to my ear. "If I pull it back like this, it brings the nose of the plane up." The craft gradually tilted up until the ground disappeared from view. We were so close together I was sure Evan could feel every heartbeat. "Or you can push it forward for a nosedive." He glanced at me, his expression sly.

"Don't even think about it," I warned, looking him straight in the eye. He laughed.

A moment later the barren field disappeared, replaced by the thick tangles of trees of the Adirondacks. Evan kept the plane at low altitude, flying just above the forest's majestic canopy.

"What's this for?" I asked, looking curiously at a straight line that scrolled continuously across a screen.

"That's the artificial horizon. It's used to check the plane's orientation relative to the horizon." Evan veered right and the line tilted, imitating his position in the sky. Just when I was almost sure I'd regained control of my breathing, a strange rumble rose from the propeller, making me flinch.

"Evan, are you sure this thing isn't too old?" I blurted, gripped by a feeling of alarm I tried hard to hide. My heart was in my throat and Evan's silence made me panic even more. But it wasn't his hesitation that worried me—it was his hands, jumping frenetically from one control to the other as the treetops grew sparser, revealing a mirror of water ready to swallow us up into its abyss. "Evan!" My voice held a hint of stifled desperation. At this point, there was no doubt about it: something was wrong.

He clenched his jaw and cursed.

"Evan, what's wrong?" I cried.

"Brace yourself!" he shouted between gritted teeth, his muscles tensed. "Oh, shit!" he snarled, clutching the control stick as his arms squeezed me in an iron grip.

"Evan!" I cried again, my voice suffocated with panic, but the plane quickly lost altitude, drowning out the rest of my sentence. My heart leapt violently in my chest as the lake below rushed toward us. Every part of me trembled with terror as I stared at the rippled water and dug my nails into whatever was beneath them. A scant few yards from the surface, I held my breath and closed my eyes, waiting for the impact.

Just then Evan's laughter resounded against my back, muffled by my hair. He confidently pulled the control stick toward him an instant before hitting the water and the plane righted itself, its wheels skimming the lake, tickling it, raising silver splashes against the windshield as we flew over the surface in perfect balance. I took a deep breath, my heart still doing somersaults, and turned to look at the gentle wake stretched out behind us. Evan was still laughing. I sighed, held my breath, and forced myself to laugh with him, my hands still shaking.

"Idiot!" I slugged his shoulder. "I hate it when you do stuff like that." I rolled my eyes, my breath still coming in gasps.

"That was fun, don't you think?" he said, grinning.

"You have a weird sense of humor," I shot back, glaring at him.

Evan nudged me with his shoulder affectionately. "C'mon, I was just kidding around. A harmless little dose of adrenaline certainly won't kill you."

"Right. As if I didn't have enough in my system already," I said, trying hard not to let him feel how much I was trembling. I took another deep breath and calmed down, letting myself smile with him. With that breath the scent that wafted up from his jacket and filled my nose distracted me from everything else. It was *his* scent.

Evan slowly pulled the control stick toward him and the fighter plane nosed up again, this time more smoothly, flying over the green treetops that disappeared below us.

PEARL OF FIRE

Whenever I'd chanced to look up at the sky when I was growing up, no matter how different it looked, I'd made the mistake of assuming it was always the same sky. But now it was like I was seeing it for the first time. I was sure that from that moment on I would never see it with the same eyes again.

Every second in the air with Evan seared itself into my memory. Once we were back on the ground it would stop burning, but it would leave a permanent mark on my heart. The ground had completely disappeared beneath us. The plane flew along through soft patches of clouds, gradually rising above a thick, continuous, reddish blanket of them. Although it was hours until sunset, the sky was a palette of intense shades, from red to orange to blue.

"Evan, we're flying!" I said, full of wonder.

"Yes." Evan smiled behind me. "We're flying," he repeated, pleased. His breath tickled my ear.

"My God. It's amazing," I whispered, enchanted. As I gazed through the glass canopy, my vision lost itself in the contrast between the orange and the pale blue. Hidden behind a fluffy cluster of clouds, the sun looked like a black pearl rimmed with fire. All around us the clouds scattered to the horizon, pierced by shafts of golden light that illuminated the dust particles in the air, making them sparkle like diamonds. Something about the sky's reddish hues reminded me of the place we'd been a few days before. It was still hard for me to conjure the thought in my mind, but I had to, because that's where I felt I was right now—in heaven.

"You don't need to tremble," Evan whispered behind my ear. "You're safe up here with me." His mouth grazed my skin.

"I'm not afraid." It was the truth. "I'm trembling because it brings up so many emotions in me."

"Give me your hands." His hot breath, as light as a caress, stirred the tiny hairs on my neck. It hadn't been a request; before I could reply, he'd already taken them in his own and wrapped them around the control stick. "If I could enfold all the love I feel for you the same way I'm holding your hands right now, I would transfer it from me to you."

I closed my eyes at the sound of his velvety voice, tilting my head back to touch his, intoxicated by his words. "You already are," I whispered.

"Hold it tighter, like this." When he squeezed his hands over mine I realized his intentions.

"Evan, don't be crazy!" I exclaimed.

"I trust you," he whispered. He smiled and cautiously relaxed his grip.

"My God," I murmured, releasing the tangle of emotions gripping my chest. "Evan, look!" I cried excitedly, but his hands were already moving slowly up my arms, caressing me. He stopped at my shoulders and squeezed them.

My heart skipped a beat. He breathed deeply into my hair and I sensed the power of his emotions: love, desire, hesitation . . . and something else I couldn't decipher. Fear? Maybe I didn't want to know. I tried to concentrate as Evan gently swept my hair back from my shoulder, almost as if it were the first time. I wasn't sure I could contain all these emotions. The heat in my chest was so intense it almost hurt.

"Bravo!" he whispered in my ear, making me tremble. The next moment, a light pressure tickled my neck as Evan rested his head behind mine, burying his face in my hair. The contact was as gentle as a caress. He exhaled deeply, his breath hot, and I shuddered again. He was still for a moment and I half closed my eyes, surrendering to the rhythm of his breathing.

A moment later, he returned his hands to mine, which I carefully slid off the control stick so he could take over. "How do you feel?" he asked.

"I don't think I've ever felt anything so thrilling before," I admitted.

Evan stole a glance at me and a tiny crease appeared at the corner of his mouth. Mischievousness sparkled in his eye just as a glimmer of alarm appeared in mine.

"You shouldn't have said that." His wolfish smile confirmed that he'd just given me a warning.

"What—"

Before I could finish, Evan pushed the control stick. The plane tilted to the right and rolled on its axis. I shrieked, my entire body tingling, and held on to Evan with all my might. A second later, the plane leveled out and we both burst out laughing with exhilaration.

"Are you sure this thing can fly so high up?" I teased, a smile still on my lips, trying to make myself heard over the sound of the engine.

"I can take you to the moon if you want." His voice filled my head with endless tenderness, reaching my heart with a warm quiver that made me half close my eyes. I'd never been this happy. Not until I'd met Evan.

"Evan," I murmured, caught between sadness and ecstasy. His laughter died away at my tone and his gaze rested on mine, listening. "Promise me you'll never leave me." I couldn't look him in the eye; the fear of losing him left me breathless.

"I promise," he whispered, his tone soothing but determined. "I'm not crazy, after all." He hid a smile in my hair.

"I'm not so sure about that," I said with a grin that faded before the serious look on his face.

"I wouldn't leave you for anything in the world." His eyes, deep and dark, were fixed on mine. "If you could read my heart, Gemma, you'd know how important you are to me," he whispered tenderly, his lips brushing my cheek.

I closed my eyes, losing all control. "I don't need to read your heart, I already know it."

For a moment, we looked at each other wordlessly.

"I'll stay with you as long as you want me."

"Forever, then," I replied with a little sigh.

"You don't know how many times I've come up here alone." His voice was tinged with pain. "You can't imagine how many times I've felt this same sunlight on my skin. But this is the first time I've felt its warmth," he said softly.

"That's because you're not wearing your jacket," I whispered, my eyes still closed because of the thrill his voice was sending through me, threatening to melt me any second.

Evan looked at me, his expression serious, and brushed his cheek against mine. "It's because you're here."

An unexpected shiver ran through me again.

As the plane taxied across the arid field I now realized was a runway, I felt emptied out, as though I'd just lost something or awakened from a fast-fading dream. And yet inside me I knew it wasn't true. I was still living my dream and would continue to as long as Evan was by my side. As long as *I* stayed by *his* side. Because sooner or later, death would return to hunt me down. I was sure of it. The thought was like a punch to the stomach.

Evan switched off the engine and I looked around. The plane had come to a halt in front of the old hangar. "You're not taking it inside?" I asked.

"You want to leave already?" he asked with a mix of surprise and disappointment.

"No," I was quick to say. "I want to stay if it's okay with you."

"That's what I had in mind," he admitted, opening the glass hood imprisoning us and climbing out onto the wing. For a second I thought it was so he could reach the ground more easily, but then he motioned for me to join him. I squatted on the metal and took a seat beside him, my legs dangling.

"This place looks abandoned," I said, glancing around.

His face darkened. "No one's come here for years," he said grimly.

"Not even Drake?" I asked impulsively.

"Especially not Drake. The memory's too painful for him. He doesn't even want to come near it." He paused. "Drake enlisted. He was a pilot." His expression grew serious as he stared into space, answering the questions I wasn't able to ask out loud. "He was eighteen when he got his orders, a volunteer fighting alongside the British in a war that wasn't his." There was something in his voice, a trace of bitterness, as if he were talking about himself, experiencing firsthand the pain he was describing. "He left everything behind, even the girl he was supposed to marry." He hid a bitter smile and I could see the disapproval on his face; he would never have done it. "Thought he could save the world. He didn't know he'd never see her again."

I shuddered, thinking of the deep holes in the side of the plane. "Drake died in the war?" I whispered, shaken.

"World War Two. He'd been fighting the Nazis for a year and regretted leaving everything to risk his life. But by then it was too late. He couldn't go back."

The revelation made my blood run cold. I'd never heard such personal details about Drake before. I'd had no idea how he had died, had never even wondered. Would I ever be able to look at him the same way again? After the last time I'd seen him, outside Evan's house, I didn't know if I would.

"After his . . . his death," I began, finding it hard to say the last word out loud. It wasn't an easy word to use when referring to people I interacted with every day. "Didn't he go looking for his fiancée, like you did with your family?"

"Yeah, but nobody was there." He looked me in the eye, his expression grave. "Later on he found out she'd enlisted as a Red Cross nurse so she could follow him, but she was sent to Normandy and died during the terrible battles there. The forces were parachuted in to support the disembarkation of hundreds of Allies, but not all of them reached the ground. The German counterattack machine-gunned them down as they were landing and she met the same fate."

"How horrible," I whispered, terror in my eyes.

"Yes. He never saw her again," he repeated, pausing on the last words. The glimmer in Evan's eye told me why he felt the pain as his own. It was the tragedy that most frightened him: losing me and never seeing me again.

I was afraid of the same thing, more intensely than I feared death itself.

"That's not going to happen," I assured him, touching his knee. I knew I was replying to what he was thinking. "You won't let it," I insisted, trying to convince myself.

His eyes wavered for a second, then his lips touched mine in a gentle kiss. "I'll never let it."

I stroked Evan's chest and clasped his dog tag in my fingers. He looked down at my hand. "That belonged to Drake too," he said, taking me by surprise.

"I didn't imagine it was Drake's. I know you never take it off."

"Because it's really important to me. He gave it to me himself, although I wish he hadn't."

"I don't get it. That doesn't make sense."

"It would have been better if it had gone to the person who was supposed to get it." He looked at me again and went on. "Drake has one identical to it. Most of the time he keeps it hidden under his shirt."

"You're right, now I remember seeing it. I didn't know they had the same story," I said, searching my mind for a picture of Drake.

"It hurts him to see it but he's never taken it off. It's like somehow he just can't let it go." He studied my reaction. "One of the tags was for him and the other was supposed to go to his fiancée Stella—I think that was her name. We never met. Drake was saving it to give to her when he returned from the war. He couldn't afford anything more."

"But he never made it back," I said in a tiny voice.

"Exactly," he sighed.

"So why do you have it?"

Meanwhile, Evan had lain down on the wing on his back, his knees raised. I lay down too, head to head with him, and we rested our heads on each other's shoulders.

"I was the one to find Drake."

His comment startled me. I hadn't thought of that. I couldn't imagine Evan during wartime or in any era other than our own. It still seemed so crazy.

"In those days evil spread quickly. A lot of people were dying and we were really needed. We worked nonstop, wandering the battlefields to help those in need, those who couldn't let go of their bodies—and we carried out orders too, naturally."

I shivered, hoping Evan wouldn't notice.

"And then I spotted Drake. He was alone and in a state of shock. It was hard for me to make him leave his bullet-riddled body. Before dying he'd managed to bring the plane down without crashing it. He's never talked to any of us about what happened."

"You were the one who read it inside of him," I said, anticipating his words.

"I was the first, and then Ginevra read his pain through his thoughts. He was tormenting himself about leaving Stella of his own volition when he could have protected her, for having lost the chance to say goodbye to her, and for not having been able to give her this." He turned the chain over in his fingers.

I tilted my head to look at him, then rested it on his shoulder again, brushing his cheek with mine.

"I bonded with Drake right away. I didn't know why. Maybe it was because I'd been the one to save him. Maybe Simon felt the same way about me. When you take someone under your wing you end up bound to them forever, I guess. Drake felt the same way about me and after a few days, when he started to recover, he decided to give me the dog tag that should have gone to her. He erased his name and engraved mine on it. When he gave it to me he told me I was the only person he had left in the world. I remember it like it was yesterday. His eyes were empty, but grateful at the same time, and what he said . . . It's all still crystal clear in my mind. I haven't taken it off since and neither has he."

"Maybe I shouldn't say this, but if it's something so important to you and Drake, why did you decide to put our names on it?" I asked, puzzled, my eyes fixed on the sky.

Evan laughed. "I knew you'd ask that. He gave it to me instead of the woman he loved because I was the only person who mattered to him. I wrote your name on it because *you're* the only person who matters to *me*. It seemed right that you be a part of it."

"Now that I know, what you did means even more to me," I told him, struck by the story. I rolled onto my side and rested my head on my elbow.

All Evan had to do was tilt his face to bring his lips close to mine. I wanted to kiss him but before I could he was already kissing me.

"It must be terrible to lose the person you love," I whispered, heartbroken.

"I can't imagine anything more painful." He looked deep into my eyes and fell silent.

ICE IN THE HEART

Evan and I had been driving back for some time now. The sun hadn't set but the cloud cover had thickened as if to make up for our absence in the sky. The upholstery was covered with crumbs. At first I'd refused the sandwiches Evan had taken out of the glove box because I was afraid I'd get his car dirty, but he'd deliberately sprinkled breadcrumbs on the red floor mats, leaving me with no excuse.

"Planning to hold me hostage much longer?" I said, grinning as I waited for his reaction.

"Something like that," he said, a cunning look on his face. "You don't seem to mind."

I shot him a glance and found him doing the same. "At this rate I'm afraid all the time you have left with me today is going to be wasted here in the car," I said jokingly. Evan looked at me and raised an eyebrow. "You're driving at a snail's pace!" I pointed at the speedometer, which read seventy-five miles an hour. A normal speed for anyone else, but not for Evan.

"Oho!" He seemed struck by the provocation. "*I'm* as slow as a snail?" he repeated deliberately.

"It's not my fault you got me hooked on excitement." I looked at him, emphasizing the last word provocatively.

He cocked his head and returned my look. "Think you can do better?" There was a note of challenge in his voice.

I held his gaze until I found my voice. "You don't need to ask twice," I warned, my eyes fixed on his in search of confirmation. What did he expect me to do, drive his Ferrari? Had he seriously lost his mind? It was crazy . . . and yet the idea stirred something in my blood. I couldn't wait to do it.

"I let you fly a fighter plane. I don't see why you shouldn't drive this," he said encouragingly, raising his thumbs from the steering wheel to indicate the car. Maybe he didn't think I was actually up to accepting the challenge, because the subtle note of mockery in his voice persisted. But then again, Evan knew me well enough to know I wouldn't back down.

He pulled over and took his hands off the steering wheel. "It's all yours," he told me, the grin never leaving his face. At that point I really couldn't say no. He walked around the car, watching me steadily through the windshield. I climbed over the gearshift—Evan preferred a stick to an automatic—and settled into his seat. By now my excitement had eclipsed my bewilderment.

"Whenever you're ready," he said with mischief in his voice once he'd slid into the passenger seat. Stunned, I looked at the leather steering wheel and stroked it. Driving Dad's old Audi was definitely nothing in comparison.

"You sure you can do better?" he said in the same challenging tone. Was there encouragement behind his mocking expression? I doubted it. "You're still in time to change your mind."

But I'd already pressed the ENGINE START button on the steering wheel and the Ferrari's aggressive roar drowned out half his sentence. I turned and shot him a defiant look, my answer to his question. "Whatever you say," I replied with a smile.

I pulled casually out onto the road, my fingers clutching the wheel because they were trembling and I didn't want Evan to notice. Excitement gripped my chest, adrenaline rushed through my veins, and my stomach was upside down, but I forced myself to appear calm to Evan's eyes.

The road was empty. Fate was on my side—or on the side of whoever might have been driving in front of me, depending on your point of view.

Once we were on a straight stretch I jammed my foot down on the accelerator, attacking the asphalt like a wild beast. The car lunged forward, pressing me back into the driver's seat and leaving me breathless.

"Whoa, whoa, whoa! Take it easy!" Evan warned me with a little smile as the arrow on the speedometer shot to sixty miles an hour. The wind whipped his words away. I couldn't slow down; it was too much of a thrill. I felt like an arrow shot from a bow. I accelerated more, reassured by the fact that Evan was there to protect me. Every inch of my skin tingled, vibrant and alive. It was like I had the world in my hands, like I could do anything, go anywhere. *I felt safe.*

"Well?" I asked Evan, keeping my eyes glued to the road. "Still think I can't do better than you?"

We were already going a hundred and twenty miles an hour. Evan was used to far greater speeds, but I'd already beaten my own record in the first five seconds of driving. Evan pressed his lips together and shook his head, almost as if he still weren't entirely convinced. His reaction compelled me to press my foot down even harder on the accelerator. I wouldn't have done it—I knew I'd already reached my limit—but I was beyond being able to resist the voracious urge that drove me on.

A hundred and thirty an hour. The road was a blur, but I was determined not to let my anxiety show. I camouflaged it with a mocking tone. "You're lucky, Evan." My eyes narrowed on the asphalt, razor-sharp as an arrowhead, while the landscape raced by in a river of hazy color. Deep in my heart, a feeling of uneasiness began to shout its dissent.

"Why lucky?" Evan asked, his voice calm.

"Now we'll be getting home sooner," I said roguishly. "You should be thanking me." Evan frowned, apparently unsure of what I meant. "This way we'll have more time to ourselves," I explained. From the corner of my eye I noticed that his lips had instinctively curved upwards in approval. I couldn't resist the urge to turn to him and smile. Evan smiled back, raising the corners of his mouth at the same time I did.

Suddenly all hell broke loose. The steering wheel jerked under my hands and spun out of control. I was hurled against the car door as though hit by an invisible train. I tried to speak but the air seemed to have been sucked out of my lungs and the car too. I tried to turn the steering wheel but the force with which it was spinning was too great to control.

"Evan!" I shrieked.

I heard him curse as terror flooded through me. "Damn it!!!" he shouted, attempting to grab the wheel. His voice also filled with panic as the car spun out of control, forcing us back in our seats. I didn't understand why he couldn't use his powers to make it stop.

A bridge was coming toward us at incredible speed.

"Evan!!!" I let out a desperate scream and met his terrified eyes. There was a sudden, brutal impact.

Then, darkness.

"Ge . . ."

His voice sounded far away, as if he were talking on a cell phone that kept cutting out.

"Hang . . ."

I tried to open my eyes but it was too difficult. Like sound, images faded in and out: flashes of light alternating with moments of total darkness. Another brutally harsh noise tore me out of the darkness and I glimpsed Evan beside me. He'd torn off the Ferrari's door with one hand.

"I'm here . . . here . . . here . . ."

At times the sounds repeated themselves in an endless echo. Again, darkness.

"Ge . . ."

I felt Evan's arms beneath me and my limbs felt heavy, as if they were dangling.

" . . . with me."

Another flash: Evan leaning over me. I felt at the mercy of the forces around me, dragged like a seashell on the shore: at times light, when the current was carrying me away from the beach; at times heavy, when the water receded, leaving me stranded on the sand. Then the pain arrived from every direction. It inundated me, making me long for the water to return and carry me off, leaving the pain behind. I tried to follow it and abandon myself to its current, but something continued to bring me back.

I could no longer see anything. Oblivion was claiming me. I wanted the pain to stop. It was too much.

Enough! Enough!

" . . . your eyes . . . eyes . . . eyes . . . ook at me!"

The desperate sound made me hurt even more. I felt a light pressure on my head, where the strongest pain was coming from. A strange heat filled my temples, burning like fire. I clenched my teeth.

The heat grew stronger, driving out the pain. Another burst of light crossed my eyes. Evan again. There was an unfamiliar edge to his voice: desperation.

Now I could see them, between the darkness and the flashes of light: his hands. Yes, now I could feel them. The warm touch of his hands on my head. It felt so nice.

Again, I felt myself slipping away. Again, darkness.

" . . . Please . . . ease . . . ease . . . " His voice shook. " . . . eave me."

His face appeared to me for a brief second, his expression tormented, agonized, almost in tears. I couldn't stand the pain. Not mine, his. Not any more. I couldn't bear to hear the anguish in his voice.

The darkness pulled me down again but I clung to his voice with all my strength.

"Ge . . . you hear . . . *Look at me.*"

I felt a whirl of energy bearing me up. The light arrived violently. I wasn't in the darkness any more. I'd re-emerged.

"Evan . . ." It was the first thing I managed to murmur, the only one I could think of. I finally saw him clearly. I was lying on the asphalt. He was leaning over me, his hands on either side of my body. When my lips whispered his name, he dropped his head toward my chest and his hair tumbled over his brow. Neither of us said a word for a long moment. I wasn't sure where we were or what had happened. I was too dazed to speak.

Evan gently brushed his forehead against my chin and looked at me, his eyes filled with a desperation I'd never seen before, his sooty skin streaked with tears. He took my face in both hands and rested his forehead against mine, closing his eyes, then let out a long breath, blowing warm air on my face. "I just died for the third time," he whispered, so softly I could barely hear him.

Bizarre as it might sound, I couldn't help but smile as his forehead continued to press gently against mine. "When was the second?"

Evan gave a deep sigh and smiled. "When I walked into the living room looking for you and you were gone."

The memory flashed through my mind like a fiery bolt of lightning. The thought of Faustian and the way he'd tricked me into running away from Evan still made me shudder. "You should reconsider being in a relationship with me," I said with a grin. "It doesn't seem to be very good for your health."

He smiled, our foreheads still touching, and kissed me cautiously, as if afraid he'd break me. "The fact that you're already kidding around is a good sign."

I blinked, still confused, dazed. "What happened?" I asked, unable to remember.

Evan didn't answer, just moved aside so I could see behind him. The whole world froze before my eyes.

"Evan!" I whispered, filled with terror.

Steps away, crumpled against a torn guardrail, Evan's Ferrari was totaled, its body twisted, its windows shattered, a tangle of scrap metal left unrecognizable by the violence of the impact. The front end had broken through the guardrail and the back end dangled over the edge, teetering between the asphalt and the water below the bridge.

"Your car . . . " I whispered, my voice full of regret.

The door lay some distance away. I remembered glimpsing Evan as he'd ripped it off its hinges.

"I don't care about the car!" he growled. "Your life is the only thing that matters." He stood up and put his hands to his head, looking nervous, as if the nightmare he'd just lived through was still tormenting him. His bloodstained hands left a smear on his forehead.

"I'm sorry," I murmured in a tiny voice, moving closer to him. A devouring sense of guilt rose from my stomach. *I* had been driving. It was all my fault. I'd totaled his car.

"Don't feel bad." His expression hardened. He turned and looked into my eyes. "It wasn't you."

Although the meaning of his words eluded me, something inside me trembled as Evan grabbed his hair in his fists. Something was tormenting him but I couldn't tell what, exactly. From the look on his face, it seemed to be a mix of emotions, with anger and shock struggling to outdo each other.

"Damn it!" he growled furiously. He slammed his fist violently against the roof of the car, crumpling the metal. The brutality of the blow made me flinch.

Worried, I stared silently at Evan as he rested both hands on what remained of the roof and lowered his head, his hair falling over his face. He turned slowly and looked at me with a distraught expression. Something in the way his eyes looked right through me made me shudder.

"They've found you."

The blood in my veins turned to ice.

GUILTY FEELINGS

"What? You, you mean—" I stared. My lips trembled convulsively and I felt I'd lost all control over my body.

"Damn it to hell! It's all my fault!" he cursed himself, his voice breaking with remorse. "I've been such an idiot!"

I still couldn't speak.

"Come on." Evan strode over. "I have to get you out of here." He picked me up from the ground gently as though I were made of crystal.

A metallic groan caught his attention, but his angry expression didn't alter. He turned toward the noise just in time for another loud creak from the Ferrari, which appeared to be teetering. A second later, it slid over the edge of the bridge and crashed into the water, sending a spray of droplets as brilliant as diamonds into the air.

The wind lashed at my face, leaving me breathless, and I buried my head in Evan's chest. He was already running, a silent missile darting through the trees like a ghost. I inhaled his scent and forgot everything else for a long moment—a single, comforting moment of relief before my body began to shake uncontrollably again at the memory of Evan's devastating remark.

They've found you.

I could think of nothing else. Someone was after me again, someone who wanted to kill me. I was on the run again. I was being hunted down again. Though I attempted again and again to drive it away, one thought filled my head incessantly: *would I survive this time?*

The wind stopped. I'd been so lost in my obsession I hadn't even wondered where we were headed. What could it matter now? No matter where I went, no matter where I hid, they would find me. I couldn't escape death. Evan couldn't protect me forever.

The air was cool and I was sure the sky would soon be shedding tears for me. I wished I could cry, but terror had paralyzed my senses and not even my tears could find a way out to help ease the pain.

Evan knelt down and laid me on the damp ground, then turned his back to me, his fists clenched at his sides. I reached out and stroked his arm. For some reason, it felt like I was the one who needed to comfort him. Guilt emanated from every inch of his body.

"Evan," I said, my voice barely audible and my eyes brimming with tears.

"How could I have let this happen?" His voice was a whisper of pain. "It's all my fault." His expression made me cringe with terror. I'd already seen that look in his eye. It only took a second for me to realize I'd seen it just once before: when Evan was leaning over my lifeless body, mangled from Faust's torture. When he thought he'd failed. *When I was dead.*

Was that what he saw in me now—a body already dead? Was there really no hope for me?

I wanted to squeeze his hand but my strength was gone. Unexpectedly, he took mine and looked up. "Come with me," he murmured.

I looked around for the first time and instantly recognized our hideaway, the lake house, a few yards ahead. Evan led me through the trees to the shore. Letting go of my hand, he walked out onto the strip of land at the water's edge and sat down on a rock covered with large roots that snaked all around it. Without a word, I did the same and sat down at his side on the rock. Neither of us said anything for a long while.

I focused on the harmonious movement of the water stirred by the breeze and tried to overcome my fear. Evan stared into space as I looked absently at a dry leaf floating on the water. It rocked gently like a feather borne along by the wind.

The lake was a mirror that reflected everything upside down: the sky, the clouds, the trees, almost as if another world existed under the water, a parallel dimension beyond its surface. I wished I could hide there. A raindrop rippled the surface right before my eyes, distorting that perfect image and reminding me there was no reality other than this one. Concentric circles formed around the place the raindrop had landed, growing wider and wider until the water returned to its former mirror-like state.

A second raindrop stirred the water. All around us, silence reigned. A third hit the surface, followed by a fourth, until the surface of the lake was dimpled by countless raindrops, making the upside-down image tremble.

I felt frozen inside, as if something had emptied my body and filled it with ice that stung painfully. The tree branches hung low, right over our heads, their dense leaves forming a canopy over us as the rain came down even harder, seemingly wishing to wash away the pain afflicting us both in that desperate silence that paralyzed my soul.

I opened my mouth for a second and then closed it. Choosing silence, I reached over and rested my hand on Evan's. He squeezed it, then raised it to his cheek and closed his eyes. He appeared to be devastated—so devastated that my desire to console him made me forget the reason for his torment.

Unexpectedly he exhaled in a barely perceptible sigh. "I've failed miserably."

"You haven't failed, Evan. I'm still here with you. You saved me," I said quietly, hoping to convince him.

He squeezed my hand even tighter as if afraid I would slip away from him. "No. That's not true. It's all my fault. I shouldn't have let it happen!" he hissed.

"I was the one driving the car, Evan. Why do you want to take the blame?"

He snorted as if I'd said something ridiculous. "The car has nothing to do with it. It could have happened any other way." Finally his eyes rested on me. "Don't you see? It's my fault they came back for you. I should have been more careful and instead I lowered my guard. I let myself get carried away by my feelings for you." He seemed to be struggling with himself. "I was too reckless."

"What are you talking about, Evan?" I asked, confused.

His face grew grave. "I shouldn't have broken the rules. I should have protected you and instead I took you into my world." He looked miserable. "I put you in danger. It was a mistake. Forgive me."

His words left me astonished. I finally realized why he felt so guilty. A series of images flashed before my eyes: the crazed horse, the falling tree trunk, the out-of-control motorcycle. They hadn't been coincidences. The events had begun right after that afternoon. And the shadow I'd seen . . .

I went ice-cold. So I hadn't imagined it. Was this the price I was going to have to pay for visiting his world: my life? My instinct had been right. It had been risky to challenge fate like that.

"They tried before too," I whispered, still caught in my memories.

"Huh?"

"They tried before." The faint voice that issued from my mouth was as cold as the blood in my veins. "This morning, and also before, when

I was out in the woods with the others. Luckily I was with Ginevra. My God . . ."

Evan clenched his jaw as if that hadn't occurred to him yet. "When I think of what might have happened to you—" He looked away, beside himself with anger.

"You said they wouldn't notice my presence."

"They shouldn't have, but something went wrong. I don't understand. No one should've noticed, damn it! How could I have been so stupid?" he growled, raising his fists to his forehead. "We could have gone on living our lives without any problems, but I went and complicated everything. I shouldn't have run the risk."

"Evan, it wasn't your fault," I said, but my attempt to reassure him failed utterly. He barely seemed to have heard my voice.

"I put your life at risk on an idle whim!" He clenched his jaw, furious with himself.

"That isn't all it was for me, Evan." I took his hands and moved in front of him. Finally he looked at me. "I wanted to do it and it was worth it, because now . . ." I closed my eyes, struggling to voice my thoughts. "Now I know what's waiting for me. You gave me a gift." A tear slid down my face. Soon I would be dead. I would lose Evan forever.

"Don't even say it," he hissed. What I'd just said almost seemed to have made him angry. Then his tone softened. "If I lost you, I'd—"

"Evan, you think there's still hope that—"

"Hope is for people with no certainty." His eyes burned into mine, his tone adamant.

"How do we stop them?" I asked warily.

No matter how hard Evan tried to lie to me, no matter how hard he tried to lie to himself, I could sense his torment and it wasn't difficult to interpret it: he was afraid of losing me. "I don't care how," he snarled. "I'm going to exterminate them all. No one is getting close to you. What happened today caught me off guard, but it's not going to happen again. He's alone, but we've got Ginevra on our side. That's a huge advantage. It won't be hard." His eyes glittered as he laid his plans, his tone ominous.

I wasn't so sure it would be that easy. Given what had happened the first time, they were bound to send someone more skilled, more cunning, and more powerful than Faust. Now they knew who they were dealing with and to what lengths Evan was willing to go to protect me. It was stupid to think they wouldn't have an ace up their sleeves this time.

After a moment of silence, I turned to Evan and asked in a tiny voice, "Was it really about to happen?" He frowned and avoided my eyes. He already knew what I meant, but I had to say it aloud before it exploded in my head. "Back there, I—I was about to die." Unable to phrase it as a question, I let the statement hang in the air. Evan didn't reply. "It was you that brought me back." It was a confession, but he didn't know it.

"I know. I healed you. You'd smashed your head against the glass."

I gulped.

"No one else could have done it."

His words skimmed my consciousness, leaving a shiver on my skin, but that wasn't what I'd been referring to. "No. I wasn't talking about that."

Evan looked at me, puzzled.

"It was your voice. I held on for you. In a sense, it's like I *chose* to. I could have let myself go, let myself slide into the darkness that had enveloped me, taking away the pain. For a split second I almost wanted to. But then I heard your voice." I sought his gaze. "*You* brought me back, Evan."

He laced his fingers with mine, squeezing my hand as his face darkened into a mask of torment. "You have no idea what I went through in those five minutes. I was deathly afraid of losing you. You have no idea how much I suffered, Gemma."

Now it was me who squeezed his fingers. All at once a doubt surfaced in my mind, clouding my certainty. I sat down again next to him. "There's something I don't understand. The last time it happened, when I died, you were afraid you wouldn't be able to bring me back in time because you weren't there to protect me. This time you were with me, so you could have saved me no matter what, right?" I studied his expression.

"I wasn't sure I could heal you all on my own. Your condition was too serious." My stomach lurched. How was that possible, if I was there now without even a scratch? "I only succeeded because you didn't give up. As long as your heart continued to beat I had a hope of healing you." Evan swallowed, his gaze empty. "But if you had died . . . I don't think I could have managed to bring you back all on my own."

I shuddered. "You didn't sense his presence?" I made myself ask in a steady voice.

"No," he said, frustrated. "My guard was down. I was too focused on you, on protecting you from the other dangers, the normal ones. There was no way for me to know he was there until it was too late."

"I shouldn't have gotten behind the wheel," I said guiltily.

"It would have happened anyway. I tried to keep the car from crashing, to stop it by controlling the air, but I couldn't. Under normal circumstances I would have been able to take control of the car before it even risked going off the road. You weren't in any danger. I didn't expect to meet with resistance. That's when I realized what was going on, but it was already too late."

"What do we do now?" Fear had gripped my stomach.

"Gemma, listen carefully. From now on it's important that you always stay near one of us. You need to be under our constant supervision, otherwise we can't protect you. If I can't be there, someone else has to stay with you—Simon, Ginevra, or Drake, it doesn't matter who. You'll be safe with us. But you can *never* be alone. Is that clear? *Never.*"

"Okay," was the only word I could utter.

"Let him try now." Defiance glimmered in his eyes. "I'll be here waiting for him."

I looked at Evan for a moment, digging my fingers into the earth. The rain fell slowly in a steady rhythm. From time to time a raindrop slid off the leaves near me, almost in slow motion, and sparkled through the air.

Our absent gazes were lost beyond the lake. Evan reached for my hand and smiled, as if for a moment he'd banished every thought, as if he wanted to forget everything and move forward, pretending it had never happened. But the problem wasn't what we'd been able to overcome or what I'd managed to survive. The problem was what we had in store for us.

What should I expect from that moment on? I decided it didn't matter. Whatever it was I had to face, Evan would be there at my side, every minute. Even if it was my last one.

That was enough for me.

HIDDEN SIGNS

"What's your favorite season?"

Evan's question surprised me. We'd never talked about the weather before. I looked at the foliage above us. The trees were still green but in a few weeks they would turn into bouquets of warm colors. I wondered if I'd survive long enough to see them again. As early as October, the leaves of the sugar maples in the forest turned to an array of red, orange, and yellow, framing Lake Placid and painting a stunningly colorful picture around the lakeshore. I closed my eyes and inhaled deeply, trying to engrave the image in my mind forever.

"All of them," I replied when I opened my eyes again.

"All of them?" Evan asked, curious.

"Does it surprise you?"

"I thought you'd say summer, or winter," he said, "like anyone else would."

"But I'm not anyone else." I watched the raindrops fall onto the lake.

"You definitely aren't," he answered with a smile.

"I think nature is perfect. Winter lasts just long enough for me to want summer to arrive and vice versa. I couldn't live in a world with only springs or summers. Each season has its scents, its colors, its charms."

Evan laughed. He seemed fascinated by my explanation. "So you really don't have a preference?"

I thought it over. "This," I told him, jutting my chin at the landscape around us. Evan frowned. It felt like a century had passed since I'd barely avoided death, but it had only been a matter of hours. The sun was about to set behind the clouds and only a few strong beams shone through.

"What do you mean?" he asked, puzzled.

"This. The summer rain. When the seasons combine. I like the strong smell of the damp earth." I breathed in the cool air. "The thunder sounds different, more comforting. Do you think I'm weird?"

Evan smiled to himself, but I wasn't lying. I'd always had a strange connection with nature, as if it were a part of me and I of it. When I was a little girl and got mad at my parents I would run off into the woods. After a couple of hours I would forget everything and go home. It was as if the forest spoke to me.

"You're adorable." He leaned in to kiss my forehead as I continued to stir the earth with my fingers.

We sat in silence for a few minutes, giving ourselves time to put our ideas in order. I continued to draw meaningless figures in the dirt as Evan stared at some vague point across the lake. Despite the distant, blank look on his face, it wasn't hard to imagine what he was thinking about.

My fingers mechanically clasped a little stone. I picked it up and studied its gray, angular details, then drew my arm back and threw it into the lake. It hit the surface with a soft, harmonious *plop*, raising a tiny splash. Spying another stone—a flatter, smoother one—beside my foot, I reached down to grab it, but Evan snatched it up first, our hands touching for a second. He gave me a sweet smile and stood up. "Want to see something?"

The rain was falling more gently now. It dripped onto his dark hair as I watched him pull back his hand with a studied movement and skip the stone across the water.

One. Two. Three. Four. Five. *Plop.*

A gasp of admiration escaped me. I'd never seen anyone skip a stone so many times before. In any case, if there was a rock-skipping record, I knew Evan could beat it with his eyes closed. He turned to look at me with a smug expression.

"Beginner's luck," I teased. My sense of competition wouldn't allow me to let him see how much he'd impressed me. Or more likely, it was my pride. I could never match that. Chances were my stone would sink without skipping even once. "Bet you can't do it again," I said. He looked so handsome with his damp hair clinging to his forehead.

"How many do you want?" he asked calmly, accepting the challenge.

I ventured an impossible number: "How about twenty-five?"

He smiled as if nothing could be easier. God, his smile was gorgeous. I wasn't ready to lose it forever. For a moment it had made me forget how sneaky he could be. By controlling the elements he could keep the stone from sinking into the water and make it skip across the surface forever if he wanted to. He continued to smile at me as I realized I'd lost before the challenge had even begun. Turning his back to me, he held a stone between his fingers and threw it confidently. I felt a tickle on my neck and shrugged my shoulder without taking my eyes off the skipping stone.

"Check it out," he told me, sounding pleased, a little smile on his lips.

I didn't reply, distracted by the annoying tickle on my back.

" . . . Seven . . . eight . . . nine . . ." Evan said. "Do you want to count or should I? Twelve . . . thirteen . . . fourteen . . ."

Out of the corner of my eye I noticed a strange blur on my shoulder and realized the tickling sensation was coming from right there.

" . . . Seventeen . . . eighteen . . ."

Evan's voice faded to a confused murmur. Focused on the tingling sensation, I wasn't paying attention to him any more. I tilted my head back and the blur moved into my field of vision. The tingle instantly spread throughout my body, galvanized by an internal shudder that triggered a wave of bone-chilling terror that ran through me from head to toe. The blur had suddenly taken shape and become clear.

A tarantula. I shuddered again. There was a tarantula on my shoulder.

"Evan." My voice was a mere thread. Or maybe I'd only imagined I'd said his name. I wanted to scream but couldn't produce any sound. I was paralyzed. Spiders had always been one of the things that terrified me most, and the knowledge that such a huge, hairy one was on my shoulder froze every muscle in my body.

" . . . Twenty-four . . . twenty-five!" Completely unaware of what was happening, Evan turned around with a giant smile, but his face instantly blanched when he saw my imploring gaze. He stood without moving for a second, his eyes glued to the creature.

"I—I have a tarantula on my shoulder." My voice trembled, my head filled with racing thoughts. Old memories suddenly resurfaced.

"Don't move," Evan said cautiously as if to avoid scaring the creature. The thought of its hairy legs on my skin made me itch all over, but I found the strength not to move a fraction of an inch.

My pleading gaze was locked onto Evan's. I swallowed slowly, afraid even that tiny movement might set it off. Though fear clouded my mind, I tried to make a mental list of everything I knew about tarantulas. From what I could remember, they weren't poisonous. Also, they were black, whereas this one was brown. Then again, I'd never seen one with my own eyes before so I couldn't know for sure. Still, I was certain their venom wasn't deadly. So why did Evan have that look on his face, as if a mountain lion were about to pounce on me?

"Don't move." His voice was ice cold. "That's not a tarantula."

I stiffened. Something in his tone told me it was even worse than I'd imagined. I began to have trouble breathing. "Evan . . ."

"It's a Brazilian wandering spider," he said matter-of-factly as if I should know what that was. "It's very fast, very aggressive, and—most importantly—very poisonous."

My heart was caught in an iron vise and an uncontrollable trembling threatened to overwhelm me, but I forced myself not to move even a muscle. I saw the spider raise its front legs and panic left me breathless. It was preparing to attack.

"Evan!" My voice broke in a desperate plea, my eyes brimming with tears.

Evan's expression hardened, his eyes trained on the spider. He rushed at me at warp speed, snatched up the creature, and flung it across the lake into the distant treetops on the opposite shore.

My heart trembled with terror. I still couldn't breathe. When I looked at my hands I saw they were shaking.

Evan turned back to me, looking worried. "Did it bite you?"

I shook my head but instinctively looked back to check.

"That kind of spider has the natural ability to control the amount of venom it injects into a victim. It regulates the dose based on the circumstances. A Death Angel could make it inject a fatal dose." He sighed and hung his head, then looked up again, his gaze fiery. "It lives in the jungles of South America," he explained grimly as if the information might be useful. Right now, its origins seemed totally irrelevant to me. "It wasn't here by chance," he explained, his gaze resting on mine.

The more alert part of my brain grasped his meaning and I shuddered. Neither of us wanted to believe it. For my part, I hadn't wanted to see reality. Fear is like a boomerang: no matter how far you throw it, it always comes back at you. Sometimes it feels like the best thing to do is ignore what frightens you, but all that does is make the blow even more devastating. It's not a choice, though, but rather, a defense mechanism our brain automatically activates to try to protect us. I was being hunted again. Neither of us wanted to accept it.

Evan didn't move a muscle. His eyes narrowed to slits, scanning the trees, carefully observing every last inch of the forest surrounding us. All at once he seemed to hone in on one spot in particular, too far away for me to make out. His eyes still fixed on the forest, a corner of his mouth rose and his expression turned sharp, threatening. *Lethal.*

"Gotcha," he hissed. Before I could open my mouth he disappeared into the forest, leaving behind a cloud of dust and cold air that sank into my bones.

A suffocating ache in my heart, I stared at the spot where Evan had disappeared. There was no sign of him, as if he'd vanished into thin air. Somewhere inside me I shuddered violently. Right now Evan was with another Soldier of Death. Not just any Executioner, not like Faust, but one who was more prepared, more aware, *more dangerous.*

I couldn't bear the idea that something might happen to Evan. Faust hadn't known what he'd been up against, but this other Subterranean certainly wouldn't be caught unprepared. He would have taken precautions, and the awareness that Evan was running this risk for my sake hurt me all the way down to my bones. I would gladly have surrendered to my hitman rather than put Evan in danger. His life mattered more than mine.

I shifted awkwardly in my spot, my eyes wandering nervously around, looking for some sign of him—any movement among the trees would be enough—but everything was still. Evan seemed to have disappeared. The forest had swallowed him up. The woods were silent, listening to my desperation. Tears welled up in my eyes in spite of my efforts to hold them back. I couldn't see anything any more. Forcing down the lump in my throat, I continued to focus on trying to spot him.

Deep in the forest, a sudden movement made my heart leap. I wasn't sure whether I had actually seen him or just imagined it, because when I looked closer everything was perfectly still. My anxiety rose by the second, preventing me from thinking straight. I didn't know what to do. My impulse was to set out and search for Evan as long as I had air in my lungs, but it was possible that might just complicate things. One way or the other I always managed to do that.

There was nothing to do but wait. Yes, I would wait for him, heart in hand, until he reappeared safe and sound. He was destined to come back, I was sure of it.

Another movement distracted me. This time I was faster and caught sight of it before it disappeared among the trees. Two dark figures that shot back and forth across the forest like bolts of black lightning. The movements were blurry and confused.

I squinted but they were too far away and the light was too faint for me to make them out clearly. It looked like one of them was chasing the other, but I couldn't tell who was who. The rain plastered my hair to my face. Finally I heaved a sigh of relief. Evan wasn't the one being pursued—he was chasing the other Subterranean. I couldn't explain how exactly I managed to figure that out, but I knew I wasn't wrong. I could feel it inside. They were too fast for my human eyes to follow their movements. At times I saw them disappear and then reappear in another spot farther off in the forest.

Evan was always on the verge of catching his adversary, who always managed to elude him. He was fast, faster than Evan, but he seemed afraid to stop and fight. Every time Evan popped out in front of him, the other Angel disappeared and the endless chase resumed. It got harder and harder for me to tell them apart. Sometimes their shapes seemed to merge together.

Gusts of cold air shook the trees, reaching me as they rustled the leaves on the branches. What the hell was going on? Suddenly I couldn't see them any more.

The terrifying silence made me shudder down to my bones. I trembled like the leaves on the trees had a moment ago. Shifting my weight from one leg to the other, my body began to move forward on its own, driven by instinct—or, more likely, my heart. Another step, and another, as my gaze darted through the trees in search of any sign of them, no matter how small. Only when my breathing accelerated did I realize I was running. I couldn't feel my muscles at all any more. My mind was honed in on a single thought and my body had reacted to that thought, desperately seeking Evan.

A flash of light caught my attention and my eyes shot in that direction. At that precise instant, an explosion hit me in the chest and hurled me into the air, knocking the breath from my lungs. I collided with a tree and crumpled to the ground. I felt disoriented, as if my brain had momentarily been switched off.

Moving my head slowly from side to side, I felt a sudden pain in my chest that didn't feel like a normal physiological response. This pain was tearing me up from the inside, crushing my heart as if someone had it in his hands and was squeezing it, suffocating me. Where was Evan? What had happened to him? I sank my fingers into the earth and clenched my fists so tightly they throbbed as the first tears streaked my skin and the rain coursed down my bloodstained hair.

I couldn't have said how long I lay there on the ground. I had no idea where Evan was, what had happened to him, or what the blinding light had been. Something had exploded. It had been too far away for me to make out what it was, but it had sent out a shock wave powerful enough to send me flying.

My palms and knees sank into the damp earth as tears silently slid down my face and spattered the ground like raindrops. I snuffled and forced myself to reason. No explosion, no matter how powerful, could have killed Evan. Only a Witch's poison had the power to do that. So why was my heart in tatters?

"Gemma."

His voice sounded gently beside me as the rain continued to course down my hair. My eyes went to his face. "Evan!" A wave of relief hit me more powerfully than the explosion had, filling my whole body and wiping away every trace of pain. I pulled myself up and threw my arms around his neck, almost afraid he was only a mirage, a projection of my anxious mind. "Evan," I sobbed into his chest, the word muffled.

He stroked my hair as if I were a little girl in need of comforting. "Everything's okay," he whispered. For a second I almost hoped he'd killed the other Executioner. I wouldn't be able to bear another moment like this.

"He got away."

His words sent a tremor down my spine. So it wasn't over. This wouldn't be the last time Evan put himself in harm's way for my sake. I held him tighter, knowing he sensed my apprehension. "I was afraid you weren't coming back to me any more," I murmured, desperation in my voice.

"Hey." Evan lifted my chin to make me look him in the eye. "I will always come back to you."

I buried my face in his chest again. His muscles stiffened and a groan escaped his clenched teeth. Worried, I instantly relaxed my grip and leaned back to look at his face. His lips were pressed together, though he was trying hard to smile. When he saw my alarmed expression, which instantly told him more than any words could, he gave a slight shake of his head and was quick to reassure me. "It's nothing."

"Evan!" I whispered, lowering my eyes to his abdomen. "You're hurt!" Looking closer, I noticed a rip in his green shirt at the level of his ribs. Through it, I glimpsed an ugly burn mark, as if something had torn first through the fabric and then through his skin. When I reached out toward it, Evan pulled away from my touch, unsuccessfully concealing a grimace of pain.

"What happened? I thought nothing could injure you," I gasped.

"We were just playing around a little." He forced a faint mocking smile, then took me by the hand. "Come on. Let's go somewhere safer."

I followed him through the trees along the same course I'd taken. Earlier the distance had seemed longer, but I'd been so disoriented by fear I'd probably run in circles. The trees parted, revealing our hideaway just yards from us. I continued to steal glances at Evan's pain-stricken face. I'd never seen him look like that before and it seemed to transmit a part of his suffering to me. Although he was trying hard not to let it show, his eyes filled with pain from time to time.

The wooden front door opened wide before us. Evan continued to look around him in all directions. When the door closed behind us I felt a strange sensation, as if a bubble of bulletproof glass had suddenly surrounded me, a protective sphere that kept out panic, pain, worry. All at once I wasn't afraid of anything any more—even the terror of dying had disappeared. Evan had banished my fears from my mind, I was sure of it. Just like I was sure he'd tried, without success, to ease the one concern filling my mind right now, the only thing that really mattered to me: the bleeding wound on his abdomen.

I'd seen other marks on Evan's body before—small cuts, burns, scratches. They generally healed even before I could get more than a glimpse of them. This injury, on the other hand, seemed pretty deep and didn't show the least sign of improving. I wondered how it was possible.

I looked away from it and stole a glance at Evan's face when he wasn't looking at me. Dark and rebellious, his drenched hair hung over his forehead and his clothes were sopping wet—no less than my own, of course. My heart beat harder just looking at him.

"He's sneaky." Evan's voice shook me out of my thoughts. "He wants to make it look like an accident, even to us. It's like he doesn't want to come out into the open."

"Maybe he's just afraid of you," I said.

Evan shook his head, unconvinced. "It has to be something else. He must have a plan—otherwise I can't explain it." He stared into space, thinking aloud. "He always keeps his distance, just far enough away that I can't detect his presence and intercept him." His face went rigid and fire glimmered in his eyes. There was something he wasn't telling me, I could feel it. "But I'll be more careful from now on."

"What happened, exactly?" I asked cautiously.

"I tried to catch him." His tone went dull again, making me instantly regret my question. "But I couldn't." He looked away.

"It doesn't matter, Evan. How are *you*?" I reached toward the wound without touching it.

"It's nothing," he said reassuringly.

"Evan, why haven't you healed yet? I thought your wounds always went away quickly."

"Only the common ones. Things get complicated if the person to injure you isn't human. The bastard threw a fireball at me, a totally extreme measure." Evan's eyes seemed to grow more pensive, but his face was set. "He didn't want to fight and he wasn't trying to kill me."

I started. "But he couldn't have done that, right?"

Evan was silent for a moment. "No, but death isn't always the worst outcome. He only grazed me and I'm sure he did it on purpose."

Another silence.

"Then why did he attack you?" I asked. "Evan, why didn't he try to hit you full on?"

"He wanted to get away." Again that pensive look. "And that's what I don't get," he reflected aloud. "It's really strange. Too strange. I had the impression he didn't want to confront me. He kept running away and wouldn't let me see his face." Evan shook his head. "No, it can't be . . ." he murmured, barely moving his lips.

"Maybe he doesn't want you to know who he is," I suggested timidly, "so he can—I don't know—operate undisturbed."

"Maybe." His gaze was still distant, lost in thought, as if he'd come up with an explanation but wasn't convinced. "Or maybe not."

THE SKY IN A ROOM

"Does it hurt?" I asked, lightly touching the wound. His sopping-wet shirt clung to his body, outlining his chest, and the burn lacerating his skin showed through.

"Only a little," he murmured at my touch. From the look on his face I could tell he was lying. An icy shiver ran down my back, reminding me I was still wet too. My clothes felt frozen to my skin.

"You're cold," Evan said, his voice low, gently rubbing my arms to warm them. He released them and went over to the fireplace. When he raised his palms toward the blackened stone hearth, a spark flickered amid the stacked firewood. Soon a fire softly illuminated the room. Outside, the sun had already set. In moments the fire was blazing, emitting a wave of hot air that startled me. Shivering again, I eased into the pleasant sensation of warmth against my skin.

I looked at Evan, captivated by the golden glow the fire was casting on his face. He opened his palm and before I could ask what he was doing something took my breath away: another spark, rising from his hand. Taking the form of a tiny crystal sphere, like a will-o'-the-wisp, its white light glimmered silver before my enchanted eyes as he raised it to his mouth and blew it off his hand. The luminescent sphere exploded in a myriad of tiny, diamond-like sparkles that looked like little stars. They floated through the room, finally coming to rest above us, twinkling just below the ceiling.

I looked up to contemplate the mantle of stars, then looked back down at Evan. No one could take this moment away from us. It was just him and me, with a microcosm of the universe shining down on us from above. I wouldn't have given up this moment for anything in the world. There was nowhere else I would have wished to be but there with Evan in our private little universe.

It wasn't the first time I'd seen him create a sphere of light, but seeing so many tiny fragments of it all gathered together made me feel I was a part of something infinitely large.

Evan gazed at me as though I too were a star. *His* star. He smiled, his face illuminated by the warm glow, and I lost the power of speech. In the silence he gripped the bottom of his shirt, pulled it off over his head, and shook his wet hair. At this unexpected action my heart leapt to my throat. His dog tag jingled against his sleeveless white undershirt, which was wet and clung to his chest. His firm muscles rippled in his arms.

I moved closer to examine his wound, challenging my self-control as the flames in the fireplace burned on my cheeks, concealing my blush. "Does it still hurt?" I asked softly, touching the gash from which blood had trickled onto the white fabric. Evan pulled back slightly, stifling a grimace. "Can't you heal yourself?" I asked, unused to seeing him this vulnerable.

"Not on my own," he said, his voice unsteady from the pain he was trying to repress. "It's not a human wound."

"Let's go to the others, then!" I said, looking at him sharply.

"No!" His wild dark eyes mesmerized me, putting an end to my attempts to take him to his brothers. Then his expression softened. "I want to stay here with you." His eyes probed mine intensely, promising to take me places I'd never been before. "It's almost healed," he reassured me in a low voice. "I just need to bind it."

Without giving me a chance to breathe, Evan reached behind his head and pulled off his undershirt with a groan, baring his pecs. An electric charge surged from my heart to my throat and stomach, his golden skin taking my breath away. With a single swift movement of his well-defined muscular arms, he tore the white fabric into strips as easily as if it had been a sheet of paper.

"Here, let me," I murmured, looking at him encouragingly and taking the bandage from his hands.

Without a word Evan gave it to me and raised his elbows slightly so I could dress his wound. Though I was focusing on his side, I felt the heat of his gaze on me the whole time. My heart was beating so hard I was afraid he might hear it. I wrapped the bandage around his middle with careful movements, wondering why I couldn't stop shivering. It felt like something was on the verge of changing forever. My movements grew slower as I felt his breath moving closer. A delicious warmth filled my head, but I knew it wasn't coming from the fire. I tied the bandage in place and swallowed, unable to look him in the eye.

I couldn't stop trembling. Not because of the cold, I was sure of that, but because Evan was there with me. Of their own volition my hands began to move over his ribs, rising with extreme slowness until they were caressing his chest. Evan's eyes were on me all the while. His skin was incredibly warm. He tucked a lock of hair behind my ear as he lightly stroked my cheek. I looked at him with a strange shyness. When my eyes met his intense gaze I felt as if I were seeing him for the first time.

"God, you're beautiful," Evan whispered. My heart skipped a beat. I felt it tremble and half closed my eyes as he rested his forehead against mine. "Everything's going to be fine."

I nodded slightly without replying. He gently clasped both my hands in one of his. "Come nearer the fire." His tone was even gentler than his touch. "You should dry off."

With a hint of embarrassment I took off my shirt. Evan looked away until I'd straightened my camisole that had gotten pulled up in the process. I sat down on the big red rug in front of the fireplace. He came over, sat behind me, and wrapped his arms around me protectively. The silence in the room, a comforting silence full of promises, was broken only by our breathing. I stared at the flames that rose higher than our heads as I listened to the crackle of the burning firewood.

"I'm sorry for everything you've been through," he said.

"It's not your fault, Evan," I told him firmly.

"It is. I shouldn't have taken you to my world. You're seventeen. These should be the best years of your life, and—"

"They are," I interrupted quickly. "*This* year," I stressed, "has been the best year of my life. *Meeting you.* Evan, over the last few months I've experienced more with you than anyone else could in an entire lifetime."

Evan's gaze was lost beyond the flames. "When I saved you, you were given a second chance. It's my fault they're hunting you again." There was pain in his voice. "Maybe we shouldn't have gotten involved."

I suddenly felt my heart freeze as if the fire had been replaced by an iceberg. The bitter chill penetrated my bones. "Are you saying you should have left me?"

Evan smiled. "I wasn't talking about *me*. I could never do that, ever. I could kill myself, but I could never think of leaving you. It's just that—you shouldn't have to be going through all this. I'm so sorry. I don't know how you can stand it."

His words took me by surprise. Did he really not know I would run a thousand risks if it meant I could stay with him? I turned slowly to face him. "I would go through it all over again, Evan, because all of it led me to you. Meeting you turned my whole life upside down, but being part of your world, being with you, has been the most wonderful thing life could offer me," I confessed, hoping he could read the emotion in my heart.

"I'll never leave your side, Gemma." His gaze melted me with its bold tenderness.

"I know. You gave me your promise." I let myself linger in the memory of that moment. It was so recent but felt so distant—he and I soaring through the sky, touching the clouds, forgetting the rest of the world.

"I mean I'll never let them hurt you," he said. I rested my chin on his upper arm as he held me closer and added, "I'll be there to protect you."

It was strange to be there with him after everything that had happened. Experiencing this magical moment with Evan banished all my worries, all my pain. This morning I'd left the house not knowing what was in store for me, not knowing death would return to track me down. Yet for some inexplicable reason, right here, right now, it didn't matter. It had been a long day full of conflicting emotions, but oddly enough all I could remember were the unforgettable moments I'd experienced with Evan. His warm body holding me close was the only sensation I wanted to focus on.

Those moments of panic had taught me one thing I would never forget: even if it's raining outside, the sun is always behind the clouds, even if you can't see it. You can never tell exactly when it will come out and shine again, but no storm can eclipse the sun forever. Not even the ones that rage in our hearts. You just need to wait for a gust of wind to blow away the clouds and allow the sun to shine again, even inside yourself. And that was what Evan was for me: my gust of wind.

I was staring at the flames in front of me when I felt his lips touch my shoulder, sending a tingle all the way down my spine. He delicately swept my hair back and his touch made me quiver again. His lips brushed my skin tenderly, moving from my shoulder to my neck. Tiny hot shivers spread through my body with each kiss. I closed my eyes as the emotion trembled all the way to my heart.

"You know . . ." The words were barely audible but I was sure Evan could hear them. I turned to look him in the eye. "Despite everything,

237

this has been the most romantic afternoon I've ever spent." He pushed a lock of hair off my forehead and, without leaving my gaze, gently tucked it behind my ear, caressing my cheek. I half closed my eyes, letting the feelings wash over me. "I wish it would never end," I whispered even more softly.

His eyes half closed too, Evan leaned forward and brushed my cheek with his. "It doesn't have to," he whispered, his lips on my ear. The warmth of his voice tickled my skin, sending an uncontrollable tingle surging through my body. God, I was so happy. I wished I could stop time and stay there with him in our little hideaway, our little world where I would be safe forever.

I inhaled deeply, his scent enveloping me as if for the first time. His mouth slowly reached my face, touching my cheek and moving on to my lips with incredible sweetness. I closed my eyes and followed his movements as my body melted like warm honey and his mouth burned against mine. He gazed at me and I lost myself in those intense eyes that were as dark as night while inside me the sun rose, a sun that would never set. I was at war with the world outside, but I didn't care. As long as I was with Evan, I knew nothing could hurt me.

He kissed me with incredible tenderness. As if it had a life of its own, my hand stroked his skin. I trembled at every movement of his lips on mine, every breath, every heartbeat, as the two of us melted together into one.

I watched Evan's hand slowly caress my shoulder and gently move the strap of my camisole aside, leaving it dangling against my arm. I held my breath as his mouth moved to where his hand had just been, burning my skin. When he slowly pressed his lips to my neck, I closed my eyes and tilted my head, surrendering to him, savoring his sweet fruity taste that lingered on my lips.

I knew what was about to happen. We both did.

My skin knew it from how it quivered at his touch. My eyes knew it from the moment they'd met his in the brief silence full of meaning that had left me dazed. And so did my heart, which longed more than anything to melt into his. Every inch of me longed for this moment and I could sense that Evan wanted it just as intensely.

"This, above all else, flouts every rule," I whispered slowly.

"There's no rule that isn't worth breaking for you. I don't care about the rules." His tone was gentle and his gaze burned into mine as his hand sank into my hair and his mouth sought mine again, this time more fervently.

I rested my palms on the rug that was as soft as down to the touch. Our lips brushed playfully as I slowly slid backwards, almost unconsciously, guided by Evan's body as it pressed ever closer to mine. Once I was lying on the rug Evan looked into my eyes, accelerating my breathing. He was suspended over me, his hands resting on either side of my head and his dog tag hanging down between us. I stared at his body and the full, firm muscles lining his arms and torso. Stroking his chest, I felt my gaze return to his as if drawn by an irresistible summons. His velvety voice filled my brain. "There's something in your eyes that drives me out of my mind," he whispered with infinite sweetness.

I knew perfectly well what he meant because I felt the exact same thing. There was something in the special way he looked into my eyes, his hard gaze that softened only for me—it drove me wild. Against all logic, it made me lose myself.

Evan continued to kiss me as he delicately unbuttoned my jeans. I longed only for him. The clothes gently slid off our bodies and at last his bare skin was against mine. He swept my hair back and I felt safe.

His voice whispered inside my head, sweeter than ever before: *"If only you could see inside me, you'd know what I feel right now."* The thought echoed intensely in my mind, his voice tinged with torment, his gaze chained to mine.

"I feel the same," I whispered onto his mouth. It felt like I'd just told him a secret. My love for him was uncontainable; I was afraid my heart would swell so much my chest wouldn't be able to hold it any more.

I put my hands over my head, abandoning them on the rug. Evan's powerful arm reached up and clasped them in his right hand with boundless tenderness as his left caressed my body, barely brushing my neck and then my breasts, slowly. He stroked my belly and his hand slipped under my back.

An invisible cord bound my heart to his. Sensation overwhelmed me. His smell, the feel of his skin against my body, the delicate touch of his lips on mine. My skin burned beneath Evan's hand, consumed by a fire that could never be extinguished.

He pressed his lips against my neck and clasped my hands against the rug more firmly as a soft breath of air blew out the fire next to us and an overwhelming emotion swept me with unexpected intensity, an internal explosion that filled my heart and shattered every tiny fragment of my being only to reunite it with Evan's in a single, inseparable entity.

Evan was inside me.

I closed my eyes and let the sensations spread through me. Fire, earth, heaven, hell whirled inside me in a tumult of emotions. The universe had swallowed me up in its infinitude and I wandered within it together with him, entwined in our forbidden love. Hidden from everyone, sheltered in our own little corner of paradise where no one could reach us. Forever connected, softly crying out our love for each other.

No one could take me away from Evan. My flesh was his flesh and my spirit had merged with his like two metals forged by the flames of love into a single indissoluble element. I was his and would be forever.

Evan, Gemma, me, him: tonight all of that had been wiped away, becoming *us*, just us. Two worlds that had combined to become one reality, all our own, where no one could hunt down our love. Two perfectly fitting halves that formed an indivisible whole, so closely united it was seamless, so deep we could forget where one ended and the other began.

Evan moved above me with infinite tenderness, treating me like a delicate piece of crystal. My lips followed his and his mine, brushing together gently at one moment, locking together ardently at another. I'd never known my heart could withstand the intensity of such powerful emotions.

I felt the delicate touch of his hand beneath my back. Never before had he been so tender. His gaze lingered on mine as he swept a stray lock of hair from my face. He spoke, and the tenderness of his voice as it issued from his lips was entirely new. "If my heart could beat, right now it would be out of control," he whispered.

The soft curve of his full lips mesmerized me as they came closer. Tilting my head to offer him my neck, I realized that the pale light that barely illuminated the room was coming from the sparkling spheres, which were no longer fixed points of light below the ceiling. Now they were swirling, moved by the energy that united us, gliding slowly around our bodies like fireflies in the darkness.

I no longer felt like a single particle in the universe; the entire universe was inside me, locked in my heart that had swelled large enough to contain it. I felt a river of emotion flowing from me to him and back, connecting us eternally. It was as if we'd waited forever for this moment.

Making love with Evan was so intense, so incredible. He was so confident in everything he did, yet every movement, every caress was so gentle. Now, like never before, I felt I could see inside him. It was as if we had each walked a separate path that had brought our souls together and now the two paths had merged into a single one.

The more time passed, the more intense the feeling inside me grew, plucking strings I didn't even know I had as Evan ran his lips over my breasts, burning my skin with every touch. His mouth stroked my ear and his voice was a warm, velvety whisper that tickled my skin, making me tremble: "I love you to death."

I half closed my eyes and allowed the emotion to sweep me away.

CONNECTIONS BENEATH THE SKIN

I'd never experienced such intense emotion in my whole life and I knew nothing could ever match it. My heart was ready to burst. Evan was lying at my side, contemplating me. The fire in the hearth had returned to warm us. The dancing firelight played over our bodies.

"It was then that the Angel saw heaven for the first time," he whispered, stroking my neck.

I looked into his eyes and bit my lip to conceal a smile. "A reckless Angel."

"I would die for you," he said, his eyes probing mine.

"Don't even try it," I warned, and he smiled at me, the sexy little creases that drove me wild appearing under his eyes.

"My God, your eyes are so enchanting." He sighed. "When I look at you all my defenses fall away. I feel like you could ask anything of me and I would grant it."

My gaze had strayed to his mouth but I returned it to his eyes, resisting the urge to kiss him. "I thought there were certain transgressions forbidden to Angels," I teased, whispering against his lips, my gaze chained to his. "Shouldn't your moral code keep you from giving in to this particular kind of temptation?"

Evan stifled a laugh. "I thought a lot of things before I met you, but you turned my whole world upside down. When you're near me I don't even know who I am any longer." He leaned closer and whispered the words onto my lips: "I lost my mind and nothing makes sense any more." He kissed my bare shoulder and his soft voice caressed my neck under my ear. "My moral code tells me I shouldn't feel what I feel and that I should resist certain urges, but my instinct tells me I might die if I don't give in to them." I rested my forehead on his, his velvety voice putting me into a trance. "If all I had was you, I would still have everything."

I closed my eyes and swallowed, lost in the spell of his warm, penetrating gaze. Making love with Evan had been an otherworldly experience, not because he was an Angel but because of the boundless love that united us. The energy was still flowing through my body. I was in heaven. Suddenly I remembered when Evan had explained that his body perceived emotions more powerfully than a mortal's. I couldn't imagine how it was possible to experience a sensation more intense than the one still stirring in my bones. My body wouldn't have been able to bear it.

Evan sank his hand into my hair, demanding my attention, as I struggled to find my way back from the dimension I was in. I turned my head so my face was close to his and gazed at him as he continued to stroke my hair.

"Before, you said you loved me." My eyes locked onto his.

Evan smiled. "What, hadn't you figured that out already?" he whispered, playfully brushing a lock of my hair back and forth on my face.

"Of course." I smiled. "It's just—you once told me you weren't going to use that word. You thought it was—how did you describe it? Superficial," I teased. Instantly, though, the memory of the intensity with which he'd said those words banished all the mockery from my face, making my heart skip another beat.

"There's nothing superficial about us or what I feel for you, Gemma." His mouth moved to my ear. "We were made to be together," he whispered, "and no one can ever separate us. Not even Death." He gently slid his hand down my belly, his eyes following the lines traced by his fingers, back and forth, reaching the edge of my panties. Unable to tear my eyes from his face, I studied its outline, observing the way his wavy hair hung over his forehead, grazing his eyebrows that were as dark as his eyes, as deep as night.

"How did you get this scar?" he asked, pushing aside the edge of the fabric and stroking the silvery streaks on my lower belly.

"It's not a scar, it's a birthmark. Huh—" I took a closer look. "It usually looks paler." It was strange to see how it glowed in the warm firelight. "I could have your name tattooed there to cover it." I shot Evan a challenging look. "But then you'd have to do the same for me," I teased, trying hard to sound serious.

"Your name is already branded on my heart," he whispered tenderly. He stroked my palm with his thumb and I returned the gesture. I loved it when he did that. The simple touch drove me wild.

My fingers slid to his wrist and began a slow exploration of his forearm as I studied his tattoo. I'd never seen anything so fascinating and frightening at the same time. The letters were so small one could barely be distinguished from the next. They seemed to form a single design. Actually, there were different lines consisting of strange symbols that wound up to the inside of his upper arm. From a distance they looked like scratches made by sharp claws or roots that branched out as if to imprison his arm.

"What are these symbols?" I swallowed, studying them carefully as though I could decipher them.

"It's Devanagari, a very ancient alphabet," he said. "Some say it's the language of the gods."

"They're tiny." I continued to stroke his arm, following the lines on his skin as he turned gradually toward me, letting me examine them. For a moment, we both watched my fingers as they moved on him.

Evan looked into my eyes, his own intense. "It's a map of what we are."

I stroked the symbols in the center from which all the others seemed to emerge.

यमराज

"That one appeared first," he explained, seeming to recall the moment. "From there it spread out all over my arm."

I touched his skin, imagining the pain he must have suffered when he was branded with the mark of the Children of Eve.

"*Yama*," he murmured in a barely audible whisper. "He who irremediably draws souls to himself and to whom is entrusted their guidance and passage from one world to the other."

Looking into his eyes, I saw them light up as if he'd been looking forward for some time now to revealing to me what was written there. "At first I didn't know what it was. It all happened so fast. The mark appeared, then the Witch, and then I saw my lifeless body. I thought I'd been cursed—and I wasn't altogether wrong. When Simon found me and made me eat of the tree, I looked at my arm and everything was instantly clear: I could read it." He frowned, pulled into the memory despite himself. "Some of the marks are the same for all Subterraneans, while others define who we are and what our individual powers are."

After a long moment, he pointed out one of the words:

कमदशभत

"*Karmadeshabhuta*. It means 'spirit that determines fate.'"

I touched the symbol, fascinated. Branching out from it were five small lines. I slowly traced the first one.

"*Jala*, water," Evan said. He looked at me and I moved my finger again, stopping on the next line. "*Teyas*, fire," he whispered, staring at my mouth, in his eyes the memory of the fire that had just consumed us. "*Vayu*, air. And this one here is the power of earth, *Bhumi*. We're spirits of nature and can control its elements." He turned his arm until my fingers were touching another word. "Life, *Ayus*." He moved it again, focusing on another. "Death, *Mrty*. They're all part of nature."

"What about this one?"

"That's pronounced *Mantra*. It means 'free the mind.'"

The fire danced in the hearth, illuminating his tanned skin, his muscles flexing with each movement. I touched a symbol that looked more threatening than the others and Evan hesitated.

अमृत

"*Amrit*," he murmured grimly. "Deathless."

"Evan," I whispered, but he smiled at me, calm again.

"You'll like this one. *Svapna*. It indicates my special power to enter others' dreams."

"*Svapna* . . . You're right. I like it."

"It's different for each Subterranean. Drake has the symbol for transformation, shapeshifting. Simon has the one for deepest memories." He pointed at other symbols. "These, on the other hand, appear on all Subterraneans. *Guhya*, hidden. *Tamas*, darkness. *Pranama*, obedience. *Amrta*, ambrosia. *Jyotis*, light. *Naitya*, eternity. *Atmanas*, souls. *Moksha*, salvation."

I stroked his arm slowly, tracing the lines on the inside of his elbow.

With a shiver he closed his eyes and took a deep breath. "*Bhoga*," he whispered, pointing at one of the symbols. "Sensual pleasure." His dark eyes probed mine, holding me captive.

I gave him a smile and went back to studying the symbols, fascinated. "What does this one mean?"

Evan fell silent, looking troubled. "*Vyaya*, loss."

"*Vyaya*," I repeated, touching it again, my heart heavy. It represented what we most feared. Tracing the mark with my finger, I noticed that the symbols forming it were interwoven with another word. He explained before I could ask about it.

"*Abhaya,* fearlessness."

"You mean you've never been afraid?"

"Never. Not until I met you." He looked at me intently and I held his gaze.

A smile escaped me. "Are you saying you're afraid of me?" I teased, grinning.

He pulled me on top of him, only our underwear separating us. "I'm saying the thought of losing you is the only thing that's ever terrified me," he murmured onto my mouth. He touched my leg, slowly sliding his hand up my thigh, then clasped my rear and pulled me against him, sending a shiver through me.

"*Kama,*" he whispered, looking me in the eye. "Desire."

I raised an eyebrow, mischief in my eyes. The heat of his erection pressing against me left me in a trance. "Desire? Is that what's written there?"

With a laugh, Evan raised my hand to his neck and slid it down to his bare chest. "No. That's what's written *here.*"

It made me smile. "I think it's written a bit farther down," I teased. My eyes were drawn to the last word, which ran up his bicep. "And this one?"

Evan smiled and touched it, his finger brushing mine.

आनन्द

"*Ananda,* bliss. It's what makes all Subterraneans hope for a reward and for Redemption," he said.

I stared at his tattoo, realizing for the first time that some of them weren't simple words, but sentences interconnected in a single design. I lay down on my side next to Evan. His face filled with intensity as he recited the words like a prayer.

Devānāṃ bhadrā sumatirṛjūyatāṃ devānāṃ rātirabhi noni vartatām devānāṃ sakhyamupa sedimā vayaṃ devā na āyuḥ pra tirantu jīvase.

"Ah, of course. It's all so clear now." I smiled to myself.

He laughed, easing the gravity of the moment, and proceeded to translate the quote: "May the auspicious favor of the gods be ours, on us descend the bounty of the righteous Gods. The friendship of the gods have we devoutly sought: so may the gods extend our life that we may live."

"Amazing. It's basically the path to Redemption!" I exclaimed.

Evan remained calm. "That's what they say."

For a moment he seemed lost in thought while another question arose in my mind. "When did you realize I could see your tattoo?" I asked. When a Subterranean manifested himself, mortals couldn't see the mark. Only I could, for some reason neither of us understood.

"It was at school, when you were stealing glances at me from your desk. You looked at me and then at my tattoo. I couldn't believe it." Evan shook his head, still bewildered by my ability. "It's amazing." He laced his fingers with mine and guided our hands up, looking into my eyes. We lay there facing each other, palm to palm.

"Did you know the palm is full of nerve endings that connect to the entire body?" He moved his fingers and a tingle ran up my arm. "From here I can feel all your energy."

An image crossed my mind: Drake claiming the soul of the boy on the street. I'd only been able to make myself look away for a moment, so I'd seen it happen. Drake had touched the spirit of the boy, who had then vanished. Did that mean their power to guide souls across worlds lay in their hands?

"There's—there's something I've always wanted to ask you," I said.

"I'm listening."

"How do you . . . take people's lives?"

Evan paused before answering. He probably hadn't expected this question, given that I'd always avoided talking about it. "It's an impulse I feel inside."

"Could you end up killing me by accident? Do I run that risk?"

"Peter has run that risk lots of times," he admitted, laughing. I punched him on the shoulder for not taking me seriously. "So did Daryl Donovan. I definitely would have liked to kill him."

"Daryl I can understand. I mean, he tried to molest me at the prom. And then he provoked you at the party Jeneane threw at the end of the school year. But *Peter!* When?"

"Whenever I see you with him," he admitted, leaning in to kiss me. "I can't stand it when he's around you."

"You can't feel the urge to kill him just for that!"

"Sure I can. It doesn't mean I'll act on it—unless he really makes me mad." He laughed and looked at me again, his eyes roguish. "You, on the other hand, make me feel another kind of urge."

"Mmm, what kind would that be?" His provocation took my mind off his threats toward Peter.

"Let me show you." He arched an eyebrow and pinned me beneath him, his mouth touching me below the ear. A shiver ran down my neck and then another one, little tingles that tickled my heart. I laughed and pushed him back by the shoulders, but he continued to kiss me.

"Evan, how do you say 'You're inside me'?" I asked, remembering the words he'd said to me at the foot of the sacred tree.

He looked into my eyes, probing them. *"Antar mayy as."*

"Antar mayy as," I whispered, enchanted.

"Yatha tvam mayy asi . . . Just as you are inside me," he replied, holding my gaze. He raised my hand to his chest and his chain dangled between us. *"Mama hrdi* . . . In my heart." He laced his fingers with mine and squeezed my hand as the throb of my heartbeat melted me. *"Mamatmani* . . . In my soul."

I half closed my eyes because Evan had expressed exactly what I felt: he was inside me. In my heart. In my soul.

Unnoticed, time flew by like a silent thief who with every minute that passed stole another fragment of our incredible afternoon. I was happy, and when the thought that I'd had a brush with death crossed my mind, all I had to do was meet Evan's gaze and everything else vanished.

God, how I loved him. His deep, dark eyes touched my soul every time they rested on me. Lying on the rug, I followed my instinct to stroke his hair. He circled my waist with his arm and my skin burned beneath his hand.

"Think we can spend the night here?" he said, his eyes never leaving mine. His unexpected suggestion left me wordless. I wished I could say yes—God knew how much I wanted to—but I couldn't.

"My dad would kill me," I said, smiling.

He touched his lips to my throat with incredible sweetness, trying to persuade me. "We can always find a solution," he said between one light kiss and the next.

"I don't think Drake is going to like being our pimp."

He kissed me again. "I'm sure he would understand. I want to stay here alone with you." I propped myself up on my side and Evan tucked my hair behind my ear. "I want to kiss you until you fall asleep and hold you all night even if you can't feel it."

"Is that all?" I cast him a sidelong glance and a sly smile escaped him. "You can always come to my house tonight," I said.

Regret flashed across his eyes as if I'd made him remember something he didn't want to recall. "That's why I wish I didn't have to leave you tonight. Because I'm going to have to face reality again and be apart from you."

"Tonight too?" I didn't even bother to hide the dismay in my voice.

"You'll find me at your side when you wake up," he promised. "You won't even notice I'm gone." Holding back my disappointment, I tightened my lips. It was hard to believe his absence could go unnoticed. Whenever Evan left me alone the nightmares returned to haunt me. Everything I was living, everything I forced myself to repress during the day, came crashing down on me with full force. Still, I couldn't blame that on him.

"I don't want you to be alone, though. Things have changed and we can't afford to run any risks. You'll sleep at my place. Ginevra will stay with you and Drake will fill in for you." I nodded, relieved. "Nothing is going to happen to you," he whispered, stroking my hair. "You're under our protection."

"How are we going to get home?" I asked, concerned by the steady ticking of the rain against the walls of the hideaway.

"Don't worry. I've already contacted Simon telepathically. He's on his way. I tried to contact Drake too, but couldn't find him. He must be . . . out somewhere. Let's hope he gets back soon."

Trying not to think of the words Evan had decided not to say, I started to get up but he pushed me down onto my back and held me tight. "Where do you think you're going?" he whispered, a sly look on his face as he barred my way.

"I should get dressed, shouldn't I?" I asked.

"Uh-uh," he said. "Why should you? You look so good like this." He kissed my neck and then my shoulder as his muscled arms flexed at my sides, holding me captive.

"Your scent drives me wild," I said with a moan.

Evan smiled against my lips. "I never wear cologne."

I shook my head, brushing my nose against his to challenge his statement. "It was the first thing I sensed when you used to sneak up on me." His chain dangled between our bodies. I grasped it in my fingers and slowly drew his face closer to mine until my mouth was brushing his earlobe. "Do you want Simon to see me naked?" I whispered provocatively in his ear. Simon would be there any minute and all I had on were my panties.

Evan shook his head slightly and tightened his lips. "You know how to persuade me. I would hate to have to kill one of my brothers," he said, breathing the words onto my skin. He kissed me again and fell silent, his eyes suddenly serious. "But there's no limit to what I would do for you."

I rested my forehead on his and we both smiled, our lips a breath away from each other. "I don't think Ginevra would ever forgive you," I warned.

Evan looked away, pretending to consider it. "You're right, she wouldn't. I have no choice but to give in." Reluctantly, he lifted his hand from the floor and propped himself up on one arm, leaving me free. "You win."

A smile still on my lips, I finished dressing just as the now-familiar hum of the BMW broke the steady sound of the pounding rain. Evan held me tight by the front door as if he wanted to keep me there with him. I kissed him and all of a sudden a terrible feeling gripped my stomach: once outside, I would have to face reality. I didn't know what might happen after crossing that threshold, and as if that weren't enough, Evan wouldn't be with me tonight. I would have to face my demons on my own. Death was right around the corner, waiting for me. How much longer could I avoid a collision with destiny? No one could say—not even Evan.

The wooden door opened, admitting a gust of cool air that struck my still-warm face. I took a deep breath and crossed the threshold, taking shelter under the jacket Evan held over our heads. I could barely see where I was putting my feet until the sound of the rain was muffled by the stillness of the BMW's interior.

"Gemma." As Simon greeted me he glanced at my bloodstained clothes.

"Simon," I replied, looking down, a bit embarrassed. For some strange reason I blushed, as if he could see in my face what had happened between me and Evan, though I knew it was impossible. Simon was always the last to know things. It was Ginevra I was worried about. While I was relieved Evan hadn't asked her to pick us up, I couldn't avoid her forever and wasn't sure I could block my thoughts from her. No, I could never manage to do that. She would know everything the minute she saw us.

Simon and Evan fist-bumped and Simon shot him a sidelong glance. "Something go wrong? Where's your car?" he asked his brother, his face serious.

From the back seat I saw Evan's jaw tighten. "We have a bigger problem than the car," he said somberly.

Simon laughed. "What could be more important to you than your car?"

Evan turned to look at him and Simon's expression altered drastically. His eyes went wide. "They found her?" he whispered, looking horrified, still staring at Evan. He turned his eyes back to the road, his expression blank as Evan clenched his fists so hard his knuckles turned white.

Silence fell. The whole way home, the only sound was the tapping of the rain on the windshield. When Simon switched off the engine in the garage, nobody moved for a moment, all of us sunk into our seats in utter silence.

Simon was the first to speak. "Do you already have a plan?"

"Not yet," Evan muttered.

"We need to tell the others."

Evan nodded. "Gemma can't be left alone." His eyes sought Simon's. The tone of his voice left no room for doubt: it was an order. Their eyes remained locked for another moment, making me guess that their conversation was continuing.

Simon quickly confirmed my suspicion, replying to a question I hadn't heard, his tone firm. "It's not going to happen."

It wasn't hard to imagine what he was referring to. After he'd left the garage, I couldn't resist the urge to ask Evan. Climbing out of the car, I leaned against the door, knitting my brow. "What did you say to him?" I asked timidly, instantly feeling embarrassed for prying. My eyes wandered nervously around the garage, but my discomfort disappeared as soon as Evan cupped my face in his hands and leaned against me, pressing me against the car door.

"Just that they have to protect you. *At all costs.*"

Something in his eyes told me it wasn't the whole truth, just like I knew he'd excluded me from their secret conversation to avoid upsetting me. I accepted his explanation, even though no matter how hard he'd tried to hide it from me I already knew the real answer. The words echoed inside me as if I'd heard them for myself: *I don't want to lose her.*

As Evan and I walked to the door hand in hand a single thought filled my mind: Ginevra. I could practically sense her champing at the bit in the room next to the garage, as if she were waiting for me just behind the door, anxious to hear the details. I knew her by now. Or maybe it was just my fear putting me on edge.

Evan seemed to notice and squeezed my hand as a little smile spread across his face, suggesting he realized the reason for my nervousness. "Don't worry. It won't be so bad," he said, unsuccessfully trying to reassure me. The closer we got to the door, the faster my heart pulsed in my temples. He took the handle and opened the door. "After you," he whispered.

Warily, I peered around the living room, but it was empty. Just as I began to breathe normally, a cascade of golden hair flowed down the stairs. Ginevra. She stopped on the last step, her hand still on the railing. My heart sank when her eyes rested on me and I had the feeling I was under scrutiny, like when the teacher asks you a question the one time you didn't study. Why the hell did I always have to be so emotional? Ginevra's mouth fell open slightly and the indecipherable expression on her face made me wish the earth would open beneath my feet and swallow me up. Her eyes shifted to Evan and back to me as I tried hard to act casual and block my thoughts, but it was no use.

About three seconds had gone by.

"Oh." She closed her mouth, looking pleased. "So there's been a change of plans." Her eyes were glued to mine. I felt completely naked.

Evan let out a low laugh and his face hardened. "Gin, there's no need for me to explain anything to you. Unfortunately I've been summoned." He turned toward me as if to apologize. "I'm leaving her in your hands," he said sternly, his eyes burning into his sister's.

Ginevra nodded but Evan didn't seem convinced that she understood how important this was. *"She can't be left alone."*

"Don't worry," Ginevra said in a carefree tone, her eyes darting to mine. "We'll have loads of fun."

Evan's expression relaxed. He cupped my face in his hands and kissed me lightly on the lips. "I'll be back soon," he murmured. I nodded and he turned to take one last look at Ginevra. "Don't torture her, okay?" he said with a wink.

A broad smile spread across his sister's face. "Can't promise you that," she said to the now-empty wall. Evan had already vanished.

I nervously ran my fingers through my hair and looked down, another rush of embarrassment rising in me. Ginevra pounced on me and grabbed my hands. In the blink of an eye she'd pulled me up the stairs and into her room, looking like she was about to explode with enthusiasm. "For Lilith's sake! What are you waiting for?! Tell me everything!" she exclaimed impatiently. For a second, the innocent, enthusiastic look on her face made me think of Peter. Her bedroom door closed behind us.

"Shh!" I warned, scanning the room.

"Sorry! How did it happen? I want to know *every last detail!*"

I wasn't used to talking about myself. I'd never liked doing it. Her eager face was waiting for me to answer. But why? Wasn't probing my thoughts enough for her? "Why should I tell you what you already know?" I said awkwardly.

"Come on," she pleaded. "Nothing like this has ever happened! Imagine being the only girl in an all-boys club for such a long time!"

I opened my mouth to speak but quickly closed it, unable to reply. Her eyes lit up expectantly as she sat down beside me on the bed. What could I tell her? I looked down, wondering exactly how red my cheeks were right then.

"You're right, I always know everything," she admitted, coaxing me with an angelic expression. "More than people want me to know. But sometimes it's nice to hear someone simply *tell* me things. It's nice to have someone decide of their own free will to share what's on their mind with me."

I shot her a reproachful glance. "In this case it's not like I'm exactly *deciding* to tell you. You're not giving me much choice," I pointed out.

"A negligible detail! C'mon, please?" she said, taking my hands and growing serious. "What did you feel?" She waited, staring at me intently. She wasn't being nosy, only conspiratorial. How could I explain to her what I'd felt? I couldn't even conceive it myself. How could words express something so intense, so deep?

That afternoon with Evan had been all our own, and part of me didn't want to give up even a little piece of it or share it with anyone else, but right now I felt a strange pressure in my chest. My bond with Ginevra was pushing me to indulge her. At long last, I had a girlfriend—no, Ginevra was more than that to me. I had a sister.

"It's hard to explain what I felt," I confessed. "It was like exploding and melting at the same time. And he—" My cheeks burned and I felt flushed again. "Evan was incredibly tender."

Ginevra shot me a smile brimming with pride. "I'm so happy you're part of our family. Evan is so different from how he used to be and it's all thanks to you," she said, piquing my curiosity.

"Really?"

"You can't even imagine. Think of a soldier, a proud warrior, a merciless executioner, and you'll have the exact picture of what Evan was like before he met you. You put a new light in his eyes. You brought him back to life. I've never seen him like this before." Her voice was pensive, as though something she'd said had summoned a memory. "When I found Evan and looked him in the eye for the first time, his face held an emptiness I'll never forget. It was like he'd lost everything, even himself. Over time that look was replaced by a tough, impenetrable mask, but occasionally that original part of him would resurface from behind his armor. You wiped that empty expression off his face forever. It's like he's finally found the place he belongs. When he met you I could see how desperate he was because he couldn't understand what was going on. Deep down, right from the start I knew what would happen, because I recognized the storm of emotions in him that had hit me when I met Simon." She snorted, amused by her own thoughts. "Honestly, I never imagined there could be one speck of romanticism in him. My God!" she exclaimed with a grin.

"Are we talking about the same Evan? He's the sweetest person I could ever hope to meet."

"Only with you," she was quick to say. "He was always a tough guy, a fighter. Nothing could ever stop him, but with you it's different. The way he looks at you, it's . . ."

"Special?" I guessed.

"Unique," Ginevra said.

"That's what I feel for him too," I admitted. Strangely, I wasn't embarrassed any more; having this conversation with Ginevra seemed perfectly normal—comforting even. When she leaned forward to hug me, it was natural and instinctive for me to return the gesture. At the contact I felt the oddest sensation, like the tingle under your skin when you get an electric shock.

I had it all, everything I could ever have wanted. Why did fate want to take it away from me? What had I done to deserve that? Maybe it was the price I had to pay—my life in exchange for everything I'd been granted. I couldn't complain. Wasn't it a fair trade?

"Evan couldn't have chosen better," Ginevra said, releasing me from her hug.

"Gwen—" The unfamiliar name popped out of my mouth.

Ginevra's eyes opened wide, stopping me short. She looked as mystified as I felt. Where had that name come from? And why had Ginevra reacted that way? "Did I say something wrong?" I stammered.

"No, it's just that—one of my Sisters always used to call me that. No one's done it since.

"I'm sorry . . ." I said hesitantly.

"No, that's all right, I'm happy. You can call me that whenever you want. Anyway, what were you going to tell me?"

"I just wanted to say thanks—for everything. This is the first time I finally feel part of something."

Ginevra smiled mischievously. "For the first time, I'd say you've done pretty well. An Angel who's hopelessly in love with you and a Witch and two Executioners who are prepared to do anything to protect you. Can you think of a better team?"

I smiled, running my hand through my hair distractedly. "Definitely not. But what do you say we continue this conversation later on? I could use a shower." All of a sudden I was exhausted. I wanted to feel hot water on my skin, on my neck muscles, my back. I wanted to focus only on my thoughts and be alone to reminisce about this incredible afternoon. The unforgettable memories brought a smile to my lips the instant they reappeared in my mind: Evan's hands on my body, his mouth pressed against mine, his heat against me . . . inside me.

"Oookay!" Ginevra said, interrupting my train of thought. "I think I've heard enough."

I blushed, realizing I'd abandoned myself to more memories than I should have in her presence.

"You deserve five minutes of privacy." She smiled regretfully.

Privacy? Did she even know what the word meant? I smiled to myself and shook my head. "Five minutes? How about twenty?" I said rebelliously, hoping to convince her.

"You know where the spa is." She got up and walked toward the door. "I've already prepared everything."

I blinked in surprise. "Um, when, exactly?"

Ginevra smiled and rested her hand on the doorknob. "Now." She shot me a sly glance and disappeared, leaving the door ajar behind her.

Whenever Ginevra smiled and narrowed her eyes like that, it was incredibly sexy. I wished I had even half her allure. She was gorgeous and you could feel her charisma a mile away—it was so strong it was almost tangible.

I got up from the bed and went down the hall to the spa. The room was built to resemble a cave. The walls were tiled in slabs of sand-colored rock in varying thicknesses while the floor was Rainforest Green, an exquisite green marble from India shot through with brown- and ivory-colored veins that created the impression of being in a forest. At the back of the spa, three steps led into the Jacuzzi built into the rock that sparkled under the recessed lighting. The wall behind the Jacuzzi was also stone, but slanted. Water flowed over the irregular surface like a waterfall. With the exception of the recessed spots above the Jacuzzi, the room was candlelit. Spicy-smelling steam filled the air.

For a moment I considered not sinking into the tub and instead using the glass-stalled shower in the center of the room that was more practical and familiar, but the gentle sound of the flowing water was too inviting for me to ignore. Besides, Ginevra had been so thoughtful to prepare it for me.

I moved into the cloud of steam, dropped my clothes to the floor, and tested the water with one foot. It was scalding hot. Bubbles rose continually to its surface, wafting a delicate floral aroma through the room. I immersed myself completely and found instant relief. The warmth filled me, penetrating my bones.

What a delicious sensation. I lay back and closed my eyes, abandoning myself to my memories. Memories of me and Evan.

VIOLATED EMOTIONS

The Jacuzzi kept the water at a constant temperature, and the heat felt too good on my skin to get out. I'd lost all track of time. Still, it wasn't fair to make Drake replace me just so I could soak in their hot tub all night. I was already taking advantage of him enough. I reluctantly climbed out. There was a red bath towel lying beside the tub; Ginevra had thought of everything. I rubbed my hair dry and wrapped it around my body.

I was bending down to pick up my clothes when a gust of cool air made me shiver. My head shot up and I noticed steam billowing by the door. Someone must have opened it.

"Gin, is that you?" I asked warily, putting on my shoes.

The room seemed empty.

"Didn't anyone ever teach you to lock the door?"

I cringed with embarrassment. "Drake!" I wasn't sure what color my face had turned. He was definitely the last person I'd expected to see there.

"Sorry," he said, his tone solicitous as he came closer, "I shouldn't have barged in like that. Sometimes Ginevra leaves the door open. You know what she's like. I didn't think anyone was in here, and I couldn't have imagined it would be you."

Nervously, I smoothed my hair behind my ear. "No, no," I stammered, "no need to apologize. This is your house. It's my fault I didn't lock the door." *Had I really forgotten to?*

Drake stepped in front of me. I looked away, unable to meet his eyes. Now that I knew about his past, it was as if I were seeing him for the first time. I'd always thought of Drake as the fun one—the carefree, swaggering brother who never took anything seriously. But now, after hearing what had happened to him and knowing what he'd lost, I saw him in a new light. In a way, I felt closer to him than before, as if the feelings that bonded him to Evan were now bonding him to me a little too.

Somewhere inside me I found the courage to look straight at him, and flinched. There was something different in his eyes—a glimmer I'd never seen before—something totally undecipherable. Had he found out that I'd learned about his past?

The heavy wooden door thumped closed.

I tried to say something, but all that came out was an incomprehensible stammer. Regaining control after a few attempts, I said, "I—I . . . I think I'd better go now." The remark hung in the air as I walked around him with my head lowered.

Suddenly he shot out his arm, grabbed my wrist, and jerked me against him. My heart sent me a desperate warning, but it was too late—his mouth was already on mine, soft and parted against my sealed lips. I shoved him away, bewildered when he let go without protesting.

"What the hell is wrong with you?" I shouted. My heart was beating wildly. How could something like this happen? One minute I was lost in the memory of the magical afternoon I'd spent with Evan and the next Drake was kissing me?

His expression turned sly and a flash of cunning appeared in his eyes. "I thought you wanted it too."

My rage boiled up until it burnt my skin. "What? My God, no!" I put both hands to my forehead and pushed back my hair. "Drake, do you realize what you've done? For God's sake, don't you care about Evan?" My eyes suddenly fell to his neck. His dog tag was gone. Was it possible he'd misinterpreted my looks of compassion? Was it possible that what he felt for me could be that different from what I felt for him? "Don't you care about Evan?" I repeated, articulating each word. *Had he even forgotten about his Stella?* I thought, without daring to say it. The strangest thing was the look in Drake's eye. He didn't seem the least bit worried. In fact, he seemed more amused than anything else. His expression irritated me, feeding my anger. How could he thrust his affection for his brother aside so heartlessly? Was it possible he didn't love Evan back? Or even worse, that Evan had never realized it?

"I don't care about anybody."

Drake's cold, merciless voice made my hairs stand on end as his gaze burned into mine. Something behind me near the door caught his attention. I turned around to check but no one was there. Puzzled, I frowned. "Drake, if you think—"

When I turned around again Drake was gone. My words hung in the empty room. He'd disappeared, leaving me alone with my pounding heart. I knew well the nature of what I was feeling and could think of only one word to define it: guilt.

"Gemma, you done?" Ginevra called from the stairs, making me jump. "I heard noises. Everything okay?" I stared into space, petrified, not knowing what to say.

"Gemma?" Ginevra slowly came through the door as I looked blankly at the floor. When I felt her in front of me, I looked up into her eyes.

It took her only a moment to understand everything, to know every detail. We stood there in frozen silence. She continued to stare at me without a word, her eyes bulging. Meanwhile, my heart hadn't stopped galloping.

"No. It's impossible," she hissed, shocked. She wasn't the only one in the room in that state.

I stared at her, anguished, confirming everything. No matter how insane, inconceivable, or unexpected it was, no matter how hard it was for me to believe, it had actually happened. Drake had kissed me.

"It's—it's not so serious," I said, hoping to downplay it. I didn't want a relationship to be ruined because of me.

"Evan's not going to see it that way." Ginevra said it so assuredly it sent me into a panic. My alarmed gaze shot to hers. "You have to tell him," she stated, her tone cold.

The words poured from my mouth at lightning speed. "No! I can't tell him. Neither can you. He would be crushed!"

"But you *have to* tell him." Ginevra articulated each word as if realizing my brain couldn't handle them all at once right now.

"I don't want to ruin what they feel for each other." In my voice, regret, indecision, and frustration battled to prevail.

"You're not the one who ruined it. Drake did, a moment ago."

"Don't you see?" I whispered, feeling devastated. How could I tell Evan without destroying their relationship? I remembered the look in Drake's eye when he'd told me he didn't care about anybody, and shock burned my stomach. For some time now I'd noticed a change in Drake, in the way he stole glances at us. Evan's meeting me must have reopened past wounds and brought back painful memories for him. I couldn't find any better explanation. Everybody makes mistakes. Drake's kiss meant nothing to me and I was sure he'd just acted on impulse, that he already regretted it.

"That doesn't change the seriousness of what he did, and Evan needs to know. If you don't tell him, I will," Ginevra warned without a trace of hesitation in her voice.

"No—all right, but let me be the one to tell him," I said hesitantly, still not sure it was the best thing to do. I just hoped Evan would be able to understand and forgive his brother for doing something so foolish. There was no other way to describe it.

I thought of tonight's plans and a shiver ran through me. At this point, staying there at their house was impossible. I couldn't get Drake to take my place any more, so I had no choice but to go home where I would be in danger.

"Don't worry," Ginevra was quick to say, replying to my thoughts. "Do you think I'd ever leave you all alone?"

"Where is he now?" I asked, thinking of Drake.

"I don't know. I can't sense him or even detect his thoughts. Actually, he's been avoiding me for a while now. It's like he's a ghost," she said, thinking aloud.

"Why didn't you sense him before? When he was here in the spa with me. Before it happened, I mean. Why didn't you stop him?"

"I was downstairs with Simon. We were busy in the workout room. It's soundproofed, remember? Unfortunately it also has an effect on my mind. Somehow it blocks the sound of people's thoughts and"— she smiled to herself—"we were making a lot of noise, if you know what I mean. When I heard something strange I came straight up here to you. In any case, you can relax. He's not here any more."

"Will you stay with me tonight?" I asked, though I already knew the answer.

But Ginevra surprised me. "I can't," she said regretfully.

"What? Why not?" I asked, desperately hoping to make her change her mind.

"If something happened to you, I wouldn't be able to heal you. Trust me, it will be better for Simon to be there instead. If I sense a problem I'll be there in a flash. I can hear his thoughts even from here if I concentrate, whereas he wouldn't be able to hear mine."

"But I'll feel horribly uneasy!" I whimpered just as Simon called to us from the stairs.

Ginevra put her mouth to my ear. "Don't worry. You won't even notice he's there. He won't make you uncomfortable. He'll only be there to protect you."

Standing in the doorway, Simon stared at us with a bewildered look on his face.

Ginevra instantly noticed his reaction to our expressions. "I'll explain later. There's been a change of plans for tonight," she said.

"You mean you don't want a rematch any more?" he said, grinning.

"You're obsessed!" I said to her, amazed.

Ginevra shot me a glance and spoke under her breath, as if that would be enough for Simon not to hear her. "He's lying. He knows perfectly well I outdid him."

My bedroom ceiling looked so unfamiliar, a million miles away from what in a few months had become my new world. Evan's house had become a hideaway even more comforting than my own home. Or maybe it was his absence that made my room seem so cold and empty.

Gripped with anxiety, I tossed and turned under the covers, unable to fall asleep. I recalled Drake's face so close to mine, how ardently he'd pulled me against him, like I belonged to him. During that brief moment, I'd gotten the impression I'd never known him, that I didn't even know who he was. And yet he was still Drake, Evan's fun-loving brother, the only one who never worried about anything. How on earth had it even occurred to him? Why had he kissed me? Maybe what made me angriest was that tonight all I should have been thinking about was the incredible afternoon I'd spent with Evan. I should have been losing myself in the memory of the two of us locked in an embrace amid a thousand fireflies of light, making love as if we were in a dream. Instead, all I could think of was Drake and the fierce look on his face when he pressed his lips against mine. For a moment I was relieved Ginevra wasn't there listening to my thoughts.

I couldn't believe Drake had kissed me. As if that wasn't enough, I couldn't think of a good way to break it to Evan—because there *was* no good way. Still, I had no choice. I knew I wasn't to blame for what had happened, so why did I feel so responsible about their relationship possibly being ruined forever?

Where would I find the courage to tell Evan his best friend had betrayed him? How could I avoid the irreparable damage? It takes two to tango—I was aware of that—but inside me I didn't feel at all complicit in what Drake had done. From that perspective I hadn't betrayed Evan. When you truly love someone you can't imagine desiring anyone except that person.

My eyelids grew heavy and relief washed over me. Falling asleep would finally hush the deafening echo of those exhausting thoughts.

Another blink of my eyelashes, this one softer and slower. I couldn't see Simon but I knew he was there and his presence made me feel safe. The light from my bedside lamp dimmed and went out and the darkness swallowed up my thoughts. "Good night, Simon," I murmured, my lips barely moving.

"Good night." The whisper floated through the dark room, but I was already asleep.

PREMONITIONS

The ice-cold air slashed my skin like a blade. I felt it on my cheeks while my hot breath hid my mouth in puffs of white vapor. I didn't know what I was running from or where I was headed, but I ran and ran, dodging the trees. I was tired, my body was about to give up, and yet a little voice in my head kept me from stopping. I knew if I did it would be the end of me. Someone was chasing me—I sensed their presence, heard their breathing among the trees.

Without slowing my pace, I looked over my shoulder. No one was there, but I *knew* he had come to kill me. When I looked forward again the sky had grown brighter. A moment later I noticed that the thick treetops were no longer blocking it. I'd left the forest behind.

I slowed down, realizing I'd been in this place before. I frowned at the sight of Evan's car on the side of the road. Filled with the sensation that something wasn't right, I continued to run toward it. When I was quite near, my heart turned over; the front end of the car was crumpled around the broken guardrail. I put my hands to my mouth. The Ferrari was totaled.

Desperate, I ran up to it, a burning ache in my chest. My heart beat fast, outstripping the tempo of my footsteps on the asphalt. The closer I got, the more tightly terror clenched my stomach.

I stopped and walked toward the driver's window. Shards of glass were everywhere. They crunched beneath my feet. Someone was in the car. I drew closer, stunned, and my heart throbbed in my temples with a wild, unsteady beat. When I recognized the head that lay motionless on the steering wheel, all the blood drained from my face.

It was Evan.

Unable to breathe, I tried to keep myself from fainting as I saw the streaks of blood on Evan's face dripping onto the road in a scarlet puddle. I felt all my muscles trembling—small, uncontrollable spasms that turned my blood to ice. It couldn't be true. I was horrified by the pain—so devastated, so drained that not even my tears could find their way out, lost in my endless torment.

I reached out a trembling hand and gently pushed him back into the driver's seat. His head fell back, revealing his face, and an onslaught of emotions shot through me. But when I took a closer look at the bloodstained face, the most powerful emotion I felt was relief.

It wasn't Evan—it was Drake.

The pain vanished as quickly as it had come, replaced by confusion. A whisper drifted through the air and brushed my ear—a sweet sound, like a deep sigh. I let myself be distracted, distanced from everything else. It filled me. I felt as if it could carry me away from there.

Then I remembered Drake and shook my head, but something strange bothered me when I turned around to look at him again. I took a step back, confused by the old, dark-gray conveyance that had taken the place of the Ferrari.

His burned and blackened body was in his warplane. Blood covered his face and what was left of the shattered windshield. Gripped in his hand were the two dog tags he wore around his neck.

No. He wasn't dead. His body was still quivering, his lips barely moving.

"Ste—Stella," he gasped. My heart went ice cold. His body slumped over the controls, lifeless. The entire side of the plane was riddled with bullet holes, more than I'd seen before.

A pungent, metallic smell filled my nostrils. I looked around, disoriented, and heard the sigh once again. It felt like it was inside me; I sensed it in every fiber of my being, like it belonged to me. Some part of me recognized it. I could feel the breath on me almost tangibly. It was so intense I turned my head to follow it.

My eyes met the gaze of a woman who stood there perfectly still, staring at me.

I heard the sound again and flinched: it was my name, shrouded in a soothing murmur. It was coming from inside me, in my head, my thoughts, my gut. The sound was everywhere.

For a moment I looked into the woman's electric-blue eyes as the wind made her long hair billow behind her. It was black, with white tips. The energy she emanated was so intense and hypnotic that it took me a moment to notice the hundreds of dead bodies piled one atop the other on the dry earth beneath our feet. Everywhere I looked were lifeless bodies.

"Naiad . . ." My name echoed through my thoughts again like a melody wafted on the wind. The woman stood there, her eyes fixed on me. Her eyes were ice, yet so comforting at the same time.

A moan caught my attention. My thoughts flew to Drake and I instinctively turned to look for him, but immediately felt as if someone had stabbed me in the heart. The plane had disappeared, as had Drake. In their place once again was the twisted wreckage of Evan's car, but this time it was me behind the wheel, lying in a pool of blood.

I tried to breathe but the air was trapped in my throat. I began to sob. Trembling like a leaf, I moved closer to see if maybe it wasn't true, it wasn't really me. As I looked at the body, spasms of terror gripped me and the voice whispered my name again. Horrified, I couldn't tear my eyes away from the face in front of me: my own, splattered with blood.

Suddenly its eyes opened wide, making me jump.

I tried to scream, but suddenly found myself in my bedroom, gasping for air. Remembering all the blood, I touched my forehead. It was wet. I checked my fingers that trembled before my terrified eyes, afraid I would find them tinged with scarlet, but my fingertips were only beaded with sweat. Then why was my heart still pounding? Why had I had to dream not only of my own death but the deaths of the others as well?

I took a deep breath and told myself it had just been another nightmare. I always had them when Evan left me on my own.

It was dark outside the window. I nervously checked my alarm clock and saw it was only four in the morning. Under other circumstances that would have been a relief because it meant I had more time to sleep. That night, however, the thought of closing my eyes again terrified me; another nightmare awaited me, I was sure of it. But still, I was so tired.

I tossed and turned under the covers but couldn't fall asleep. I noticed a faint light just above my bedside table and remembered Simon must be somewhere in the room, watching over me. The thought calmed me a little.

His voice echoed from the ceiling as if he'd heard me. "Everything okay?"

"I've had better nights." I heard him chuckle in the darkness.

"I'm sorry Evan isn't here in my place," he admitted, sounding sincerely regretful.

"No, it's all right," I was quick to reply. "It's not your fault he's not here."

No matter how much I missed Evan, I was happy his family was so protective of me. From the bottom of my heart I appreciated that Simon was here, willing to confront my enemy in order to protect me.

"You were tossing and turning the whole night." Simon fell silent for a long moment, making me think he'd finished speaking, but then he continued. "I can protect you, but there's nothing I can do about your nightmares. I can't help you with those."

Judging from his rueful tone, I must have been seriously restless.

"Those aren't your fault either. Don't worry about it," I said, not wanting him to feel bad.

His reply took me by surprise. "He would rather be here instead of me too, and it's not his fault that he isn't."

"I know."

"No, maybe you don't, actually. I know Evan really well. I was there when we found him and we've been together ever since." He paused for a few seconds. "What we do—" He hesitated again. A movement in the half-light caught my attention and my eyes darted to the window. Simon was standing there, staring outside. He seemed to be searching for words as I watched his silhouette shrouded in darkness. "I understand it might seem frightening, but if you look at it from the right perspective it actually isn't so terrible." He turned toward me. "Our task is to free the spirit from the body in which it's trapped so it can return to where it belongs. Humans see death as the end of everything—I was human once and well remember the feeling—but it's not. Not for you. For you mortals, it's only the beginning."

He stared out the window again as I listened in silence. I'd never thought about the fact that Evan's brothers were going through the same kind of suffering he was. They had been condemned to the same fate, but neither Evan nor even Simon had reason to complain. At least not as much as their brother. Drake was alone, condemned to Earth forever, forced to give up Stella, the woman he loved. It must be terrible for him.

The thought made me remember the night before and a shiver ran down my spine. How could I take away the only thing he had left—his family's love? I shook my head to banish the thought. I was about to pick up our conversation where we'd left off, but Simon spoke first. "In any case, it's not up to us. We must act against our will. We're not the ones who decide."

"Who does, then?" I asked uneasily.

"Orders are imposed on us." His tone was hard, as if intentionally avoiding an unspeakable secret.

"By *whom?*" I insisted firmly. I'd never broached the subject with Evan, having always had the impression it was something better left unsaid. Or maybe I simply hadn't been brave enough. With Simon, on the other hand, it all seemed much simpler.

"By the Elders," he replied, looking me in the eye.

"You guys always seem afraid to talk about them, but who are the Elders, anyway? What do they have to do with all this? And above all, how do you know what they want you to do?" The intimacy created by the dim light made me brave and I finally gave my curiosity free rein.

"We just know, that's all. We feel it inside, like intrinsic knowledge, a thought coming from our own minds. They communicate with us even if we can't hear them. It's as though they insert the information directly into our heads."

"Is it the same for everyone?"

"From the first time we eat of the tree. Many of us don't survive, but those who do are acknowledged—it's as if a connection is created—and we begin to serve them. The Elders never intervene personally. They send us out instead to make sure each person on Earth meets the destiny that's been ordained for him or her. No one has ever seen them—or more accurately, those who have didn't survive long enough to tell the tale."

My heart pounded harder as I realized I'd paved the way to finally asking the question I'd been harboring for some time, too terrified to hear the answer. "Simon?" My voice trembled as I said his name. "Why do you think I have to die?"

His eyes wavered, avoiding mine. "I can't answer that." For a moment, the silence drowned out every sound. "But there's a reason for it. Nothing happens by chance."

I stared at the floor, thinking about what he'd said. I honestly couldn't imagine what good my death might do.

Simon interrupted my thoughts. "The Elders were chosen to maintain order, to determine who is to return. They're the ones who make the decisions, but none of us know the reasons behind their choices."

"What happens to the people who don't redeem themselves, the ones who can't return?"

I'd never seen Simon so serious before. The dim light cast a grim, mysterious halo on his face. "We don't receive orders for them."

"What happens to them?" I insisted.

"They become slaves."

The darkness in his eyes made me shudder. A bitter instinct warned me not to travel further down that path because it led through a minefield. And yet there was another part of me, hidden somewhere deep inside and thirsty for more knowledge, that made me go on. "Why didn't they find me before? All these months, what kept the Elders from finding out I wasn't dead yet? Can't they see everything?"

"No, they're not omniscient. They send us out to make sure destiny has been fulfilled. We're the arm of Death, the shadow of fate."

"But who are *they*, exactly?" I hoped Simon would stop dodging the question and finally tell me.

Seeming to summon his courage, he looked at me. "They're the Màsala," he explained, his tone so serious it sent a shiver down my spine. "No one dares speak their name. It's as if it's forbidden among us: an unwritten rule. They're the purest angels, members of the Order, a dark, secret brotherhood as old as the world itself. It might seem paradoxical, but they're the messengers God uses as instruments to implement His plan, celestial creatures appointed by the Supreme Being to maintain order in the universe. Long ago they were called devas. Some call them *those first to come* and for others they're the ancients or the elders. You humans call them archangels."

I shivered. After all the bizarre experiences I'd been through over the last few months, it was strange to feel all this emotion at just one word. It was easy to pretend nothing existed, that the spiritual realm wasn't real but just a figment of the human imagination built up over the centuries and handed down as law. God, archangels . . . Eden. But then, when reality finally hit you, no matter how insane or shocking it might seem, there was no denying it—all you could do was accept it and tremble.

Simon's silhouette began to fade before I had the chance to figure out if it was him or if I was starting to fall asleep again. I lay down face up on the mattress. As my eyelids struggled to stay open I heard Simon's smooth, gentle voice in my ears: "Now get some rest."

A BURDENED HEART

My legs tangled in the sheets as I rolled over and a moan of pain escaped me. It felt like something was forcing my head down into the pillow.

"Finally!" Evan's cheerful voice brought me back to reality, but all I could do was let out another moan. I glanced out the window, my eyes still half closed, but couldn't understand if it was too early or too late.

"What time is it?" I grumbled, raising my torso slightly.

"Five in the afternoon."

I shot bolt upright as if someone had thrown a bucket of ice water on me. Evan's sweet eyes met mine and the walls of the room closed in around me, crushing me.

Suddenly I remembered everything. Evan noticed the change in my expression and misunderstood. "Did you have another nightmare?" he asked with concern.

I took a moment to answer. "I think so, but I'm not really sure any more." Last night's terrible dream—so distant now—had lost all importance in comparison with the real world, which would definitely be far more grueling.

"Gemma, is something the matter?"

His eyes probed mine again and I looked away. The devastating memory of yesterday throbbed in my temples. It felt as if the secret had taken shape inside me and was trying to get out with every heartbeat as I struggled to force it back down. It was a massive boulder between us, one that couldn't elude Evan's notice for much longer. I couldn't hide the truth from him. I had to find a way to tell him everything.

He looked at me, puzzled, and I tried to pick up the conversation where we'd left off. "I must have dreamed something terrible." Deep down it wasn't a lie. I tightened my lips and stared down at my bare knees. I couldn't even bring myself to look him in the eye.

"I'm sorry." He caressed my cheek. When I felt his touch, I closed my eyes, tears stinging beneath my eyelids. After taking a deep breath I tried to speak but my voice trembled. Evan noticed and seemed to misunderstand yet again.

"This always happens when you're gone," I explained, referring to the nightmares. Actually, I couldn't remember my dream any more except for a few fragments that were already fading. The real world was what frightened me the most now. The thought of Drake's lips on mine and how Evan would react to the news was worse than any nightmare I could imagine.

When you love someone, you open up to them completely—you give them your heart and your entire being. You think you can tell them everything, no matter what, but it's only when you discover how much the truth can hurt them that you realize how difficult it is to face it. But you have to do it all the same, because lies are huge boulders blocking the path that unites you—boulders destined to grow larger and which you're bound to trip over. The larger they are, the smaller your chances of getting up and moving forward.

"How long have you been here?" I asked to distract him from the conclusions he must have been drawing. From the way he'd narrowed his eyes I could tell he realized something was wrong.

"A while." He smiled again, boosting my spirits. "I took over for Simon at dawn."

"Why didn't you wake me up?" I protested, embarrassed about having slept so late.

"I wanted to," he admitted. "There were times when I couldn't resist and came over to wake you, but then I went back and sat down again. You looked so tired," he whispered, sitting on the bed and leaning toward me. His mouth brushed mine. "I missed you."

I tensed, self-loathing filling me. The last lips on mine had been Drake's.

No! I couldn't react like this! I couldn't let this thing come between us. Not now, right when everything was going so well, not after making love with Evan.

"Everything's going to be fine," he whispered, resting his forehead on mine, again misunderstanding my tension.

"I have a headache, that's all." I forced a smile as my heart pounded in anticipation of confessing everything. "Where are my parents? How come they didn't wake me up for lunch?" I asked, so confused I couldn't even remember what day it was.

"We convinced them you were eating at my place. They didn't even notice you were still here."

"*We* convinced them?" I asked with alarm.

Evan smiled. "Drake gave me a hand. Sometimes I can barely—"

My heart lurched. "Drake was here?" Aghast, I felt the blood drain from my face.

Evan frowned, disconcerted by my reaction.

"You should have woken me up," I said sternly.

So they'd seen each other.

"You needed to rest," he replied. "Yesterday was a tough day for you, Gemma. Too much happened."

More than he could imagine, actually.

"Simon told me you'd had nightmares so I made sure you slept in soundly."

I couldn't object. My last few hours of sleep had been deep and dreamless. Forcing another smile, I tried to banish the thought of Drake from my mind, at least for a while. "So how many did you kill off last night?" I asked bluntly in an awkward attempt to normalize things, but even I was shocked by the bitterness of my sarcasm.

Evan frowned and I struggled to decipher his expression. He was right—this wasn't like me. "S-sorry, it sounded funny in my mind and obviously it wasn't." Grimacing with regret, I nervously ran my hand through my hair. What was happening to me? Why was it so hard to utter the simple words that continued to scream inside my head?

"Feel like going for a drive?" I asked out of the blue. "I could use some fresh air." Evan nodded, still bewildered.

I went to the bathroom, turned on the tap, and splashed scalding-hot water on my face. Still trembling, I clutched the rim of the sink. For a minute I stood there staring at my reflection, almost not recognizing myself. Then, resigned, I continued to wash up.

I had to find a way to make the weight in my stomach go away. I couldn't bear to see the worried look on Evan's face. Who knew what was going through his mind. I hated myself for never having learned to hide my emotions. If something made me happy or upset, trying to hide it was hopeless. Anyone could see it.

When I walked back into the bedroom, Evan's expression relaxed and a roguish smile appeared on his face. All it took was one glimpse of his eyes to understand his intentions. I hadn't gotten dressed yet. I raised an eyebrow and let the towel I was holding fall to the floor. My camisole matched my scarlet panties. Their lace edging was similar to the lace on the black panties I'd had on yesterday at the hideaway and aroused a dangerous look of interest in Evan's eye. I'd never worn these before, but last night I'd almost instinctively searched for them in my underwear drawer, knowing Evan would be there when I woke up.

He watched me as though he'd forgotten the rest of the world, as though only I existed. Taking my hand, he pulled me gently against him, brushing a lock of hair from my face. "Sure you want to go for a drive?" he whispered, his dark eyes on mine.

I looked down again, unable to hold his gaze for more than a few seconds. "I—I think we'd better." I pulled away, leaving him with his hand in midair at the height of my cheek. Out of the corner of my eye I saw his arm drop to his side and his expression turn blank. Our eyes met and I forced a smile.

"Does this have something to do with what happened between us yesterday?" His disappointed, hesitant tone floored me, hitting me straight in the heart. I blinked nervously. This couldn't be happening. Evan had misunderstood in the worst possible way.

"No!" I exclaimed instantly. "What are you thinking?" I went and took his hand. What on earth was I doing? How could I let this terrible secret ruin this moment?

"What's wrong, then?" he asked, exasperation in his voice. "You're so strange today and—"

"You were right. Too much happened to me yesterday." My voice broke on the last words. "More than you realize. You have no idea how I feel."

"Shh," Evan said, cutting me off and pulling me to him. He wrapped his arms around me again in an intimate embrace and I let myself be enveloped in his warmth. I could do it. I had to tell him. I'd finally found an opening to release the poison. I looked into his eyes . . . and sank back down into the pit. Why did this have to be so difficult?

"You can tell me about it later if you feel like it. Let's get out of here."

Part of me had yearned to hear him say just that. Somehow, putting it off was the most tempting solution, though I knew it would only prolong my torment.

"Feel like seeing what the others are up to?" Evan asked, behind the wheel of the BMW. Scenes from the nightmare suddenly reappeared distinctly in my mind, jumbled with images of reality. I shuddered at the thought of his Ferrari at the bottom of the lake.

"Or we could spend some time alone," I put in, instantly alarmed by his suggestion. I wanted to stay as far from their place as possible. What was even more important was to make sure Drake was far enough away when I told Evan. I honestly couldn't imagine how he would take it. Deep in my heart, I hoped to find a way to make the confession less bitter. I didn't want Evan to be mad at his brother forever, and Drake's presence wouldn't help the situation.

Evan smiled at my proposal, once again misunderstanding my intentions. This time, though, I went along with it.

Immersed in my private nightmare, I hadn't realized Evan had already pulled into his driveway. I squirmed in my seat. "I thought we'd decided to be alone." I tried to hide my nervousness but there was a hint of reproach in my voice.

Evan leaned toward me, his lips curved in a pleased smile. "I just need to get a few things," he whispered, kissing me before I could reply. "If you can hold out." He got out of the car and opened my door.

"I'll—I'll wait here," I stammered sheepishly. I didn't want reality to come crashing down on me because I'd probably end up crushed. I wasn't ready yet.

"Don't be silly," he said.

I got out of the car and immediately went into panic mode. My breath grew short as we walked, my heartbeat accelerating as the distance to the front door lessened. I heaved a sigh of relief when I found the living room empty and silent. Still, with them you could never tell when they'd turn up. I hoped Evan would be quick. I tapped my foot, enduring the nerve-racking wait. Drake might appear at any moment—or maybe he was already there and I didn't know it. I waited for Evan in the kitchen, anxiously peering around the empty room.

Ginevra came up behind me with feline stealth, making me jump out of my shoes. "Hey! You scared me half to death!" I accused her.

"Or maybe you're just a little on edge?" she asked, her glacial eyes trained on mine. I half closed my eyes under her searching gaze. Aware that she was probing me, I desperately tried to raise a wall between our minds. "What?! You haven't told him yet?"

"Told me what?" Evan appeared behind her, looking puzzled.

My heart skipped a beat. My eyelids fluttered from the strain and I felt myself being dragged down into a dark vortex from which there would be no escape. I felt Evan's impatient gaze on me but didn't have the courage to face him.

"What's she supposed to tell me?" Evan repeated.

Ginevra sensed my hesitation and looked him straight in the eye. "That Drake kissed her."

The words struck me in the chest like an arrow shot straight at my heart.

Evan's eyes, as gray as a stormy sky, sliced through me. For a moment I felt like a ghost of ice, invisible to his gaze. A shudder ran down my spine.

"Evan," I murmured. He stood paralyzed in front of me.

Ginevra clearly hadn't expected this reaction from him because she suddenly looked alarmed. "Evan, calm down," she whispered.

His expression was indecipherable to me but she knew exactly what was going through his mind. I would have given anything to be in her place right now. No—actually, I wasn't sure I really wanted to know.

"There's no need for that, Evan!" his sister said, her voice turning loud and harsh. My heart beat wildly. Without saying a word, Evan rolled his hands into fists and clenched his jaw, his eyes narrowing to menacing slits.

The only one privy to his intentions, Ginevra continued to beg him to calm down but her voice had grown faint in my ears, drowned out by the deafening panic that threatened to crush me. Abruptly, she fell silent.

Evan was furious. His implacable rage frightened me. He seemed as hard as ice and ready to kill. All at once he vanished, leaving us in the silence of the kitchen. Ginevra and I looked at each other and for a moment I thought I saw my panic reflected in her eyes.

"What's going on?!" I cried in alarm.

"Simon!" she shouted into the empty room.

A second later Simon appeared beside us. "You told him," he guessed, looking nervous.

"It's worse than I imagined," she said.

"Would you mind telling me what's going on?" I wanted to shout, but all that came out of my mouth was a hysterical noise. *It's worse than you imagined?* What the hell did that mean?

Ginevra's gaze sliced through me and she said the last thing I wanted to hear: "He went to find Drake." My body froze from head to toe.

"We've got to hurry," Simon spoke up, heading for the door.

Moments later the wheels of his car were skidding through the gravel. I was terrified and in shock. I wanted to be mad at Ginevra for telling Evan the truth so abruptly, because I hadn't been ready to face his reaction, but deep down I was relieved she'd lifted the burden from my heart.

"How do we find them?" I asked, torn with anxiety.

"He went to Roomer's," Simon replied.

"The night club? How do you know?" I asked, my nervousness growing.

"That's where Drake is."

"But I can't go in there!" I said in alarm. "I'm underage."

Simon's eyes narrowed in the rearview mirror. "Consider it one of the advantages of being with us," he said, flashing me a charming smile.

The car sideslipped on the asphalt, cutting the curves in half, as I chewed the inside of my cheek.

"He's there," Ginevra said, clearly picking up on Evan's thoughts through the distance.

Simon slammed on the brakes. "He's angry. My God, he's absolutely enraged. But I don't sense Drake."

"What do we do?" I said timidly, my nerves on edge.

Once again, it was Simon who answered. "Gemma, come with me. Maybe you can talk some sense into him." His face was grave.

When Ginevra opened the passenger door, Simon turned and glowered at her. "Stay here," he ordered, his face set. I'd never heard him speak to her so sternly before.

"Simon, the place is full of people. He's not going to do anything stupid," she said.

"He's dangerous. I can feel his energy and I don't know if he'll be able to control it. You need to stay here," he growled.

Following my impulse to rush toward the door, I left them behind. A bouncer stood there staring at me. I was afraid he was about to stop me, but he unexpectedly stepped aside and let me through. I turned around. Simon was a few steps behind me, his eyes locked on the bouncer's. The door opened just in time for me to see Drake standing by the pool tables and Evan charging him with unrestrained violence.

I shouted Evan's name, but he seemed to see nothing except Drake. My shout did, however, draw the attention of everyone else in the club. They turned to watch the scene as Evan shoved Drake against the wall, which cracked beneath the blow. A murmur spread through the room.

I sensed Simon's tension. He stood at my side as still as a statue. His hopes that Evan might stop if I was there had gone up in smoke and he clearly didn't know what to do. There were too many people there to intervene. Suddenly he stepped between the two, struggling to hold Evan back. "Evan!" he shouted, attempting to get his attention, but he was entirely focused on Drake. "Evan, you've got to calm down. Now!" he ordered firmly. "Look around you." Simon's eyes burned into his brother's. "We're not alone," he whispered. At this point Evan's gaze shifted to Simon's and he seemed to see him for the first time.

I was still trembling. For a moment no one in the club moved, as if they were all holding their breath. Drake stood there, his back pressed against the wall as Evan's eyes shot back to him. He was still irate, but he seemed to have snapped out of it. Evan leaned in and Simon moved his shoulder aside to let him. Drake's eyes were glued to Evan's, their faces inches apart. "I never want to see you again," Evan said between clenched teeth, his expression murderous.

His brother tilted his head in an unspoken challenge, never taking his eyes off Evan, who turned and walked out without even looking at me. It hit me straight in the heart.

He was mad at me too.

Simon and I exchanged worried glances. He slipped his hand into his pocket, pulled out a big wad of bills, and rested it on the bar before the owner's surprised face. "For the damages," he added, looking him steadily in the eye. "This should cover it."

The man reached over and picked up the money without saying a word. I was sure that soon no one in the club would remember anything of what had happened.

I came out of the club just in time to see Evan get behind the wheel of the BMW. I walked up to the car and he glanced at me through the window, then nodded for me to get in. I searched Simon and Ginevra's faces for their approval.

"He wants to be alone with you," Ginevra said encouragingly. "See you later." I hesitated a moment, staring at Evan in the driver's seat waiting for me, then opened the car door and got in, fearing the worst. The BMW left Lake Placid as the failing light around us magnified our silence. For a while, neither of us so much as breathed.

"So that's why," Evan said, his tone grave and his eyes on the road.

I looked down to gather my thoughts. "I didn't know how to tell you. I didn't want to ruin what you two have between you."

"Ruin what we have between us?" he said bitterly, turning my words around on me. My heartbeat faltered when I heard the resentment in his tone. "I thought we had a deal: no secrets," he growled, his anger superseded now by disappointment.

It was more than I could bear. "Evan, I wanted to tell you and I would have! It was just so difficult. You've got to believe me!" He shot me a glance. "It all happened so unexpectedly. He caught me off guard." I stopped short, realizing that if I kept defending myself like this I would only be making things worse for Drake. "You saw how nervous I was. I could never have kept it a secret from you. And I didn't intend to."

Again, silence. It was even harder to bear.

"Say something, please?" I begged.

His expression was stony. It was dark out now, but as I looked out the window I recognized the small, steep road Evan turned onto. A moment later, the car stopped.

"Why are we here?" I looked around, confused. Now that darkness had fallen, the long, arid field where we'd been the day before made me shiver. As I got out of the car, Evan, who was already at my side, sensed my tension and squeezed my hand. The warmth of his skin eased my nerves.

"Don't worry," he whispered, his face serious.

I'd missed his sweet, protective tone of voice. For a second tears of relief filled my eyes. I'd been worried this would go miserably, but maybe he wasn't so mad at me after all.

I followed him into the hangar. A faint light flickered on as we entered. We passed the plane and I lingered by its tail, looking straight into Evan's eyes. "You need to tell me what you're thinking," I said. It was an order, but it came out as a plea.

Evan stifled a humorless chuckle. Disappointment was plain on his face, and no matter how self-centered the thought was, I hoped his resentment was directed only at Drake. "What do you imagine I'm thinking?" he said bitterly.

"Still angry?" I asked warily.

"Angry? I'm beyond angry." His eyes burned. "But not with you," he added. His tone softened, as did his face.

"I'm sorry. I would never have wanted something like this to happen, but I'm sure you'll manage to forgive Drake and everything will go back to normal," I promised, but it was only my hope talking.

"Nothing will ever go back to normal. Drake is out for good," he said sternly.

"You can't be serious," I said, though in his eyes I could see the reflection of the proud warrior Ginevra had talked about.

"Why can't I?" he shot back.

"He did something stupid, that's true, but try to imagine what he's going through. You have me, and Simon has Ginevra. Drake, on the other hand, lost the person he loved forever! Don't you think that's a lot for him to deal with? Besides, everyone deserves a second chance," I said decisively.

"You're too good a person, Gemma." His tone made it sound almost like a rebuke, but then his voice softened. He came up and wrapped his arms around my waist. "But I don't care about anyone but you."

"Not even your brother?"

Evan tensed. "No. Not even him. He made his decision. And every decision entails a sacrifice." His tone was cold.

I couldn't stand to see this rupture separate them forever, not if I was the cause. And yet, no matter how hard Evan tried to appear stoic, I could see a glimmer of pain in his eyes that he was clearly struggling to force down. Yes, with time Evan would forgive Drake. I would do everything in my power to make that happen.

"There's just one thing I need to ask you." His eyes studied me intensely as he stroked my cheek with his thumb. I looked at him, puzzled by his afflicted expression. "I already know what you're going to say but I need to hear you say it," he whispered warily.

"What?" I lowered my head at the touch of his fingers so he would caress me a second time. It was good to feel him so close again. Actually, he always had been—I was the one who'd raised a wall between us.

"When Drake—when he kissed you," he began, forcing out the words, "what did you feel?"

I exhaled all the air I'd been holding in my lungs. *Evan was jealous.* Was he actually worried I'd felt even the slightest thing for Drake? I found the very thought ridiculous. Of course, he couldn't know that. He couldn't read what I had in my head or my heart. He couldn't know he would always be the only one to make it beat. The sight of him right now, his eyes glued to mine, anxious to hear my answer, filled my heart with tenderness.

As he waited for my answer, perfectly still, I leaned in and brushed my lips against his. I couldn't think of a better reply. I rubbed his nose gently with my own and shot him a mischievous glance. "Let me get this straight," I whispered slowly, a fraction of an inch from his mouth. "You want to know if I felt the same heat that burns my skin when *you're* near me?" I stared at his mouth and looked into his eyes again. "If I felt the electricity that runs through my body when your mouth"—I stroked his lip with my finger—"is on mine?" I kissed him.

Evan stood there, under my spell. When I moved to one side his mouth followed me, wanting more. This time I was directing the game. "Or"—as I looked him in the eyes I slowly took his hands and slid them down my body to my hips—"when your hands touch me . . ." Evan gripped my waist, slipping his fingers under the hem of my shirt. ". . . and it makes me lose my mind?" I whispered as he half closed his eyes, breathing deeply, holding back.

I'd created an electrical current between us that tingled on the surface of our bodies. I felt his desire for me and wanted him just as intensely. Slowly moving my mouth to his without touching it, I allowed our lips to linger a fraction of an inch apart. The longer I delayed, as if contact were forbidden, the wilder its lack made me feel. My heart pounded in my throat with impatience. My instinct was urging me to kiss him like never before, but I made myself repress the primitive impulse, bend it to my will—and the tension grew even greater.

Our lips touched, just barely. The accumulated energy surged through my body, igniting everything inside me. I brushed my mouth against his again, this time a little longer, but when I pulled away his lips followed me avidly and his hands grasped me firmly by the hips, refusing to let me go.

Something exploded inside me. I wouldn't be able to control myself much longer, but Evan couldn't resist another second. His mouth was on mine, hastening my loss of control. He swept me up off the floor. I instinctively wrapped my legs around his waist, my lips on his the whole time. My head was spinning.

"I wasn't joking when I said it: you're all mine," he breathed directly onto my mouth. He buried his face in my neck and the contact sent another electrical charge—wilder and more powerful—racing through me, melting me. Evan locked his fierce gaze on me. "No one else is allowed to touch you," he whispered, tender and commanding at the same time, as if his words were law. His tone made me even dizzier. It was still hard for me to believe Evan could be jealous on my account, and the sensation sent a delicious tingle through every fiber of my body. I was his. Inside, I knew it couldn't be otherwise, but it was exciting to hear him say what he'd just said.

I surrendered to his arms as he slowly laid me down, one hand under the small of my back and the other caressing my hip. I sank into something soft. It felt strange, and I realized it wasn't the floor, but I was too wrapped up in Evan to care.

"I want to be with you and no one else," I whispered against his lips, my breathing ragged.

His mouth slid down my neck and I glimpsed the military fabric beneath us, piled into a fleecy cloud of green cloth. His lips didn't stop moving against mine for a second and I let myself be guided, giving in to all their decisions. As his hands moved over my body, unfastening my clothing, I grabbed his shirt and pulled it off him. My body was in flames. The only thing left between us was a single thin layer of fabric.

As Evan prolonged his kiss, his hand continued to roam over me. For a moment his fingers fastened on the lace of my scarlet panties as though he wanted to rip them off me and was trying to restrain himself.

I burned with a fire that couldn't be quenched—not as long as Evan was there on top of me, fanning the flames. Not as long as he continued to press me against him with a sensual single-mindedness that drove me out of my mind. My lips were warm from his breath.

His hand slipped down my back and into my panties, clasping my rear as he kissed me passionately. He pulled down the silky fabric and I felt his knee press against my thigh in a gentle but firm movement that brought down the last of my defenses. And then he was inside me, triggering a hot shiver that swept me into a world of pure sensation. Fire burned beneath my skin—a fire that consumed me. My body trembled, exploding in a wave of pleasure that filled me all the way down to my toes. The flames invaded every part of me. I was burning, consumed in a blaze of passion.

"Jamie," Evan whispered. No one except him had ever called me that.

I let myself drift away on the current of electricity and his voice enveloped me like warm velvet as his mouth set my neck on fire.

"Marry me."

A tingle ran over my skin, taking me to heaven again.

They say your first time is the one you never forget. I couldn't figure out why no one ever mentioned the second or the third because from what I'd already experienced, forgetting such a powerful emotion would be inconceivable. I was also sure that making love with Evan would be just as unforgettable every single time. Forever. There was no way I could touch the moon and return to earth without remembering it. Sometimes, afraid someone up there might notice and decide that so much happiness was too much for just one person, I tried to make myself repress the emotions and keep them locked up inside. But then my eyes would meet Evan's and I would betray myself.

"I wasn't kidding, you know." His voice sent a tingle straight to my heart. Had I really not just imagined his words? Had he actually asked me what I thought he had? "I want you to be my wife, Gemma. I want it more than anything else in the world," he whispered, stroking my ear with the tip of his nose.

"Evan—" My throat was tight with emotion as I looked into his tender gaze.

"We'll do it in secret. Simon will marry us and when you're eighteen we can tell everyone. I don't care who else knows it; I just want to exchange vows with you before God," he murmured as the intensity in his eyes made me melt. "Wait—I don't want you to answer right away. I've had time enough to realize that my life used to be meaningless. Now that I've found you I don't need any more time. Still, I know it might be different for you. I'm just asking you to consid—"

I passionately sealed his lips with my own as tears filled my eyes. "I don't need time to realize you're the most important thing to me, Evan," I sighed, resting my forehead on his. "If I had only one day left to live, I would want to spend it with you."

Evan pulled my hip and rolled me on top of him. My hair hung down, forming a curtain around us that shut out the rest of the world. We both smiled, our lips still touching. The feeling in my chest was so intense it almost hurt.

"I've been thinking about it for a while now. I wish I could have done things right—with a ring and everything. I wasn't planning on what happened with Drake last night."

"It's already perfect," I whispered. "I don't need a ring. I already have you—I don't need anything else."

"No, I want to give you my mother's ring." Evan looked into my eyes. "It's belonged to my family for a long time. It would mean a lot to me if you wore it from that day on, forever."

"Evan, I—" His words and penetrating gaze were so intense that for a moment they left me speechless. "It's really too much."

"You mean the ring or my proposal? You still haven't given me an answer, you know." He smiled.

I returned his smile and let my weight fall on him, burrowing into his body. His warmth was so wonderful, it made me feel like the cold didn't exist. "You're wrong. I gave you my answer before you even proposed." I kissed him on the lips and rested my head on his chest, forgetting the outside world.

STRANGE ENCOUNTER

I got out of bed and a shiver ran down my back. The temperature had dropped drastically over the last few weeks, but this morning my body was particularly sensitive to the cold. I guess I'd been more sensitive in general lately.

When I looked out the window I saw Evan already waiting for me, leaning against the hood of the BMW. I smiled at him and my breath left a mark on the glass, a white halo that lingered even when I walked away. Minutes later I was outside, my green backpack slung over my shoulder.

"Good morning," I said, kissing him lightly on the mouth.

His lips smiled against mine. "It is now," he whispered sweetly before opening the passenger door. It was a habit he'd never lost.

The recent weeks had been easier to bear. Though I could never forget Death's icy breath on my neck, the connection between Evan and me took my mind off everything else. Thinking of him—*being* with him—was like having a hideaway somewhere far from the rest of the world, far from danger, a place where I could be safe because the very thought of Evan made me feel that way.

We knew that the Angel of Death, whoever it was, was not going to give up the hunt and we were all waiting for him to make his next move. Sooner or later he would strike again and we would be ready. That's what everyone kept telling me.

In a little corner of my mind I harbored the hope that there really was a chance everything would work out in the end. But maybe it was just wishful thinking; there was another part that wasn't entirely sure.

Almost a month had gone by since we'd seen Drake. There had been no message, no phone call, no unexpected appearance. As far as I knew, he'd disappeared from our lives. The thought that it was my fault left me with a bitter taste in my mouth and a strange churning sensation in my stomach. All my attempts to persuade Evan to forgive his brother had failed. Each time, though, the regret I glimpsed in his eyes persuaded me to keep trying and so I did, with the feeble hope that one day I might be able to set things right.

When I got out of the car something cold touched my neck. I looked up and saw snowflakes drifting down from the sky like soft feathers cradled by the air. I held out my hand and stared at the flakes, enchanted. The first snowfall of the season, when the wind blew away the remaining leaves, always had this effect on me. Every time felt like the first time, despite the fact that Lake Placid was almost always covered with snow as soon as the weather turned cold.

"You like the snow?" To Evan I must have looked like a silly little girl, my hand held out to catch the flakes, my chin raised toward the sky. His mocking smile confirmed my suspicion.

I lowered my damp hand and wiped it on my jeans. "You don't?"

He laughed. "Now I know I do."

"Why?" I asked, my breath freezing in a cloud in front of my mouth. "You don't have to like everything I like, you know."

Evan smiled as if I'd just said something nonsensical. "Actually, that's not why. You know I don't like Strawtella," he shot back teasingly.

"Then why?" I asked, puzzled.

His smile softened and he looked at me tenderly, the sexy little creases under his eyes making an appearance. "The cold air brings out your eyes. It's stunning. I didn't know that before," he whispered in my ear. "But I do now."

Although my face was freezing cold, I felt warmth spread over my cheeks. Evan smiled. It was bizarre how he still managed to make me blush. There had to be something in his tone of voice that caused this instinctive, uncontrollable reaction in my blood.

Snowflakes continued to drift down, increasing in number as the morning progressed. From time to time I would stop to watch them through the school windows, mesmerized when a few crystals landed on the glass and let me admire them.

By the time classes were over, a blanket of white covered the whole campus and every surface. I hurried to the car, dodging the snowballs the students were throwing every which way across the parking lot. One of them was heading straight for Evan. I tried to warn him but he'd already noticed it. His arm shot out to grab it, but the snow melted a split second before it hit his hand. Incredible. Attempting to figure out where it had come from, I noticed a grin on his face and followed his gaze. Ginevra was across the street.

"Just wanted to cool you down a bit, little brother," his sister teased.

Her subtle innuendo—unless I'd misunderstood—made me blush again. I hoped neither of them noticed. Damn it, with all this snow it was even easier to see the color rise in my cheeks.

"It's a shame you didn't hit me then!" Evan was quick to reply, bending down. I blinked as I watched a snowball form without his even touching it. He threw it at Ginevra who in the meantime had whipped up an arsenal. The white spheres began to fly toward us at a speed I could barely follow, but none of them hit me—they all melted inches from my body, so close I could feel their chill. I didn't understand what the two of them found so amusing, since neither of them managed to hit their target even once, though one time, while Evan was protecting me, an unexpected snowball hit him right in the head. All three of us burst out laughing as he shook his damp hair.

The snow continued to fall all day long, becoming a blizzard in the afternoon. I ate a late lunch at home with my parents. Ever since my life had been under siege I'd tried to spend time with them too, though work at the diner took up most of their waking hours, especially since Dad had started baking cakes and doughnuts for the neighboring towns. Orders kept pouring in.

At three, Evan pretended to stop by to take me to his place— although actually he'd never left me. Every day he secretly stayed with me to protect me from anyone who might try to get close. This afternoon he would be gone, something he'd already warned me about yesterday morning before leaving calculus. I'd sat there at my desk, a little shaken like I always was when Evan brought up what he did. But then I'd opened my notebook and found a message from him, written in Devanagari.

अन्तर्मय्यसि मम हृदि ममात्मनि

I recognized the words at once because he'd said them to me after our first time together and the memory warmed my heart. *You're inside me—in my heart, in my soul.* I stroked the symbols, imagining Evan writing it there. He knew I liked to know in advance when he had to leave me. He'd been so sweet it made me forget everything else. Besides, I didn't mind spending a little time with Ginevra. The hours I spent with her flew by, a bit like they had when I used to hang out with Peter.

Peter. Although I saw him at school every morning I sometimes missed his constant presence in my life. We'd been inseparable for too long for me to feel otherwise. I still called him to see how he was doing, but nothing was the same any more, not even his tone of voice. The delicate balance had been upset and the change seemed irreversible.

"Will you be gone long?" I whined, sitting cross-legged on Evan's bed.

"A couple hours. I'm not going far."

"I haven't seen Ginevra yet," I said.

Evan smiled, no doubt privy to something I didn't know. "She's downstairs with Simon."

From his expression I instantly grasped what he was talking about. "I bet she's leaving him black and blue."

"Simon knows how to defend himself," he said, grinning.

"It would be fun to watch you sometime," I blurted, hoping he'd agree to my millionth request, but I already knew how he felt about it: the workout room was off limits for me when they were training.

"It's too dangerous for you," he said, his tone serious.

"From the looks of him I can't believe Simon is as dangerous as you say," I joked.

"Actually, he's always very careful with Ginevra. One mistake, one second of distraction, and he could kill her. You should have seen him fight Dra—" Evan stopped in mid-name as if he'd just remembered it was no longer part of his vocabulary.

And it was all my fault. Guilt was devouring me.

Evan's face had hardened. I knew him well enough to realize how much he was suffering though he would never have admitted it. I tried to get him to look me in the eye but it was no use.

"I let Ginevra know you'd be here before they started. She won't be much longer," he said, changing the subject. "Meanwhile, go downstairs if you want. The water in the pool is hot. You're safe here in the house."

"Don't worry, I'll find a way to keep myself occupied. You just try to get back fast," I threatened, pulling him onto the bed by his shirt.

Evan fell on top of me, his arms outstretched, and kissed me for a moment, then pulled back and rested his forehead against mine. "I have to go. Try not to drown in the pool while I'm gone."

"I'll do my best, but I can't promise anything." I smiled.

"Then I'll come back as soon as I can." He kissed me again.

"That was all part of my plan," I whispered onto his lips.

He disappeared and the room was instantly filled with his absence. I sat there a few minutes, contemplating the empty wall, then fell back onto the bed and closed my eyes, taking a deep breath. Without Evan, the silence was oppressive.

I got up from the bed, uneasy. Maybe going for a swim wasn't such a bad idea.

I tested the water with my foot before immersing the rest of my body. It was hotter than I remembered it being last time. Not even in the swimming pool, though, could I shake my uneasiness. The room was too large for me to lose myself in my thoughts—the sound of the water slapping against the sides of the pool echoed off the walls.

I swam for a few minutes, watching the snow fall on the other side of the huge picture window that overlooked the garden, but the silence soon made me antsy. I climbed out of the pool and wrapped a towel around my black swimsuit, a monokini that left my back bare.

"Don't do that. You totally look better without it," a sensual voice rang out behind me.

I jumped and spun around. "Evan!" I sighed with relief, breathless from the surprise. "What are you doing here?"

"You don't seem too happy to see me. If you want, I can leave," he said, raising an eyebrow, but his hands were already on my hips.

"N-no," I stammered. "I just—I thought it would take you longer than that. I was expecting to have to spend a couple of hours without you." Evan took a step toward me, looking hesitant. "You're back sooner than I'd hoped." A half hour at most had gone by since he'd left me.

"Really? Seems like days to me. I just couldn't stay away from you," he whispered onto my neck. "Actually, I can't stay long. I just thought I'd stop in and see how you were doing. You know, with one thing and the other."

"Good thinking," I said, pleased.

"Well? Mind telling me what you're doing with *that* on?" he asked, nodding at the towel wrapped around my body.

I looked down at it, a bit puzzled. "I took your advice. The water's great."

"M-hmm." Evan shook his head, amused by my remark. "But I meant what are you *still* doing with it on," he said, his voice low as he undid the towel and dropped it to the floor. His evocative gaze brimming with desire, he stepped forward and I moved back until my bare shoulder blades were pressed against the ice-cold wall. The chill made me flinch.

"Uh-oh," Evan whispered, resting both hands against the wall on either side of my head, blocking my way. "Now you're trapped," he whispered, his gaze as sensual as his tone.

"I'll let myself be tortured, if that's what you're getting at," I shot back, raising an eyebrow.

"You read my mind." His hand rested on my bare waist and he kissed me passionately. The cold returned, giving me goosebumps. No—not the cold. Something else. Evan's hands began to roam over my body in an unexpected manner as his lips explored my neck and descended to my breast. I looked around, strangely uncomfortable. "Evan," I murmured, but he was too absorbed to listen to me. "Evan, stop it," I whispered, not very convincingly.

"I have no intention of stopping," he said firmly, pulling me against him. I'd never seen him this aroused and unrelenting before.

"Someone might come in," I insisted. "Simon and Ginevra are in the next room."

"I don't care," he said, his breathing ragged as he continued to kiss me.

Pressing my hands against his chest to make him stop, I looked him straight in the eye, my face serious. "Well, I *do*. What's gotten into you?" I asked, puzzled.

"You're so surprised I want you?" he asked, arching his eyebrow.

My eyes wandered, checking the room. I kept feeling a strange sensation on my skin, as if there were a foreign or hostile presence somewhere in the vicinity. But it was impossible—Evan would have detected it.

I happened to glance at his neck. "Where's your dog tag?" I asked in alarm, pulling his shirt open slightly. Evan's eyes wavered.

He never took off his dog tag. For a moment I was afraid he'd lost it in who knew what part of the world. All at once an even worse thought crossed my mind, but I banished it instantly; it was unlikely Evan would have taken it off because of his falling-out with Drake.

He felt around on his chest. "I must have left it in my room."

"But you never take it off," I said.

"Yeah. Well, don't worry, I'll put it on again as soon as I get back," he whispered, pressing me against the wall. "I can't stay much longer," he warned before kissing me passionately again. I kissed him back and he disappeared without warning, his lingering voice echoing through the empty room with a hint of mischief: "See you soon."

I remained leaning against the wall with a strange sensation on my skin and the memory of his intense gaze that soon began to fade. A sudden cold shiver gave me goosebumps. Without Evan's heat to warm me, I realized I was still wet. Unsettled, I picked the towel up from the floor and quickly dried myself off.

It had been a weird encounter. Evan hadn't made me feel the sensations I always felt when he kissed me. I wasn't used to him being so insistent, and I wasn't sure I liked it.

SUBTLE DECEPTION

I pulled on my clothes, still confused, and knocked on the door to the workout room, from which came sounds so muffled they seemed far away. No one opened. I cautiously gripped the handle and opened the door just a crack to peek inside, but something struck it and slammed it shut. Before I could catch my breath Ginevra was beside me. "Gemma! What were you thinking? What are you doing here? It's dangerous for you!" she said, worried, almost reproaching me. I was about to reply but she cut me off, peering over my shoulder with an alarmed look on her face. "Someone's been here," she said, paying no attention to me.

"It was just Evan," I said, but she didn't look reassured.

"I thought he was gone."

"I thought so too but he surprised me." Ginevra continued to scan the room uneasily. "He had some spare time," I said. "Is Simon in there?"

A proud smile formed on her lips. I already knew what she was thinking. "Give him a little while to recover." She leaned toward me and lowered her voice. "I think I overdid it this time."

I shook my head and looked more closely at her body. There wasn't a scratch on it. It must be awesome to be a Witch. The door to the workout room opened behind Ginevra, who shot me a conspiratorial look.

"You're all in one piece, it seems," I said, smothering a laugh.

Simon looked at Ginevra, who shrugged. "Not a scratch," he shot back, throwing his girlfriend a challenging look.

"Good thing you heal fast," she taunted him. "We can go back in if you feel up to it."

"Okay, okay!" I said, smiling. "Don't you two ever get enough? I propose a truce. What do you say we go to the kitchen?"

Ginevra didn't take her eyes off Simon's for a second. "Sounds like a good idea." She smiled slyly. "Angels' bodies have their limits too. I wouldn't want you to exceed yours." Her sensual eyes sparkled at

Simon, who tilted his head as he held her gaze. Suddenly he grabbed her wrist, yanked her toward him, and pinned her against the wall.

I'd seen Simon shirtless before but had never noticed how muscular he was. His tanned skin glistened with sweat. "See?" he whispered onto her lips, his strong arms tensed as they barred her way. "To catch you off guard, all I have to do is distract you."

I winced at the memory this scene brought to my mind. Blushing, I looked down, embarrassed. Ginevra sensually brought her lips close to Simon's without touching them, lingered a moment, and then nimbly inverted their positions, slamming him against the wall. "What makes you think I was off guard?" she whispered in response to his provocation.

Being able to read Simon's thoughts in order to know exactly when to strike was definitely an advantage for her. I shook my head as Simon smiled at her stubbornness; he clearly liked this aspect of her. "You never give up, do you?" He smiled against her lips, amused by their little game.

For Ginevra everything inevitably became an endless challenge, a competition in which she couldn't stand the idea of losing. Maybe it was part of her nature as a Witch. It was nice to see them together, but the more I watched them, the more I missed Evan. Though it had only been a few minutes since I'd last seen him, it felt like hours.

"I don't know about you, but I'm getting kind of hungry." I hoped one of them would take me up on the proposal. My eyes rested on Ginevra, who was quick to accept.

Simon shot me a glance and smiled. "You really have a Witch's appetite, Gemma," he teased.

Head down, I followed them upstairs. "It's the pool," I explained, feeling awkward. "Swimming makes me hungry."

The next two hours flew by so fast I almost didn't feel their weight on my heart. Simon and Ginevra were good company and our mutual affection was unconditional. Even so, Drake's absence was still keenly felt in every corner of the house. They all missed him, I was sure of it. Whenever one of us happened to mention his name a sad silence instantly filled the room.

Evan's lighthearted voice shook me from my thoughts. "Did you guys miss me?" I smiled. "Not much, it would seem," he said sarcastically, looking at the table that was covered with a cornucopia of leftovers. I threw my arms around his neck. "I guess somebody was celebrating without me," he teased, rubbing his nose against mine.

"What?" I exclaimed. "We would never celebrate without you." I shot a glance at Simon and Ginevra, urging them to back me up.

"Of course not!" Ginevra said as she popped another morsel into her mouth and chewed with delight. "How could you think such a thing?" Evan laughed and I kissed him as the others silently turned to go.

"Oookay, looks like we should leave you two alone," Ginevra said.

"No need," I was quick to reply.

Evan smiled and I noticed him wink at her.

"Someone doesn't agree with you, Gemma. Please, Evan. Spare me the details!" she groaned, pulling Simon by the hand. "At least wait until I've left the room!"

Evan laughed and turned to face me. Finally we were alone again. "It felt like an eternity," he said, gazing at me tenderly. I was in danger of melting whenever he looked at me that way. He almost seemed like another person compared to the last time I'd seen him. "Sorry I kept you waiting. It took longer than expected."

"You found it!" I cried with relief, noticing his dog tag was back in its place.

Evan didn't seem to understand. "Found what?" he asked, gently resting his lips on my neck.

"Your dog tag," I said.

"I never took it off," he whispered casually, his mouth making its way up toward my chin.

"Yes you did," I insisted. "You weren't wearing it by the pool." Evan froze and looked at me, frowning. "You said you'd left it up in your room," I reminded him, baffled as to why he looked so bewildered.

His eyes wavered in alarm as the truth began to dawn on me. "I don't remember saying that," he replied, standing stock-still and staring at me as if he were hoping to hear me say I was wrong. "Gemma, I've been gone for hours, you know that." He almost seemed to be trying to convince me it was true.

"No, you were—So, by the pool—" I put my hand to my mouth and felt my body turn ice cold with shock as I watched the rage grow in Evan's eyes. Hatred glinted in them.

"He came back," he snarled, tensing his muscles.

My hands trembled. "What—You mean it was Drake?" I whispered, horrified by the thought of our encounter. Evan fixed me with a wary gaze and I sensed his anger growing by the second. My body felt trapped in a block of ice.

It hadn't been Evan.

"What did he do to you?" he growled, his tone so harsh it made me flinch. "What did he do to you, Gemma?!" he repeated, raising his voice. A black fire burned in his eyes.

"I don't think you want to know," I barely murmured.

"Yes I do," he insisted through clenched teeth. "Did he touch you?"

I looked away and closed my eyes, unable to answer. Evan growled and slammed his fist into the cement wall. It cracked beneath his knuckles as I stood there, petrified. The look on his face told me there was no doubt about it: this time he wouldn't hold back.

"Evan—"

"He's crossed the line. It's not going to happen a second time," he said, his tone implacable.

"Evan!" Ginevra shouted, racing into the room. She stopped in front of us and looked him in the eye. "I need to talk to you."

"Not right now," he snapped.

"It's important. You need to listen to me. Drake is the least of our problems right now," she insisted. She'd read in our minds what had happened, but she didn't care; it seemed what she had to say was far more important. Finally Evan straightened up and paid attention. "The vial with the poison." Ginevra's tone was as grave as the look in her eyes. "It's missing. I can't find it anywhere, Evan!"

Her brother's face paled instantly.

"He was here!" Ginevra exclaimed. A cold shiver ran down my body. The Executioner sent to kill me had been in this house. "I don't know how he managed to get into my room without me noticing it," Ginevra said.

"Are you sure about all this?" Evan asked in alarm. "When was the last time you saw it?"

"I don't know, it's been too long. Since I gave you the poison to use on Faust, I guess. I haven't even thought about it since!" Ginevra cried in panic.

"But it was empty. You put the only drop of it onto the dagger—I saw you do it," Evan said, thinking.

"Evan, you're underestimating how potent it is. You have no idea how little it takes to kill a Subterranean."

"You should have destroyed it then!" he yelled. He fell silent for a long moment, lost in thought. "We don't know whether the Executioner came back after the last time or if he'd taken the poison even before that. We can't know if he intends to attack. We have to stay alert."

Simon nodded as he walked into the room. "Think you have a plan?" he asked.

Evan stood motionless for a moment before answering. "Something doesn't make sense. Too much time has passed since the last time he tried to kill Gemma." He continued to shake his head, processing the information.

"Maybe he wants to catch us off guard," Simon suggested.

Evan didn't seem convinced. "No. He's sly. He knows we'll never let down our defenses. He must have a plan." Evan's eyes narrowed to slits as if trying to see our enemy's intentions. "He has something in mind, but I won't let him get away with it. We need to stay alert and wait for him to make his move." A sudden spark ignited in his eyes. "When that happens we'll be here waiting for him."

"We don't even know who we're up against, Evan," Ginevra cautioned, "or even worse, what his power is."

Evan gave her a hard look. "I think I have an idea," he murmured to himself.

A frozen silence fell among us. I stared at Evan in shock, trying to decipher his expression. He came to me as if I'd called him, pulled me against his chest, and covered my head with his hand. "Don't worry," he whispered. "Everything's going to be fine."

A cold shiver raced over my skin because deep down I knew it wasn't true.

FIREFLIES IN THE NIGHT

I went to bed early and fell asleep without realizing it as the trees outside scratched at my window with their branches and the stormy wind howled like an angry wolf.

"Gemma . . ."

A voice echoed in my head, whispering in the silence of the night. I flinched. There was no way it could be morning already.

"Shh, don't worry. It's me," he whispered tenderly.

"Evan," I mumbled, my eyes still closed. I noticed him next to me and bolted upright in bed. "Evan, what is it?" I asked in alarm, wondering what could have happened to make him wake me up in the middle of the night. I blinked several times to allow my eyes to adjust and looked out the window where darkness reigned over the silent night. It had stopped snowing. "It's not morning yet," I said.

"Get dressed," he ordered, his voice kind.

Trying to understand, I looked into his eyes so he could see my concern, but he smiled reassuringly. "Are we going somewhere?" I asked, puzzled, continuing to look at the darkness outside the window.

Another smile spread across his face—this time a sweeter one. "Trust me," he whispered, never taking his eyes off me. "There's something you have to see."

I got out of bed and did as he'd told me to. "We're going out the window?" I asked in surprise when Evan opened it.

"As always." He smiled at me, but I still wasn't completely convinced of his proposal. It wasn't the first time we'd snuck out in the middle of the night, but when we'd done it before things had been different. Death hadn't been hunting me and we could count on Drake to replace me. Circumstances had changed.

"My folks might wake up! What if they notice I'm gone?"

He smiled disarmingly at my reluctance. "Why so worried all of a sudden? Come on, Gemma. We've done worse." I couldn't disagree. "I've already visited your parents. They won't wake up before dawn. I made sure of it."

I couldn't find any other objections to make, so I joined Evan at the windowsill. He cradled me in his flexed arms and a moment later we landed gracefully on the walk below. I didn't even feel us touch the ground. He must have defied gravity by controlling the air so it would waft us down. The only thing I felt was the cold wind stinging my cheeks.

The blizzard had subsided, leaving the yard blanketed with snow. The pure white mantle over everything was a beautiful sight. In the car I noticed two pairs of ice skates on the back seat—one pair small, the other almost twice as large—and instantly realized Evan's intentions. I stiffened in my seat as he glanced at me with a smile.

I thought of the Olympic Oval in front of the school. Every year when the temperature dropped it was filled with water that froze into a skating rink. What was he thinking? "It's three in the morning!" I said. "They'll think we've lost our minds!"

"There's nobody where we're going," he said, careful not to tell me more.

I was wrong; the car turned in the opposite direction from the school. I tried to pry more information out of him but gave up after a while and waited in silence to see where he was taking me. We continued toward the woods, away from Lake Placid and the city lights.

The darkness gradually swallowed us up as the car wound its way through the trees, the headlights casting a solid beam of light in front of us. A moment later I thought I glimpsed a soft glow deep in the woods, but it immediately faded. I leaned closer to the window, curious, trying to figure out where Evan was taking me and what had emitted that silvery light. He continued to steal glances at me, grinning the whole time because of my reaction.

The car stopped in the middle of nowhere and Evan opened my door. I looked around in bewilderment, daunted by the darkness. "Evan, what—" I stammered, unable to see anything.

His laughter rang through the night and his tone grew gentle. "Ready?" he whispered behind my ear. With a delicate touch, he lifted my chin.

As I stared at the dark leaves overhead, a silvery sparkle winked on. Slowly, the thick canopy came to life as hundreds of twinkling, luminous points appeared.

I was no longer sure if I was awake or dreaming. My eyes were dazzled by the incredible display. Like an infinitely large, delightful cave filled with fireflies, the forest had lit up all around us, thousands of brilliant specks shining through the treetops. From their pure white glow I could see they were tiny spheres of light. There were so many of them they banished the night, tiny little stars floating in the trees as though the heavens had descended and hidden there to watch us.

I pivoted slowly, my face to the treetops. They were a fascinating sight. I couldn't find the words to tell Evan how touched I was to know he'd already been there to prepare everything for me. I noticed he was staring at me, a smile still on his face as he waited for me to say something.

"Is all this real?" I murmured. "You know I don't like it when you confuse me like that—are we really here or are we in my mind?"

Evan laughed. "No, you aren't dreaming. If you were, I wouldn't have been able to take you wherever I wanted. Don't forget, in your dreams you're the one who calls the shots."

"You know how to take my breath away. It's beautiful," I exclaimed. "But why are we here?" I thought of the ice skates on the back seat of his car. There weren't any skating rinks in this area, and the school was far away.

Evan came up behind me and rested his hands on my hips. He glanced briefly at the lake through the trees, then looked at me, his expression uncertain but full of promises. "Have you ever skated on the lake under the stars?" he whispered, his lips brushing my ear. His hot breath tickled my skin.

"Of course," I said, thinking of the dozens of times Peter and I had stayed up late, skating on the lake and around the Oval outside the school.

I bit my lip, instantly regretting my impulsive reply, but Evan was quick to ask, "Have you ever watched it freeze over?" he whispered, pointing at Lake Placid in front of us.

Up until now I hadn't even thought about the lake. From the distance I'd seen the moonlight sparkle on its surface, but I hadn't been sure if it was frozen or if Evan was planning to make our skates glide across the water. With him, anything was possible.

"Are you kidding?" I said, turning my head to look at him. His chin was resting on my shoulder and my cheek brushed his. I already knew he wasn't, but his smile confirmed it. "You're not kidding," I murmured to myself.

"Come with me." Evan took my hand and led me toward the shore. I followed him. He let go only when we were at the water's edge, when he looked at me for a long moment, either to encourage me or more likely, to pique my curiosity even further. This was the part he always loved most. I watched him kneel down and reach out his hand until his palm was almost touching the water. I held my breath as the surface of the lake trembled below him, rippling slightly. Suddenly the water froze under his palm. I gaped as the ice spread out, stretching across the entire surface of the lake in crystal ripples, transforming it in seconds into a perfectly smooth mirror.

Evan turned toward me with a satisfied look on his face and I blinked, entranced. "You froze the lake," I whispered as if what he'd just done wasn't clear enough already.

"Nothing escapes you," he teased.

I opened my mouth, still amazed, and pointed at the shiny surface in front of us. *"You froze the lake!"* I repeated, dumbfounded.

"Yeeeaaaah." Evan frowned, looking puzzled. "I've done worse things in my life."

"I can't believe it."

"You don't like it?" he asked, sounding confused and concerned.

"No—Yes—It's just that it seems—" I struggled to find the words. "Unbelievable," I said, entranced. "It's really too much just for me, Evan."

"Nothing is too much for you," he was quick to reply, as if what I'd just said was silly. He stroked my cheek and disappeared. In a fraction of a second he was back and handed me my skates. He'd already put his on, though I was sure he didn't even need them. When I'd put mine on I took the hand he held out to me.

"Ready?" he asked, looking at me encouragingly.

I stared at the sheet of crystal that stretched out in front of me. "I'm not sure," I admitted, a bit worried.

"Trust me." He squeezed my hand. I rested one foot and then the other on the icy surface of the lake, moving hesitantly. It was harder than I'd imagined.

"Careful," Evan said softly, still clasping my hand. I'd always been good at skating, but he seemed like a pro in comparison. "This will be a bit different from the other times," he warned.

"I'd imagined that," I shot back sardonically, feeling like I was sliding across a soapy surface. No matter how hard I tried to keep my balance, it was impossible to maintain arm-leg coordination. The ice beneath us was perfectly smooth, as crystal clear as the icicles that hung like jewels from the tree branches.

"You'll get used to it in no time. Meanwhile, don't let go of my hand," he said, his voice deep.

"Okay." I struggled not to fall as I awkwardly made my way forward.

The air was so cold I couldn't feel my cheeks any more. My hand clasped in Evan's, instead, felt cozy and safe and its warmth spread all the way up my arm. I tried not to think of the cold, deep water beneath us; the layer of ice was thick and there was no reason for me to worry. With Evan I wasn't running any risks.

"Okay, I'm ready." When I felt fairly sure I could stay standing without his support I took a deep breath. "You can let go now," I told him. I didn't want him to leave my side, but I wanted to show him I could do it.

"You sure? It might be dangerous." My expression had probably given away my uncertainty. Evan relaxed his grip.

"I'll manage," I said in a low voice, mostly to reassure myself. He let go of my hand and I found myself teetering on my own.

It seemed easier when he was near to instill me with courage, yet I knew I could do it. I made my way forward determinedly, digging the blades in one after the other, faster and faster, pretending to have mastered the ice. The lake was immense, but it didn't matter how far out I went—Evan would be there to bring me back. In an instant he was at my side, skating in sync with me. Then, with a decisive movement, he swung out in front and skated backwards as if it were the most natural thing in the world. I'd always wondered how people could do that.

"This is fun!" I murmured, in spite of feeling a little dizzy from watching his face as we moved.

"You got used to it pretty quick," he said, pleased.

"Did you doubt me?" I grinned, finally finding my feet again.

"I'm still not so sure, actually."

Was he challenging me? With my next steps I pushed harder against the ice and moved faster. "Let's see if you can catch me," I said, taking up the challenge though I knew I'd already lost the race. Evan's laughter rang out behind me as I narrowed my eyes and focused on the ice in front of me. The air was so cold it took my breath away, but all I was worried about was not falling. I could hear his strokes behind mine as I gathered all my energy to stay out ahead of him. I knew perfectly well it was only a little game we were playing and that if he wanted to he could catch up with me in the blink of an eye.

Carelessly, I turned around to see how much of a lead I had. Wrong move. In a second I'd lost my balance and tripped over my own feet. Why did I always find a way to make a fool of myself? At this speed the impact with the ice was bound to be violent and painful. I instinctively put my hands out in front of me and tensed my muscles, bracing for the pain. From the corner of my eye I saw a blur shoot toward me at warp speed a second before I hit the icy surface and something cushioned the blow. I opened my eyes. It was Evan. He'd grabbed me and slid beneath me, his back on the ice, my body on top of his. For a moment I lay still, panting, my lips on his ear, my heart racing. Then I raised myself slightly and looked him in the eye, a cloud of breath escaping my lips.

Evan smiled, his expression tender. "Got you," he whispered, his eyes fixed on mine, his hands encircling my waist.

I bit my lower lip. Evan wasn't just talking about my fall. "I could have beaten you," I said defiantly, unable to handle defeat.

"No doubt about it," he said, an impish sparkle in his eye.

"Don't tease me. It's not my fault you're way faster. I'm just a mortal soul."

His smile softened and became more tender. With his hand he followed the curve of my face as he pushed back a lock of hair that had fallen over my forehead and swept it behind my ear. "You aren't just a mortal soul, Gemma. You're much more than that to me." My gaze locked onto his. "Otherwise I would never have fallen in love with you. You're—" He stared at me intently as if searching for the words inside me. "You're like a flower that blossomed from the snow." He stroked my cheek again.

I slowly lowered my head toward his face.

"A beautiful flower, so strong it defies the cold," he whispered, "but so delicate and fragile it needs protection."

I rested my lips on his. When I pulled back, he looked me in the eye, his expression proud. "And I *will* protect you from everything, at all costs," he said with determination.

I trembled at the memories his words conjured in my mind. There were moments when I could forget about everything else. At those moments Death stopped haunting me—there was no Executioner hunting me, threatening to kill me. There was nothing for me to be afraid of because Evan would always be with me. No one else. Just me and him, forever.

Then I would come back to reality. I couldn't escape my fate forever. Sooner or later I would have to pay the price. Deep in my heart, the only hope I nurtured was that I could avoid death as long as possible and spend what time I had left with Evan. That's all I wanted.

SCARLET DEATH

A snow flurry drifted through the air, caressing our faces as we lay on our backs, gazing at the sky. All around us, the spheres of fire glowed with their white light, hidden in the trees like fireflies peeking down at us from behind the leaves. Who knew how long we lay there on the ice, one next to the other, looking at the dark mantle overhead. I couldn't even feel the cold any more. Or maybe I simply didn't care. The warmth in my heart was enough to keep away the chill.

Evan had taken off his skates, disappearing and reappearing with his shoes on, but I'd decided to keep my own skates on a little while longer to prolong this magical experience. We hadn't spoken for a while now, maybe because the pure white moonglow had absorbed my thoughts, releasing them in a thousand reflections that touched the sky.

I wondered if there was some other place, apart from the earth, where Evan and I could live together without the constant threat of being separated. A world where my fate would be different from the one in store for me here. Then reason brought me back to the present. There was no other place I could seek refuge, and no matter how hard Evan tried to hide me, no matter how he struggled to protect me, Death would never stop hunting me down. It pursued me like a hungry feline, pulling down all the branches I managed to scramble up onto. I was its prey. How much longer would I have breath enough to run? It was impossible to say. But one thing was inevitable: the day would come when I wouldn't be able to endure it any more. I could only hope it didn't come too soon. I didn't want to lose Evan.

"What are you thinking about?" Evan rubbed his head against mine as he continued to stare at the sky.

I didn't want to drag him into the melancholy depths of my brooding mind. "Ice sculptures," I lied, but he must have realized it because he studied me silently for a long moment as if trying to probe my mind.

"You don't have to prove you're brave through all this. No one expects that of you, Gemma." I didn't reply. Nothing escaped him.

302

"Besides, I already know you are. In fact, you're a lot braver than you imagine. It can't have been easy to face everything you've been through, but you've never given up."

"How could I? I had no choice, Evan," I said sadly.

"You know that's not true. Others would have broken down if they'd been in your shoes, but you've always taken everything with your head held high."

"Only because you're here to protect me."

He squeezed my hand and I understood what he was trying to say: he would always be there for me. We turned to look at each other and he smiled. For a fleeting moment, his smile seemed to be telling me everything would be fine—but now he was the one who was lying.

"So what were you saying about ice sculptures?"

I smiled at his attempt to change the subject. Playing along, I lost myself in my story. "I remember one in particular. I must have been seven or eight but I remember it like it was yesterday. It was this huge carriage made of ice—or maybe I was just really little so it seemed big to me. In any case, I remember going to touch it. It was so smooth and transparent it looked like crystal."

"I wish I could have seen you back then. And to think I was who knows where in the world, living an empty existence, while you were here," he reflected, the thought saddening him. "You must have been adorable."

"Actually, I was a little monster," I admitted.

Evan burst out laughing and propped himself up on his elbows. "I don't believe it."

"Ask my mom and dad. They'll be happy to tell you." I did as he had done, sitting up on the ice. My back was damp. "When they would come looking for me I was always out climbing trees with Peter. I was a total tomboy! It must have been his influence."

Mischief glimmered in Evan's dark eyes, so deep I risked losing myself in them. "A tomboy?" He raised an eyebrow. "That's hard for me to believe, especially after the other night."

Blushing, I changed the subject. "Anyway, there was this huge carriage and I assumed there were a prince and princess inside it. Peter made fun of me but I kept insisting. I can't believe I actually told you that, it's so stupid!"

My sudden embarrassment made him throw back his head back and laugh, but then his laughter became gentler. "I was right, though.

Behind that tomboy façade, my sweet thing was already hiding," he said, grinning.

I tightened my lips, blushing at the confession I'd just made, revealing a tiny part of me I'd kept hidden among my memories.

"Hold on." Evan pulled himself up and rested one knee on the ice. I stared at him, puzzled, as he focused on the frozen surface, holding his palms over it.

"Evan, what—"

"Watch this," he whispered without looking at me, his sweet tone not allowing any objection.

"It's not another of your mind-blowing tricks, is it?" I joked nervously. He ignored me. "It's another of your mind-blowing tricks," I murmured. I stared at his hands, but nothing happened. Nothing except . . .

I squinted at the puff of white steam that rose from the cold surface beneath his palms, trying to remember if it had always been there. No, it was the ice that was steaming. The mist thickened beneath Evan's hands until I couldn't see through its silvery veil any more. It looked like something was moving inside it. I didn't understand. Evan's hands slowly moved up and the fog thinned out. The rest of his body followed his hand movements, straightening up as the ice changed shape at his command, leaving me breathless.

Only a moment had gone by. Before me stood a large statue that looked like it was made of crystal. I couldn't believe it—he'd sculpted it out of the ice as though it had been trapped inside it all along and he'd only freed it.

Despite all the astonishing things I'd already seen Evan never failed to surprise me. He'd left me wordless. "Your prince and princess," he announced with a flourish of his hand and a pleased smile on his lips. In silence, I looked from him to the sculpture, which was so perfect it was like I was seeing two actual people captured in the ice.

"Don't look at me like that—you know I can control the elements."

Without replying, I walked around it cautiously, complete astonishment on my face. I'd seen lots of ice sculptures in my life, but none of them came close to the graceful beauty before me now. It was perfect, right down to the smallest detail. There were no words to describe it. A prince was kneeling before his lady, holding a crystal flower out to her.

Reading my mind, Evan walked over to the prince and gently took the rose from his frozen hands. The flower came away as smoothly as if the prince himself had handed it to Evan. He offered it to me.

I hesitated before accepting it, not saying a word. Holding it in my hand like a precious gem, I examined it. "It's beautiful," I said, my voice barely audible. Each transparent petal was perfectly defined, the half-opened bud sparkling like a Swarovski crystal in the silvery moonlight.

How was it possible that all this was happening to me? It felt like I was living in a dream. I brought my other hand closer to trace its contours and stroke the petals with my fingertips.

"Careful," Evan warned me gently—but it was too late. I flinched at the sight of the blood. The petals were as sharp as they were beautiful. I hadn't even noticed I'd cut myself—there had been no pain. A scarlet droplet formed on my pointer finger, grew and slid down, leaving a crimson streak on my skin. As I watched the tiny red droplet, mesmerized, time seem to slow. I carefully observed every instant of its fall to the snow-covered ice. It struck the pure white surface and my heart skipped a beat as though I'd heard it make impact. Though the sound was imperceptible, it silenced my heart for a second.

A premonition. A horrible premonition writhed in my chest.

Evan watched me with concern but seemed unaware of the dark sentiment that throbbed in my veins, demanding my attention. Time froze as the strange sense of foreboding gripped my chest and stopped my heart.

"Everything okay?"

His voice pulled me back to his side as though someone had deactivated the mute button, snapping me out of my trance.

"Gemma, are you okay?" he insisted, alarmed, as I continued to stare blankly at the scarlet spot that had spread on the white carpet of snow.

"I'm fine. It's nothing," I stammered. What was going on with me? Why was I having these weird reactions? Why did time seem to suck me into a black hole where I couldn't breathe? Why did I feel these bone-chilling sensations on my skin? Was it a consequence of defying death and coming back to life?

"Let me take a look." Concerned about the cut, Evan examined my finger for a second.

"Beautiful and dangerous," I said, looking into his eyes. I wasn't talking about the flower.

Evan returned the look. "I can heal it in no time," he said solicitously.

"There's no need, really. It's just a scratch. It'll be fine," I reassured him.

Evan shot me a glance. "I told you you were brave." I wasn't sure whether or not there was mockery in his half smile. "But why wait?" Before I could reply he brushed his thumb over the cut. It closed at his touch. He flashed me a little smile and his expression abruptly changed.

I could tell from the expression on his face that something was wrong. He looked lost. Standing perfectly still, his muscles tensed, he moved his eyes as if to peer over his shoulder.

"Evan—"

"Don't move," he ordered.

My heart lurched. Inexplicably, my instinct had warned me. I'd foreseen it. The sensation I'd felt beneath my skin had been a premonition after all. All at once, I heard a strange, creaking sound. My heart pounded, making it difficult to breathe. Something moved on the slab of ice, too fast for me to make out what it was. I tried to get Evan's attention, but he looked through me, his face full of fury. I could see he was listening for something, but I couldn't tell what. Then I saw it on the ice: *a crack*. It was racing toward me.

"Evan . . ." I whispered, my heart in my throat. A whimper escaped me. He didn't move. The crack stopped at my feet and an eerie silence fell, hushing even the wind around us.

It was a threat.

I looked around, trying to control the panic filling my mind. My instinct already knew what to look for though my eyes hadn't yet managed to spot it anywhere on the ice. It had to be *him*. He must be here.

The Reaper Angel had come to kill me.

My alarmed eyes flew to Evan's. Up to now he'd worn a tough, focused expression but when I looked at him I saw a cunning smile spread across his face. He was ready to kill.

Bewildered, I stared at him, trying to understand, as he clenched his fists at his sides. Suddenly his voice rang out, breaking the icy, ominous stillness. "I should have expected this from a traitor like you." He spoke without turning around, as if someone were behind him.

"Nothing personal."

I jumped at the sound of the voice and whirled in the direction it had come from. My heart skipped a beat when my eyes met his.

Drake.

"Wha—How—" I stammered in shock. He was the Angel who wanted to kill me? No. It couldn't be true. I had to be wrong, yet I saw him clearly a dozen yards away, his cold, detached gaze fixed on us. In his shadowy face there was no hint of the fun-loving, carefree guy I had come to care about. My heart refused to accept it and yet there he was, his hostile gaze locked onto mine.

Drake was there to *kill me*. Something inside me shattered. For the first time I realized what was so different about the look in his eye: it was the look of a predator—and I was his prey. He'd just been waiting for the right moment to attack.

Drake took a step in my direction and Evan, his back to me, shielded me with his body, glaring at him threateningly. "I suppose it wasn't anything personal when you kissed her either," Evan accused him, bitter poison in his tone.

The corner of Drake's mouth rose in a crafty smile. "You mean the first time . . . or the second time?" He was clearly trying to provoke Evan. "Because I have to admit things were a lot more exciting by the pool. You should have seen the way she touched me."

"You pervert!" I accused him, stunned.

He tilted his head and locked eyes with me. "Come on, you mean to tell me you didn't like it?" There was a wicked glimmer in his dark gaze.

"I thought you were Evan!!!" I cried.

Drake shook his head as if to disagree. "Actually, I think part of you knew," he said.

I glared at him. This couldn't be happening. I couldn't believe those words had just come out of Drake's mouth. This had to be a trick—it was all too bizarre. He'd never spoken to me like this before. It couldn't be the same Drake who'd helped me so many times. I simply couldn't accept that he'd betrayed us all, that he, of all people, was my Executioner.

It hurt too much.

"Why?" Evan snarled, his muscles tensed.

"You know what?" Drake shot back in a mocking tone. Evan waited silently, his eyes narrowed to slits as he followed Drake's every movement. "I wanted to see what there was about her—what was so special about her, an insignificant mortal soul—that she deserved the protection of three Subterraneans and a Witch, against everyone and everything."

I winced at his harsh words. I didn't want to listen to him any more. It was too painful.

"And at what cost." He laughed to himself. "I thought maybe if I got close to her I could figure it out. But as I expected, she's not such a big deal—although I can't promise you I won't try her out again." His tone was even more provoking and a smirk spread across his face as he continued to challenge Evan with his eyes. "You know what I'm like— with me, bad habits die hard."

"Why?" Evan repeated in a snarl, his tone fiercer now. His resolute attitude made me guess he'd suspected this horrifying deception for some time now. There was no trace of surprise on his face—just rage.

Drake turned serious. "I'm a servant of Death," he said, as if Evan might have forgotten. "Just like you. Orders come first. There's nothing I can do about it. I can't deny my own nature."

Evan stifled a bitter smile. It was plain from the look in his eyes how difficult Drake's unfaithfulness was for him to accept, how much his brother's betrayal pained him. "You're right. I can't blame you for what they've ordered you to do," he said calmly, "but don't think I'm just going to stand by and watch you do it. You know I won't let you."

Drake cocked his head, his evil eyes locked onto his brother's, a look of amusement on his face. "You going to kill me like you killed Faustian?"

Evan clenched his fists. It had been difficult for him to kill Faust, and doing the same thing to his brother would be infinitely more so. Drake was aware of this and was using it to his advantage. Something flashed through my mind and I turned pale as my heart raced wildly. The poison. It had been Drake who'd taken it from Ginevra's room, and he would be prepared to use it against Evan if they battled. Panic left me breathless. I wished Evan could read my mind so I could warn him. I trembled at the thought of what might happen.

"I'll do what I have to do," Evan said, his tone steely. Vapor rose from the ice on which he stood, as if the fire burning inside him was melting it.

An evil smile spread across Drake's face, making me shudder. "Why don't you try it right now?" he said.

"No!" I cried. I had to prevent it. Drake clearly wanted to seize this chance to catch his brother off guard. I moved closer to Evan, alarmed. "Evan, don't do it," I whispered. "He's the one who took Ginevra's poison."

Evan didn't bat an eye. He attempted to reassure me in a low voice as he shielded me with his body, but there was nothing he could say to ease the panic consuming me. Terror descended on me, almost blocking out his words. His fierce gaze sought Drake's.

Without warning, the ice trembled and lurched beneath my feet. I jumped, a cry escaping me as I lost my grip on the flower I'd had in my hand the whole time. It shattered against the ice with a disquieting sound that penetrated my bones. Evan turned toward me.

"Evan!" I screamed in a desperate warning, but it was too late—I had distracted him.

A blast of ice-cold wind struck him in the chest, hurling him against the sculpture, which exploded in a thousand pieces beneath his weight. I tried to run to him but hesitated when he thrust his arm out in my direction without looking at me. He was already back on his feet. "Get out of here, Gemma. It's dangerous!"

I retreated, remembering the moment I'd distracted him.

The surface of the lake trembled beneath my feet again. All at once the ice exploded and a thousand fragments flew toward me. Evan hurled a fireball into the air, melting most of them, but a few remaining shards lodged in the ice. I turned toward Drake. His fiery gaze met mine, making me shudder with terror.

Evan charged him. They moved too fast for me to make them out clearly. All I could see in the dim light were two blurs battling it out on the ice. Drake hurled Evan in my direction as I watched, my heart shrinking in my chest. I felt small and powerless as he crashed backwards into a tree. It toppled over behind him, uprooted from the frozen ground. When he got up, there was something different in his look. He turned to me and winked, his face shrewd, evil.

I shuddered and recoiled. It was Drake in Evan's guise. The real Evan shot toward him like a bolt of lightning, stopping in front of him. I started. They were identical, like a reflection in a mirror.

Evan's fury was apparent. A vortex of wind blew around him and the ice steamed beneath his feet, creating spirals of fog that encircled him.

Drake changed his physical appearance again, his body smaller. "Why don't you attack me now?" Terror pierced my skin at the sound of my own voice: Drake had taken on my appearance. In his new body he challenged Evan. "Bet you can't." He laughed, an evil laugh that rang out icily through the chill night.

The air around Evan swirled restlessly as if expecting him to rush Drake from one second to the next. He was more enraged than ever.

"Nah," Drake said, "you don't have the guts. You're so predictable."

Evan ignored his provocation and his eyes seemed to ignite. All around him a vortex of air rose up like a barrier. The solid mass of air became fire, then earth, water, and again air. He hurled it at Drake, who still had my appearance, and it flung his brother far into the distance.

Evan turned to me. "Run! Gemma, you need to go!" His tone permitted no objections. "Hurry! Take the car!" he ordered, worried.

"No!" I protested. "I'm not leaving you here, Evan!"

"Gemma, do as I say!" he growled, glowering at me.

"I said no!" I insisted.

"Then at least get away from the lake. You've got to get off the ice!" he said agitatedly. "Go back to shore and wait for me there."

I flinched, realizing I needed to obey—staying there would only distract him. I rushed to him and kissed him desperately. "Be careful, I'm begging you." Evan rested his forehead on mine. "The poison. Watch out for the poison!"

"Wait for me," he said. His gaze hardened and I realized he wasn't speaking to me any more. "I have some dirty business to take care of," he added, raising his voice.

Out of the corner of my eye, I spotted Drake watching us, perfectly still, not far away. "What a romantic scene."

Evan gave me a gentle push, urging me to leave. "Jealousy can make life bitter. I have what you couldn't have. What's wrong, can't you accept that?" His tone had turned harsh and cruel. "You need to face facts—just because you lost Stella doesn't mean others don't have the right to love."

I glimpsed a glimmer of pain—fleeting yet intense—in Drake's eyes when he heard her name. I wasn't sure, but I thought I saw him flinch—or maybe it was just my imagination. This new Drake seemed incapable of feeling emotion. This Drake hadn't hesitated to wage war on his brother. He'd betrayed him. He'd betrayed us all.

I took a step back, slipping awkwardly on my skates, and skated as fast as I could toward shore, trying not to call attention to myself. I was stunned by how incredibly far away it seemed. All at once a low rumble put me on alert. A second later the ice cracked beneath my weight, bringing me up short. I fell with a crash and lay dazed, as a piercing pain gripped my belly and tore the breath from my lungs. I curled up to ease the pain. After a moment it began to lessen and I tried to get up, but the blade of one of my skates was stuck in the crack in the ice. I attempted to yank it out, shuddering at the metallic squeak it made each time it met with resistance from the ice.

I glanced nervously in Evan's direction, hoping he hadn't noticed. I didn't want to distract him; one false move and Drake could kill him with the poison. Cringing, I saw a tall, powerful figure towering in front of Evan, who staggered back at the sight, almost losing control. Drake had taken on yet another appearance. He was now shrouded in a red mantle that covered his entire body down to his feet. A broad hood concealed his face. Something inside me trembled unexpectedly as I watched the scarlet figure against the pure-white snow.

A deep, hoarse voice issued from the dark hood, uttering words that were incomprehensible to me, though Evan didn't seem to have a problem understanding them. I concentrated harder, a tingle spreading steadily over my skin. I could feel a dark, ancient energy flowing through those unnerving, primordial words that seemed to spring directly from the center of the earth as if they had existed since the beginning of time. Another shiver rushed up my spine. Some obscure instinct told me a much graver danger lurked behind this mysterious creature.

Drake resumed his appearance and Evan hurled a fireball at him. He crashed onto the ice a hundred yards away and the battle began again.

The crack in the ice advanced with an ominous groan, making my heart tremble again. In the blink of an eye, before I had time to realize what was happening, a gap opened and I slipped through it. I held my breath to avoid screaming, then gasped from the chill that sank into my skin. The water was so cold it took my breath away. "Ev—" I sputtered. Water filled my mouth, freezing my lungs. Something was dragging me down. I resurfaced for a few seconds, coughing up the water I'd swallowed, then gasped, filling my lungs with air. My legs felt heavy. I looked around, moving my arms in the water. I had just enough energy to hope I could do it alone, without drawing Evan's attention.

I grabbed hold of a slab of ice that had broken free from the surface and tried to catch my breath but slipped over and over. Something still seemed to be dragging me down. With difficulty I kept myself afloat, at times sinking into the icy lake, on the verge of blacking out.

The water was too cold. I felt like I was drowning. My legs had gone numb and my hands were starting to do the same. Just breathing took a tremendous effort. My chest expanded and contracted slowly and heavily, as if a strap were squeezing my ribcage. I clung to the slab of ice with all my strength but kept slipping.

"GEMMA!"

I heard my name being shouted in the distance. "Ev—" came from my mouth, barely audible. My throat filled with ice-cold water as the lake enveloped me in its freezing mantle. *Don't worry about me*, I wished I could reply as I surrendered to the darkness. But my wish was feeble, full of pain; Evan wouldn't be able to hear me any more.

Suddenly I felt light. My body was so cold now I could no longer feel the cruelty with which the water was freezing me. A wave of heat filled me like an electric charge and my body trembled in response.

I opened my eyes. I was once again on the surface and Evan was kneeling at my side. I felt the warmth of his touch but before it could sink in, something sent me flying. I crashed down onto the ice, where I lay sprawled for a moment, my energy drained. Moving was too painful and too difficult. Just opening my eyes took too much effort. My body wouldn't be able to resist the cold much longer, I could tell.

"Evv-vvv-vvv—" My teeth chattered so hard I couldn't even pronounce his name. Though I couldn't see him, I heard the sound of blows as he continued his battle with Drake and wondered if it would ever end. I struggled to keep my eyes open, knowing that if I fell asleep it would be the end of everything. For a moment the idea seemed comforting.

No. I couldn't lose consciousness, otherwise all Evan's efforts would have been in vain and Drake would win. I couldn't let that happen.

Slowly I forced my eyes open. Their lids were so heavy. Perhaps my eyes were deceiving me, but Evan and Drake seemed miles away, barely visible as they savagely battled each other. It was too difficult to bear. What would winning mean? Killing Drake? What a miserable price victory would exact.

No, there would be no victory in this battle.

I was devastated. I'd pitted two brothers against each other. My life wasn't worth this much. I was too tired to think. Every breath was exhausting and I couldn't tell whether darkness was all around me or if I was about to pass out again. Keeping my eyelids open was becoming more and more difficult; they felt as heavy as lead. All at once there was silence. I couldn't even hear the incessant spasmodic chattering of my teeth from the cold.

"Gemma!" As distant as an echo, Evan's voice tore me out of my isolation and I opened my eyes again. He and Drake were closer now, but it was still hard for me to make them out clearly. "You've got to keep awak—"

Darkness.

"Gemma! Stay with me, please!" he shouted again, desperation straining his voice.

I focused on Evan's face, twisted into a mask of hatred and suffering, bitterness and torment. His eyes mirrored his pain. I couldn't die now, of all times. This couldn't actually be the end of everything. And yet I was so tired . . .

My eyes went to Drake who was staring at Evan with a triumphant expression. If I died, Evan wouldn't be able to keep him from taking me with him. I couldn't let that happen. Gathering the little energy I had left, I fought as hard as I could to stay awake and lucid. I was determined not to surrender to my destiny.

Drake abruptly froze as if he'd seen something terrifying over Evan's shoulder, and vanished. His parting words, "We'll meet again soon," hung in the air. The warning note in his tone made me tremble.

Evan rushed to me, his face filled with concern. "Everything's going to be fine," he whispered tenderly. I opened my eyes and winced at the sight of the wounds on his face and body. Seeing the anxiety in my eyes, he shushed me before I could speak. "It's over." His tone softened, as did his expression, and my eyes closed again.

"You need to warm her," someone said in a kind, authoritative voice. Ginevra? I hadn't realized she was there too. I still didn't have the strength to open my eyes and make sure. Someone took off my skates.

"My God," Evan murmured.

"Her body won't hold out much longer. Look at her feet! She needs warmth."

Evan was already on top of me. "I'll take care of her," he said tenderly.

Heat spread slowly inside me, growing stronger and more comforting until it burst into a powerful energy that warmed every fiber of my being, filling my body from head to toe. A moment later, blurred images raced by in my mind as if my thoughts were whirling on an out-of-control carousel.

I opened my eyes. Evan's face was the first thing I saw. Simon and Ginevra were also leaning over me. "You're all here," I murmured, still dazed. "I sure keep you guys busy, don't I?" I joked, then became serious again. "Where is he now?"

It was Evan who answered. "He's gone." His eyes went to Ginevra's. "Seems he's afraid of you," he said intently, holding her gaze as if privately communicating with her.

"This is insane," Ginevra muttered as if to herself, a desperate look in her eyes. "Evan, tell me I'm wrong. Tell me your thoughts are lying, Evan!" It sounded like an order, though there was a pleading note in her voice.

Evan's expression hardened and Ginevra looked devastated.

"Would somebody mind telling me what's going on?" said Simon, intruding on their silence.

"It's Drake," I answered in a tiny voice, my heart crushed by guilt. I swallowed, trying to loosen the knot in my throat. "He's been the one behind it the whole time. He's the Executioner sent in to kill me."

A glint of ice flashed in Simon's eyes. He looked horrified by the revelation. "No," he whispered, gazing blankly over the lake, "you guys must be wrong." He continued to shake his head, seeming overwhelmed by shock and pain.

"I wish we were," I said slowly.

"It's impossible!" Simon insisted.

Evan looked directly into his brother's eyes. "No. It isn't." His hard tone banished every doubt. "The only way to get at Gemma was from the inside. The Elders knew nobody could get close to her with us around."

"Nobody except one of us," Simon broke in. He looked devastated by the reasoning behind the nefarious plan that had pitted us against each other.

"Exactly. Drake's the youngest member of the family and they knew it."

"No. I can't believe it. He would never do that," Ginevra said, looking as crushed as the others by the painful betrayal. "The fact that he's been with us for less time doesn't make him easier to influence. I can't accept that."

"You have to," Evan ordered in a growl, giving her a hard look. "Drake's made his decision. No matter how much he meant to me, I'll do whatever it takes to stop him."

"Evan!" Simon gasped reproachfully.

"Don't forget, Simon, *he* was the one who attacked *us!* He was about to kill Gemma tonight," Evan snarled. "And it wasn't the first time he'd tried."

"The poison," Ginevra said, suddenly gripped by the realization. "He's the one who took it from my room! I wonder why he hasn't used it yet."

"I don't know, but he won't hesitate to use it next time. That's why we need a plan," Evan stated, so determined, so confident it seemed impossible he was talking about killing his own brother.

"The last time you said that, things didn't turn out so well," Ginevra reminded him, sarcasm in her voice.

"This time we won't make any mistakes. What Drake is doing is reprehensible, but I can't blame him for not standing up to the Elders. I understand. I was on the verge of making that same decision to follow orders myself, though I already knew I loved Gemma. Why would he have disobeyed them?"

"For you," Ginevra was quick to say.

"His soul is on the line," Evan said, resolute.

"Still, it's insane. I would have bet no one would ever manage to separate us," Ginevra whispered, gazing sadly into space.

"Looks like you would have lost that bet." Evan's tone was matter-of-fact, as if he weren't bothered by the situation, but I knew that wasn't the case. "Drake was faced with a decision: with us or against us. He made up his mind, and we're going to act accordingly."

This time I couldn't justify Drake, not even to myself. What he'd done was inconceivable.

"Bullshit!" Simon burst out, overcome with rage. "Drake's never believed in Redemption! He would never have betrayed us for that."

"Seems he changed his mind," Ginevra said coldly.

"Evan," I ventured, goosebumps rising on my skin at the haunting memory, "who was that man with the hood? Why did Drake take on his appearance?" My words sliced through the air like the crack of a whip. They seemed to sting Simon and Ginevra more than the freezing air. Evan's face turned grim.

"It was an Elder," he said somberly.

Beside him, Simon tensed. "What are you talking about, Evan?" he said, shocked. "How can you be so sure? No one's ever seen an Elder!" I could hear in his tone that he wanted an explanation.

"You're wrong," Evan replied coldly. "I've seen an Elder before — when I summoned the Màsala to ask to be relieved of the mission to kill Gemma."

We could read the shock in Simon's eyes. His face turned to a mask of ice. "I thought you'd summoned them in your mind! My God, Evan, it was enough of a suicide mission as it was. But they —" Simon pressed his lips together as if trying to hold back a curse. "They *showed* themselves to you, for God's sake? Why didn't you tell us?"

"I didn't see any need to," Evan said.

Simon let out an exasperated sigh. "Where did it happen?" he asked.

"In the woods. What do you want me to say? I wasn't expecting it myself. They already knew what consequences there would be if I deserted, they already knew the feelings hidden in my heart. They'd already perceived them before I was aware of them myself, and they knew how many Subterraneans would pay the price. I guess that was why they thought it was best to personally intervene and try to change my mind, persuade me that it had to be done. They talked as if the fate of the whole world depended on Gemma's death, like it was a question of the utmost importance." Evan snorted, his lips twisted into a grimace, then faced Simon again, his eyes intense. "Not only did the Màsala refuse my request, they *demanded* I carry out their order—but I didn't."

"Wait a minute," said Ginevra, who looked as if she hadn't dared interrupt until then. "During the battle what you saw wasn't actually an Elder . . . but how could Drake have known what they look like?"

Our baffled faces shot to Evan's in search of an answer to the mystery but his expression had already darkened, shrouded by an impenetrable veil.

"He said something," I told Simon. "I couldn't tell what language it was, but it sounded ancient."

"Sanskrit," he deduced, looking grim.

"Evan, did you understand what—"

The darkness of Evan's expression made me cringe and the words died in my throat. He clenched his fists at his sides and his jaw tightened as he answered my unfinished question. "He's not going to stop until he kills you."

An eerie silence enveloped us all. A silence that extended to our hearts.

DARK OMEN

The sun hadn't yet risen over the silent town of Lake Placid. Snow blanketed everything in a fluffy white mantle. I stared at it through the picture window in Evan's living room, but all I saw was the dark halo encircling my heart.

Still in shock, the others continued their discussion, searching for a solution. Their conflicting emotions were keeping them from formulating a plan to kill the brother with whom they'd lived for such a long time—longer than my entire life.

I was miserable. Guilt gripped my heart like a tether pulled so tight it made it bleed. Even so, I tried hard to hide it, maybe because I was afraid the others would finally realize it was all my fault. Regret burned me like acid corroding my stomach. The feeling was unbearable.

From time to time, reflected in the window, I saw Evan steal a glance at me as Simon healed his wounds. Only after Evan had taken off his shirt had I seen the bloody gashes on his body.

"My God, look what he did to you," Ginevra had said, her voice broken with dismay over Drake's brutality. "I still can't believe it was him." Her comment had been met with silence.

Ginevra returned to the subject now, a new awareness in her eyes. "You already suspected him," she said, turning to Evan. It wasn't a question. "How could I not have picked up on your suspicions?" she wondered aloud, self-reproach in her tone. "When did you figure it out?"

I turned to look at Evan too, waiting for him to answer. He hesitated a few seconds, staring blankly ahead as if recalling the memory were painful. "He attacked us when we were in the café, but at that point I wasn't suspicious at all. I didn't sense the presence of any Subterraneans except him, but I thought he was there for the guy who'd been riding the motorcycle. That's what he wanted me to believe," Evan said as if just figuring it out now. "Then he caused the accident with my car. That's when I realized it wasn't over, that it was happening again." Evan paused, still shaken by the memory. "That afternoon he tried it again, in the woods."

"I still don't get it," said Simon. "What made you suspect Drake?"

"That afternoon, before the car accident, we went to a hangar not far from Lake Placid. I took Gemma up for a ride in the old fighter plane that used to be Drake's." I instantly noticed the surprise on Ginevra's face. She was wondering how Evan could have kept it a secret from her. "I was expecting to be attacked at any moment, although I tried not to let Gemma see how worried I was." He glanced at me. "What happened in the café had alarmed me. But then nothing happened."

We all gazed at him in silence.

"So I figured my suspicions were unfounded and that they hadn't come back to hunt Gemma down after all. It would have been the ideal opportunity for anyone who wanted to kill her. I'd offered them the perfect chance to attack. And if they had, I would have been prepared—but nothing happened." He stopped, gazing into space again. "Later the car went out of control and someone kept me from stopping it. That's when I thought of Drake and something he'd said just a few days before when I'd told him where I was going to take Gemma: he said he didn't want to see that plane ever again. He wanted me to get rid of it. I knew how much he suffered whenever he went near that place. Still, I couldn't accept the idea—it was so far-fetched. When he kissed Gemma my suspicions grew stronger, though I still wasn't completely sure. I went to Roomer's because I was furious about what he'd done and what I suspected he meant to do. I wanted to give him a warning, make him change his mind while there was still time. Or maybe deep down I still hoped I was wrong. Clearly I wasn't. In that case, I could at least have gotten him away from the house — that was already something."

"How did you manage to keep me in the dark about all this?" Ginevra was shocked. She still couldn't believe it was possible.

"I've honed my skills over the years," he said with dull sarcasm. "I can block my thoughts and keep anyone from getting into my mind. Besides, don't forget I have my powers too, including the power to influence *your* mind. I didn't want to worry you guys until I was sure. Until tonight," he repeated bitterly.

"What do we do now?" his sister asked.

I listened to them distractedly, staring blankly out the window as the first timid rays of sunlight began to illuminate the garden. Their voices reached me like a distant echo, almost as if I weren't part of the group right now. Maybe taking part in their pain was too much for me. Maybe I couldn't handle being the cause of it. I'd never seen them so upset before.

"First of all you two need to choose whose side you're on," Evan said steadily. I turned to look at him. The others' eyes were fixed on him. "You and Simon aren't obligated to stand by us. I won't ask you to do it. You're free to choose or declare your neutrality. I won't blame you if you decide not to get involved. Gemma and I can handle this on our own."

"No," Simon replied firmly. "What Drake has done is underhanded, atrocious. He had no right," he said, his voice stern. "He might have sided against us and chosen to follow orders, but he still should have treated her differently." He looked at me for a moment, righteous anger in his eyes. "Drake showed you no respect."

"I barely recognize him," Ginevra murmured distractedly. "Now I know why he was avoiding me all the time—he didn't want me to read his mind and find out his true intentions."

"The Elders thought of everything," Simon went on, still stunned. "I mean, he clearly isn't acting alone—I suspect he's working under someone's guidance. He's too young. They would never let him tackle all this on his own. It would be a suicide mission and *they* can't afford that. Besides, some of his behavior just isn't like him. He's always loved being surrounded by beautiful girls, but he would never have done anything so wrong to Evan, of all people."

For a moment a grim silence enveloped us. Simon and Ginevra still hadn't given a definitive answer, and the tension they felt about their decision was plain to see in their faces.

"We're with you," Ginevra stated, speaking for both of them.

Evan's face instantly relaxed and he let out a long sigh, as if he'd been holding his breath the whole time. Having Simon and Ginevra on our side was a far-from-negligible detail.

Simon rested his hand on his brother's shoulder. "We could never abandon you. You can count on us," he confirmed, though Ginevra had clearly spoken for both of them. "You're part of a team as long as you're playing on the right side of the field. Drake isn't on our side any more, though it pains me to accept it." His voice broke. "Personally, I don't feel like standing around doing nothing when someone needs me. Ginevra and I will be on the playing field with you," he concluded, sounding more confident.

"What do we do now?" Ginevra asked, turning to Evan. "We can't sit around waiting for him to attack. It's too dangerous. We need to be in full control of the situation." Her green eyes began to sparkle. "We need to act, and act fast." Evan looked absorbed in his sister's words. "But most importantly, we can't forget he stole my poison. That means that unless we stop him before it's too late, he'll use it against us. It's not just for Gemma any more."

"I wonder why he hasn't used it yet," Simon added, voicing the question we all shared.

"We're all wondering that," Ginevra said.

"The vial seemed empty," Evan said. "Maybe he thought it wouldn't be enough, that exposing himself that much was too risky. I mean, he was counting on our trusting him, and if we'd caught him with the poison it would have ruined that. No, it's crazy."

Ginevra shook her head. "Its odor was still strong. I could even smell it with the vial closed when I opened the drawer I'd hidden it in. I seriously doubt any Subterranean could survive if Drake decided to use it on them."

Evan and Simon exchanged puzzled glances, obviously not understanding. Then why had I understood instantly? I remembered perfectly well what Ginevra was talking about—the pungent smell was branded on my memory. Sometimes I even thought I could smell it when I woke up in the morning. It was probably because of the shock connected to the memory, the trauma I'd undergone that day. But I knew for a fact that Evan had told me the poison was odorless and tasteless. Was it possible it had a different effect on humans? Maybe it was a punishment for the Subterraneans—not being able to sense the only weapon capable of killing them.

Their conversation snapped me back to reality.

"He hasn't used it yet, which means he still has it, and that complicates everything." Ginevra was leading the discussion again. "We had an advantage over Faust, but this time we're fighting on equal terms." As she spoke, she shot Simon concerned glances, probably worried about him.

I stared at the floor, feeling guilty again. No one had anything else to say.

"Damn it!" Evan's furious voice sliced through the dismal silence we were lost in. "Not now!" he said through gritted teeth. After a moment, his expression became more resigned.

Ginevra gazed at him regretfully for a second. To my dismay, I understood. He had to leave. I looked him in the eye, forcing myself not to seem alarmed, though the idea that he was leaving me right now made me tremble. After everything that had happened today, I wasn't sure I could face anything else, especially without Evan's support. I was exhausted and couldn't even remember the last time I'd slept or eaten.

Evan looked at me, a mix of devastation and rage in his eyes. Without coming closer, he clenched his fists, his eyes on mine. The intense silence seemed to fill with his unspoken words.

"Evan," I murmured, almost to myself, in a frail voice.

"I'm not leaving now," he growled.

"We'll be here with her," Ginevra reassured him. "There's nothing for you to be afraid of."

Evan shook his head. "No. I said I'm not leaving," he insisted. "I can't. I can't leave her now, of all times."

"He won't attack right away," Simon pointed out. "He'll need to recover after tonight's fight too, and we still don't have a plan for how to face him. We need time."

Evan clenched his jaw, deep in thought. He looked torn. "To hell with it! I don't care!" He looked at me again and moved closer. "I'm staying here with you."

I wavered for a moment, confused by his expression. It had become tender but still had a touch of desperation in it. I didn't know what to say, though I was sure of what I wanted and sure of what would be best. Unfortunately, the two things weren't the same. "You should go," I said, my voice dull. It wasn't convincing enough. I tried to regain my self-control, even though I knew someone else in the room was aware of exactly what I was feeling. "Nothing's going to happen to me. I don't want you to compromise yourself for me even more than you already have." For a second, I thought my words had been almost believable.

"Screw the rules!" he exclaimed, still furious. Then his tone sweetened for me. "I have nothing more to lose if I stay, but I could lose everything if I go."

"It's not true you have nothing more to lose," I said. "You've already risked enough for me." Evan came closer still and my voice began to waver. "I won't—I won't let you throw away your only hope of redeeming yourself," I said in a desperate whisper as he rested his forehead against mine. "I want to know you'll be there when . . . one day—I don't want to lose you forever."

Ginevra spoke up. "Evan, she's right. We'll be here with her. You've been gone for far longer periods in the past, even days at a time."

"That was different," he snapped.

"We'll protect her. It's only a few hours," she insisted, trying to reassure him. Her concept of time was a little different from mine, though. What were a few hours to someone to whom time was of no importance? For me it would be an eternity. I could already feel the burden though Evan was still there with me.

He seemed to consider what Ginevra had said. After a moment he looked at me, his expression grim, and nodded slightly, though he didn't seem entirely convinced. He stroked my cheek and slipped his fingers into my hair, his face close to mine. "You sure?" he whispered, studying my face.

I nodded, hoping my eyes weren't giving me away. "How long will you be gone?" I asked timidly. I had to know.

"Until this evening. I'll be back at six." He glanced at the clock on the wall. "It's already seven in the morning," he said reassuringly.

"Seven? School!" I exclaimed.

Evan cut me off, his expression stern. "You're not going to school today. It's too risky. Besides, I'll be calmer if I know you're here with the others. Promise me you won't leave the house," he whispered, articulating each word.

"All right," I said. "Of course I promise. I promise." After all, skipping another day of school wouldn't be the end of the world. "Although my parents—"

"I'll use mind control on them," Evan said. "Don't worry. I'll stop by your place before leaving."

"Okay," I said, resigned. "See you back here at six, then." I forced a smile. There was something different in the way he looked at me: a profound sadness, a bitterness, shone through, as if he were afraid this would be the last time he saw me.

"I won't be a single minute late," he whispered, lifting my chin. He gave me a little smile, locking his gaze onto mine for a long moment. "I have to go," he said, louder, so the others could hear him too. Turning toward his brother and sister with the most serious expression I'd ever seen on his face, he said, "Protect her at all costs. I'm counting on you two. We've got to make the first move this time. Think of a plan while I'm gone. Meanwhile I'll do the same."

When Simon and Ginevra nodded, Evan turned back to me. I looked at him, a terrible feeling deep in my chest. My eyes locked onto his and a profound sense of desperation grew in my heart as tears welled up in my eyes. Suddenly I didn't want him to go any more—I wanted to keep him there with me. Part of me was screaming at myself to stop him. "Kiss me," I begged, forcing back the tears.

Evan moved his lips closer to mine, seeming to sense that I shared his desperation. Gripping my face in his hands, he kissed me ardently, as if no one else were in the room. For a moment the contact with his mouth made me dizzy. His lips, softer than ever, moved gently against mine. Small, tender kisses alternated with ones that were longer, more passionate—*desperate*.

When he pulled away and rested his forehead on mine, a shiver of terror ran down my spine and I felt a deep sense of loss. My gaze met his and again the terrible sensation that this would be our last kiss came over me. I shuddered from the power of the ghastly premonition.

Evan ran his hands down my arms and rubbed them gently because I had goosebumps. He took my hand and smiled at me, but it didn't dispel the awful feeling. Could it really be a premonition? Would I really die during the few short hours Evan would be gone? I looked into his eyes but couldn't see him; my mind was elsewhere, adrift.

He ran his thumb over my lower lip to bring me back to reality, shaking me out of my fog. I looked him in the eyes again, forcing a smile that he returned.

"I'll take the taste of your lips with me," he whispered, his face an inch from mine.

"And I'll be here waiting for you to renew it with another kiss," I said, hoping against hope it was a promise I would be able to keep.

His gaze didn't leave me for a second as he began to disappear before my eyes. The strange agitation stirred more fiercely inside me and my heart responded by accelerating its rhythm. I felt a sudden, desperate impulse to squeeze his hand and keep him there with me before he vanished entirely, but it was too late. Evan was gone. A blade of ice pierced my heart. Never before had I felt so alone.

EXTREME DECISIONS

"Don't worry," Ginevra told me. Though I could feel her close by, I barely registered my surroundings. Evan had been gone only a moment, during which I hadn't moved, staring blankly at the spot where he'd been, my mind wandering who knew where. It was as if a black hole had swallowed up all my thoughts. I felt alone without him, and the horrifying certainty that I'd lost him forever stubbornly persisted. Would I really never see him again? The very thought was enough to drain me of all my emotions.

"Gemma." A hand stroked my arm in the same place Evan had touched it a moment ago. I instinctively pulled back as if to protect the memory and looked at her, dazed. "Everything's going to be fine."

I looked into Ginevra's eyes and felt like I was seeing her for the first time. My eyelids fluttered nervously, as if I'd just awakened from a state of shock.

"We won't let anything happen to you. You'll see, the day will go by fast." Evan had said the same thing, but I wasn't convinced. "You should eat something."

"I'm not hungry," I said automatically. My stomach was in knots.

"Yes you are," she said sternly. "You can't afford to get weak now, of all times. You need every last drop of your energy." Her voice was raised in reproach and I didn't have the strength to put up a fight. "Besides, you look exhausted. You need to get some sleep. Let's go to the kitchen. I'll make you something to eat and then you'll go rest," she ordered me firmly.

Not wanting to waste my breath, I did as she said and followed her into the other room. After all, she wasn't all wrong. Maybe it was weakness that was clouding my mind, and that was the last thing I needed.

The silence in the kitchen made it seem even larger than it was. That it felt so empty, on the other hand, was for a completely different reason. I missed Evan. Unable to stop thinking I'd never see him again, tears stung my eyes. I could feel his absence in my stomach.

"The only absence you feel in your stomach is lack of food!" Ginevra said, replying to my thoughts and trying to boost my morale—but the look on my face told her it wouldn't work.

Only a few hours had passed, the minutes ticking slowly by. It seemed like an eternity since Evan had left. Simon and Ginevra moved around the kitchen nervously. I hadn't moved from my seat the whole time, listening to them. I wanted to help, but for some reason all I could think of was the look on Evan's face right before he'd disappeared and the terrible feeling of emptiness and loss he'd left behind.

"There must be something we can do to put an end to this whole thing," Simon was saying.

"Nothing that doesn't involve the one thing you're refusing to think about," Ginevra told him frankly. "You've got to accept it, Simon."

"You think I don't realize that? I'm not denying what has to happen."

"So why don't you say it out loud?" she rebuked him. "You can't, that's why! Simon, if you aren't convinced—"

"Of course I am," he said firmly. "It's just that—it's hard." His expression turned sad.

"I know, but we've already chosen sides. Now we just need to figure out how to play the game: offense or defense. As I see it, we can't wait for Drake to make the first move. Don't forget he has poison and he'll use it against you guys. We're all involved at this point. He might decide to use it on Evan." Ginevra paused a moment, looking troubled. "Or on you." Her eyes glimmered on his. "And I'll never let him do that. I'm not putting your life in jeopardy. Drake is perfectly capable of making his own decisions and so are we. I'm not going to risk anything happening to you, Simon. We're going to do what we need to do." She looked straight at him, in her eyes a sharp light that shone with all the coldness of her true nature. "We're going to kill him."

At that moment she was a Witch and Drake was her ancient enemy, a Subterranean to kill. Her prey. The thought hit me so hard I shuddered.

Simon's face turned grim, but the gleam of pain in his eye showed me he knew Ginevra was right. They would do what they had to do, no matter how painful it was.

Sitting in my corner, I felt smaller and more insignificant than ever. It wasn't fair that my survival was causing so much grief to the people I loved most. Maybe there actually was some reason I was destined to die and they were making a terrible mistake by defying fate. How many more lives would be cut short because of me? How many more Angels would be killed so I could live? Who would be next? Because I was certain—it would never really be over. I wasn't so sure any more that my life was worth that much. And yet I couldn't stand the thought of losing Evan forever.

Hidden behind my feelings of guilt, my egotistical survival instinct reared its head from time to time, eclipsing everything else, urging me to fight, to cling to life tooth and nail, to do whatever it took to avoid losing Evan.

I couldn't give him up. Not for anything in the world. Not for *anyone* in the world. I didn't care how selfish or even evil what I wanted was; I wasn't going to lose Evan, not even if prolonging my life meant sacrificing the lives of many others. Everything had its price. Someone else would pay the price of my destiny. I had to accept that because the alternative was inconceivable.

A shudder ran down my arms and for a moment I felt an odd sensation under my skin. Excitement mixed with something else I couldn't decipher. Power, maybe? I quickly composed myself, shocked by my own thoughts, and looked around in alarm, hoping Ginevra hadn't heard them. She was still talking to Simon, so wrapped up in their conversation she didn't seem to be paying attention to me, though I couldn't be completely sure.

I silently reflected on the strange, uncontrollable sensation I'd just had. It was like there was another Gemma inside me, one I'd never known, and my mind had temporarily shut down, letting her emerge, allowing some primitive instinct to take over—a dark instinct I could feel in my bones. It scared me because it felt like an integral part of me. The sensation wasn't entirely new to me—it wasn't the first time it had happened. I'd felt it before during the last few weeks, like a secret switch inside me had been flipped, instantly filling me with unfamiliar wrath. It was a rebellious, uncontrollable feeling that made me unexpectedly boil with rage. The last time it had made me scream at Ginevra.

What the hell was happening to me? Was it some kind of side effect of having come back from the dead? Maybe Evan was wrong—maybe I wasn't as strong as he thought and I was falling to pieces.

No, I was just under stress. It was an understandable reaction. The emotional pressure I'd been subject to was clearly too much for me. After all, everybody has their limits. No matter how hard I tried to hide it, even from myself, I actually felt so fragile, beyond exhausted. My nerves were as taut as a strand of hair against a razor, trembling at the faintest puff of air. All it would take was one tiny movement for me to touch the razor's edge and snap. It felt like that moment was about to arrive.

"You're not getting involved." Simon's voice rang through the room, his fiery eyes locked onto Ginevra's.

"I know how to defend myself," she retorted. "Don't think I'm going to stand by doing nothing while Drake hurts you."

"I've already told you, nothing's going to happen to me."

"My poison is lethal to you too!" Ginevra shouted.

"Just like his fire is to you!"

"We've trained hard and we'll keep on training hard until the time comes. I'm ready. It won't be the first time for me—I've battled lots of Subterraneans before."

"That was ages ago!"

"You can't protect yourself against the poison, but I can protect myself from his attacks. Besides, you're forgetting that he's afraid of me."

"No," he repeated firmly. "It's out of the question."

"Simon, we'll train harder. Trust me, it's the best choice. Let me do this," Ginevra said, trying hard to persuade him.

Crushed by a feeling of powerlessness, I looked directly at Simon for the first time just as his crystalline eyes flickered and a sly smile spread over his face. It looked familiar for some reason, and I realized it was the same smile that appeared on Evan's lips whenever he had an idea. I tried hard not to let myself be overcome by nostalgia, since it threatened to drag me into the vortex that led to Evan. Maybe it was natural for every thought to lead me back to him.

I turned to look at Ginevra. Her eyes had narrowed to slits as she studied Simon's mind with keen interest. "What are you thinking?" I said, speaking for the first time.

They turned toward me as if they'd forgotten my presence. I looked at each of them in turn. Simon hesitated, giving Ginevra time to carefully assess his idea.

"Interesting," she whispered, deep in thought.

I glanced at Simon and then turned back to Ginevra, waiting for one of them to answer me.

"Drake is expecting a battle." Simon's expression gradually became more cunning and determined as he explained. The plan began to take shape outside his mind. "But he's in for a surprise."

"It's a desperate plan," Ginevra cautioned him, still probing his mind.

"Desperate times call for desperate measures."

They both turned their eyes on me. I looked back and forth between them, puzzled. The whole time they'd pretty much excluded me from their conversation, talking to each other as if I weren't there, but now they had a strange light in their eyes as they stared at me, as if I were the key to everything.

"What?" I asked in alarm, but their attention to me disappeared as quickly as it had come. I was invisible again.

"Would she go that far?" Simon asked Ginevra, almost in a whisper, without taking his eyes off me. I had the impression they were both studying me. "It might work but we need to assess all the risks," Simon warned her. "It would take incredible courage."

"I don't think that's a problem. She can do it. I know she can."

"How can you be so sure?"

"I just am, trust me. I can't explain why—it's like an instinct. Just believe me on this," Ginevra told him.

"But you saw how she reacted the first time!"

"This time it'll be different," she said, determined. "Things have changed."

I was lost. Simon wasn't so convinced of his own plan any more?

"Besides, I'm not even sure Evan would allow it."

"Would you guys mind telling me what you're talking about?" I blurted. "What wouldn't Evan agree to?" They both stared at me again. "What do you have to tell me?" I realized my voice was trembling. "You have a plan, don't you?"

"Not necessarily," Simon answered.

Ginevra rephrased his answer: "You'll be the one to decide that," she said gravely.

I looked at her, bewildered. What was going on? "I'm too tired to play guessing games," I said. Their mysterious discussion had left me exasperated. "What is your plan, exactly?"

They stared at me for a long moment, as surprised as I was by how calmly I'd asked. Ginevra was studying me, I was sure of it. There was nothing I could hide from her. "Simon has an idea." I waited for her to go on, my impatience mounting. "I think it's a good plan, but you would be directly involved." Her gaze, deep as a stormy sea, lingered on me.

"That's why the decision is up to you," Simon added. "No one will blame you if you decide to refuse."

They were both gazing at me attentively. What was going on? Could Simon read my thoughts now too? From the way he was looking at me, it certainly seemed like it. My heartbeat accelerated unexpectedly. What was with all the tension I saw on their faces? And why would Evan not accept their plan? My instinct gave me the answer: I was going to have to do something dangerous.

"Would you mind telling me what's going on?" I asked again, though I wasn't so sure I wanted to know any more.

"The idea might work. In fact, I *know* it'll work. It's an excellent plan," Ginevra exclaimed, "but it requires a courageous decision on your part." She moved a few steps closer. "And I know you're capable of handling it."

"Tell me something I don't already know," I shot back, out of patience.

"Gemma," Ginevra began cautiously, "you already know my poison is the only weapon that can kill Drake." I nodded without speaking. "But open battle might be too risky at this point for any of us. You know Evan won't hesitate to fight for you."

"We're almost positive somebody's got Drake's back," Simon added. "He isn't working alone, and that's definitely not to our advantage. We might lose." His tone hardened.

Was that really a possibility?

"And we can't forget he has my poison with him—enough for a lethal dose." Ginevra said. She paused to study my reaction and read the thoughts that whirled confusedly in my mind like a helium balloon at the mercy of the wind. Their plan must be far from pleasant if it was taking them this long to explain it. She continued. "That's why we need to avoid a direct battle . . . and set a trap for him. We need to catch him off guard," she concluded firmly.

"All right," I whispered, my voice barely audible, "but what's my part in all this?" I was starting to feel seriously worried.

"Actually, that all depends on you," Ginevra said gravely.

I turned to Simon who was staring at the floor as if avoiding my eyes. The idea had been his, and yet on his face was a look of . . . uncertainty? Guilt? I couldn't tell. And what were we talking about, exactly?

"I'll do whatever it takes." My voice trembled. I wasn't completely sure I would be able to keep that promise, but after all it was entirely my fault they were in this situation in the first place. "Tell me what you have in mind," I said, my tone more convinced this time.

"Good," Ginevra murmured, almost to herself, "because you're the only one who can slip Drake the poison without his noticing."

Her words hit me hard, like a punch to the gut. "Me? What are you talking about? H-how could I?" I asked, confused.

"With a kiss."

I jumped in my seat, my blood running cold. It was finally clear why they'd been so hesitant and mysterious. A mind-numbing panic filled me and I tried not to show how incredibly shaken I was. "You're saying I would have to *kiss* him?" I shot nervous looks at Ginevra and Simon, who was still avoiding my eyes.

"No one is forcing you, of course," he said, "but that's all we've got. For now, it's our only hope. We can't put the poison in a glass of water—Drake has no need to drink and would be suspicious if you asked him to. Not to mention how dangerous it would be if he discovered our plan."

It took me a moment to grasp what he meant. They had wondered out loud if I was brave enough and now I was wondering the same thing. Ginevra seemed convinced, but how could they be so sure, if not even I knew the answer to that question? I would have to let Drake come near me, and he could kill me with a wave of his hand. That in itself was enough to make me hesitate.

The thought of kissing anyone other than Evan of my own free will was hard enough already, but it was impossible to wrap my brain around the fact that this kiss would be fatal. No matter how many times Simon and Ginevra told me I wouldn't be forced to do it, I knew it wasn't true, at least in part. I had to do it whether or not I wanted to. It was my turn. I had to protect Evan.

It was up to me to kill Drake. I calmly repeated the thought in my mind as the two of them assessed my silence. Simon, who had stood aside, was also waiting for me to speak.

When I finally opened my mouth, I'd made my decision and it was final. "I'm the one who set you against each other. I'll do whatever you ask."

"Don't speak too soon," Simon warned. "First you need to hear the hardest part."

His harsh tone made me flinch. "What could be more terrible than kissing Drake . . . and *killing* him?" I asked, forcing out the last two words. How would I be able to kill Drake if I could barely stand the mere thought of doing it? I studied their faces and waited.

After a silence that felt endless, Ginevra explained all in one breath: "You wouldn't be immune to the poison."

A cold, bitter wave crashed over me even before I'd fully grasped what she'd just said. My body had understood and reacted instinctively. "You're saying—" I murmured in shock.

"The poison is going to kill you too," Simon said ruefully.

I was stunned. My thoughts echoed in my mind as they continued talking, freezing everything inside me. For a moment I felt cut off from them, like I wasn't in the room any more. I was alone—alone in my desperation.

So death would come after all, and not by chance. I felt myself wandering through the darkness of those absurd words. My mind seemed to be lost, or maybe it didn't want to return at all. I wished I could run away from this place, from these people, even from myself, and hide somewhere dark and safe.

I heard something in the background and barely managed to realize someone was talking to me, but I couldn't make out the words, still deafened as I was by the last ones. They whirled through my head, drowning out everything else. Everything was so distorted, so confusing . . .

Their voices echoed in my head, shouting the bone-chilling words I didn't want to hear: I had to die.

All at once the murmur stopped and the sudden silence tore me out the trance I'd fallen into, dragging me back to the room. "You're saying that—" I stopped, unable to go on.

Simon and Ginevra continued to watch me silently. "We told you it would be difficult," Ginevra said.

"And we'll understand if you decide to back down, though we don't have much time to come up with another plan. If Drake attacks again, we'll have to face him, and we're not sure how that will turn out," Simon explained.

I winced, thinking of Evan. He was all that mattered to me. Everything else—including my own life—was less important.

"Simon's plan is really good," Ginevra added, "and there's no way it can fail, unless you're discovered."

Did they really think I was capable of this? I would ruin everything like I always did one way or another, and put them in danger for the millionth time. Why didn't they realize that? Why did they trust me so much?

"The only person who doesn't trust you is you," Ginevra said, replying to my thoughts.

"What if I fail?" I murmured, the knot in my throat growing tighter.

"You won't. We trust you, Gemma," Simon assured me.

"What happens afterwards?" I said, my voice barely audible, forcing myself to hide my trembling.

Simon walked over to me and looked me in the eye for the first time. "You don't need to worry about that." There wasn't a trace of fear or doubt in his voice. "We'll be there with you, even though you won't be able to see us. When the right moment comes we'll get there in time. You just need to focus on what you have to do and it will all be over. We'll take care of the rest. We've already done it once before. We know now how to handle the situation and we'll be able to bring you back without any problems. You'll return, but he won't."

Simon's reassuring tone eased some of my tension. I felt drained. In a way, I had no words to say or questions to ask.

"You can always say no," Ginevra repeated.

I turned to look at her. *No, I can't,* I replied in my mind. I owed it to him—to them all. "I'll do it," I announced, forcing myself to sound determined. "Tell me what I have to do."

Simon shook his head. "This is insane," he burst out. My eyes shot to his. "Forget we even said it. We'll think of something else."

"Simon, there's no time," Ginevra rebuked him.

"Evan will never go along with it. We're wasting our breath."

"Why? Don't forget his last plan entailed risks, and they weren't any less drastic than yours. He was aware of the dangers but he accepted them." Simon looked torn and Ginevra studied his silence. "Fine. Do you have a better idea?"

Simon clearly didn't. "All I'm saying is that it's insane! We can't let him get so close to Gemma."

If they didn't even believe in the plan, how could I?

"It's dangerous, that's true, but we'll be there with her. It'll work and none of us will get hurt. Now cut it out, Simon—you're confusing her!"

"It's up to me to decide, right?" I said. They looked at me. "Simon, is there any possibility you won't be able to bring me back?" I asked, just in case.

Simon glanced at me, seeming unsure whether or not to relieve my doubts with his answer. "No. Your death will only be temporary. As far as that goes, you have nothing to worry about. It would be even briefer than last time."

"But last time," I said cautiously, "there were three of you there to heal me."

My point left him wordless for a second, but he composed himself. "We don't need Drake. This time we won't need to heal wounds all over your body, so it'll be easier. You'll only die from the effect of the poison. Other than that, your body will remain intact and unharmed."

"I don't see a problem then," I said firmly. I looked him in the eye, almost as if I were the one reassuring him. "I can do it," I said in a determined tone even I didn't recognize.

"You sure?" he asked, still wary.

I looked at him and then at Ginevra before answering: "I'm doing it." I stared at them hard to emphasize my decision.

"Fine. We have to act fast then. We can't risk his making the first move, so you need to be prepared to face him when the opportunity presents itself."

I flinched when I realized it was actually going to happen. I'd agreed. The *end* would be the solution. "When do you think he might show up?" I asked anxiously, turning to Ginevra.

"We can't know for sure. He'll need time to recover and I doubt he would decide to attack too soon, but meanwhile he might use his powers to get close to you again. I'll give you some of my poison. You'll need to take special care of it. You must keep it with you *everywhere* and *at all times*. Then, when the opportunity arises—and I don't think it'll take that long—you can't hesitate for even a second or Drake might guess our plan."

I trembled at the thought. Ginevra had been clear in the strict orders she'd given me. They were all counting on me. I couldn't let them down. "We need to tell Evan," I said, worried there wouldn't be time.

"We'll tell him when he gets back," Simon reassured me. "Don't worry."

I sighed with relief. I wasn't prepared for the possibility of carrying out the plan without his support.

"I wouldn't be able to bring you back without him," Simon continued. "I just hope Drake doesn't take advantage of his being gone to get near you," he said, looking concerned.

"What should I do if that happens?" I asked in alarm.

"Nothing risky," he warned. "You can't use the poison until Evan knows about the plan, otherwise you'll complicate things." Simon looked me in the eye to make sure I followed his instructions. "You risk actually dying, Gemma. I can't do it all alone. It's imperative that both Evan and I reach you in time to save you."

"We'll be there even if you can't see us," Ginevra explained. "We'll have to keep a certain distance. That way Drake can feel safe enough to get close without being able to sense our presence. Still, we'll be close enough to get to you in time."

"Fine. I'm ready." I swallowed and looked confidently at Ginevra. "Give me the poison."

She nodded slightly, her eyes fixed on mine. "Come with me."

I did as she said, but after a few steps I turned to look at Simon, puzzled. "Aren't you coming?"

A bitter half smile escaped him. "I don't think that would be a good idea."

"Right." I opened my mouth but closed it a moment later.

Simon was still smiling. "Don't get bitten before it's time or we'll have to scrap the whole plan!" he warned with a wink and a touch of sarcasm.

"If that happens I guess you won't need a plan any more," I reminded him in the same tone, returning the smile and leaving the room.

MYSTERIOUS INSTINCT

Ginevra opened her bedroom door casually, disregarding the furious beating of my heart that I was sure she could hear. My blood was pumping so hard I felt my veins throbbing in my temples. This was all so bizarre.

I'd been in this room a hundred times and knew it well—I'd memorized its every detail. Except one, obviously: the vault, which had always been strictly off limits. I'd never paid much attention to it, but now the door seemed larger and heavier, as if it continued to grow out of proportion before my eyes and wanted to crush me. Or maybe it was me who felt smaller and more helpless than ever. In a moment I would walk through that door toward an encounter with my fate.

I'd heard them mention Ginevra's serpent before, though rarely. Usually they preferred not to dwell on the subject. Ginevra came to a halt in front of the door. I was right behind her.

"You can wait outside if you want," she said.

"I'd rather go in," I replied quickly, yearning to give in to the strange instinct that continued to push me toward danger.

With a clack so loud it penetrated my bones, the lock opened and the vault door swung open. Shuddering as I followed Ginevra in, I looked around and realized we weren't in a room, but rather, an enormous, unearthly garden under a lead-gray sky. It was as though the door had opened into a parallel dimension.

When Ginevra moved I followed close on her heels, staying alert. I didn't want her serpent to lunge out and bite me. Of course if it did, it would spare them a few problems. In reply to my thoughts, Ginevra cast me an amused frown. "Just kidding," I said with a grin and a shrug.

All at once her expression turned serious—not worried, just serious. "Don't move," she warned, stopping in front of me calmly. At her words I froze in my tracks. Out of the corner of my eye I noticed a movement just over my shoulder. "Don't worry," she reassured me. "He won't hurt you."

Every fiber of my body trembled as the movement continued. I stood rigid and saw it: her serpent. It moved with Ginevra's grace, weaving in harmonious patterns through the branches above my head.

"He's under my control," she continued to reassure me. "He won't do anything to you. He obeys my thoughts."

I weighed her words and something dawned on me: it wasn't fear I was feeling. Something else was trembling inside me, some emotion I couldn't put my finger on.

The serpent moved toward Ginevra, slithering over a large branch so smoothly he almost seemed to float through the air. Ginevra held out her hand and the creature obeyed, sliding sinuously onto her arm. I would never have imagined it, but seeing them together was electrifying.

The serpent coiled gracefully around Ginevra's forearm. "Scared?" she asked me, her voice comforting as I stared at her, fascinated.

"No, I don't think so." It was the truth. "I think it's something else. He's so . . . *magnetic*," I replied as the animal formed a perfect spiral, gliding elegantly up to Ginevra's elbow. When he reached her upper arm, something unexpected happened. My eyes bulged as the serpent fused with her skin.

A glimmer spread over Ginevra's eyes, making them even greener. Their emerald-like light was hard to describe. For a fraction of a second her pupils narrowed and lengthened in imitation of her serpent's, leaving me breathless. She turned to me with the satisfied look an inventor might have when showing off their newest creation for the first time. Unable to believe what I'd just seen, I opened my mouth to speak, but not a sound came out. Ginevra continued to smile at me like someone who's just finished a long journey through the desert and finally quenched their thirst.

The serpent had disappeared beneath her skin, leaving a spiral-shaped silver mark around her arm. *Magnificent* was the only word my brain could come up with.

"You really think so?" she asked, looking honored.

I was even more convinced than before: there was something magnetic about her creature, so powerful and extraordinary. I nodded, unable to take my eyes off the spot on her arm where her serpent had disappeared.

"He's part of me," she whispered, her smile widening as she looked me in the eye in search of understanding.

I flashed her a reassuring smile. After all, I didn't need to read Ginevra's mind to guess how she felt. For centuries her only company had been three Subterraneans, and on top of that she'd always hidden the existence of her creature from them. She'd had to conceal an important part of herself and although Simon had always known her secret, Ginevra could never have shared with him the feelings that bonded her to her serpent. She'd even had to create an impenetrable barrier to separate them. It must have been nice for her to finally be able to share something so important, so personal.

The serpent rematerialized, gliding across Ginevra's skin before my captivated eyes, as if he'd also heard my thoughts and wanted to give me the chance to see him more closely. He spiraled down her arm toward me. Ginevra reached her arm out, a pleased look on her face.

I instinctively moved nearer. The serpent triggered a strong attraction in me, a powerful energy that even the most hidden part of my brain could detect.

We were so close. For a moment, the serpent swayed in front of my face as I gazed at him in fascination. His venom was deadly and he could bite me so quickly I would be dead before I knew it. Yet I wasn't frightened. There was no trace of fear in my body. Quite the opposite—it felt like the serpent was summoning me. The more I looked at him, the more I longed to touch him. It was a visceral need, a need I couldn't control . . .

"Don't get too close," Ginevra warned cautiously. This must have been a completely new experience for her too.

"So small yet so powerful," I murmured, my eyes riveted on the bewitching creature.

"True greatness doesn't depend on size. Sometimes the greatest power resides in the most hidden things, unseen to our eyes. This is the first time I've shown him to anyone in who knows how long."

"Yeah, that's what I would imagine."

"I even keep him away from Simon," Ginevra said as though she needed to explain. She had the serpent slide down into her hands and showed him a tiny glass container the size of a thimble. I admired her movements. I would have given anything for an ounce of her gracefulness.

"He's too dangerous for Simon," she went on, frowning in response to my thoughts. She thought it was crazy that I sometimes looked at her with such admiration. *I* thought it was crazy that she considered *me* to be on the same level as her.

"I thought you said you could control him," I said aloud after our silent disagreement.

"Yes, but I can't guarantee his reaction in such an extreme situation. Simon is still a Subterranean, after all, and it might be too much for a serpent to bear. If his survival instinct kicked in, I would have to—" Ginevra stopped abruptly. There was no need for her to finish her sentence—I already understood. "I do it to protect both of them."

As she said this, the serpent sank his fang into the vial, drawing my attention. The scent was so powerful and immediate it made me dizzy. I almost lost my balance, it was so intoxicating. It was just as I remembered it: intense, overpowering . . . *irresistible*. Who knew what it would be like to taste it. For a second, it almost felt like I was savoring its flavor. I would find out soon enough.

Ginevra raised an eyebrow and looked at me. "It's strange that you can smell it," she said with surprise.

"I thought Subterraneans were the only ones who couldn't," I said, confused.

"Actually, I've never tested it out on a . . . human." She said the last word cautiously.

"Go ahead and say it—I'm not offended. I know perfectly well I'm a human," I reminded her.

"It's just that Angels generally can't smell it."

"That must be an advantage for you Witches."

"I guess."

"Since they can't smell it, they can't anticipate the danger, or something like that," I said, still dazed by the scent. Who knew why humans were allowed to smell it? From the look on Ginevra's face, I deduced that she was wondering the same thing.

"Done," she told me, setting her serpent back on a large branch that hung directly over our heads. "We have the poison." She raised the vial to show me its contents and a sparkling droplet slid ominously to the bottom, almost dancing—elegant and lethal, just like Ginevra. It was hard to fathom how much power was contained in that tiny vial. I stared at it for a long moment, struggling against the seductive power that tried to pull me into its black coils.

Ginevra tore me from my thoughts. "Still think you can do it?" she asked. "You won't be able to change your mind. Once you've taken the poison you'll have to see it through to the end."

"Explain everything to me," I said without hesitating.

After a long, silent, intense gaze, Ginevra took my hand and cautiously placed the vial in my palm. A shudder ran through me at the contact with the cold glass—or more likely, the awareness of what it contained had triggered my reaction. I had just signed a contract with death and in my hand I held the weapon with which I would take my own life. The key to my own end—or might it be a new beginning? I wasn't sure.

"It's essential that Drake not realize your intentions," Ginevra warned as if I didn't already know that.

"Are you sure I'll have the chance to use it? Who says he won't attack me right away? He might not give me the opportunity to get close enough to kiss him."

"We create our own opportunities. Don't forget he can't come into our house in his real appearance and I don't think you have any intention of leaving for the time being. That means the only way he can get close to you is to take the guise of one of us. He could take on my appearance or Simon's, but that wouldn't make sense, given that he can get a lot closer to you by transforming into Evan. Unless, of course, Evan is already there with you—but I doubt he'll try that again, after what happened last time. My guess is he'll want to approach you when you're alone—that would make more sense. You'll have to seize the chance. Once Evan knows about our plan, we'll set the trap and pretend to leave you alone. I'm sure Drake won't let the opportunity pass him by. At that point you'll have to use all your powers of seduction to lure him close to you. It'll be an invitation I'm sure he won't be able to refuse. Then, making sure he doesn't notice, moisten your lips with the poison. You'll have a few seconds to kiss him."

As Ginevra gave me my instructions, I stared at the little vial and gulped. She rested her warm hand on my shoulder. "Don't worry. I'm sure you won't even have to make an effort. From what I've gathered from your memories, you won't even need to persuade him. It's Drake, remember. This is all part of the game for him. He'll kiss you first, but it will be too late for him by then."

I looked up in time to see a glint in Ginevra's eyes, preceded by a bitter smile. "We'd better not make Simon worry. He's still downstairs waiting for us. I can feel his impatience even through the walls." Ginevra locked the mighty vault and we left her room.

"Yeah, we'd better not." I shut the door behind me.

"You have it on you?" Simon asked, poorly concealing the nervousness in his voice.

I tightened my lips in confirmation and unconsciously gripped the little vial in my sweatshirt pocket. From the contact with my skin, the glass had grown warm and my fingers seemed to quiver with tension.

"Make sure you hold on to it," he warned me with a sardonic grin.

"Don't make me angry or I might kill you too," I teased, my tone serious.

"You want to kiss me too?" he shot back, grinning. "Because I don't think Ginevra would like that very much." He tipped his head at his girlfriend next to him, encircling her waist from behind.

"No offense, but one brother at a time is enough. I was just dying to say it, that's all."

Ginevra smiled and they exchanged a light kiss. "Aren't you tired?" she asked, worried about me as always. "You should get some sleep."

"I don't think I could manage that. Not now, at least." The blood was churning through my veins.

Simon and Ginevra glanced at each other. I noticed her nod slightly as if answering a question I hadn't heard. "Gemma," Simon began, his tone kind, "it would be wise if she and I used the next few hours constructively."

"We need to train," Ginevra said, turning to me, straightforward as always. "Until we tell Evan about the plan, there's nothing else we can do. We have to be ready in case something goes wrong. You can never be too prepared. You have the poison on you and you've got to be ready to use it at any moment. But now you need to get some rest," she insisted, giving me no choice.

"Can't—can't I go with you two?" I asked timidly even though I already knew the answer. I really didn't want to be alone, not in this state of alarm.

They exchanged another look.

"Okay, you can come with us, but you have to be extremely careful," Ginevra warned, her tone serious.

I could barely believe my ears. The workout room had always been off limits to me. It seemed impossible that Simon and Ginevra were being so accommodating. Or maybe I should consider it a bad sign— they were so afraid to leave me alone they were willing to bend the rules. Then again, her vault had always been off limits too and she'd just taken me there. It seemed as if all bets were off today, as though all the boundaries had been brought down.

Soon even the one between life and death would be obliterated. And it would take me with it.

The heavy door to the workout room closed with an ominous clang like the barred door of a prison cell. I kept looking around uneasily, unsure of what was going to happen. It wasn't the first time I'd been in this room—Evan had shown it to me over the summer, and a couple times we'd hung out there with the others, laughing amid the black punching bags filled with cement and the mats covering the dark marble floor. But I'd never been there when any of them were seriously training. When they did, for my own safety I wasn't allowed to enter for any reason. Now, for the first time, a sinister shadow descended on the room.

"Ready?" Simon stood in front of Ginevra. His tone was both challenging and determined.

For a moment their eyes frightened me: an Angel against a Witch, each prepared to receive the other's deadly blows.

"Always," she hissed, a smug look on her face.

My heartbeat suddenly accelerated. Had they forgotten I was here? I nervously shifted my weight from one leg to the other, not knowing what I was supposed to do in the meantime. Why had nobody explained it to me? All those times they hadn't let me in there were making me awfully uncomfortable right now.

"Gemma, stay behind me," Ginevra ordered, her tone far from comforting.

"Huh?" She couldn't be serious.

"Do as I say," she hissed, her eyes never leaving Simon's.

Ginevra actually wanted me to stand in the trajectory of Simon's blows? From the look on his face I could tell I didn't have much time to consider alternatives that might be just as risky. I followed Ginevra's order and darted behind her back. The tension between the two of them grew as taut as an electrical current across a silver wire.

Before I knew what they were planning to do, a violent explosion burst from Simon's body and a trail of fire came at us at breathtaking speed. I stifled a scream and held my breath, instinctively covering my face with my arms. The overwhelming force made Ginevra's hair fly back and the scorching heat of the fire hit me full in the face. My stomach felt as if it had been turned inside out. Ginevra's foot squeaked against the floor as she countered his attack.

I couldn't breathe. Suddenly the heat disappeared, leaving me trembling. I heard amused laughter and opened my eyes, allowing myself to inhale.

It was Simon. "Relax!" he told me, grinning. "I'm not planning on killing my girlfriend." I looked at Ginevra, disoriented. My breathing came in irregular gasps as if my body couldn't get enough oxygen.

"Did you think he was going to roast us?" she admonished me.

"I didn't have much time to think about it," I said, still in a state of shock. "The fear was enough to fry my neurons. But what—" I was dazed.

"The enemy never leaves you time to think—remember that. You always need to be prepared."

"Why weren't we hit?" I asked, still confused.

"Because I prevented it. I created a barrier and removed the air around us, which is why you couldn't breathe. Fire can't cross through it. That's what protected us," she explained, looking proud of her demonstration.

I stared at her, wordless with amazement. "It's incredible," I murmured to myself. "By the way, thanks for warning me," I scolded her, not hiding my sarcasm.

Ginevra snickered. "That was nothing. Managing to do it when I'm moving and under more difficult circumstances is even harder, but we've learned to defend ourselves. If you know the things that can destroy you, you can learn to protect yourself—some of the time."

Her discussion with Simon popped back into my mind. Ginevra was right—Subterraneans had no way to defend themselves against Witches' poison, whereas Witches could escape Subterraneans' attacks. *Witches were more powerful.*

I gaped at Ginevra, blown away by this new awareness, but she instantly rushed off, disappearing from sight. I tried to follow her with my eyes as she darted through the room, dodging the fireballs Simon hurled at her like lightning bolts, threatening to reduce her to ashes.

My heart in my throat, I flattened myself against the wall. The room must have been reinforced with a special material, because the missed shots hit the walls without leaving a mark. I couldn't remember ever having heard such a din.

Scaling the walls at warp speed as if gravity had no power over her, Ginevra deflected the fireballs even while spinning through the air. Occasional silver lights burst from her body and rushed at Simon like bolts of lightning, but neither of the two ever managed to hit the other. The floor trembled under their blows.

Ginevra chased Simon and when she reached him their bodies collided in a wild battle that led them from one end of the room to the other. They were spectacular, especially Ginevra. I couldn't stop staring at her in frank admiration. I'd never seen her like this before. One moment she was dodging Simon's blows with feline grace and the next she was on the offense, leveling swift, violent attacks against him. She was like a cougar ever ready to pounce. The power she emanated was perceptible, like an aura. It was everywhere, so evident I could almost see it.

I could barely follow them with my eyes. For a moment the whole room seemed to spin. All the noise had thrown me off balance, and both Simon and Ginevra noticed. They stopped and looked at me.

"Something the matter?" Ginevra asked, looking concerned.

I hadn't realized it was so obvious. "No, I'm a little tired, that's all," I said. "I feel kind of dizzy."

"You need to get some sleep," Simon said, almost reproachfully. "I know only one person who's more stubborn than you, and the two of you make a nice couple."

I smiled. "I guess you're right, but this whole thing is making me so nervous I don't know if I'll be able to—"

"I'm sure a hot bath will help," Ginevra suggested, her tone kind.

"Maybe that's what I need," I finally said.

"It's ready and waiting. Want me to come with you?"

"No, you guys go ahead and keep training. I'll be fine." They had already done enough for me.

"When you're finished, you can lie down in my room or in Evan's, if you prefer. Take all the time you need."

"Okay, thanks," I said.

I left the room, their concerned eyes still on me, climbed the stairs, and walked down the hall without relaxing my grip on the vial. Having it with me made me feel safe, to a certain extent. When I opened the door to the spa, a cloud of hot steam hit me. The room was filled with that particular spicy scent that made me think of Ginevra. The soft candlelight made the atmosphere so relaxing.

I carefully took the vial out of my pocket and rested it on the edge of the tub. With my hair tied up so it wouldn't get wet, I let my clothes slide to the floor and sank into the scalding-hot water. The relief was instant.

I rested my head on the edge of the tub, closed my eyes, and surrendered to the comforting sensation, letting myself be cradled by my thoughts. It was insane—I'd spent so much time and effort trying to escape death only to decide now to seek it out of my own free will. But it was what I had to do, a flaming hoop I had to jump through in order to bring the show to an end.

I'd made up my mind. No matter how much Simon's plan frightened me, I'd already made too many mistakes, rash decisions for which we would all have to pay the consequences. I couldn't continue to put the others in jeopardy and stand on the sidelines while they fought a battle that should have been mine.

The last time I'd acted on impulse and refused to accept Evan's plan, I'd almost lost him. It was a risk I was no longer willing to run, not if I could help it. If there was something I could do to prevent it, I wouldn't let Evan fight Drake again.

It was up to me now.

Evan was right. None of them were being forced to protect me and yet neither Simon nor Ginevra had ever shown a second's hesitation about it. From the very beginning they had always been prepared to support Evan and me. Even when Evan's decisions had seemed questionable to them, they'd been there. For that I would be eternally grateful to them.

But now I had the chance to do my part.

In spite of the circumstances, none of them were treating me like a fragile piece of glass. I could play a role in their lives just as they had in mine.

That's what I felt now—like one of them. We were fighting a war for my sake and only mine. It was only fair that I be the one to walk onto the battlefield. I would be the one to kill the Reaper Angel who was after me.

Of one thing I was finally sure: the constant fear of being hunted, of feeling him breathing down my neck, had made me tremble for months, but now that I was the one choosing death, I wasn't frightened any more.

When I came down the stairs I found the living room empty and silent. Simon and Ginevra must still be down in the workout room. I could have joined them, and would have if I hadn't suddenly felt sleepy and drained. The hot water had soothed every muscle in my body and I wasn't even sure I'd be able to find the energy to climb back up the stairs to Evan's room. I couldn't remember the last time I'd gotten any sleep and I'd never felt so tired in my whole life.

I took my phone out of my sweatshirt pocket and put it on the glass coffee table, sure that a few hours would be enough to get me back on my feet. Letting my body sink into the leather cushions on the couch, I forced my eyelids to remain open one more minute. All my body wanted was to lose consciousness.

I rested my head on a cushion, my fingers still gripping the vial I'd hidden protectively in my pocket. A second before my eyes closed, I glanced at the light-blue digits on the Blu-ray player. It was one o'clock. Only five hours left until six. When I woke up, Evan would be there.

EVAN

SPLINTERS IN THE HEART

Dark specks on the gray asphalt, sounds and silences dissolving in the air; my fists clenched so tight they hurt, my body as tense as my heart. From atop the building I absently watched the slow progression of thousands of bodies flowing like water in a river a thousand miles away. In my ethereal form I could even hear their heartbeats and footsteps. The sounds were so close and yet so far from where my mind was.

I knew I wasn't alone. None of them were there by chance. I could almost feel their ice-cold eyes on me, demanding I concentrate. It was almost time. The wind lashed at my skin, trying to snap me back to attention, but without success—because I wasn't really there. Or rather, my body was, but my heart was elsewhere, struggling with disappointment, grief, and fear.

Devastating disappointment over a brother I'd lost. *Brother*—maybe it was time for me to stop using that word.

Grief, bound up with her, with Gemma—the person whose life had become my sole purpose, the only one who could make me breathe again and take my breath away with a single glance. There are billions of people in the world, yet you can feel infinitely alone if you're deprived of the one who's important to you. I had lived for a long time, but only now did I realize it.

I felt so powerless when I was away from her, I felt I was going mad. I imagined her threatened by a thousand dangers and me unable to do anything to protect her. Without her, the frustration was tearing me to pieces, as unbearable as whiplashes against my naked, fragile heart.

And finally, fear. Fear of what might happen—of what was bound to happen. Because no matter how things turned out this time, no victory would be celebrated in my soul. With my heart bloodied from the pain I would sacrifice my brother, but part of me would die with him. Maybe it had already died from disappointment.

Deep inside I continued to struggle to accept the painful, ineradicable truth. Part of me still insisted on denying Drake's betrayal, considering it one of night's deceptions, nothing more than a nightmare. Like I might wake up any minute now and find it had never happened, that it had all been just a projection of a fear buried in my heart, a lie . . . and then Drake would be by my side again, as always, and we would fight this war together.

But that wasn't the truth. It was just an illusion to alleviate the unbearable pain that tormented me—as if that feeble hope might be enough to erase everything else. *Nothing could.* I couldn't go on lying to myself forever.

Up to the very end, I had repressed my doubts and reproached myself for my suspicions. I had hoped I was wrong—I'd hoped it with all my soul, which was why I hadn't said a word about it to anyone. Deep down I'd been afraid that giving voice to the unspoken thought would make it more real.

I'd known that sooner or later someone would come to claim Gemma's life. I'd lived with this torment every single moment, hoping she wouldn't notice as I'd forced myself to fill her days with memories of the two of us—special memories, unique experiences I didn't want her to forget.

My need for her was so insatiable I even stole her nights, like a greedy thief jealous of his treasure. I'd always wanted to keep her close because I was afraid someone would soon come to take her away from me.

But not him; anyone but him. Never had I imagined I would have to fight a member of my own family. Never, not even for a second. Not until that first, terrible suspicion—and even then the thought had been too painful. That night by the lake my heart had turned colder than ice when my suspicions had taken shape before my eyes like a nightmare come to life to torture me.

I didn't dare imagine where I would find the strength to kill Drake. I tried to stop thinking about it by visualizing Gemma's face in my mind, but there was no way to banish the terrible image.

I'd already put myself to the test in a battle against him and it had felt like every blow I dealt Drake had come back to strike me as well with just as much force, cutting through me like a double-edged blade.

What I couldn't understand was why the same true wasn't true for him. The merciless, detached coldness in his eyes was what hurt me most, as if someone had erased every memory of me from his heart along with the affection I'd thought he had for me. But maybe that was my mistake and I'd just been kidding myself, thinking I'd found in him the brother I'd never had. Now it was so difficult, so painful to accept the truth.

If I hadn't had Gemma to protect, Drake's betrayal would have destroyed me. She was the strength I clung to to avoid drowning in despair, in this cruel, grim twist of fate. No—fate was to blame for many things, but not for this. Fate guided us to certain events and led us to forks in the road, but we were the ones who ultimately chose which path to take. Our decisions led us to our destiny. I had learned that.

But no matter how terrible or painful it was, I couldn't be angry at Drake. When all this was over, would I also be able to forgive myself for my own sins?

I already knew the answer.

No. I would never be able to forgive myself for my brother's death. Nevertheless, I would keep on living. For her. Because nothing was more important.

Wars, epidemics, massacres . . . For long centuries, my heart, as hard as metal forged in the fire, had borne ever more difficult trials. It had carried too heavy a burden as souls slipped through my fingers—souls I tore away from their families, staining me with guilt I could never wash away. My eyes had witnessed tragedies I could never forget. And yet in the single blink of an eye my heart had stopped. I had surrendered to love at one look from a sweet, delicate, mortal soul. My life depended on this.

It depended on her.

Time crept by at a glacial pace. Never in my existence had it been so cruel. Ten endless hours of waiting. How would I be able to bear the last few minutes that separated me from her?

I had no reason to believe Gemma was in danger—I knew I could count on Simon and Ginevra—but that wasn't enough. For some reason, the painful thought that I wasn't there to protect her threatened to overcome me with every passing moment.

Nevertheless, I couldn't shirk my duty.

I had to make sure destiny was carried out, not because I was a Soldier of Death with no choice—not any longer—but because if I didn't keep Death from robbing me of Gemma, I wouldn't be able to join her after this life. It was the only thing keeping me away from her. I couldn't afford to give up the possibility. But neither the oceans nor the continents nor any execution order Fate could give would be enough to keep me from thinking of her every second—of the special way she looked at me, as if I were important—*me*.

Didn't she know that without her I was no one? I never had been. Yet at her side I felt so strong, so safe. All those lifetimes I'd wasted in the blind assumption that I had lived—God, how wrong I had been. You can't realize you've always been in the darkness until you find a spark that finally makes your heart beat. My blind eyes had been used to living in the dark. Then I'd discovered an unknown world full of light and hope, and only at that point had I realized I'd been wandering in the shadows.

It had taken only an instant to realize how devastating and irreversible the feeling was. I'd known in a heartbeat that it was impossible for me to return to the darkness. I knew I could never let anyone take from me the most precious thing I had in the world, the only spark that could light up my life: Gemma.

No. I would never let that happen. My eyes had been dazzled and I could never go back to the darkness I'd once known so well. Not any more.

Everything had changed since I'd met Gemma. I myself had altered, and the change inside me had been so deep, so radical, that I couldn't even remember who I'd been before I met her—as if I hadn't even existed. With all the emotions that had stirred inside me since she'd been in my life, this handful of months had been worth more than all the centuries I'd lived.

I didn't know how much longer we had to live together, but I would treasure each memory forever, her smallest gesture, the symphony of her voice, her radiant smile, her sparkling gaze, the warmth of her skin, the fragrance of her hair, the soft touch of her lips . . . Kissing them drove me wild and each and every time my desire, my need for her was stronger, deeper, impossible to deny.

And then that day at the lake house . . . I'd felt like I was losing my mind. I'd feared my heart wouldn't be able to contain such emotion, like it was on the verge of exploding.

I'd yearned for her for centuries without knowing it. It was as if all my life I'd wanted nothing other than that moment, nothing other than to be with her, holding her close, feeling her warmth against my skin. To merge with her. To disappear inside her. God, what a sensation . . . How could such a deep emotion be wrong?

I should have felt guilty for feeling this way—after all, I was still an Angel—but I couldn't. Not even the tiniest fragment of my spirit regretted a single instant I had spent with Gemma. There was nothing more *right* than being with her. It was as if I had been born for her and she for me—I could sense it in her every breath, because it was in her breath that I found my own. Simply embracing her in the silence of the night to hear her heartbeat was enough to make me breathe.

And then there was the incredible attraction that electrified me whenever her eyes met mine—so powerful it devastated me. Every time her deep, dark eyes gazed into mine I lost myself in longing. I surrendered to that desire because it was all I wanted, all I needed. I loved her so much even looking at her hurt. Was love so overwhelming, so absolute for everyone?

I was fighting a battle I couldn't afford to lose. What would become of me if I did? How could I continue to live without her? Like a tree stripped bare, its roots ripped from the earth, I would die along with her. I couldn't see any other solution. I would be consumed like wood on a fire until nothing was left of me but ash, what we had been burnt to cinders by pain.

No. I would never let that happen. There wasn't much time left now. I could sense it in this body that had never felt so mine before. Days, maybe hours, and it would all be over. We would belong to each other properly, without anyone hunting us down.

I would protect her forever, whatever the cost, and soon I would make her my wife. I would make my vows before God and with a trembling heart put my mother's ring on her finger. It couldn't belong to anyone but Gemma. I knew that now. With that simple act, her soul would be united with mine forever.

I already belonged to her just as she belonged to me. I could feel it in Gemma's every heartbeat. The thought that Drake or anyone else might go near her again made me crazy. The kiss that miserable traitor had stolen from her was enough to drive me insane. I would have killed him without batting an eye if it hadn't been Drake. Or maybe I might have anyway, if Simon hadn't come to stop me. At this point it was hard to say.

I'd been consumed with rage, overcome by a furious jealousy that had gripped my chest, a deeply rooted hatred impossible to eradicate. At that brutal moment I'd even lost control of my reason. I couldn't tolerate the idea that someone else might touch my Gemma—or even desire her. I was prepared to kill for her, even to die for her. No one would take her away from me. Fate wouldn't be enough to separate us.

Drake would be the last one.

No other Executioner would come looking for her because I would prevent it. In silence I had racked my brains for months, seeking a way to keep Death from taking her away from me, and had finally found a glimmer of hope for our future: the forbidden fruit. Ambrosia, the vital essence that nourished me. I was almost sure it would allow her to live forever too.

It would be dangerous. I had scrupulously evaluated every possibility and in the end I'd reached the right conclusion: if she ate of the tree, her soul would be forever barred from entering Eden. It would make her immortal. It would make her mine for always—if she wanted it.

It didn't matter whether or not the rest of the family approved. It didn't matter if I had to leave them all behind. My mind was made up.

I wished I could control time, bend it to my will so I could return to her. The thought that Drake might take advantage of my absence and visit Gemma made me frantic. Today might have been the longest day of my life, and my frustration rose every second as I bore the slow passing of the hours that separated me from her. But it wouldn't be long now. I just had to hold out and bear the torment a little while longer.

I could already feel the tension in the air—the kind I felt on my skin just before it was time to move into action. Looking up, I met the eyes of one of the others who was crouched on the roof a few yards away, staring at me with a puzzled look on his face as if he wanted to understand my secrets and frustrations.

He didn't understand, nor would he ever be able to—I realized that now. Our race had been created solely to kill, to liberate the soul from the shell that protected it during its brief stay on earth. Not to give up everything, like Simon had. Or me. We had a different objective: Redemption. Driven by such a motive, no Subterranean would give up everything to look for love among the extremely rare cases of women who bore the gene of the Subterraneans. And bonding with a mortal soul was inconceivable. No one could understand the devastating power of love until they had personally been swept away. None of these Angels could imagine the nature of my frustration.

There were lots of us today, maybe more than forty, scattered over a five-hundred-yard radius. I could sense them all around me. We were all there for the same reason, and for many of them it was their sole purpose in life—but not for me. Whereas they were eagerly awaiting the moment to carry out their orders and second the hand of Fate, I was longing for everything to be finished so I could return to Gemma. It was the only thing that mattered to me. But by now the worst was over.

We had spent most of the first hours making sure each of these people would end up in the right place at the right time. That was usually the hardest part. My ability to control people's unconscious minds gave me an advantage over the others; once I'd tracked down the mortal soul entrusted to me, making it go where I wanted it to had never been a problem. I could bend anyone's mind to my will with a simple glance. They all obeyed.

Sometimes a minor decision was enough to change someone's destiny. Missing a train, running a red light, going back for something left behind—trivial actions that determined their fates, mere seconds that decided everything, whether someone lived or died. All I had to do was look them in the eye to get them under my control. They couldn't see me, but their spirits would obey.

A high-rise. Today a high-rise would collapse, consumed by flames. We also had to take care of the people who weren't supposed to end up trapped in the fire, because there was no such thing as coincidence. Or better said, if it did exist, we were the ones who acted behind its mask, hidden in the fuse that started a fire, the breeze that fanned the flames, the first gust of wind that whipped up a storm capable of wiping out entire populations.

Our intervention was subtle and no one ever noticed us. The preparation in cases like this one took a long time. In these hours I'd discovered that the woman entrusted to me was a thirty-eight-year-old American named Jodelle with a successful career in Bolivia. She'd started at the bottom and had worked her way up, assuring her two children a good future.

That morning she'd dropped her kids off at school. Still in her car, she'd been about to leave for work when a strange instinct had made me suggest she call them back. They'd spent the whole morning together enjoying La Paz while I prepared the others. It was a gift I wanted to give her and her children. I couldn't do anything more. I was just Death's Soldier, a slave to its will. I didn't have the power to defy fate.

Death itself was a part of life, like the due date on a contract for eternal freedom. Because no matter how unfair it might seem, it actually wasn't. Humans had always feared death, mistakenly considering it a punishment, overlooking in their blindness the true key to happiness on earth: enjoying the journey. No one ever realized that death was only a new beginning. I was convinced that if we revealed this secret to mankind, the world would be a better place; once the awareness that life was transitory had rid them of their oblivious skepticism, every mortal soul would be more careful of their actions. You needed to know evil to be able to choose which side you were on.

We were ready, each of us in our place. Within seconds the fire would be kindled and no one would be able to determine the cause. Still I couldn't concentrate.

Gemma. She was the only thing on my mind. The more time that passed, the more agitated I became about not being there with her. I tried to focus on the building in front of me before the fire consumed it. Jodelle had just gotten back. The mirror she was looking into had to be the one in the bathroom. No one else was home; her husband had offered to take the children to their karate lesson that had been rescheduled for today. Once again, the delay had nothing to do with coincidence.

Everything was ready. Death was poised to engulf the building and we, its Soldiers, were ready to assist destiny. I didn't need to look at a clock to see what time it was. Jodelle would be waiting for me at ten to six, twenty minutes after the fire had trapped her in her home like a mouse in a deadly cage.

Suddenly, the air went silent. An instant later, I felt warmth dispersing from the bodies of my companions as a golden flicker in the building told me the device had been triggered.

It was the beginning of the end. The end of my wait to be with Gemma.

DEADLY TRAP

It took only minutes for the spark to become an inferno. The wind fanned the flames, driving them higher and hotter, and the building was soon engulfed in an impenetrable wall of fire.

I stood perfectly still, watching their eyes fill with the fear of death. But no one could escape, not if one of us was there waiting for them. Panic filled the streets. People ran from every direction and helplessly watched the building go up in flames. Some of the ones inside jumped out the windows and clung to the scaffolding outside the building. Though they didn't realize it, they would be the survivors that day. None of us were there for them.

Then I sensed her. Jodelle. She exhaled her last breath, drawing me to her like a magnet. Before I knew it I was in the thick of the blaze, surrounded by flames that whipped all around me, threatening to devour me. They couldn't, of course, because I was the one who controlled them.

Jodelle was facing me, looking down at her hands. I took a step toward her and her bewildered eyes locked onto mine for a long moment. Some instinct made her begin to turn around, but I reached out my hand just in time to stop her. I wanted to spare her the tragic sight of her body being consumed by the raging fire.

Though Jodelle was lost and disoriented, I could tell that somehow my presence was comforting to her. I could read her every thought, her every fear. Her lips moved slightly in the deafening crackle that surrounded us. "Who are you?" she whispered, terrified.

"I'm here to help you." I spoke reassuringly, my voice low and cautious, as I gave her a kind smile so she would trust me.

"Help me," she repeated to herself as if she didn't understand what I'd just said. Her expression changed abruptly and her eyes widened at the sight of something behind me. I didn't need to turn around to understand her sudden look of terror. She'd seen her body reflected in what was left of the broken mirror on the wall behind me. Her head began to waver, moving almost imperceptibly from left to right.

"Jodelle," I said.

"I—I can't," she whispered, in shock. "I can't leave them. I need to go back." She broke off, falling into a stupor, her unseeing eyes still locked on mine.

"There's no need. Your time is up, Jodelle. You did it. You can come with me now," I reassured her, my voice soft as I slowly held out my hand. "Everything's fine. You're going home." At my words, her eyes lit up and she finally seemed to see me for the first time. She stared at my hand, hesitating. "Give me your hand, Jodelle," I said, "and all this will be over."

Inside her I sensed a new emotion: hope. She looked at me again, but her face was calmer now, like she'd finally understood why I was there. Reluctantly, she began to extend her hand to me but then stopped. I waited without moving. I didn't want to pressure her. Each soul reacted differently and it was only fair for me to respect her personal need for time. It was the least I could do.

I sensed her intentions before she moved. Her hand drew closer and touched mine as I smiled at her warmly to let her know everything would be fine. The moment my fingers grasped hers, her silhouette changed shape like a cloud of smoke moved by the wind. She disappeared before my eyes, her gratified murmur echoing in my ears: *"Thank you."*

I smiled to myself before disappearing. My ethereal body was automatically pulled back to the last place it had been before Jodelle's soul had asked to be saved—the rooftop of the building across the street. The sweet awareness that my tormenting wait was about to end warmed me. I checked my phone. It was a few minutes to six in Lake Placid.

Bitterness unexpectedly filled my mouth, wiping away my joy like the swipe of a sponge. *"Goddamn it!"* I growled ferociously, my eyes stinging with disappointment. "No! No! No! Not now! Not now . . ." I raised my hands to my head, consumed with desperation, shaking with indecision. What was the right thing to do?

I wasn't sure any more. I'd been counting down the seconds waiting for this moment to arrive. They couldn't do this to me—not now, of all times.

"Another order." I sighed, my energy draining away. I felt powerless. Gemma was expecting me at six and I didn't want to break my promise. I had to explain my absence somehow, let her know I'd be late so she wouldn't worry.

Resigned, I picked up my phone and called her. Since I expected her to answer right away each new ring sent my mind racing to a thousand thoughts, a thousand dangers.

I tried again and again with no results and began to fall into a panic verging on madness. "Damn it, pick up!" I hissed. What had happened to her? What was keeping her from answering? When I tried to contact Simon and Ginevra all I heard from their minds was silence. There was no time, but I had to make sure she was all right before I went to carry out my next mission. Why the hell had they waited until the last minute to let me know I had another one?

A thought struck me and I went cold: it was a trap. They wanted to keep me away from her so Drake could work undisturbed. I cursed again, blaming myself for not realizing it sooner. They'd lured me into leaving her on her own and I'd fallen for their dirty trick hook, line, and sinker.

A shudder of desperation gripped me, making my skin crawl. I might already be too late and it would be all my fault because I hadn't been there to protect her. I was the only one who could prevent it. A sudden flash of certainty illuminated my mind: if anything had happened to her, I would turn heaven upside down, tear it apart. Because of their deception, no one would survive. *No one.*

Seething, I glared at the flames roaring up from the building across the street as a fire that was even more violent and consuming rose inside me. I concentrated on Gemma in order to reach her, wherever she was, and vanished.

The relief I felt was so overpowering it made my body ache: she was asleep. My legs shook from my misplaced rage. There had been no trick, no deception. I dropped my head into my hands, undone by my fear. Unfounded suspicion had blinded me completely and made my entire world collapse.

Gemma was right there, lying on the sofa in a deep, peaceful slumber. I couldn't stop staring at her. My whole life was enclosed in that single delicate being. I moved toward the sofa, noticing her phone on the coffee table. I'd imagined the worst, but she was just sleeping so deeply she hadn't heard it ring.

I reproached myself for how impulsive I'd been—I might have woken her. Who knew how long it had been since she'd last slept? I forced myself to take a deep breath, filling my lungs with air though I had no need of it. The fear of losing her had driven me to imagine some sort of conspiracy when the truth was that Drake and I were the only two in this battle. Soon, only one would be left. And there was no way I was going to lose to him, because I had something more important to go back to. Never again to see her adorable face that I couldn't take my eyes from now was out of the question.

I went to her. Stroking her cheek, I pushed a stray lock of hair out of her face. The touch of her warm skin sent a jolt through my entire body. It had always been like that with her. There was some sort of magnetism between us. Even back when I hadn't known her and sworn I would keep my distance, I could never fight my urge to touch her. Physical contact with her felt essential. It was an indispensable need for me. Even though I knew it was physically impossible, it felt like my heart started beating inside me again every time I gave in to my instinctive craving to touch her. Pressing my lips against hers, feeling the warmth of her body, sliding my mouth across her skin until I was kissing her belly . . . all it took for me to feel alive was simple contact with her. For me to feel my heart throbbing in my throat, beating so hard it almost hurt.

Fighting the urge to steal the kiss she'd promised me when I got back, I caressed her again. At my touch, Gemma moved her head, following my hand. I froze, not wanting to wake her for anything in the world.

I could have stayed there for hours, watching her sleep, but I had to go.

"Evan . . ." she murmured, still asleep.

Her eyes moved beneath her closed eyelids. She was dreaming of me. The peacefulness in her voice melted my heart. I could have joined her in that dream. Every last bit of me wished I could, but I didn't have time and I knew that if I didn't go soon I wouldn't be able to find it in my heart to leave her.

No. I wouldn't be able to. I would leave her a message. I had to let her know I would be late, but without disturbing her sleep. Gemma expected me at six, and if she woke before I got back she would be worried.

I picked up a sheet of paper and let the pen move under my fingers.

Fate is against us; it keeps trying to separate us, but don't worry—it can't. Nothing in the world could ever keep me away from you. You can't separate a body from its heart without killing it. One more hour, my love. Just one more hour and I'll return to you.
Yours forever,
Evan

I would definitely be back before she woke up. As I placed the note on the coffee table the light of the display on the Blu-ray player caught my eye. It read exactly six o'clock. I would be back by seven.

The air was filled with her scent. I inhaled it deeply. An hour—just one more hour. What could possibly happen in an hour? Calmer now that I knew she was safe, I looked at her one last time, feeling a pit in my stomach for having to leave her again. If it had been up to me, I would never have left her alone to begin with. I wanted to engrave in my mind the sight of her face as she slept so peacefully and have the memory to keep me company while I was away.

I would always be there for her, as long as there was breath in my body. I wouldn't let anyone near her. I would rewrite her destiny, binding her life to mine, defying fate. I didn't care how much longer I needed to fight or how many of them came looking for her—I would be there to protect her. I would kill them off until there wasn't a single one left on earth. But Gemma would survive.

I leaned down and touched my lips to her forehead. It was painful to pull them away again.

"This will all be over soon," I whispered. With bitterness in my heart I vanished.

GEMMA

A MASK UNSEEN

A violent sense of vertigo woke me up. I opened my eyes groggily and realized I wasn't alone in the room. It took me a few seconds to make out my surroundings clearly. Finally I saw him. Evan.

I smiled and studied him for a moment. His back was turned to me and he was holding something, a piece of paper, maybe.

"Hey," I whispered tenderly.

He started and turned toward me. "Hey," he replied, smiling.

"What's that?" I murmured, my voice still sleepy, nodding at the piece of paper in his hands.

My curiosity seemed to surprise him and he hesitated before answering, then smiled. "Just a note for Ginevra. Nothing important," he said casually, folding the sheet in four. He tossed it into a stone vase on the coffee table and held his hand over it. The paper began to burn.

I looked at him, puzzled. My thoughts were still bleary after my long nap and I didn't understand why he'd done that. Raising my head from the cushion, I turned toward the clock. It read twenty after six. "You're late," I said with a grin, not taking my eyes off his.

"I didn't want to wake you." Evan held out his hand. When I took it, he helped me up from the couch, gently pulled me against him and clasped my hips.

"Well? What are you waiting for?" I asked, a hint of naughtiness in my tone that he didn't seem to catch. He looked a little tense—maybe he was frustrated that we didn't have a plan. Simon and Ginevra probably hadn't spoken to him yet. They must still be downstairs, and Evan had likely come to see me first thing after getting back. "I owe you a kiss, remember?" I whispered, pressing my lips against his and sinking my fingers into his wavy hair.

"I think I deserve a little more than that, don't you?" he whispered back. He finally seemed more relaxed. His arms pulled me closer as he kissed me.

I smiled against his mouth and pulled back gently, resting a hand on his chest. "Hey, give me a minute. I just woke up."

"I've already waited too long," he said, his breath uneven, pulling me to him again.

"I mean it," I whispered with a smile, finally managing to pull away from his embrace. I took him by the hands and led him to the couch. "There's something I have to talk to you about." I sat down and pulled him down next to me. Now that he was there beside me, I felt calmer, stronger. Nothing could stop me. "I was afraid you wouldn't get here in time."

"In time for what?" he asked warily. "What are you talking about?"

"Drake."

I noticed that his pupils dilated slightly at my mention of the name. "We have a plan," I announced proudly, as if the plan didn't involve my death. But that was how I felt. For once, I wouldn't have to hide. I wouldn't have to fear my hunter any more. I would no longer have to dread death. And I couldn't wait for Evan to know every last detail.

He blinked several times, clearly not expecting this. "That's great news," he finally said with a nervous look on his face as if he already suspected the danger I would be facing. "I'm listening."

I swallowed, my throat suddenly dry. "Ginevra is convinced Drake will try to get near me again in your appearance."

"I agree," he replied, clenching his fists.

"Good. So you'll also agree we can use the situation to our advantage."

"How, exactly?" He tensed.

A knot in my stomach made me hesitate. Having agreed to the plan didn't necessarily mean banishing all my fear. "Since I'll be closest to him, I'll be the one with the best opportunity to kill him," I blurted out all in one breath.

Evan didn't laugh like I'd expected him to. "What? How do you plan to do that?" he asked, seeming shaken.

I hadn't imagined he would actually consider the plan so quickly though, judging from the look on his face, I wasn't sure he liked the idea.

"That's absolutely ridiculous," he said, frowning.

"No it isn't, and unless you've come up with something else it's all we've got." I touched the vial in my pocket, then took it out and showed it to him. Evan went rigid, his head snapping back instinctively. "It's not ridiculous if I have this." My eyes were sparkling from the power I held in my hand.

"Is that what I think it is?" he asked, still frowning, his eyes riveted on the little glass vial. He looked anxious.

I nodded and tucked the poison back into my pocket where it couldn't hurt him. "I can do this, Evan," I reassured him.

"It's risky," he said, his gaze abstracted.

"I know, but I have to do it."

"How do you plan on making it happen, though? Do you really think Drake would be that stupid?" There was a note of bitterness in Evan's voice.

"I'll pretend I don't realize it's him." I swallowed. Having seen Evan's reaction to the first time his brother had stolen a kiss from me, telling him I would have to kiss Drake again might end up being the hardest part of all. "I just need to wet my lips with the poison," I explained softly, letting him guess the rest of the plan.

Evan didn't react as I had expected him to. Continuing to stare into space, he slowly rolled his hands into fists.

"Evan, I can do this, trust me. Let me do it. I'm not afraid to face death." Finally he looked at me. "I'm not afraid, because I know you'll be there to bring me back."

He was lost in thought.

I waited. Suddenly, a glimmer appeared in his eyes and he looked at the clock. I did the same. Six forty.

"It's shrewd," he murmured finally.

"It'll work," I said, possibly more to reassure myself than to convince him.

"We'll make sure it works," he replied. "Now listen carefully: Drake is going to try to find out what we're planning, and we already know how he manages to get close to you. From now on you can't trust anybody—not even Simon. You have no way of knowing it's actually him. You need to be absolutely certain who's in front of you. With Ginevra it won't be hard—you can always ask her to tell you what you're thinking. Drake can take on her appearance, but he can't mimic her powers. He'll definitely try to trick you to find out what we're planning."

"Okay, but how do I know if he takes on your appearance?"

After a moment of thought, Evan took my hands and looked me straight in the eye, inches from my face. "How did you feel without me?" he asked, his voice hard.

"What?" I said, puzzled.

"How did you feel without me?" he repeated, articulating the words carefully.

"Terrible, like always when you're gone," I stammered nervously, still confused by his question. "Why are you asking me that right now?"

"Because that's what I'll tell you whenever you ask me that question. Remember the words carefully, Gemma—it's absolutely critical. You need to remember them to be sure it's really me. This is a decisive moment. My brother could be here any minute. We can't make mistakes. His eyes, his voice—everything will lead you to believe he's me. So before you use the poison, before you kiss him, you need to test him by asking him what I just asked you. 'Like always': that will be the right answer, your key to recognizing me. Otherwise it doesn't matter how much he looks like me or how much he acts like me,"—Evan looked me straight in the eye, deliberately articulating each word—"you'll know it's not really me. Do you understand?"

I nodded, surprised by the hard note in his voice. He tensed and searched the room with his eyes, then looked at the clock again. I wondered why he kept doing that.

"It's time," he warned me, his expression sharp. My heart began to race. "He's close. I can sense him," he whispered.

I blinked as panic gripped me. "What?! He's here?" I asked breathlessly, wrapping my arms over my chest.

"Not yet, but he will be soon. I'm sure he's waiting for just the right moment." He looked me in the eye. "Ready?" he asked point-blank.

"How soon?" I asked, my voice trembling.

"I can't say. Just don't forget anything I've told you." He got up from the couch.

"Where are you going?" I asked in alarm, too quickly for my anxiety to escape him.

"Don't worry." He took my hands. "I won't be far, but I need to get out of here or he won't come near you."

"Right," I murmured, shaken. "That's what Ginevra said too."

Evan nodded. "Because it's true. I'll go tell the others that I know all about the plan. We need to be ready when the time comes to bring you back."

I swallowed, my mind suddenly blank. He leaned over and kissed me on the forehead. His expression unexpectedly turned sly and I flinched at the dark glint that flashed in his eyes. "It's going to be the most unforgettable kiss he's ever been given." He smiled to himself. "Because it will be his last," he hissed, his eyes narrowed to slits.

A cold shiver gripped my stomach.

CRIMSON KISS

The room around me seemed to expand infinitely once Evan was gone. I sank my fingers into the leather couch cushions and clenched my fists. It was really about to happen. Everything was about to end. A shudder ran through my heart as the knowledge that the time had come sank in.

I was going to kill Drake, all alone. I didn't know why I hadn't been able to picture it in my mind before now. Maybe part of me had expected Evan to refuse to let me go through with it. What had I been thinking?

It was right that I should do it. The fact that Evan hadn't objected only showed how much he trusted the plan. Otherwise I was sure he would never let me run such a risk. So why was I trembling? I tried to get up but my head started spinning again, making me pause.

It was a few minutes before seven and I hadn't eaten for hours. I was sure it would do me good, but not so sure my body would be able to handle food. All this tension had left me nauseated. The room spun around me and I felt a pit in my stomach, showing that my body was protesting my decision. I leaned back, sank into the couch, and closed my eyes. The silence around me was bone chilling.

My hands shook. I couldn't remember ever being so nervous before. A million things whirled in my mind. I just wanted to get off the merry-go-round, just for a few minutes. That's all I was asking for.

I tried to think of Evan, the love I felt for him, the unforgettable moments we'd shared, and for a few seconds my tension eased. But that brief moment of peace made room for another thought that burst unexpectedly into my mind with devastating effect.

I bolted upright as the thought raced through my aching head, triggering a storm of conflicting emotions I wasn't sure I could handle, especially not right now.

A question throbbed in my temples.

When had I had my last period?

I desperately tried to do the math, to sort through the dates, but anxiety overwhelmed me and I kept getting confused. For a long moment I couldn't breathe.

The day Evan and I had made love for the first time had been the day I'd discovered they'd found me. Ever since then, my fears about their coming back to hunt me had absorbed all my energy and I hadn't had the time or the strength to think about anything else. Still, it was ridiculous—it couldn't be. Evan was an Angel, and I was just a mortal.

I instinctively rested my hand on my belly, my eyes unfocused as I considered the absurd notion. I hadn't had any symptoms, any pain or discomfort that might make me suspect. Or maybe I'd been too wrapped up in everything else to pay attention to the signals my body had been sending me. I wasn't sure.

The more I thought it over, the more I realized there was no mistake about it: my cycle had always been regular, and I was several weeks late.

How the hell could I not have realized it? My suspicions turned to certainty. I cautiously covered my belly with both hands and uttered the words in a whisper: "A baby."

I was expecting a baby.

Tears filled my eyes—tears born of a myriad of conflicting emotions. But foremost among them was a new fear: it wasn't only my life at stake any more. How could I also risk our baby's? Would Evan and Simon be able to save its tiny life too? My fingers gripped my belly more firmly as though that might protect it.

I blinked as three tears slid down my face. I had to tell Evan. All my certainties had slipped away and everything was more complicated now.

My legs trembling, I got up from the couch and headed into the kitchen. The clock on the wall was the first thing my eyes fell on as I dragged myself to the sink. It was seven sharp. The clock struck the hour just like the realization had struck my heart. Turning on the tap, I hung my head, leaning against the edge of the sink. I let the water run, listening to its comforting gurgle and hoping it would wash away my thoughts, my worries.

I couldn't focus.

Out of the corner of my eye I saw a glass near my hand. Almost unconsciously I picked it up and held it under the faucet, watching it as it filled. Turning off the tap, I drank a sip, then set the glass down and leaned over the edge of the sink again, resting all my weight on my arms while bowing my head and trying to think straight. But it was no use. It was like I'd fallen into a dark chasm. I looked for the light, but no matter how hard I tried I couldn't find the way out. The walls were closing in on me and I couldn't breathe. The chasm was so deep and dark it cut me off from my surroundings, and I didn't hear him arrive. I jumped at the touch of his fingers on my waist.

"Miss me?" he whispered sweetly in my ear.

I spun around and found myself pinned between his body and the sink. I paled violently. It was Evan . . . or was it? I was riddled with doubt.

His lips smiled at me, but my heart rate accelerated and my breath came fast. "Hey . . . calm down. It's only me." He stroked my cheek, drying the tears on my face.

"Evan," I whispered in a tiny voice filled with uncertainty. Suddenly I didn't know what to do any more. I felt uncomfortable, confused, and not at all ready for this.

"Hey," he whispered again, sweeping my hair over my shoulder. "Relax. You're on edge. You don't have to worry any more. Everything's going to be fine. I'm here with you now." He cupped my face in his hands.

His words aroused my suspicions. The real Evan shouldn't have been there. He'd gone to alert the others. He moved closer until our bodies lightly touched, blocking my way by resting his hands on the sink behind me as he gently kissed my neck. I stood there, petrified.

"We'll figure out a plan and everything will return to normal." He leaned back and looked into my eyes. "Do you know if Ginevra or Simon came up with any ideas while I was gone?"

Drake is going to try to find out what we're planning. Evan's voice rang in my head like an alarm bell. There he was, attempting to discover our plans as Evan had warned me he would. I looked into his eyes and tried to find Drake in them, but didn't see a trace of him. Anxiety stifled my breathing.

"N-not yet," I stammered.

Another kiss on my neck, this one more wary.

"Evan . . ." I whispered, almost without moving my lips.

"Yes?" he said softly.

My breath came even faster. I needed air. "How did you feel without me?" I whispered into his ear, my voice trembling.

He exhaled against my neck and his tone filled with pain. "Like I was in hell."

My heart constricted. *Wrong answer.*

He took my hand and squeezed it, rubbing his cheek against mine tenderly. "I felt like I was going mad," he said in a barely audible voice, his tone almost desperate, as I stood there unable to move.

Everything will lead you to believe he's me. The real Evan's words whirled through my head. *It doesn't matter how much he acts like me.*

I shook my head, in torment. It was obvious that after our last encounter Drake would be gentler, more cautious. I had to realize he would do or say anything to seem like Evan. Now I knew this wasn't the real Evan. He was lying—I knew it.

The vial felt like a ton of bricks inside my pocket. The others knew by now. Evan had gone to warn them. It was time.

"Your heart's beating so hard." He rested his hand on my chest.

He was so sweet, and yet I knew he wasn't really Evan. Why, then, was this still so difficult? Though I'd been trying hard not to do it, I inadvertently looked directly into his eyes, so close to mine, and my heart stopped. I wasn't sure I was brave enough. After all, it was still Drake. But then again they were all counting on me. I couldn't let this chance slip through my fingers. Drake was right there in front of me and the poison was burning a hole in my pocket. I couldn't back down. I had to do it. I owed it to Evan, to Ginevra, to Simon. I owed it to the baby growing inside me. I owed it to myself.

He rested his forehead against mine. The gesture broke my heart in two. Raising his hand with mine still clasped in it, he looked into my eyes. Palm to palm, forehead to forehead. "It'll all be over soon," he whispered, his gaze locked onto mine. "I promise."

I slid my free hand into my pocket and clenched the glass vial between my fingers. "I know," I murmured, resting my chin on his shoulder so he wouldn't see the teardrop streaking my face. "It'll all be over soon." I took the cap off inside my pocket. The smell of the poison rose into the air, so pungent it burned my throat. It took effort not to react. The aroma had suddenly captured my every thought. I felt an almost irresistible desire to move the vial closer and fill my nostrils with its scent.

Though I tried not to let myself get swept away by the strange sensation, there was no ignoring it. It was like a primitive instinct hidden in my gut.

This was wrong of me—I had to focus on Drake. But I could smell it, and it was going to my head.

I focused my attention on the body holding me close. I didn't want to give him a name any more.

Evan's voice whispered shyly in my ear: "You haven't answered my question: did you miss me?"

I cringed in silence at the tenderness in his voice. I thought of Drake, remembering his real face, all the moments I'd shared with him, the sincere affection that had connected us before he'd gone over to the wrong side.

I dipped a trembling finger into the poison. "I'll always miss you," I breathed into his ear as I brushed my finger over my lips, feeling an iron weight on my heart. It was over. We were both about to die. "Evan," I murmured, seeking his gaze. "Kiss me."

His mouth moved toward mine, stopping a fraction of an inch away. I closed my eyes as a hot tear slid down my cheek and I felt his lips part and then press against mine.

"Jamie," he whispered in my mind with infinite sweetness, his lips still on mine.

A dagger cleaved my heart. I froze and tore my lips from his, my bulging eyes filled with shock and despair. A second later, his body jerked as if an electric charge had surged through it.

Simon and Ginevra appeared at the other end of the room. "NO!" Ginevra's shriek died in her throat. She covered her mouth with her hand, her eyes petrified.

My heart burst in my chest, forcing me to hear its message of desperation. Overwhelmed with panic, I grabbed his shirt collar and bared his neck. The dog tag jingled against Evan's skin. It was there. In its place.

No. It couldn't be true. What had I done?!

"Evan," I murmured in anguish, my tears overflowing while his eyes stared at me, full of terror. "Evan, no . . ."

His body began to shudder and he staggered backwards to the kitchen table. He tried to grab its edge but fell to the floor. I rushed to him, my hands shaking as I caressed his face and hair.

No! No! No! This was all wrong. Not Evan. No. Profound, violent torment consumed me. "You—You came back," I sobbed. "You told me to—"

Almost imperceptibly he shook his head as his body jerked again. "I left you a message," he murmured between spasms as I moved my hands over his body desperately. I had no idea what to do.

"Evan, no—Please!" I struggled between numbness and despair.

The spasms racking his body grew more violent. I grabbed his face with both hands. "Look at me. *Look at me!*" I pleaded. "Evan, I'm begging you—" Tears filled my eyes. *Maybe I can take back the poison,* I thought. "Kiss me." In torment, I pressed my lips to his, but his body continued to shudder. "Evan . . ." I sobbed.

"It doesn't matter," he whispered, kissing the palm with which I had been caressing his cheek. He pulled his dog tag off his neck and pressed it into my hand. "Maybe this is my punishment, but it"—his face was a mask of agony though he tried to hide it—"it was worth it."

"No!" I shook my head over and over, my eyes locked onto his in a hopeless attempt to keep him there. "I'm begging you, Evan, don't die! Stay with me!" My tears fell on his face as I clung to him in desperation. "Don't leave me, please. You can't leave me now!" I sobbed. "You can't, because . . ."

He rested his finger on my lips, his eyes probing mine. Like a miracle, a crystal tear slid from his eye. *"I love you,"* his voice whispered in my mind. *"Wherever I go, that will never change."*

I squeezed his hand tighter, but I couldn't keep him with me. "You can't . . . I'm having your baby!" The desperate whisper broke through my tears, but Evan vanished before he could hear it.

I fell forward, desolate, paralyzed by his sudden absence. I pressed my palms against the ground, my eyes staring unseeingly at the empty floor beneath me. My heart shattered. A maelstrom of memories hit me like a tornado, dragging me back in time. The first time he'd smiled at me, his gaze sweetening only for me, him shaking his wet hair as he came out of the lake, his body entwined with mine.

His voice filled my head like a distorted echo, putting me into a trance. *My name is Evan James . . . I love you—love you—love you . . . Damn me, then, with a kiss . . . Close your eyes . . . Those are Sephires . . . —phires—phires . . . God, you're beautiful . . .* To punish me, my mind was pulling me back through time. *Hold on tight—ight—ight . . . The Angel saw heaven for the first time . . . Everything's going to be fine . . . You're my star . . . Just to see you breathe—eathe—eathe . . . Don't forget us—us—us . . .*

I wanted it to stop; it was too painful. But Evan's words continued to whirl in my head and tighten around my heart. *Did you miss me? . . . You're all mine—ine—ine . . . I'll always be at your side . . . Jamie . . . Marry me.*

The torrent of jumbled memories was killing me. They pierced my chest, as painful as thorns wound around my heart. The way he tenderly pressed his lips to mine, the scent of his skin, the gentle touch of his mouth when, behind the wheel, he would turn to look me in the eye while kissing the palm of my hand—he'd done that so often. It was a gesture that drove me wild—and one I would never experience again.

"It can't be . . ." I murmured to myself as Simon and Ginevra stood frozen a few steps away, their incredulous faces filled with horror. "This can't be true." I looked up at them. The pain was making it hard to breathe. *This can't really have happened!* I begged them with my eyes.

Something moved at the other end of the room.

Drake.

Simon's eyes, brimming with hatred and disgust, locked onto his. "How could you do this, Drake?" he screamed in outrage, fighting back tears. "He was your brother!"

Ginevra's icy voice cut him off. "That isn't Drake. It never has been."

I looked up, stunned, just in time to see Drake's evil smile vanish, along with the rest of his guise. In its place appeared a Subterranean I'd never seen before, his eyes filled with terror. An instant later, a flash of light shot across the room like a bullet.

Ginevra.

I held my breath. The Angel was gone. Where his feet had been was Ginevra's serpent. It slithered back to her and coiled around her ankle. They had disintegrated him with a single fatal blow. He hadn't even seen it coming. Her power was awe-inducing.

I could barely see through the veil of tears covering my eyes. My heart frozen, shattered into infinite shards that tore me apart with each breath, I stared at my hands, shocked and bewildered. "Why am I still alive?" I murmured, trembling.

It wasn't a question—it was a desperate protest.

I clutched Evan's chain in my fist as an infinite, agonizing pain settled into my chest.

My heart was bleeding. It would bleed forever.

ACKNOWLEDGEMENTS

With all my heart, I thank the two people I love most in this world: my son Gabriel Santo, who's so kind and sweet to let me devote time to this great dream of mine; and my husband Giuseppe Amore, who supports me every day, encouraging me and bringing out the best in me—not just because he's always in the front row cheering me on, but because he's my biggest inspiration. My love, if I know in my heart that men like Evan exist, it's because I met you. You are my Evan. Thank you for everything you do. Thank you for everything you are.

Special thanks go to my entire family for having brought me up surrounded by love. To my parents, whom I love immensely: my mother, who passionately follows every new development in the saga; and my father, who can't watch an interview without being moved. To my sister Ketty, who spends more time at my house now than ever, helping me with the thousand tasks that a book launch entails; and my sister Rosanna who, though she now lives far away, is always in our thoughts. Thanks also to my nephews Filippo, for the aviation insights, and Luigi, for all the enthusiasm he's shown.

I can never thank the entire team at Nord publishers enough for having welcomed me so warmly, especially Cristina Prasso, the sweet editorial director, and my irreplaceable editor Giorgia di Tolle. My thanks to Barbara Trianni and Laura Passerella in the press office who supported me in all the interviews and did an incredible job. My gratitude to all those who worked on the original book: editor Paolo Caruso, journalist Luca Crovi, Giacomo Lanaro from the marketing office, Uti for the careful corrections, the graphic artists for the beautiful cover they created, and the rest of the team. There are some of you I've never met, but I know you worked behind the scenes for me and my book, and for this I thank you from the bottom of my heart.

A huge THANKS to my translator Leah Janeczko, who not only translates my words but truly understands the souls of my characters, enabling her to bring them to life in another language without losing any of their passion or tenderness. Of course, I have to thank the person who has helped me most in this adventure: my wonderful, sweet editor Annie Crawford. I love you, dear! She is a very talented author in her own right, so check out her books *The Curse of the Jade Amulet* and *The Ring of Leilani*.

I thank Orietta Strazzanti for her priceless advice on the texts and Gino Strazzanti for technical support. Thanks to Tabitha Suzuma, the author of *Forbidden*, for kindly allowing me to mention her novel. As always, thanks to Alex McFaddin and Rhiannon Patterson for their invaluable information about Lake Placid. My gratitude as well goes to all the owners of the commercial establishments in Lake Placid that welcome Evan, Gemma, and the other crazy members of the group: Generations Restaurant, Bookstore Plus—where Gemma buys all her novels—Bazzi's Pizza, Ben and Jerry's, and Roomer's Nightclub. A huge thank you goes to Professor Saverio Sani who teaches Sanskrit at the University of Pisa, for his valuable help with the translation and transcription of Devanagari. Thank you to my lifelong friend, architect Salvatore Nicolosi, for his indispensable contribution.

I couldn't write these acknowledgements without including James Blunt and Lana del Rey, who inspired every little scene in *Unfaithful: The Deception of Night*. Thanks are written on my heart in permanent ink for Martina Lo Riso, a reader who not only got a tattoo of words from the book, but also wrote me that those words give her courage and faith in herself every day. To me it was a beautiful gift; if you'd like to see it you'll find it on the saga's website along with the one of Elisa Florio, another reader who got a tattoo of Evan and Gemma—again, my thanks. A big hug goes to my sweet friend Beatrice Luzi. Meeting you was so amazing! Many kisses to Consuelo Cedioli and Bliss Silverleaf for going wild about Evan and Gemma and their crazy conjectures about the future of the saga. To Valentina Canella for her original ideas, to Georgeta Susan Mitzgan, who's become a loyal *Streghetta*, to Maria Calafiore for how affectionately she followed Evan and Gemma's story, to Susy Follero, founder of the fan club (and who also had some of Evan's words prominently tattooed on her body), to Federica Cia, to Alessia Garbo, Sonia Cannarozzo, Franci Cat, Stella Ferro . . . I would love to mention absolutely everyone, but there are too many of you! But please know that you're in my heart.

A giant, infinite THANK YOU to all the readers and supporters of the saga, to all those who sent me their drawings or made videos, figurines, or other things inspired by Evan and Gemma, and most of all to the Witches and Subterraneans in the fan club who have developed a passion for Evan and Gemma's love story. Your constant affection fills me with joy. I really didn't expect such a warm response, and I'm grateful to everyone from the bottom of my heart!

Just one more moment: I'm not done yet. My biggest thanks go to YOU as you read these words. Heartfelt thanks from me, Evan, and Gemma for devoting a little of your time to us. Before saying goodbye, there's one more thing I'd like to share with you. I'm often asked, "Why do you write?" I searched inside myself to find the answer, and it came to me: it's because writing makes me dream. That's the truth. I write because I dream. I dream because I write. And I hope that my words have made you dream too, just a little—because dreams are the language of our souls.

Until next time!

BROKENHEARTED

Nightmares. Premonitions. Obscure Secrets

Death Has Never Been So Ominous.

Through dark and forbidden worlds

Are you ready to defy Fate?

"The most passionate saga of recent times." –Coffee and Books

2016

***

Want to be the first to know when *Brokenhearted* will be released?
Sign up for the Touched Saga Newsletter and you'll automatically be
notified.
http://eepurl.com/bR8EuT

PRESS

"As seductive as *Meet Joe Black*. As mysterious as *City of Angels*. As powerful as *Twilight*."

"Elisa S. Amore is one of the few phenomena in Italian self-publishing." **Vanity Fair**

"Girls who dream of love, a new novel just for you has come out in bookshops." **Marie Claire**

"*The Caress of Fate* is the literary success of the year." **Tu Style**

"A winning novel that's fresh and interesting, one that belongs on your bookshelf." **Io Donna**

"Italy, too, is seeing the rise of the fantasy genre served with a side of romance. Its undisputed queen is thirty-one-year-old Elisa S. Amore." **F Magazine**

"A sensationally successful debut." **La Sicilia**

"Elisa S. Amore is an unquestioned star of the supernatural fantasy genre." **Metro**

"For those who think emotions shouldn't die out as you grow up, this novel has a lot to offer you." **Vero**

"With *The Caress of Fate,* Elisa S. Amore makes her bookstore debut, but if you look up her name on the web you'll discover a whole world. Elisa S. Amore's narrative skills are clear; it's like reading a classic American-made saga." **Pop Up Literature**

"A truly incredible fantasy novel in which love is masterfully combined with the supernatural. A new saga whose readers are already anxiously awaiting the second—and no doubt spectacular—installment." **Il Recensore**

"A love story that goes beyond the confines of reality to unite two souls as they overcome every obstacle. Recommended for all romantics and everyone who dreams of immortal love." **Gli Amanti dei Libri**

"Elisa S. Amore has created a world around her novel, making it something unique." **Lo Schermo**

"A modern version of the Italian masterpiece *Death Takes a Holiday*." **Elena - Goodreads**

"As fascinating as *Meet Joe Black*, but for young adults. And not only." **The Bookworm**

"Following the Italian success of Alberto Casella, another fascinating story about death and love." **R. Fantasy**

Hailed by readers as a perfect mix of *City of Angels* and *Meet Joe Black*, with a pinch of the Orpheus legend.

THE AUTHOR

Elisa S. Amore is the author of the paranormal romance saga *Touched*. She wrote the first book while working at her parents' diner, dreaming up the story between one order and the next. She lives in Italy with her husband, her son, and a pug that sleeps all day. She's wild about pizza and traveling, which is a source of constant inspiration for her. She dreamed up some of the novels' love scenes while strolling along the canals in Venice and visiting the home of Romeo's Juliet in romantic Verona. Her all-time favorite writer is Shakespeare, but she also loves Nicholas Sparks. She prefers to do her writing at night, when the rest of the world is asleep and she knows the stars above are keeping her company. She's now a full-time writer of romance and young adult fiction. In her free time she likes to read, swim, walk in the woods, and daydream. She collects books and animated movies, all jealously guarded under lock and key. Her family has nicknamed her "the bookworm." After its release, the first book of her saga quickly made its way up the charts, winning over thousands of readers. *Touched: The Caress of Fate* is her debut novel and the first in the four-book series originally published in Italy by one of the country's leading publishing houses. The book trailer was shown in Italian movie theaters during the premiere of the film *Twilight: Breaking Dawn—Part 2*.

Find Elisa Amore online at www.touchedsaga.com
On Facebook.com/TheTouchedSaga
On Twitter.com/TouchedSaga
On Instagram/eli.amore
Add the book to your shelf on Goodreads!
If you have any questions or comments, please write us at
touchedsaga@gmail.com

***

If you enjoyed this book, consider supporting the author by leaving a review wherever you purchased the book.
Thank you.

CPSIA information can be obtained
at www.ICGtesting.com
Printed in the USA
LVOW11s1958171217
560109LV00006B/684/P